THIS
BLOOD
THAT BREAKS
US

S. L. COKELEY

THIS BLOOD THAT BREAKS US

S. L. COKELEY

Author's Note

This series contains content that may be triggering for some audiences. You can find an updated Content Warnings page on my website. Scan here or visit _slcokeleybooks.com_ :

Please make sure you check the warnings before reading. This book contains heavier content and themes compared to the first two books in the series.

Playlist

De Selby (Part 1) by Hozier

Long & Lost by Florence+ The Machine

Snap Back by twenty one pilots

I'm Your Man by Mitski

Dream Girl Evil by Florence+ The Machine

I Don't Smoke by Mitski

Heavydirtysoul by twenty one pilots

I Know The End by Phoebe Bridgers

My Love by Florence + The Machine

In This Shirt by The Irrepressibles

All song recommendations are solely for inspiring readers' imaginations when reading and sharing the love of music.

For every Luke and Zach—anyone in the worst storm of their life who can see no way out.

For those who have to hide their shaking hands and panic attacks with a straight face.

For those who felt they were supposed to be the hero in their own story but just couldn't make it happen.

And most of all, to those who feel broken.

You're not alone.

"All hope abandon ye who enter here."

Dante Alighieri's The Divine Comedy

PART ONE

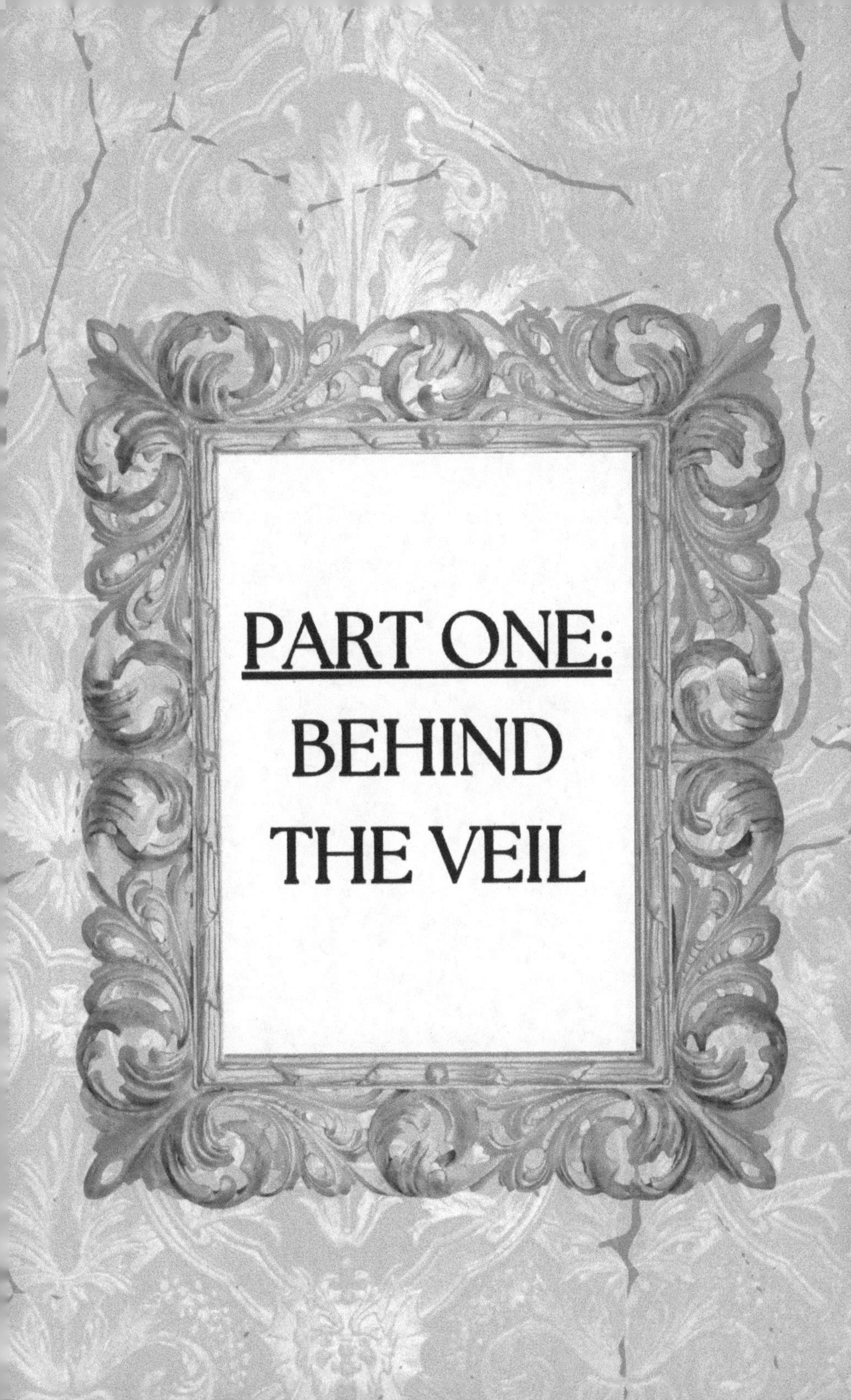

PART ONE:
BEHIND
THE VEIL

Prologue

The hot asphalt warmed the soles of my shoes, and a foreign sensation raised the hairs on the back of my neck. A cyclist sped past me. Brooklyn was full of hustle and bustle, and everyone had a place they needed to be, including me.

I searched for the cause of the disturbance, and there they were.

Two young boys, not even teens, snickering on the side of the street. One dark-haired and the other blond.

The twins. Not likely. They could have been just brothers. They didn't look alike.

It didn't worry me. Fate was ironclad. They would make it to us one way or another, but the foreign sensation was enough to make me linger there for a moment longer.

The blond was chatty and personable and talked some women into giving him five dollars for a fundraiser while the other was calm and calculated. Calculated enough to snatch a twenty from the side pocket of another woman's purse when she wasn't looking.

They interacted like two halves. *The sun and the moon . . .*

No. It couldn't be them. I'd imagined they'd be identical and much older. At least thirties like we'd all been. I checked my watch. I had a meeting at ten but couldn't pull myself away from them.

When the woman left, the two boys argued.

"I told you not to do that." The blond grimaced as he eyed the bill.

"We need the money, and now we have enough. We don't have to sit here all day."

"What if she needed it?"

"We need it more." He pointed to a woman who had set her bags down. "Wait, look. She's not even paying attention."

The older woman was too busy wrangling her kids to cross the street to notice one of her grocery bags was about to be snatched by some kid.

"Don't."

"Come on? It's easier than dealing with the cashier."

Normally, I'd keep walking. What did a couple of kids stealing groceries have to do with me? But I was frozen to the spot on the sidewalk. As if a cord was wrapped around my chest, it pulled me to them.

I had to know.

I strolled up to them with my hands in my pockets, and they froze, their guard instantly up.

"What do you boys think you're doin'?"

"Why do you care?" The dark-haired one's tone was harsh, and he pulled on the blond's sleeve like he was ready to run.

"Because it looks like you're working my street."

"You can't own a street," the dark-haired one said, more hostile that time. Like he might spit on my shoes.

"I can and I do. See all these buildings lined up here? I'm in charge of all of them in one way or another. I make sure everyone here feels safe, secure. Not taken advantage of."

"Congratulations on that."

"We were going." The blond smiled, clearly using a more agreeable approach.

I snapped my fingers. "Why don't you boys follow me inside? They've got an arcade in here."

"We don't talk to strangers." The dark-haired one smirked. *Little brat.*

"It's obvious to me you do."

"Sorry, sir, we don't want trouble, and we don't have any money for that." The blond's smile was unwavering; he had confidence about him. Like he could talk me out of anything.

I pulled out my wallet and waved a hundred dollar bill in their faces.

The dark-haired one's icy gaze softened, but the blond was cautious. "What's the catch?"

"You get to play a game without spending that money you're hoarding, and I get you off my street."

The dark-haired one waited for the blond to speak.

The blond snatched the money from my hand. "Deal."

His brother liked that idea and thawed from his stoic gaze. I followed them inside to Mrs. Prentia's little bodega with a wall full of arcade machines.

"Ezra." She stopped cleaning when she saw me. The familiar fear surfaced in her voice at first, but she hid it well. "Nice to see you."

"Hello, Mary. I'm accompanying these two to the games in the back."

Her brow bent as she eyed them with recollection. She whispered, "I didn't see them outside."

"No, they're fine." I smiled. "I want to treat them today."

That softened the wrinkles gathered on the edges of her eyes, and she turned to the boys. "You'll get a free game on your birthday. Do you boys want to sign up?"

They nodded, more excited now. Their guard was down again. They were like any other kids, easily influenced and distracted.

"My name is Zach Calem," the dark-haired one said, smiling for the first time.

"And I'm Luke Calem. Our birthday is on June 1st." They watched in awe as the cashier typed their names into her system.

My heart thumped in my throat.

Fraternal twins. Geminis.

Twins of Gemini will usher in the new Guard.

I didn't believe in coincidences. In my world, you couldn't believe in both. Coincidences were for people with no faith, no compass or greater calling. Coincidences left the world up to chance and the whims of mortals, but the whims of mortals and lowly humans only stood in the way of The Divine. The Divine's plan was the one true way.

I followed them to the back where we exchanged a few dollars for some coins, and the boys filled their pockets with anticipation. Two minutes in, it was obvious they'd never played before, as they fumbled with the controls. Luke let his brother go first, and Zach seemed to relish every minute.

"Are you going to tell me what you need all that money for?"

"Do we have to?" Luke's question seemed genuine. He hadn't trusted me for a second.

"No. But I'm curious what this big fundraising project is."

"We need money for groceries."

"Ah, is that why you were contemplating snatching that bag from that poor woman?"

"We wouldn't have," Luke said.

"You're not lying, are you?"

"No," Luke Calem said with firmness. "We wouldn't lie about that."

Now that I was closer to them, the pulling in my chest got stronger. I didn't want to leave them, and the thought of doing so was worrisome.

The Gemini twins. I'd found them at last, and so early. I pulled out my phone to dial Akira's number. We'd need to be certain. He'd help arrange a time for Her to meet them soon, to be sure, but I felt it. Like Her blood in my veins was calling to them.

"Fine. Here is how this is goin' to work." I snatched a dollar from Luke's hand. "You can stay on my street, but I'm going to come for my cut. Seem fair?"

Zach was already complaining, but Luke nodded.

"I'll see you boys around."

Then I left them to their game.

This was a shitty part of town. There were only two schools in the area, and neither were safe places to raise children. The boys likely walked, so I guessed they attended the closest one. *How were they allowed to walk all the way here?*

Fate only got you so far. It wouldn't protect them from the rapidly changing world or whims of others. The Divine's plans were the one true path, but sometimes, fate needed a little kick. Someone to help it along.

We'd need to scope out their family and decide what needed to be done. They wouldn't be changed until they were older, which meant they'd need protection. I was afraid to leave them, even with an important client meeting looming. I'd have to cancel.

The twins were the most important thing. Ensuring they got home safe was top priority.

Why were they so young? I hadn't prepared for that. It would be different. Raising kids wasn't something we were accustomed to. We'd need to make sure they didn't get themselves killed, but there were other threats too like illness, auto accidents, or natural disasters.

Her voice sounded in my head. ***Have faith, my love.***

She was right. Her plans were higher. The Divine's true path would shine through and give us favor. I only needed to be the hand that helped usher it into existence. Her plans would take care of the rest. It was already written.

Dear Luke,

I have a few questions for you.

One. Why the heck did you send us somewhere that's freezing? Were there no sunny beaches available? Frozen tundra was the only place, huh? Don't worry. I'm being good. I haven't complained once. Okay, that's a lie. But I'm trying, so A for effort.

Two. Not really a question. Aaron is a terrible driver but won't let me drive for some reason. So far, we've driven hundreds of miles. All of which Aaron insists he knows where we're going. Only, I don't think he does. Navigating the world without smart phones is torture. I wish I could call you. At least a text or something. I already miss telling you all the random stuff I did all day. You're the only one who never minded.

Don't worry, I'm writing it all down so you won't miss anything.

Three. Are you okay? I hope you're not going to tell me that this feeling in my chest is what you felt all this time because, dude, this shit hurts. I keep thinking it's going to go away, but it doesn't.

I wish I could get you this letter. Tell Zach I'm being good.

Love you forever,

Presley

P.S. Today, I saw the cutest dog.

One

ZACH

"Ezra, what the fuck are we doing here?" I squinted as we exited the plane.

He hadn't told us where we were going or why, but the smell of horse shit filtered through the air and a crowd could be heard in the distance while the drizzle of rain wet my clothes. Luke and I spent the majority of the plane ride sitting in silence, which was oddly comforting. What do you talk about when the world is fucked? When the little bit of hope you had left was run over and shot a few times to ensure it wouldn't attempt to get up again.

We needed that time to process its decaying carcass and get used to the smell.

The only solace we had was that everyone else we cared about was safe. Life was as it should be. This was the original plan before we got a little too hopeful about what was possible for us. Blackheart changed everything. Once we were there, it was hard to want to leave.

We followed Ezra through a field that was the deepest green I'd ever seen. Brooklyn was all concrete, and Blackheart was mostly trees and warm dirt. Nothing here was warm. Even with my blazer the cold air permeated the shell of my clothing. The ground was wet, and the mud stuck to my shoes.

"Welcome to Ireland, boys." Ezra straightened his jacket.

"All hope abandon ye who enter here."

I'm sure it was nice for people who grew up here—or some pretentious college students on a backpacking trip—but for me, it was one thing: hell.

I expected to see a dungeon or motes. Instead, all I saw was a wash of gray in the sky with thick clouds that matched the shit mood I was in. I nudged Luke and he smiled. It wasn't genuine, but it was just for me, so I'd take it.

"I repeat, what are we doing here?"

The roar of the crowd and the neighing of horses greeted us as we neared. We looked ridiculous as a mob of men dressed to the nines in all black trudging through the mud.

I waited for Luke to speak. He usually talked his way through these types of situations, but he said nothing and stared off into space, not sharing what he was thinking.

I was used to the dull ache of Luke's pain sitting on my chest. As if I'd broken a rib that never fully healed. After I drank the queen's blood, I felt it. Sometimes, it was faint, and other times, it was so agonizing it put me on my ass. Usually, I'd drink.

This new feeling wasn't that. It was more of a drawing toward something. A tug in my chest. A slight tingling in my fingers and buzzing that reverberated in my body. We were close to Her again. It was something undetectable when you're used to being close to Her, but now that we'd had the distance, the longing was overwhelming.

Still, we weren't there yet. We were at a horse track.

"This is a minor stop before we head home. Close to the harbor. I'll want you to get there the proper way the first time," Ezra said.

"What about Will and Thane?" Luke's voice sounded rough and far away.

"They're alive till we get there. Don't worry."

Luke and I shared a look. We didn't like that answer. I had used some of my silence on the plane to try to think of something to save them, and I'd come up with absolutely nothing, but I wasn't the plan maker. Just the one who carried out the plans.

Luke didn't argue, which I hoped meant he had an idea.

When we reached the edge of the grass, a young man kneeled in front of me and started cleaning my shoes. I tried to kick him off, but he kept going.

Ezra circled to stop in front of us. "This is your first bit of training. We have a client to meet. Introductions are important, so I'm hoping you'll both make a good impression."

His freaky blue eyes bore into mine on the last words.

"A client for?" I pushed my hands through my hair. Fuck them for cutting it short. It was too cold for that shit.

"We've got clients we attend to all around the world. Due to your stunt with the Legion, we had to move Her, and in doing so, we had to delegate our business in America. Now we're rekindling our business here. We have business partners that have held down things for us while we were away."

"Care to elaborate on what that means?"

"We facilitate things. We make things possible for others as a middleman. Which keeps us with enough money to do what we need to do and gives us enough influence to keep Her safe."

"Ezra, you do realize you're looking at two people who know nothing about that, right? For fuck's sake, a month ago I was taking Jell-O shots off a girl's stomach."

The Jell-O made me gag, but it was worth it because she was hot.

I remembered when that little lightbulb in Luke's head went off and he decided being in a fraternity was a good idea.

We were walking to the dean's office at Black Forest, and there they were. One of the bigger fraternities on campus preying on freshman and coaxing them to join. Luke had gotten this twinkling in his eye when he saw them.

I knew what he was thinking. Like, actually. I could guess what he was thinking nine times out of ten. We'd even tested that theory when we were kids.

Luke studied them with their chants and their brotherhood and wanted Aaron and Presley to have that. He was probably thinking it would help mend the giant hole when we left them on their own. Or that giving them experiences they'd remember forever would put them on the right foot and they'd have better things to remember us by.

Luke only admitted it would be *"Safer to be in the same house."*

I'd convinced him we didn't need to join the *biggest* fraternity, and we settled on OBA.

Now, I saw it for what it was. A desperate attempt to hold on. To stay. To live. I didn't think either of us expected that dream to get its hooks in us so deep. Our time in Blackheart was the closest thing Luke and I would ever get to peace. Pretending we were normal and going to college with our brothers, felt too right. And for a minute I believed it. As usual, the joke was on me.

Ezra's voice snapped me back to the present. "That's why you need training."

"And if we don't?"

"I'll kill your friends." Ezra sighed like he didn't want to say it.

"How long are we going to do that song and dance?" I sighed.

"Till it sits itself in your brain. You're here. You're meant to be here."

"We'll comply." Luke nodded, and I fought the shiver of anger that ran down my spine.

Just a small thing. Nothing you can't handle. Repeating Mom's words as my mantra, I reminded myself not to be an asshole all the time. It took actual effort. Especially toward people like Ezra who deserved it. I hated him for more reasons than I remembered, but mostly, I hated him because he had been inserting himself into my life since we were kids. He'd ruined everything, and a part of me—something tiny, insignificant, and weak that needed to be pulverized into dust—had missed the bastard.

Once we were cleaned and our blazers were adjusted, we walked on. A huge horse track carved out of warm wood and gray stone stood out in the field of green. There were three tiers of stands of people watching while below smelled like a bar.

"His name is Liam Brennan, and he owns this horse track. It's one of his many businesses he launders money through. He's easy to get along with. It will be good practice."

"And we help him by doing what?"

"By being at his beck and call. It's mostly diplomatic. If things are serious enough, we're there with support, like muscle. Whatever is needed."

I bit my tongue to stop myself from making a smart-ass comment.

We followed him into the lobby. The red carpeted floor was lush and new despite the crowd of people standing on it, and a chandelier hung overhead with tiny Edison bulbs. This place wasn't a family establishment. No place for snotting babies or little kids running to the snack machine. Everyone was dressed in a three-piece suit and scowled like a riot might break out if someone sneezed or a hair fell out of place. All eyes were on us as we entered.

Ezra parted the crowd, and we walked across the lobby and out the double doors. The noon sun peeked through the clouds, and I fought the urge to complain about the smell again.

We followed Ezra past rows of men and women, all expensive looking, and climbed the stairs to a lounge. It was full of more warm woods and deep-green velvet chairs, and covered by a canopy that hid our meeting place in shadow.

In the corner of a booth sat a man with a mustache and long brown hair that grazed his shoulders. Those around him stood in our presence, but he didn't. The man sipped his drink before straightening his jacket, then gestured with his hand for us to sit.

"The prodigal sons return." His Irish accent was thick.

I waited for Ezra's lead because the guy looked like a dick, and I tended not to get along with men who acted like dicks.

Ezra sat in a wide-legged stance and pulled a cigarette from his vest. Luke and I took an open chair on either side of him.

"Nice to meet you all. I've heard loads about ya."

"Pleasure." Luke held out his hand to shake, but I kept mine in my lap and nodded.

I could already feel Ezra's eyes on me.

"Now, tell me how it feels to be back in the home country."

"Cold." Luke smiled.

"Smells like horseshit," I added.

Ezra blew smoke into the air. "They've never visited."

"I can see that." Liam snickered. "Tell me, boys. Ever place any bets on a horse before?"

"No. We aren't big gamblers," Luke said.

I was happy Luke bent the truth a little. He didn't lie about things that mattered, like keeping promises, but when it came to safety and strangers we couldn't trust, he tested the waters.

"Take a look out. Tell me. Which one would you choose?"

We eyed the row of horses waiting around the barn next to the stalls. All were wearing different-colored numbers on their backs.

"Twenty-four." Luke motioned to a gray one.

"Ah, the underdog. And you?"

It was my turn to pick. I eyed the lineup, looking for the one I thought would be the strongest. A restless black horse bucked at another horse's legs, and I assumed it was as good of a pick as any.

"Thirteen."

"Interesting choices. Now, how far would you go to ensure your horse wins?" He plopped down a stack of hundreds on the table. "I want you to go place your bets and double this."

"Is this a test?" I spat.

Ezra grumbled to himself.

"Let's all relax. I see two boys sitting in front of me. You are young. I need to know I can trust you."

There was something about the way he looked at me. His eyes scanned me too quickly, taking in too many things at once, so I focused on his chest. He tried to hide the uneven breaths, but I'd trained myself in Blackheart to check every single person who walked past me, especially after we were caught by The Legion.

He was a vampire.

"He's one of us?" I plucked a toothpick from the table and plopped it in my mouth.

"Barely. A rat by blood in comparison to what's pumping in your veins right now. Turned out of courtesy to the cause more than one hundred and fifty years ago by an underling. Like that one standing next to you that shined your shoes."

Liam licked his teeth and eyed my wrist. It held a faint scar where my tattoo used to be. I'd worked long and hard to repress the memory of the Legion peeling it off my skin in the old church.

"Now, boys, please humor me. Ten minutes."

There was something there. *Envy.*

I didn't like being ordered around, but I followed Luke's lead.

This was our first official mission, and we needed to make it good, or I'd have to watch my friends be tortured. *Fun.*

"How are we going to do this?" I asked Luke once we got out of hearing distance, and looked out onto the track.

A large oval track with nothing in the center except a large pond stood out among the green of the field.

"Give me a second to think."

"If I need to break some jockey's knees, I will, but I draw the line at hurting horses," I said. Men were all assholes deep down, but animals were a different story.

"No one's breaking any kneecaps."

"What if we need to? That's the exact type of shit I signed up for. I'll make sure he stays quiet so you don't have to feel bad."

I'd beaten the shit out of people before. I could do it again. Though I felt a little guilt at the thought. That was the problem with spending all that time with my brothers. I'd grown a conscience and didn't like it. They made me soft, so I was out of practice.

Luke frowned. He wasn't in a joking mood. I wasn't either, but humor was the only thing preventing me from falling off the deep end.

Be helpful, I thought, wanting to get that worried look off my brother's face.

"What if we found the horse to beat and then drugged the jockey? I watched this show once where they drugged horses before a race. This is like that but no guilt."

"You are on to something . . . not with the drugging, but we do need to find the horse to beat here. We could cut the bridle or loosen the saddle so that tack breaks during the race. Then I could—"

"Luke, I don't know what the hell you're saying. Just give me a job to do, and I'll do it."

To my surprise, he smiled. "Find the horse to beat. I'll wait, and then go make our bets."

I couldn't suppress the laugh. "Some chaos might be what this place needs."

He held out his hand to me, and I placed mine on top. Our handshake was completed with one of my hands smothered by his and the other on top. I turned on my heels and walked the stands, looking for my mark—the meanest-looking fucker I could find.

An older man with gray hair and his sleeves rolled up stood out. I grabbed a drink from his hand and downed it. Straight bourbon. Next to him, an even larger man towered over me with hulking arms and red hair.

"Who are we betting on?" I couldn't wait for the buzz to hit me.

They said nothing and stared at me with gnashing teeth and blank scowls.

"You need to get back up to your suite, Mr. Calem," the older man said.

Of course they knew my name.

"Why? Afraid to have a little discussion?"

"We don't want trouble," the big one said.

"You look like you want it."

He practically growled, and his buddies avoided looking at me. They were all elegantly dressed in various colors of velvet.

"Come on. Think you can take me?"

I chewed on the ice before dropping the glass to the floor and finally grabbing the big one's drink and downing it in front of him.

How hard was it going to be to get this fucker to hit me? He had to be the one to hit me first, or Ezra would be up my ass for fighting.

"Damn. This tastes expensive." I was bluffing. All of it tasted the same to me.

He gritted his teeth. I was getting somewhere. My tactic was simple. Get someone to fight me—easy, then beat the shit out of them to tell me the horse to beat. Not subtle, but I didn't have time to be.

"Maybe you should listen to the warning."

"Should I? I think I'll stay here. Who are we betting on?"

He grabbed the collar of my shirt. *Yep, that did it.*

As I awaited the raising of his fist, another spoke.

"Word is that twenty is the one to beat." A boy no older than eighteen with dirty-blond hair and bright, golden eyes stared at me. "He's the large white one."

I swallowed the lump in my throat and tried to refocus. Moving my thumb, I pinched the soft connective tissue on the man's hand, and he dropped me with a grunt.

"Thanks kid." I turned to the others. "Was that so hard?"

I turned on my heels to find Luke. He gave me a thumbs-up, signaling he heard me, then disappeared into the crowd.

The drinks hit me at once, and I cared less and less about the sheer number of people staring at me. Even sober, I didn't care, but I was in another country about to meet the vampire queen I loathed, and everyone in our new environment looked like they were ready to snatch my soul from my body. They wanted to be me. It was comical, really.

The fact they'd probably get down on their knees and beg to be in my position. I had wondered if there was a way I could hide Luke and run, but I was over that pipe dream. They had Will and Thane, which meant we weren't going anywhere.

I ascended the steps toward our booth and stopped to watch them line the horses in the stalls. Nothing looked out of order, but I wasn't worried.

A man dressed in all black came to stand beside me. One of ours.

"Need something?" I asked.

"No, sir. I'm here for your aide."

"Oh, so if I ask you to go get me another drink, you will?"

"Yes, sir."

"Good. Go do that. Surprise me."

I smiled as he sauntered off toward the bar. Hell wouldn't be all that terrible.

A bell rang out, then the horses were off. Only, all but four had been let out a second or two late. Number twenty led the pack before slowing to a halt when his jockey fell off his back and into the dirt.

My lackey was already back with my drink, and I sipped it as the horses took the curve.

The whole place grew silent. There was big money on the line here. I scanned the crowd for the richest-looking one. I could break their arms outside until they gave me the amount I needed, but instead, I watched the race with confident assurance in Luke.

I didn't know how he did it, but Luke always got his jobs done.

Of the three left in the lead, two led: thirteen and one. My heartbeat drummed faster watching them. Thirteen took the lead at first but slowed as they neared the finish line.

Then without warning, twenty-four barreled through them and passed the finish line.

How the fuck?

I left the stand in search of Luke and waded through the thick cigarette smoke. He was waiting for me at the end of the steps with his hands in his pockets, looking pleased with himself.

"How the fuck did you do that?"

"While you served our distraction, I got everything in order for number twenty, but then I found the showrunner here. His name is Jerry. He's got two grandkids he adores. I talked with him while I had someone set up the stalls with the delay. No one noticed anything."

"You're shitting me."

"Nope."

"You amaze me, brother. But how did your horse beat mine?"

"That was luck. I couldn't rig just our horses to run, so I had to take a chance."

Luke's personable skills were scary. He was magnetic to luck and success. That bothered most people. Some asked me growing up if I ever hated being in Luke's shadow. Those people didn't understand it and probably never would. Luke wasn't my competition. He may have had skills I didn't, but he liked to share. He shared all that he had. His happiness and luck belonged to everyone around him. Standing in his shadow was the closest I'd been to happiness.

We collected our money and strolled shoulder to shoulder back to Ezra and the others.

"Well, boys, how's the pot?"

Luke laid down a pile of money that made Liam smile. Ezra did too.

"Guess I better stop calling you boy." He stood up, ushering us closer. "What do you think? Like it here?"

"I think you should be careful how you speak to me." Sometimes, I couldn't stop the words from coming from my mouth.

"Is that so?" His eyes locked with mine, then he leaned back in a roaring laugh. "I like you."

He pulled us into an awkward half-hug. Luke and I furrowed our brows at each other.

"We're all going to get along just fine. We're practically family now."

What the actual fuck?

LUKE

Sometimes, being optimistic didn't work out. You could go your whole life being the one everyone looks up to and still turn out a colossal failure with little to nothing to show for it. Sometimes, hoping too much leads you down a dark path to the one place you never wanted to be . . . miles from home. *Home.*

Brooklyn never felt like home. I was happy to leave the house at eighteen. Home for me was where peace existed. Only once in my life had I felt at peace, then that place burned.

A full moon greeted us as dusk turned into night, and the smell of smoke stuck to my skin and hair. I thought of washing it in the sink at the horse track, but I wanted it to linger a while longer.

Stop. That's not helping.

It was a curse. My inner voice never stopped trying to find the bright side. I'd spent the better half of my life pulling myself up and pushing on while packaging everything into a perfect life lesson so I could teach my brothers.

That only worked when you weren't fated to be with a vampire queen.

I'd said it more times than I could count. *"Think of what you want to be doing five years from now."*

I had hopes for my little brothers.

One: they'd be close so even if they didn't have Zach and me, they'd have each other. Two: they'd know how to identify what they wanted and go after it and not be afraid to take chances to get it. Three: they'd use the lessons I taught them and cherish the memories we had and remember me for the person I was.

I'd been planning it all before I realized that's what I was doing. Giving my life up to The Family and prepping my brothers for my departure. It started in high school. I distanced myself from them and gave up on things I'd wanted in junior high. I'd never have a normal job, and any thoughts I had about joining the military flew out the window. As a kid, I thought of myself as some hero, so going into the service was appealing. Zach would have followed me, though, and I would have loved the company, but I hated that he chose to do things he didn't want to do because he was worried about me.

I wasn't a hero.

My five-year plan never mattered, but I was happy I'd given my brothers one. Despite what Akira said about the prophecy, I didn't believe my brothers were meant to be a part of this. But this place had haunted every corner of my life. Maybe fate was real.

That explained why I stopped being able to answer *What do you want to do when you're older?* a long, long time ago.

The cold wind slinked its way under the cloth of my jacket as I stood at the edge of the boat. It was a large-windowed barge with covered seating and space to stand in the front. Ezra mentioned a ferry service going to and from the island for tourism. As the island grew closer, my heart drummed faster and faster. I wasn't ready to see Her.

"How are you feeling?"

Ezra appeared beside me, the tips of his hair frozen from the freezing rain slowly turning to snow.

Terrible was what I wanted to say.

"Fine," I said.

I should have been mad at him, but I wasn't. Especially when he was the only one who might help us. Zach made it more than clear that he didn't trust Ezra, and I didn't either, but he had aided our escape once. He didn't have to do that. Without Ezra, we'd have never made it out of Brooklyn and neither would've Mom.

"It's going to be all right. You'll be surprised how quickly things change."

"Where are we going?"

"The castle. We have a couple safe houses around, but this was Her original home. She wanted to come back."

At the mention of Her, my skin itched. A feral buzzing tore through every inch of me. My bones practically vibrated with the anticipation of seeing Her again. That brought on an eclipse of emotion I wasn't ready to unpack. There was no use in being afraid. I would soon be near Her. It had been carved in stone many years ago. I was meant to be on this boat closing the distance between us.

I had people I needed to protect. Which meant I couldn't drown in my own misfortunes yet. Not when they needed me.

I nodded. "I've never seen a castle before."

Always a positive.

Staying on Ezra's good side was the right move.

"There's a first time for everything." Ezra slapped me on the shoulder and retreated into the darkness of the ship.

That brought me back to the beginning.

Sarah and I had sat on the swings on the playground. The memory was hazy, but the smell of fresh rain brought me clarity.

We'd met in kindergarten, and in a matter of days, we were inseparable. Lunch and recess were my favorite because I got to spend all that time with her.

"*We should do all our firsts together,*" she said. Her green eyes sparkled in the sun while her dark hair blew off her shoulders.

"*First water park,*" I said.

I was obsessed with waterparks as a kid, probably because we never got to go to any.

"*First dance.*"

"*Uh, first trip to the snow-cone stand.*"

"*First roller skating party.*" Her eyes lit up.

We'd had that party for her birthday that year.

She had all the good ideas.

I had opened my mouth to say something else, and without warning, Sarah leaned in and kissed me square on the lips.

"*First kiss.*" She smiled, not even the littlest bit embarrassed.

I remembered the warmth in my cheeks, and my swinging came to a halt as butterflies fluttered in my stomach. I wanted all her firsts, even back then when I got embarrassed and wiped my lips in fear of "cooties."

"Luke." Zach shook me from the memory.

"Sorry."

I didn't like to mention Sarah. Mentioning her did nothing but make us both miserable. I looked out on the island as it grew closer, knowing my fate was awaiting me. We were almost to the queen, and I felt it in every cell of my body. The buzz from Her proximity sped up, making me impossibly restless. I tried to think of something else, but the nagging need was stronger than anything else I wanted.

That wasn't true. I had to focus and be on guard if I wanted to keep Thane and Will alive. There wasn't time for anything else.

"How are we doing this?" Zach asked.

We were stationed at the back of the barge, right by the roaring water and propeller where Ezra wouldn't be able to hear me.

"I haven't been able to talk to Will yet."

"She's going to want them dead," Zach said.

"I know. But we won't let that happen. We need to regain Ezra's trust."

"Fuck that."

"Ezra is Her right hand. Having him be a buffer and helper is our best route. Try not to piss him off too much?"

"Fine."

"We have to show him we can be trusted. Let's ask him to talk to Will. If we sneak around and do it, he's going to catch us."

"And say what? *Sorry asshole. Guess you got caught by the cult you've sworn to demolish. Now I'll get to watch as they probably pluck your eyeballs from your body?*"

"I was thinking a simple 'Hang in there. We're in this together' would be a start."

"Right. So, what if we do get them out. What about us? Are we staying?"

"I don't know. I think we need to focus on getting Thane and William out first. Making them disappear is a lot easier than us."

Zach nodded.

"Follow my lead." I tapped his shoulder, and we moved toward the front of the ship.

The other members bowed as we passed. I tried not to think about the foreign world I'd stepped into. One foot in front of the other, and one task at a time.

We found Ezra at the front of the ship texting.

"We want to see Will and Thane."

"Why would I let you do that?"

"Because what will it hurt? Who knows what will happen when we get there. Maybe She'll change Her mind," I said.

"I'd rather you not get your hopes up."

"Too late. Already up. Come on. I need to talk to Will. Please."

Ezra always softened when I said please. He may be a master manipulator, but he'd been there for us growing up, and even if it was naive, I still felt that bond with him.

He stared at my brother. "Anything to say?"

Zach pretended to zip his mouth shut.

"Fine. You get five minutes."

He walked us through a door that led to a small cargo hold under the ship.

"Say your goodbyes, all right?"

He left us and walked into a dimly lit room, and the swaying of the surging ocean caused me to grip the wall. It smelled of rust and fish.

"We're there!" Thane exclaimed when we appeared.

"No, we're not," William groaned.

They were bound to the wall by chains. Shredded pieces of clothing littered the floor, and what was left on their bodies was soaked with black blood. Multiple bite marks on their arms and necks glistened in the dim, flickering lights of the ship.

"Come to take another hit at me?" William smiled through bloody teeth, and it disappeared when he saw us. "What are you two doing?"

"We came to tell you we've got your back and shit." Zach sighed, with his hands in his pockets.

"We're fucked, then." Will smiled.

"Are we there? Or are we almost there? It can't be much longer now." Thane shook in his chains excitedly. "You two met Her. What's She like?"

My heart sank. Whether it was Thane's innocent expression or the fact he was attached to the hip with Presley and Aaron while in Blackheart, I didn't know, but he reminded me of them. The fate we'd saved them from but not everyone.

"He's been like that this whole time. I'm . . . I'm afraid they gave him too much blood to keep him from complaining. I've heard the stories and—"

"No. We can fix this," I said.

"You don't know that."

"Come on, Will. I'm fine. You'll see," Thane whined.

"I do." I crouched down in front of Will. "I promise. We'll fix him."

I had to keep going until they were all safe.

Three

LUKE

A gray stone castle stood in the distance, highlighted by the night sky.

"Welcome home," Ezra said next to me. "You both must carry good luck. It's the first and likely the only snow of the season."

Tiny snowflakes fell on my face in rapid succession. The trees around us were evergreen, and the white powder fell to the wood and grass around the dock. It was cold enough to stick. Tall, thin trees lined the shores, and an old stone building stood next to the water's edge.

"Lucky us," Zach grumbled.

I smiled at my last memory of Zach in the snow. He'd bit it in our high school parking lot.

I'd hoped to see the snow in Blackheart and daydreamed of what it would look like in the redwood trees.

Our boat docked, and we stepped onto creaking wood. The boats at the harbor looked new. A gray stone castle loomed a hill's length away, and my heart fluttered with the anticipation of seeing Her. Was it nervousness? Worry? Fear?

Zach and I waited while we watched some members pull William and Thane from the hull. William's smirk was stained with blood.

Ezra grabbed his collar to look him in the face. "Ready for your judgment?"

Will spit black blood in his face, and Zach and I had to try to hide our amusement. Ezra wiped it with a handkerchief from his pocket and motioned toward the castle.

"So, what's the plan?" Zach whispered next to me.

I had one he wouldn't like.

There were two roads in my mind. Each was a diverging path of how this was about to go. The dark road filled with peril was one in which we reached Her and She killed Will and Thane right away. It seemed the most obvious, but what would killing them satisfy? Revenge? Akira mentioned revenge as something only The Legion cared about. He wasn't a trusted source, but from what I remembered about Akira, he told the truth more often than not.

Their history made me think there was more than revenge here.

In a perfect world, the other road would be a place where they would keep them alive with a simple please, but the opposite path wasn't a sunny, happy one. It was more like a well-kept wooded trail. It would cost something, and I was okay with that because I was open to giving. The one thing I wouldn't give up was my brother, but they wouldn't ask to harm him. So, what did we have to lose?

We could navigate it if we played our cards right.

"We keep them alive at all costs."

"Ah, the Calem special. I like it."

Being in charge meant I needed to be thinking five steps ahead and have a plan. Even if that plan wasn't that great. Heavy hangs the crown, I guess.

I had a good feeling about it, and my gut never steered me wrong.

We followed along a cobblestone trail that was intricately placed over mowed grass. As we neared the castle, it broke out into a checkered pattern. The world in my peripheral vision was a wash of gray or green. A set of large hedges sat near the front of the property, and next to them was a pond the size of a hockey rink, fit with a fountain barely trickling. I was sure there was more, but it was all I could see at night. The snow flurries grew larger and larger, covering my coat.

Sirius stood at the end of the path grinning with his hands held politely in front of him. His thick brown hair was pushed away from his face, and his suit was perfectly pressed. On his hand, silver rings with emeralds and one with a small ruby laid across his warm beige skin.

"Well, well. My brothers have come home at last," he said with a smooth voice.

I hardly thought of him as a brother. Mentor was closer but not quite the nail on the head. Of the three, we'd interacted the least with Sirius. He was always with Her while Ezra and Akira handled most of the day to day.

"I wish I could say it was nice to see you." Zach smiled.

"I wouldn't expect such flattery from you, Zach Calem." Sirius smiled back.

He looked at me, and I wondered what he saw. The boy he once knew or a man who was a shell.

"I've been instructed to take you to Her immediately upon your arrival. Then we can make with the pleasantries."

"We're ready." Fire ignited in my veins as I said it. The moment was finally here, and I wouldn't cower or run away. *Fate, here I come.*

The cathedral was on the other side of the castle. Its flying buttresses towered into the night sky but didn't quite make it to the height of the castle. Sirius explained they weren't connected as he walked us toward the back until we stood in front of a large set of double doors. The stone of the cathedral was gray, but the door was a warm mahogany. Sitting above it, a stained-glass window was illuminated by the light inside. I couldn't decipher it, but it reminded me of my art history class and looked like a nymph bathing in a pond.

The doors to the cathedral opened. At the back, a tall stained-glass window overlooked the building with high ceilings decorated in the most intricate painted art.

She stood at the foot of a set of stairs near a chair fit for a queen. Her hair was a white blanket at Her shoulders, and She had a sheer ivory fabric draped across Her thin frame. I swore Her eyes darted to me first.

A wave of emotion anchored my feet to the floor until I was kneeling. My body shook from the weight of it. I wanted to run to Her. To feel Her. To apologize. To hide in Her shadow.

Zach placed a hand on my shoulder and bowed next to me. He met my eyeline. Only, he had desperation in his eyes, like he was hoping to see something in me. Something strong and sure. It was enough for me to straighten my shoulders and face Her head-on.

The emotion surging inside me was a feeling, and feelings weren't truth. It would pass.

The lace hem of Her dress trailed after Her with a long fabric train, and the ivory fabric fell from Her arms. Her slender fingers brushed a hair out of Her eyes. And Her lips . . .

Why had I been so afraid? Why had I wanted to be anywhere else but here?

Her irises, cloudy and gray, stayed steadily on me, and I waited for beautiful words to come from Her glorious lips.

"Welcome home."

Could words sever a soul from a body? They cut deep in my marrow and sinews. I tried to fight the pull, but Her words were ink to page.

"How was your journey?" She stopped looking at me to turn to Ezra, and the absence of Her attention left me empty.

"Eventful. Akira did well. He served his purpose with honor."

"And honored he shall be."

She stepped toward me, and I froze. How long had I waited for this moment? All that pacing around in my room in agony for this small sliver of time in the universe. I'd thought it had been fear. Disgust. But those words didn't exist in this place.

Her cool fingers caressed my cheek, and my chest seized.

"That's enough," Zach snapped.

"You dare speak out of turn?" Sirius said.

I couldn't stop looking at Her and feeling the ecstasy of Her skin on mine. I never wanted it to end.

"It's all right, Sirius. Let them get their bearings. You may all speak as freely as you wish."

Her thumb moved along the stubble on my jaw. I wasn't moving. I was Hers. Entirely. Completely.

"I missed you," She said in a whisper. "You look well."

My whole body was hot. My only thought was that I wanted Her to never stop touching me.

"I-I missed you too." I didn't know if I meant it.

"I mean it. Stop." Zach moved closer, but Ezra grabbed his shoulder. "Touch me again, and I'll take your fucking arm off."

His aggravation broke me from the trance, and I pulled away.

"It's fine, Ezra. He won't hurt me. He worries for his brother."

When She moved away, all the air got sucked out of the room, but I was grounded again. She reached toward my brother, and he flinched with gritted teeth.

"Don't."

"You didn't miss me?" Her lips curled into a curious smile.

"No. And I'd appreciate it if you kept your hands off me and my brother. We're here like you wanted. It's not a fucking petting zoo."

Sirius growled. "Careful how you speak to Her."

She retreated to the chair carved out of gray and white marble. The cathedral appeared bigger on the inside with pillars that arched up to the ceiling. All the windows were colored glass, and there were dark wood pews near the back.

"I suspect you're both exhausted from the journey and the changes. You'll want to settle in and get your feet set. No need to worry about being separated. You may go wherever you like and stay with each other whenever you please. I want to make this a pleasant experience for all involved."

"That's comical." Zach scoffed.

"I wish to start anew. We're to build our family. I've waited years for this moment. What can I offer that will earn me your trust?"

"A fucking time machine maybe."

"Our brothers . . . What happens to them?" I asked.

In the forest, they'd tried to grab us all, which meant they had a plan for them. My little brothers believed Akira's words about the prophecy, but I hadn't accepted it. I wouldn't.

"I see you wish to keep them hidden. I'm not concerned with bringing them here if it makes you unhappy," She said.

"That's not good enough. We need answers," Zach said. "We know about the prophecy."

"When the dark sun descends, a new era begins. The celestial dance may spell doom for your throne. Twins of Gemini will usher in the new Guard. To four, every knee shall bend. In shadow's haze, power ascends. Those who dream of your demise shall kneel in gloom's embrace. And chaos descends in all fates."

She recited the words like a well-rehearsed play.

"I wasn't expecting to dream of you two, but not soon after we lost Eros—a treasured member of The Guard, I closed my eyes and felt you. So many years away, calling to me. The Divine spoke and gave me word of your arrival. I was told you'd arrive under the light of a full moon. You were sent to me to complete the bond that was broken. So we can be a family again. And when I met your brothers, I felt that bond running through their blood. You are mine. And they are yours. They belong to all of us. However, if it is your wish to let them be separate from us, I will respect it."

"All of this so we can be together?"

"Bonds are the most important thing in this world. Only people with real power have them. To navigate this world, we must forge together the broken souls into something greater. A family where we can all be together for eternity. We do not grow old. We do not die."

Sirius and Ezra walked to stand beside Her. I wondered about that bond. The other two Guard members were absent.

"What's the point in forming a Guard and creating a family here?"

"Why does anyone form a family? For connection. For protection. For love. The Divine flows through me, and with that connection, I bring in those who were lost. And they need leaders, people like you."

Zach pinched the bridge of his nose but didn't protest. I didn't either. What could I say to that? How could I argue with fate? And as long as my little brothers were kept out of it, I might be able to accept it.

"Now, as for The Legion—"

"I'll take accountability for them." I interrupted.

The room stirred, and the candles next to Her marble chair flickered.

"You can't kill them."

"You want me to spare them?" Her eyes were soft, but Her perfect lips turned to a frown.

"Yes."

"Their fate was already decided by The Guard. We bleed them out on the lawn at dawn. For Eros." Sirius scowled at me.

I couldn't blame him. If the Legion killed his brother, I could understand that pain. I didn't believe in revenge, but for my brothers, I might.

"Sirius is right. The Legion knows too much already. Holding on to them will do nothing but cause more trouble for us all. Someone must pay for Eros's death."

"I'll do whatever you want. Name your price," I said.

"Luke," Zach said.

There was a stirring next to me, and Will wiggled to try to get his mouth free. His dark eyes met mine, but his words were muffled. I'd almost forgotten they were in the room because I'd been so focused on Her. Thane was kneeling on the floor, staring at the queen with veneration.

"You must care about them a great deal."

When it came to myself, I wasn't sure what I wanted, but I knew for certain what I wanted for others and what I'd do to make sure it happened.

"I do. I can't sit by and watch you kill them. I don't want to try to fight, but I will."

"We can't allow them to live. It's not right," Sirius said.

I stepped forward, and Zach followed with his shoulders pulled back and his chest out. We couldn't take them, but it didn't matter. Sirius dropped down to the bottom step and unbuttoned his cuff.

"Let's keep a level head." Ezra stopped Sirius with a hand on the shoulder. "This isn't how we want to start things."

"Is that all it takes for your compliance? Sparing these two. That's all you want?"

Want. When did it ever matter what I wanted?

"Yes. Well . . . one other thing."

She tilted Her head to the side and waited for me to speak again while pulling Her hands through the ends of Her hair.

"Fix Thane. Cleanse his blood and make him normal again."

"He's more at peace now than his friend. He's rightfully whole and fulfilled. But if it's to make you happy, it is done. What will you offer in exchange for my generosity?"

Ezra pulled at Sirius whose body was shaking.

What could I offer that wouldn't feel like an insult?

"I offer my unfailing loyalty as I have offered to my brothers. I promise to do my best here. To try to live here and train to be in The Guard to protect you. I won't fight."

"And I trust your brother feels the same?"

I turned to Zach with a sheepish grin. He was used to me doing this by now, and this was what he'd asked for on the plane. He wanted me to try, and this was me trying.

"Yes, Your Greatness. I agree to be at your beck and call."

Ezra shook his head at the sarcasm oozing from Zach's voice, and Will mumbled again.

"It's a start. I'll require you to see me every morning at dawn."

Butterflies filled my stomach at the attention I'd receive from Her.

"You're welcome to come." She beamed at Zach, and his teeth grit together. "This one will be yours to watch."

She moved the hair from Will's forehead, and he flinched.

"And the other will be for you to watch, My Love. They must always be under observation, and they will serve you and The Family for two hundred years at minimum. After that time, we can reevaluate that sentence. What do you think, Love?"

She looked at me again, and I felt the pull, the need to sit at Her feet and collapse in Her arms. To beg Her to make this yearning end. I should have focused on what She was saying and the importance of it, but I was caught in Her affection for me and the softness in Her features as She spoke.

"Love?" I cleared my throat.

"Yes, Love. Will that make you happy?"

Happy wasn't the right word, but I felt at peace with it. I turned to Will, and he nodded. It wasn't freedom, but it was better than death. Two hundred years was a long time to figure out an escape plan.

"For now."

Four

ZACH

It had to be a joke. God, or whatever, had it out for me. Keeping Luke from being himself in all situations would be tough. With his constant need to be good, it made protecting him way harder than it needed to be. I cared about Will and Thane, sure, but Luke always gave too much. It was a replay of Blackheart and every time he'd done it before that—too many to count. In his worst moments, he'd tell me he didn't understand the person he was. He gave everyone so much there was nothing left for him. He felt like he had no personality. When the sun came up, he knew it was bullshit, but I hated how the topic kept surfacing. He kept saying it like he believed it.

I'd already forgiven him for his lack of care for himself by the time we reached the door to our room.

"This will be your room."

After a series of arched entryways and long hallways with floral rugs, we arrived at yet another wooden door. It had cherubs and other decorative shit carved into it. I was more concerned with the vein about to pop out of Ezra's head.

They cleansed Thane's blood in the cathedral, then they brought him some blood bags. I guessed they had access to that sort of thing here. We were assured they wouldn't be hurt while receiving their instruction for what was next. I considered it a win. Alive was better than dead.

"Your friends will join you shortly after they're done getting cleaned up and fitted. I'd suggest you keep a close eye on them. No one here will be easy on them but you."

"Thanks . . . " Luke said as we stepped through the door and entered a dimly lit room.

A stained-glass window was set aglow by the fire. Underneath it sat a velvet bench with fringed pillows. On either side of the room were beds that looked way fancier than anything I'd ever slept on.

"You're welcome to separate rooms if you'd like, but I know how you two are."

"This is perfect," Luke said.

I hid my relief. Locking myself in a room alone with my own thoughts could be very bad for me. Probably Luke too. I'd have to see about getting music in the room as soon as possible. One of my little lackeys was probably dying to fetch me something.

"No phones. At least for the first couple months. Same for going out. We'll go out to town, and I'll introduce you to everyone, but we do it together. For now."

"Until you can trust us not to run away?" Luke said.

"You can't run from your own fate. It will find you," Ezra said.

We shared a glance. My brother and I were starting to believe it and were too tired to argue. I couldn't even get tired, but I felt like I'd run a marathon.

Ezra motioned to a spiral staircase that led to a loft. Along the floral-papered walls were different paintings in various frames. Every color in the room was muted, except for the orange of the flickering fire. I welcomed the smell of burning wood.

"You have your own private bathroom up in the loft."

Thank god. I was dying to get the stench of ash out of my hair.

"You two can get settled in till the morning. Explore the place. But don't leave the castle."

"Got it," Luke said as he collapsed onto his bed, and I did the same in mine.

Cool sheets and the relief of not standing had me melting into a puddle. Ezra left us in silence.

I lay back on the bed and stared up at the ceiling. It was vaulted up to a dome, and inside the dome, a skylight let the light from the moon in. Hundreds of stars painted the dark, and I let my shoulders relax. I wished for sleep, for a break from the torment of the day. I was tempted to think of my brothers. Had they made it to their destination? Luke never told me where it was. The less I knew, the better, and the less I thought of it, the better too. I rubbed the ache in my chest.

"Maybe this is what I was meant for." Luke's voice echoed from across the room.

"What?"

"They could be telling the truth. This is fate. I'm meant to be with Her."

"Luke, don't say that shit. I'm serious. I'm going to punch you if you say anything like that again."

I hated the idea of it. If it were true, there wasn't anything right in the world. Because there was no way Luke would be with someone like Her, and he didn't deserve to be here. He should have been back on that mountain baking cookies with our brothers and singing songs.

"Then why at every turn do we end up in the same place? Why does it feel truer than anything else?"

"Just because it feels like that doesn't make it true," I grumbled.

"You always say that."

"You should listen to me, then." I sat up to glare at him. "You're not the only one allowed to be right. We ended up here again. So what? It doesn't mean anything. It could be worse." *Not really.*

"We can see it as an extended holiday. We've never been out of the country. Could be a new opportunity," I said.

"For?"

"Change," I said.

I was shit at pep talks. What Luke needed most of the time was to get out of his head.

"Come on. Quit moping around. Let's do something fun." I hopped up off my bed.

"Fun? How is anything fun here?"

"We'll make it fun."

"We'll make being in a cult fun?"

"Fuck yeah."

I walked up to his bed and held out my hand to pull him up.

Luke groaned. "I really wanted to rot away in here all night."

"I know. That's why we need to get out. Where's all that team spirit?"

I used to make fun of Luke for the football thing. He'd been good at it, like he was good at everything he did. It was all in good fun. I'd enjoyed watching him play while I slunk around behind the stands and smoked.

"I don't have any little brothers to encourage anymore."

"Technically, I'm younger than you."

"Shut up."

We walked into the hallway. A man, who I'd hardly call a man, stood outside our door. He blushed before he bowed.

"H-hi, I'm Connell. I'm so honored to meet you both." He looked at the ground. "I've heard so much about you from the others who knew you before you were . . . Well, I can't tell you how excited I am to finally see you in person. If you need anything, please tell me. I'll get it done."

Luke and I shared the same wide-eyed confusion, but I knew what Luke was thinking. This kid was young. He had to be newly turned and no older than eighteen. It didn't help he had short curly blond hair and was the same height as Presley. At least he had blue eyes and a thick Irish accent. It didn't matter either way. Luke had that savior look in his eye like he wanted to wrap the kid in a hug and tell him to make better choices.

He couldn't help himself, and it wasn't just anyone who was younger but anyone weaker who needed help. It's like he could sense it in people. The only woman in the store who had a hard day and needed her groceries taken to her car. Or the old man taking longer at the bench because he was waiting for someone to help him get up because his knees were shot. He had a radar for it, and I was always there, right next to him, holding those groceries or grabbing the other hand. They'd thank me too, and I'd smile back. It made Luke radiantly happy, but for me . . . nothing.

That goodness would hurt. He would try to get this kid's story and get too attached. I needed to be the buffer.

"You new?" I asked.

"Yeah. I got inducted last week. It was exhilarating," Connell said while he scratched his freckled arm. His face was covered in them too.

"Where are your parents?"

"They're gone, sir. My mum died young, and my dad was reaped."

"Reaped?" Luke asked.

"Oh yeah, sent to Her Gloriousness, of course."

Luke's face went white.

"It doesn't happen to many. A lot of the guys here never had any family. It's an honor, really, to have someone I could sacrifice to Her Magnificence."

Luke said nothing, but I saw it all over his face. He wanted to grab this kid and run out of the castle, as if we weren't also fucked and Ezra wouldn't pop up like the boogeyman the moment we set foot outside.

"Don't look so concerned, sir. He had a bad drinking habit. I kinda hope he isn't with Her eternally like She said. I secretly hope he's rotting in hell somewhere." His shrill laugh echoed in the hallway.

I cleared my throat to stop the little fucker from talking another minute. "Connell, what's a guy gotta do to get a drink around here?"

Drinking was about the only thing Luke and I did for fun anymore. We'd never had a lot of hobbies in common, but back in Brooklyn, we could watch movies or take the girls out. None of which could ever be done again after Sarah died. Luke and I couldn't even sit still long enough to watch a thirty-minute TV show, let alone a whole movie.

Unless Presley strapped us down to watch his *Twilight* marathon.

"Oh, we could go to The Underground! That's where a lot of the guys hang out at this hour. It's downstairs. I'll show you."

We followed. Luke watched the back of Connell's head, quietly creating another plan.

"Don't do it," I said.

"I'm not."

Connell walked ahead of us talking, and neither of us listened.

"You can't save him, Luke. We can barely save ourselves right now."

"But . . . he reminds me of Presley."

That did it. My whole body ached with a sharp pain that made my stomach turn. I stopped walking.

"Okay, rule. No talking about them. No saying their names. No bringing up old memories."

"But—"

"Please," I said to the only person I'd ever whisper that word to.

He nodded and we walked on.

Connell knew it all. Where and why they selected every painting on the walls. The type of wallpaper. How old the stonework on the fountain was. Luke agreed when Connell offered to give us a tour tomorrow afternoon, and I had to act like it wasn't the worst idea I'd ever heard.

He led us through the garden. There were rows and rows of budded flowers being suffocated by the falling snow. We passed a stone gondola, and next to the castle was a wooden cellar door.

"Did you bring us here to kill us, Connell?"

He snorted. "Good one, sir!"

"Someone finally thinks I'm funny." I smiled at my brother as he rolled his eyes and pushed me through the door.

It was an old wine cellar bathed in red lights and cigar smoke, and there was music. Perfect. Only, the room went silent as we entered. Everyone fell on one knee before I could blink. Even the ones who looked too drunk to say their own name.

"This way to the bar. What'll you have? We have nothin' but top-shelf liquor."

"Whiskey. Neat."

"Beer. Any kind," Luke said.

"Plus, two shots. Surprise me," I said

Luke nodded. He needed to loosen up, and one of the only perks of being a vampire was there was no hangover. Can't poison a body that's basically dead.

A few of the guys were recognizable, but I had never really paid attention before. We went along with whatever Ezra wanted us to do. I blamed it on my brain not being fully developed yet.

Luke and I were in a different class now. It was easy to tell because we'd been members of each at one point or another. The first rung was the humans. Which we used to be. It was easy work. We'd had little jobs like collecting money for Ezra or running pickpocket schemes in the city. We were high schoolers and made games out of it. I don't think either of us took it that seriously. It wasn't until senior year that we started to realize we were in deep. We wanted to move up even though we didn't fully understand what that meant. Because while Ashley and Sarah were applying to colleges, we were too busy playing the role of criminals in the city.

Once we turned, we were above all who we used to consider peers. And we trained. That's where I learned what my new body could do. Getting turned and not understanding was scary at first, but that wasn't the part of The Family I hated. It was the best part. A new body that could move in new deadly ways. Plus, immortality didn't suck.

I'd always known things were different for Luke and me. No one ever let us forget it, with their long scowls and their whispering. Now I understood why. We were set apart for Her.

"We've awaited your return, sir." A familiar voice made me turn.

"Henderson." I threw back my shot.

Henderson leaned against the bar with a drink in his hand. His head hit the low-hanging light as he nodded to us. He was bigger than Luke in height and rivaled him in build.

"Good to see you." Luke smiled and held out his hand to shake.

Henderson licked his unusually sharp canines. "Sorry. Can't, sir. There are rules about that sort of thing now."

"Right." Luke swished his beer.

"It's nice to have you here finally. What took you two so long?"

Henderson didn't like us. It had to do with the fact that he was at least eighty years old and jealous as fuck he wasn't a "chosen one." He looked young with no wrinkles on his smooth tan skin. He'd told me his age back before I realized he only liked to keep tabs on us.

"We like to annoy you."

I downed my other drink and motioned for Luke to take his shot. The pain in my chest was finally subsiding, and I could function normally again.

"Did you see Connery?"

I saw Connery back in Blackheart when he plunged a knife into his chest. They had been attached at the hip like Luke and me. Not related, from what I remembered, but great friends. Luke was in no condition to break bad news to him, and I didn't give a fuck if he knew Connery was dead or not.

I took the lead. "Yeah. He seemed . . . happy."

I mean, he *did* look happy with his decision to plunge that knife into his chest.

"He told me he was handpicked by Akira to go. A huge honor. When he didn't come back with you, I figured it might have been something that kept him in America."

"Yeah, something like that."

"How are you?" Luke's voice was softer. "In this place?"

He was being genuine. *The fucking teddy bear.*

"Ireland is amazing. The countryside. The people. I prefer it to America. I hope to never go back. You'll both come to love it, I'm sure."

I raised my glass to my lips and let the comfort of the alcohol burn my throat. A guy could hope.

"You can't help yourself, can you?" I smiled as Henderson left.

"I really can't."

We watched the others play pool and readied ourselves to join. Most were friendly, but I felt their eyes on me when I wasn't looking. This would be different from before. Being part of The Guard was different.

I should have cared more about being forced to be in The Guard, but all I could think about was that there wasn't anything they could force me to do that I wouldn't do for my brother. If we were trapped, he needed me to make this easier for him. I wasn't sure what that would look like, but I knew I could.

I'd never imagined more for myself than here. Hell, drinking and hanging around with a bunch of assholes sounded fun to me.

After a few drinks, Luke finally smiled, and my work was done for the night.

"You were right. This is fun."

Five

LUKE

The morning came for me despite me willing it not to, and it came in the form of William and Thane knocking on our door. We spent hours drinking before The Underground started to clear. It was a nice distraction for our first night.

"Don't you say a fuckin' word, Calem." William loosened his collar.

They were dressed in all-white slacks and dress shirts. He reminded me of a butler, but I would not mention that. Thane's long hair was brushed into a clean bun, and William's looked freshly cut on the sides.

"Come on, Will. It could be worse," I said.

"No, it really couldn't. We're at the threshold of hell," Will said.

"Not even the threshold. I'd say we're cruising around level two or three right now," Zach said.

"Serving the Calem twins in hell. If you'd have told me this months ago . . ."

"We'll go easy on you. You bossed me around for months, and now that karma is back to repay you." Zach smiled from ear to ear.

"They want me to bow." Will gritted his teeth while looking at himself in our floor-length mirror.

"Well, come on. Let's see it," Zach said.

"Fuck. You."

Zach nudged him. "You can shine my shoes instead."

"I need a cigarette."

It was a sobering experience. In a matter of days, everything was different. No more late nights in the frat house listening and watching my little brothers live their lives free of burden. I loved being there for them. Did I miss college? Had I liked my classes? I wasn't sure, but I was sure I was happy then, when they were happy and we were together.

"My vote is on a big distraction. We could set fire to the castle. Will and Thane brain wipe a few, and we steal a boat," my brother said.

"The only way that works is if you're interested in watching them torture us when they catch us. From what I've gathered so far, a lot of people here are the same age or older than Thane and me. We wouldn't be able to keep them under. You're talking about four of us against more than twenty moderately matched opponents if they catch us. Not to mention the actual Guard. They could have people waiting on the mainland."

"It's too risky. We need time to have a better opening," I said. We needed time to construct a plan that might actually work.

Thane was quieter than usual, and his gaze burned a hole in my face.

"Luke, I wanted to thank you for doing that for me." Thane pulled me aside while William and Zach continued to bicker. "I'm so sorry."

"You don't need to apologize. The others are safe. That's all that matters."

"I knew you were going to say that, but I was rooting for you guys. I didn't want you to have to come back to them. So being the reason that you are here is—"

"I know."

"No. Let me say this. I've always been loyal to The Legion. They're all I have. The only good thing I've ever had in my life. And when Akira cornered me in the forest and forced Her blood down my throat, nothing else mattered. I forgot about the things I stood for and the people I care about. I thought I understood after the trial in the church. But that grew after getting to know all of you. I knew I needed to help you. And now I get it so much more. So that's what I'm going to do. I'm going to help you get out of here. I owe you. I'm in your debt."

"I'm more concerned with getting you and Will out first."

"Oh no. That's not happening. We all go or none of us do."

Before I could protest, Zach stepped in.

"Are we good over here?"

Zach wouldn't forgive Thane easily. He didn't forgive people. Holding grudges was fun for him. Anyone who wasn't immediate family didn't often get second chances. I'd come to accept it even if I didn't agree.

"He's fine." I wouldn't let him torture Thane on my watch.

Thane had been manipulated like my brother and me. In my book, there was nothing to forgive.

"No, that's good. I'd prefer one of you to be angry with me. It makes me feel better." Thane's lips tugged into a wide smile.

"Oh, perfect. See? We're going to get along great, then," Zach said.

"It's almost dawn. We should go," I said.

I'd promised to meet their demands, though I didn't have a choice.

"Do we know where we're going?" I said as we made our way into the hallway.

"Unfortunately, yes," William said. "Follow me."

I had paid little attention to Connell's brief tour. The castle was huge. We passed a lot of doors, some open and showing brief glimpses into the architecture and decor. Every window was stained glass, and most rooms had thick ornate rugs. There was no dust on the end tables or picture frames.

A magnetism pulled me toward the other end of the castle. My thoughts were speeding up again, and my pulse raced in my palms.

"Here. Thane and I can't go in." William stopped in front of the large set of double doors.

I could hear Her heartbeat, as I placed my hand on the door.

"Because of Ezra?" I asked.

"He made our deaths pretty vividly obvious if we set foot in there. We can't even go there with ya," William said.

There was a shift in his voice. His accent had peeked through.

My brother and I shared a look.

"This place bringing back the ole accent, buddy?" Zach smirked.

"Fuck off. I'm so used to hiding it. But I guess I don't need to anymore."

"Where you grew up, was it around here?" I asked.

Will revealed little about his past while in Blackheart. He was too busy telling us what to do.

"No, I lived in the South. I can't believe I'm fuckin' here. This place haunted my nightmares as a kid."

"I heard 'em too. Though I think they turned this place into a historical landmark. I overheard them talking about giving tourist tours of the far end of the property."

"Great. Glad we're stuck here in this nightmare of a place. Good reminder," Zach said.

"Stop stalling and go," Will said.

Zach and I pushed open the doors.

It opened to a large and expansive room with marble flooring. A room meant for something else, but they'd undoubtedly transformed it with lavish drapes. The linens were clean and pressed. Her bed was the centerpiece with a canopy of black sheets cascading from the ceiling and onto a rug below. There were no windows or natural light, only a sprinkling of candles and dim lights around the room. A large harp sat on the far edge of the room along with a vanity with fresh purple roses and thistle.

We bowed to the natural weight of Her gaze.

"I'm pleased to hear you were both out speaking with everyone. You're all anyone has talked about for the last few months. Your family has anxiously awaited your return."

It hadn't felt like months in Blackheart. It took me that long to feel . . . safe. As safe as I could with Akira breathing down my neck. It was odd looking back. How I'd had days where I'd spent time going to class and working at the theater. If I'd pretended long enough, I could almost forget about this place.

On second thought, I did like working and school, even if it had felt a little like playing pretend. My chest ached when I thought of it, even while standing next to Her.

Something about Her was different from the day before. Her posture was less rigid and Her smile softer. "Usually Ezra is my companion, but we thought it might be appropriate for us to spend time together. I spend many hours in this room, so I enjoy the company. I mostly rest. After the full moon, my energy slowly drains till the end of the moon cycle. This mortal body isn't able to hold the power of The Divine for long."

"Oh, I didn't know that."

We didn't see Her much before. Only when it was time to donate our blood to Her. I'd never seen Her look even the slightest bit frail.

"It's not something we want all to know."

She came up to rest Her hand on mine, and I shivered at the coolness of Her touch. I drank in the sight of Her before me. Glistening eyes; perfect lips, teeth, and tongue.

"We usually start the day in the garden before the sun is up."

She motioned for my brother. "You're always welcome to come along."

He said nothing. My guess was he had nothing nice to say.

"You want to walk in the garden?"

"Yes, My Love."

"And that's it?"

"Yes, it's nice to get out. Sometimes we go for night walks too. There are plenty of other things too, but this is my favorite. I thought you'd enjoy it too."

She wasn't like I remembered Her. In many ways, it was like seeing Her for the first time. When I got lost in Her eyes, I could almost forget about who She really was and how She'd taken the kindest person I'd ever known away from me.

The guilt brought me back to reality. "Let's go, then. I'll need some guidance, though."

She smiled and took my arm, sending a wave of euphoria through my entire body. I wrapped Her arm in mine and let Her lean into me. Zach glared. Far behind us, Will and Thane followed.

With Her skin touching mine, I wasn't scared or nervous anymore. I felt at ease. Peaceful even. The rest of the world fell away, and I floated with Her down the hallways and through arched doorways until we were outside. The chill of the early morning permeated my jacket. A blue haze lingered in the sky where the sun was dawning.

She led us out through a mossy cobblestone archway covered in snow and ivy.

"You don't have shoes?" Zach grumbled.

He had his hands stuffed in his pockets and his collar pulled up to protect himself from the bite of the cold.

"I don't have much use for them. I don't travel to many places."

"Do your feet get cold?" he asked.

"I'm used to the winter. I grew up here. Before I was what I am, I had many days spent on this very soil. I enjoyed the outdoors the most. Many hours spent with my brother playing in the hills by the cliffs."

Her foot slipped on a cobblestone, and Zach and I moved to steady Her. It was quick and instinctual.

"I'm fine. Thank you."

"Shit." Zach picked up the train of Her silk gown. "You're going to get your dress dirty."

She smiled at him, and I swear my brother blushed. Step by step, he shifted closer to us.

"I didn't think you'd remember anything before you . . ."

"Yes, me and The Divine are connected now. At times, it's strong, and at other times, it's faint. But I have all her memories . . . my memories. The human's memories. We were once two completely separate beings, and then we formed into one."

"Is that why you sound so . . . normal, then?" Zach said.

"Yes. Our body has had many years to adjust to a new way of speaking."

Together, the three of us were in a different place. A blissful trance. It was hard to remember the past or the pain. It was simple to think of Her. To fall into Her rhythm and care for Her. Something shifted within me, and I wondered if every cobblestone step was leading me on the path of The Divine. I didn't know what I wanted, but I didn't mind walking in the garden if She was next to me.

Thick flakes of snow fell onto my eyelashes. The sky had turned from a milky blue to a soft yellow. We'd walked around the entire garden that spanned the left side of the castle. Beyond it, a set of cliffs and a raging sea beckoned. Time had passed without my recollection.

"Should we stay out?" I said, with the wet from the snow seeping into my clothes.

"No, let's go inside."

We walked Her through the garden and through a stone corridor. Sirius met us halfway. He bowed to Her, then peered up at Zach through his long lashes. A small smile caught in the corner of his mouth.

Zach was still holding Her dress.

"I'm requesting Zach's presence. Will you grant him leave?"

"He's free to do what he wishes."

"You could keep holding Her dress if you'd like. Or we could start training. I'll want to see you too, Luke. But it can wait."

"Oh, fuck yeah." Zach's eyes lit up, then his face quickly fell. "I don't know if I should."

"I'll be fine," I said, knowing his fear was about me.

Zach wasn't afraid of anything unless I was involved. I hated being the one weakness of my otherwise impenetrable brother. I didn't hate that he cared. Just that it made him do wild things and prevented him from doing things he wanted to do.

He cocked his head, not saying a word, but I could almost hear his question. *Are you sure?*

I nodded. I vowed not to let him be alone with Her again—not that he didn't sneak off and do it anyway. She'd always been harsher with him than me, and I didn't know why.

Will left with them, and I escorted Her back to Her room while Thane stayed a few paces behind. Once alone in Her bedroom, I escorted Her to the vanity chair.

"Can I ask you something?" I asked.

"Anything, Love."

"Do you ever miss your family? Your parents, I mean. It's probably been so long for you."

She studied me for a minute. "Yes. My dad, in particular. A great man. He took care of me."

Kilian had run me through what he knew about Her history. The human had been married, then died three short years after. She was the daughter of a chieftain over five hundred years ago and had taken over her father's reign. Her name, Cecily Dooley. I had questions but none which seemed right to ask Her in the moment.

"He sounds like a great man. What do you miss the most?"

"My father possessed a hearty laugh. He had me and then my little brother. He was quite proud to have an eldest daughter to take his place. Not many men felt that way about their daughters then." She smiled down at Her hands, then up at me. "You must miss your brothers."

"Yes."

"I knew you'd be unhappy like this. But I respect your decision."

There was something about Her. The way She moved made me soften to Her and let down my walls.

"It will get better." She was angelically beautiful. Her face was smooth like porcelain.

She leaned into my shoulder, and Her scent and presence filled up the cool air and thickened in my lungs. "I've learned pain doesn't last forever."

"What about the prophecy?"

"The prophecy was a message from The Divine given to me one night only. After Eros died, there was a solar eclipse. It found me. The path of totality came over us, and the stars spoke to me about you two. There is another coming soon. The path will head over this very castle. The place where the Earth goes dark has found me again. I believe it will have the answers of who is to complete The Guard."

"I don't get it. There's a prophecy, but you can see the future too?"

"Only when I touch you." She ran Her fingers along my forearm. "And I can't do it all the time. Only on certain moons. There's a differ-ence between The Divine's message and what I see. When I touch you,

I can see your most likely path based on your current decisions and the decisions of others. But I can also see many other futures too. It changes quickly. But The Divine's word is the one true path."

I leaned into Her. Tethered to Her gravity. She continued to move Her fingers over my forearm and over my ear until they were in the stubble of the hair on my neck.

"Now, can *I* ask you something, My Love?"

I nodded, still enamored with Her.

"How was your time with Kilian and the Legion?"

I swallowed. She was likely angry, and rightfully so. My brother and I left. We bolted and ran to their one enemy for help. There were plans that involved us coming back here and tricking them. Kilian was vague. It all seemed ridiculous now.

"It was . . . he was . . . " I couldn't find the words to explain how I felt about all of it because it was confusing, even more so when She looked at me. I was sure then I wanted to leave, but now that I was seated next to Her, the thought of leaving Her terrified me.

"Are you angry with me?"

"No. I understand why you and your brother left. I apologize for my rash decisions with the girl. I should have never punished you so harshly. I just want to know. You could show me."

"Like . . . you want in my head?" I pulled away from Her, but She reached up to rub the skin under my jaw.

"Only if you'll allow me."

"I don't know."

"I won't hurt you. It's easier. I'm within you and you're within me."

"I want to. I'm just afraid." Normally, I'd cry, but next to Her, I wasn't sure it was possible. She kept me together somehow, with hopeful anticipation.

"I'm sorry. I promise. Things are different now. I'll only take care of you. You're so special to me." She leaned in and placed a kiss on my cheek.

"Okay." I couldn't believe my words as I said them, but I needed Her to keep touching me.

With one hand rested on my hand in my lap, She laid the other across my cheek.

I braced myself for something sick and terrible, like when She'd given me all my memories back and I learned about Sarah's death, but it was gentle as She waded through my memories of Blackheart, only lingering on the moments with Kilian. The time spent in his study where we'd meet. He mostly asked me questions about our childhood. Kilian wasn't someone I liked, more like someone I tolerated. Every exchange was a transaction of something. He liked to go through memories, and I'd let him. Hoping it would help a little of this anxious panic let go of me, but it made it worse.

I sucked in a breath as the memory faded. Her hand clenched around mine, and She stayed stroking my cheek. It helped alleviate the weight of it.

"I'm sorry he betrayed you. That must have been scary."

It was. All of it was scary. Thinking Kimberly and Presley were dead. Kilian locking us in a room, and thinking I wouldn't be able to get to them. I'd been trying to construct another plan, all the while knowing we were outmatched. All the feelings from the memories lingered in my chest, and I pinched the bridge of my nose. My hand shook from the intensity of it all. All that time in Blackheart. Every panic attack.

She continued to touch me, lightly massaging my tensed forearms.

"Yeah, it was."

"Kilian threatened your brothers. After having had a brother himself, I would have believed he'd have some understanding of what a bond like that could mean."

I drew in a breath. My chest grew tight and panic washed through me.

"I'm here." She gathered my hands in Hers. "There's nothing to fear anymore. No one here is going to hurt or trick you. And I won't keep you from your brother."

With the coolness of Her fingers, the panic left as quick as it came.

"I really did miss you." Having seen and felt the memories again, I couldn't hide from that fact. When I was alone in my room, I thought of Her constantly. If I wasn't training or busy at work at the theater, She was on my mind. There was relief in Her presence.

"I know, Love."

My weight shifted, and without thinking, I reached for Her. Cupping Her chin, I pulled Her to me. I needed Her lips on mine.

A knock on the door cut through my trance, and I pulled away.

Ezra stepped in and bowed. "My queen, I have something to discuss."

"Can I go? You'll be all right?" My whole body was hot and buzzing from head to toe.

"I'll be fine, Love. Go if you wish."

I bowed and made my way out into the hallway. I had to fight the urge to sprint.

Thane was next to me. "Hey, wait up. Are you okay?"

"I'm good. I just need some air."

Day one and I was already losing my resolve. I tried not to think. Impossible. What was wrong with me? Had I forgotten in a matter of seconds the things She'd done to Sarah? To my brother? To my family?

The feeling of doom and panic built in my chest.

No, No, Luke. Don't do it. Don't crumble.

I plowed over someone in the hallway.

Laying unmoving, Connell looked up at me, waiting for me to respond.

"I'm so sorry." I reached down to pull him up.

He popped up. "Oh no, please don't apologize, sir."

"Call me Luke."

His eyes widened. "Yes si—I mean, Luke. Yes. I will call you whatever you want."

His smile grew wide, and I saw my brothers so clearly in his face. Grief washed over me, tearing me from top to bottom. I hated this. How could I do this? How could I stay here?

Together. Keep it together.

"Connell, how are you doing here?"

"W-what do you mean?"

"Are you happy? Are you safe?"

He narrowed his eyes, then blurted. "Of course. The guys can be a bit tough at first, but I think they're warmin' to me. Henderson is rough around the edges, but he means well."

"Tell me if he gives you too much trouble. I'll take care of it."

His whole face softened. "Thank you . . ."

I grabbed his shoulder and gave it a squeeze before continuing on to my room.

"He's so young," Thane said, somewhere close at my heels.

I stopped when I reached my bedroom door. "I'm sorry, Thane. Can I have a second?"

"Yeah, of course. Tell me if I can help. I'll stay out here and wait for you."

I entered the room and sighed when I saw only my reflection in the mirror next to the door.

I think I liked my hair long, but I wasn't sure what I did and didn't like. All I knew was I didn't like the way I felt staring at myself in the mirror.

Blackheart may have been brief, but it felt like an eternity away from the past . . . from Sarah . . .

"It's beautiful," I said, watching Sarah comb her dark hair while I sat on the edge of her bed.

"I hate it. It's too dark. It doesn't suit me."

"Everything suits you."

Sarah smiled at me in the mirror. *"What if I dyed it pink, then what would you say?"*

"I'd say . . . hell yeah. Then I'd dye mine too."

"You wouldn't."

"I would if you wanted me to."

"Would you want to?"

"I don't know."

"How do you not know?"

"I don't know. I don't always know how I feel about everything. Like most things are neutral. But I know when I feel something I really do care about. You know?"

She spun around in her computer chair. *"No. I always know. Like I know I want highlights and I want them to be a level eight caramel blonde. And I want to lighten the whole thing to an auburn brown."*

"Oh. You should, then."

"Would you like it?"

"I like anything on you."

"You're sure?"

"That, I'm sure of."

I buried my face in my hands. If I could let go, I could get through this. I needed to be someone different here, but how when everywhere I looked, Sarah haunted me. Could you decide to be someone else? For that to happen, I had to know who I was to begin with, and I didn't.

Who was Luke Calem? Just some guy who ruined the lives of everyone he came in contact with.

The undying optimism circled in my blood. A curse. I shoved it down as I gripped at the short hair on top of my head. I wanted that optimism to die. This place was poisonous. I couldn't have both. I couldn't be with Her and have peace. Me and this place would never mix. No matter how much my body fought to have Her. It wasn't my fault, but I felt guilty even thinking of Her.

There was only one solution to end my torment. We had to leave. It wasn't a revolutionary idea. One we'd had over and over and tried before. It was the definition of insanity to try again. As I remembered the pull of Her when She ran Her fingers across my skin, I knew I'd never be able to avoid Her if we stayed. There had to be a way to get out of this place. And if there wasn't, I'd have to find one.

Six

ZACH

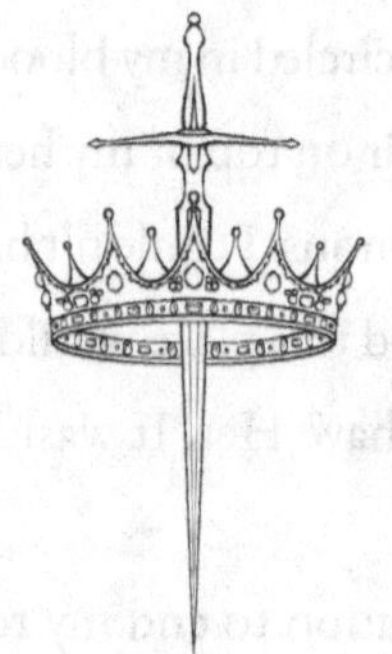

I wondered what Ashley would think if she could see where I'd ended up. She loved a man who could dress. At least I had that going for me.

I never thought I'd meet a girl I'd want to marry till I met her. And that day was unforgettable.

We had the same homeroom teacher freshman year of high school. The only thing I knew about her then was that her dad had money; she got driven to school in a nice car and always had on jewelry, like her favorite diamond earrings.

Ashley sat in front of me every day, and I didn't say a word, resolving to ignore her. I didn't resent people with more money than me, more like I couldn't relate to them. We lived in different worlds. So I'd stare at the back of her neck and wonder how the hairdresser cut her bobs so straight.

The bell rang and we'd gone through the doorway at the same time, and our shoulders bumped.

"Do you wanna let me through, princess?"

"Excuse me?"

"Did you expect me to roll out the red carpet for you or something?"

Okay, I'd resented her a little.

"What the hell is your problem?"

"I don't know. Spoiled rich girl. What do you think it is?"

To my surprise, she pushed me into the lockers while locking eyes with me. *"You don't know anything about me, so don't act like you do."*

I couldn't respond through my shock.

Luke appeared behind her. *"Hey, Ash, you good? Is my brother bothering you?"*

Of course Luke was friends with her. That was before she became best friends with Sarah. Mr. Popular could have any girl he wanted. Because unlike me, he wasn't an asshole. The girls literally flocked to him. I think knowing he didn't date made them more desperate to try to change his mind.

"I can handle it." She scowled at me, then moved away. *"Thanks, though."*

She winked at my brother as she left.

My mouth hung open as she walked away. *"Holy shit."*

"Uh-oh." Luke knew the look in my eye.

"She's . . ."

"Too good for you." Luke smiled. *"Which means she's exactly your type."*

"You gotta get her to talk to me again."

"Well, be nice. Have you tried that?"

"Shut up."

If Ashley could see me now, she'd probably slap me. She'd hate the person I was choosing to be. She'd never forgive me. Because by doing this, I was betraying her and myself, but more importantly, I was betraying Sarah.

Ash had wanted the four of us to go to college together, and sometimes, I wondered what would have happened if we had.

The college gig wasn't really my thing. I could forget sometimes and play my role as the college fuck boy, but Luke and I differed from everyone around us. Not just because of the vampire issue. I couldn't shake the feeling we weren't meant to be there. Like we didn't fit.

I scoffed at the thought. *Fuck fate.*

Sometimes, I missed certain parts—like the way most people had nothing to worry about with their petty fights about stealing girls and failing classes. There was something therapeutic about getting drunk and listening to it all. I'd gone out of my way to take the most useless classes possible. One being an entire class on the study of *Dante's Inferno and the Theology of Hell*. I took it as a joke, but somewhere in there, I enjoyed the distraction.

Dante's self-inserted story sounded like something I'd do. Make myself look blameless while deep in my core, I was a prick.

The coldness of reality brought me back to the present in my concrete prison.

I dodged another one of Sirius's punches but caught the tail end of a kick that sent me flying into the wall. The fucker didn't hold back. *Ever.*

"Can we take a break? How long have we been doing this for?"

The whole day could have gone by and I'd have no way of knowing.

My body never tired and there was never an ache in my muscles, but mentally, I was drained. There were no windows, and our training was nonstop. It was a blank slate of concrete on all sides. The main purpose being to paint the walls in black blood.

I scraped myself off the floor for what had to be the hundredth time. It was a new type of torture. Sirius had chosen me as his prize fighter—the guy loved to fight. I loved fighting too until I realized how unfun it was being locked in a room with someone way stronger than myself.

"No." Sirius came at me again, and I braced for impact.

"Well, I'm fuckin' tired of this."

He backhanded me across my forehead.

"Ow."

He wasn't even trying to hurt me; he was just that strong.

"You're such a child."

I rolled my eyes. Everyone was a child compared to his old ass.

"Come on, I don't want to keep doing this. I need a break."

"Luke is fine." He said it too quickly, knowing exactly what I was thinking about. "Now, get up."

I didn't want to. Not without proof. I planted my ass on the ground. "Prove it, then."

Sirius sighed, pulled out his phone, and started typing something. "You need to be properly trained. Your break sent you back years."

"I'm sure you'll catch me up in no time. Since you love torturing me."

He laughed. "You're so pathetic. Don't worry, we all had this phase. You'll get over it."

He finally said something that piqued my interest.

"All of you hated this place at first?"

"Well, almost. We all had our own journeys. Akira, on the other hand, he was happy from the start."

At the mention of his name, my heart ached. He needed to die. He deserved it, but it felt like a loss even to me.

"Are you pissed at me for killing him?"

Sirius smiled. "No, because She knew our day was ending. It's how this works."

"Who was the first?"

"Ezra, as you know him. His name used to be different. All of us have changed names at one point or another. You will too, I'm sure. Ezra knew Her when She was a mortal. Then came Akira, and lastly, my brother and I completed Her Guard. She said we were the perfect blend of differences and similarities. All coming from different walks of life but destined to come together for a common goal: to serve Her."

"Did you hate sharing Her attention?"

"No. We were all destined for our roles. Like you and your brothers."

I gave him a warning look, refusing to believe my brothers would be part of this.

He scoffed, probably knowing he could kick my ass any day of the week. "You'll accept your role here soon enough. And when you do, you'll know true peace."

"I don't know. I get major blood orgy vibes from you guys, and I don't think I need to tell you how that's not fucking happening with me and my brother."

Sirius threw his head back on a boisterous laugh. "You don't know what you're missing. You have no idea. Your relationship with Her will be different than what we've had. You're so young, you can't even imagine how a few years with Her will change you."

So, changing was part of it.

"Plus, I don't think that would be wise with Luke. I've never seen anyone drink as much blood as him and stay sane, let alone so normal."

"Really?"

"Yeah, especially after Akira's stunt. I don't know how he does it."

From what I could tell, it was sheer force of will. And Luke had the strongest will of anyone I'd ever met.

"How does it affect you?" he asked.

"I feel the same, mostly. Is it different for different people?"

"Yes. Her blood is a divine gift given to us so She knows our weaknesses and strengths, and it allows us to form a stronger bond. She helps us overcome."

I wasn't entirely sure what that meant.

"The bond has got to be eating you a bit. It used to be like that for us."

"With the queen?"

"No, your brother. The bond that only comes from sharing Her blood together."

"Yeah, it hurts. Like all the fucking time."

"Akira talked about it sometimes. He felt your connection."

"So you're part of that connection, then?"

"Not anymore. Ezra and I are connected to Her still in a different way than you and your brother. It's all about the blood. The more of Her blood you drink, the closer you feel. There are all levels to it. But that's not the only factor of The Guard. Your connection with Luke automatically makes your blood connection stronger with the bond."

"You felt that too, then? Before you became a trio."

Sirius grew quiet. "Yes. Eros was my brother. Back when all four of us were connected by Her. I can't explain to you the . . . euphoria. The power. There was nothing we couldn't do together. But when The Legion attacked, it was never the same. The connection between us was broken no matter how hard we tried. We couldn't mend it. It tore us apart until Ezra and I were able to shut ourselves off from the bond completely. Akira was disappointed. He liked the bond. Craved it. Having you two to feel and agonize over your pain was a treat for him."

"Bastard," I said, feeling that familiar ache of watching him die.

Sirius showed me his phone with a message from Ezra. He was with Luke on the other end of the castle. He'd even sent a blurry photo of my brother and Connell. Probably giving that tour he'd offered us. I was happy I didn't get sucked in.

I sighed, bringing myself back to my feet. "Alright. Hit me."

I think I was in that room for a full twenty-four hours. It was blissful in a way. This place didn't feel real but also felt like my true reality. The one I'd been waiting for to finally find me.

"Good work." Sirius followed me as I opened the door. "Come with me. I want to show you something."

When I opened the door, Will was waiting in that stupid white outfit from where I'd left him when we entered. Teasing him about that would be fun.

"Holy shit. You've been out here the whole time?" I asked.

Sirius raised an eyebrow at Will, and Will's features soured.

He rolled his eyes and bowed. "Of course, oh Glorious Chosen One. I've been assigned to you which means where you go, I go."

I couldn't hide my shit-eating grin. "Fuck. This is entertaining."

"Come. We don't have all morning."

Sirius led us down a corridor, and Will mouthed obscenities at me. He led us through the garden. The sun had passed the horizon and illuminated the sparkling snow that covered the rose bushes in the garden. We passed a large set of tall hedges that Sirius mentioned was a labyrinth. What they needed that for, I didn't know or care to ask. The air was cold, and there were bits of snow left on the ground. In the distance, was a two-story building of what looked to be an old church.

Sirius stopped us at the door when we arrived and glared at Will. "Stay."

"Oh fuck, please don't leave me out here for the day again."

"Why can't he come?" I asked.

"Because he's an outsider. And this place is sacred. We won't be long. Take off your shoes."

I gave Will a sorry nod and complied. I liked hanging out with Sirius. It was different from Ezra. Ezra was complicated and confusing, but Sirius's goal was always clear. He wanted me to be the strongest so I could protect Her. There was no hidden agenda. He didn't try to be fake nice or parent me, he just wanted to make me better.

It was a church. There were no crosses, but pews lined the back and rows of lit candles led to an altar.

"The candles in this building always stay lit for Her."

"What is this place?"

"It's the place where it all began for Her, where the human vessel was born."

On the ground was a blood stain, and at the far end of the room, sat a mural of Her. It had been hand-painted onto the wall. Black and white.

But instead of the light eyes I knew, the eyes on the mural were black and dripping.

Taking a step back, I could smell it. "It's . . . blood."

"Yes, art for Her. Of Her and Her magnificence. Hand-painted."

Sometimes, I forgot I was in a cult. Truly, I forgot. These people seemed normal enough until I saw something like the blood mural, then it made me wonder how I could forget.

"What exactly do you do in here?"

"We pray."

"To the wall?"

"Just get on your knees."

I sighed but did as he said.

"Do you have a god you pray to?"

"No, I don't believe in anything. Or anything that cares."

"She cares for you."

"Doubt that."

"You're blinded by your own self. If She didn't, She'd have gutted your friends in front of you."

"I'm supposed to give kudos for not killing my friends?"

"Your friends murdered a member of our Guard and caused you to be in this very position. Did you ever think of that? If Eros wasn't dead, you'd never have been called on the true path."

"Lucky me."

"Shut up and close your eyes."

"And do what?"

"Be quiet and think of Her. See what She brings you."

What a load of crap. I'd somehow escaped the hell of normal church and landed back in one. Mom was a believer. She'd wanted us all to believe, but her faith only made me want to believe less. Mom got nothing from her prayers. She was always exhausted, and her life was hard. She could never catch a break. If she had a real god, he never listened.

"Just feel. Listen."

Nothing. I heard only the flickering flames and William's pacing outside in the snow.

"This is stupid."

"Can you take this seriously?"

"Come on. I'm sitting on my knees on this dusty floor in the cold, staring at what might be the creepiest fucking painting in the world. I'm being as serious as I can. This is me giving effort."

He grabbed my hand and placed it on the ominous dried blood on the floor.

"Listen. Don't talk."

I decided to try because I had nothing else better to do. And because I felt bad William was outside waiting for me to pray to a wall.

I thought of Her. Focusing first on the way She looked. Her soft long white hair. What it would feel like to comb my hands through it, finding my way to Her hips. Her thighs. Her lips. What it might feel like to brush my fingers across Her bare stomach and up to Her chest. If this was praying, it felt like a sin to want Her like I wanted Her. It was easy not to think about it with all the changes, but there in the silence, it was absolute. I let out a breath and thought of how She made me feel. Like shit. Angry. Unwanted. Maybe I wanted Her to look at me like She looked at Luke.

Darling.

I stumbled back. "Wait, what was that?"

"Relax." Sirius steadied me. "It's alarming at first. But you'll get used to the strangeness of it all."

I scoffed. "You say that like this is going to be happening again."

"We will come every morning before the sun is up to pray. To ensure we keep on The Divine Path. When we pray, we invite The Divine into our bodies and minds. It gives Her strength. It gives us purpose."

"Oh fuck. That sounds terrible. I'm going to pass on that one."

Sirius smiled as he got up and dusted off his clothes. "You say that like you have a choice. This task is nonnegotiable, I'm afraid. When I'm gone, I need to know this place will be maintained and taken care of. Prayer is an important part of maintaining a bond with Her and keeping the strength of The Guard and our family."

"Again, lucky me."

Sirius stayed smiling. I think I was growing on him.

So what if I wanted Her? Dante didn't think lust was that big of a deal anyway.

Dear Luke,

Everything is weird now. It's so cold. I've always been one of those *cold is better than sweating* or *you can put on layers, but you can't escape the heat* type of guys. Well, I'm not too proud to say I was wrong. The cold here is intense. Is it cold where you are? I know you'd get on to me for being dramatic for the fact I'm writing these letters like I'm freaking William Shakespeare and then burning them in the fireplace when I'm done. But it's the only thing that makes me feel like you're going to get them somehow. Fireplace magic likely? Probably not. But neither were vampires, so I'm holding out for a miracle here.

I don't like when they sit on my dresser.

Tell Zach I'd write him letters if he'd actually read them. Someone's gotta be the cool, tortured one in this family. And though Aaron tries, he's cursed with blond hair. Cool, tortured bad boys don't read letters from their little brothers, so tell him I get it. Guy has a reputation to uphold.

I'm probably too old to miss you this much, but I don't care.

P.S. My chest still hurts. And I saw two dogs today.

Love you forever,

Presley

Seven

LUKE

I lost track of the days. It was easy to do since we weren't allowed any technology and Ezra and Sirius made sure we were busy at all hours. It took days of planning before we got Thane and William alone with us in our room again.

"Will, what are you doing?" I asked.

Will snipped dead leaves off the plant on my nightstand. "There's not enough light in here for this."

"Can we talk about the plan?"

"One of you has to repot this today, or it's a goner."

"Fine. I'll do it," I said. That seemed to ease the lines of worry between his brows.

"Okay, today's objective. We have to find a way out of the castle and off the island."

"Easy for you to say. Sirius is up my ass wherever I go. He beeps me." Will licked his teeth in silent disgust.

"You have a pager?" Zach chuckled.

"Yeah, everyone here is ancient."

Thane cracked a smile as he fell back onto my bed. "At least Ezra comes and finds me."

"You get to do nice things like tend to the garden, while Sirius makes me do pointless tasks like go outside and dig holes and shovel dirt. And then he makes me fill them back up again. Don't even get me started on the lack of plant care in this place. Diabolical."

"So we have to get out of here. That much is clear," I said.

Thane was eager. "I did get to explore a bit of the east wing today while I was waiting outside the queen's quarters for Ezra and Luke. I can attest to the fact that there is little to no way to get out that way. Not because of the lack of doors, but because they have a rotation of people guarding that area. I heard some of them whispering about being told to keep an eye on you guys. Oddly enough, I think they watch you guys more than Will and me. We could use that to our advantage."

"See, great job, Thane. That's the type of information we need." I patted him on the shoulder, and his smile widened.

"Thanks man."

Will and Zach shared a look, and my brother rolled his eyes.

"Fine. As I waited for Zach for an entire day while he trained with Sirius, I did get a little time alone. When I wasn't hidin' out in closets and all that shit, I checked out the garden and the main hall. I can tell ya the garden isn't going to work either. It's the main way for everyone movin' in and out of the castle. So traffic is moving down the hall at all hours."

"Great. Yes. That's good."

"Don't I get a pat on the shoulder? Not even a 'good boy'"?

"Good boy, huh?" Zach said.

"Focus. We don't have a lot of time. Who knows how much time has passed."

"It's been about two weeks," Thane said with a nod of confident assurance.

My heart fluttered with anxiety at knowing. I wasn't expecting an answer.

"How do you know that?"

"I keep track of the moon cycles. I don't always get to go outside, but I have this tiny window in our chambers."

"How is that, by the way?" Zach and I weren't allowed in their quarters, and every night, unless they were specifically assigned to us for the day, they would lock them in there.

"Humble but not a torture chamber. We have beds and stuff."

"It's dirty and fuckin' cold." William crossed his arms. "But no one bothers us for a couple hours."

"I doubt we'll be able to get out of the castle alone," Thane said, rubbing his chin. "I'm hoping for a secret tunnel of some kind."

"Right, we should check the basements while everyone is busy. Thane, are you up for it?"

"Hell yeah, let's go."

I turned to Zach. "Will you guys try to check out the north end and the harbor? We need a clear way off the island."

"You got it, brother." Zach hit my shoulder, and we went our separate ways.

Thane and I started toward the basement. The last few days were a blur. I'd spent all morning with Her every day. It started in the garden, then it grew into me staying with Her till Ezra came for me. It was always when the sun was highest in the sky.

She was lonely. Lower-ranked members scrubbed Her floors and cleaned Her room, but they could never look at Her. Not that it mattered; Her eyes were always on me.

I thought She'd be hard to understand, but She told me about places in the castle where Her and Her brother played as kids. Her hobbies. Her wants. She felt real. Like The Divine in human form, and it made this place feel easier to take in a way.

I hadn't realized I'd spent the entire walk down thinking of Her and tuning Thane out.

"Luke?"

"Sorry. Say it again."

"We should check down this way. There's this door that's locked I can never get into."

"Oh, Ezra gave me keys to almost every room in this place."

"I thought he would." Thane winked.

Something about his optimism made me smile. I tried not to let it pull me down a bad road, but it was hard not to think of my brothers daily. I wanted to know what they were doing. Where they'd been. I missed Presley's stories. Mostly, I missed how they both made me laugh. I never talked about it, but sometimes, I'd stare up at the skylight and imagine them all living their lives. I hoped they were happy.

After trying a few iron keys, the door opened and a wave of cold blew through the corridor. The smell of mold and dust lingered in the air.

Dimly lit bulbs lined the walls and illuminated an abandoned path of dirt and cobblestone.

"This must be where they tortured people," Thane said.

I think he was joking.

I led us through empty archways. Most were barren. There was nothing useful. Just dirt, old furniture, and decaying wood crates. A near silent electrical humming echoed in the walls, and I followed it to the far end of the hallway to a large storage fridge filled with fresh blood bags. I swallowed.

I'd almost forgotten about feeding. It's not like I had the calendar on my phone anymore. Luckily, I felt fine.

Thane and I split up, moving our hands along the walls for any signs of a way out.

"I'm not finding anything." Thane's voice echoed.

He was right. No secret passageways. My guess was it was an old armory hundreds of years ago, and now there wasn't a need for one.

"There you are." Ezra stopped us. "What are you doing?

"Uh, exploring," I said.

Ezra's eyes flickered to Thane, who was getting good at bowing.

I'd need to be more convincing. "I was looking for blood. Connell told me I could find it here."

"Next time, tell me." His eyes seemed to soften as he opened the fridge and handed me a bag. "Here."

"What about Thane?"

"Luke, you don't need to—"

"Fine." Ezra grabbed another and handed it to Thane. "Drink quickly. We have somewhere to be."

After biting into the plastic, I let the blood fill my mouth. It was cold like everything else. I closed my eyes, willing myself to be anywhere else, and She came to mind. I missed the taste of Her. I couldn't drink any blood without thinking of Hers. My heart raced at the thought, and in seconds, every last drop was drained.

"Good. Come on."

"Where are we going?"

"It's the day before the new moon, we have a time of prayer."

"Oh."

While readying myself, I mulled over the new information. I knew She was The Divine, but I'd never considered praying to Her before. Zach had mentioned Sirius making him "pray to a wall" every morning, but Ezra had never spoken of it to me before.

We followed him to the cathedral, where he had Thane wait outside with Will. Snow flurries disappeared into the white linen covering his shoulders. He simply nodded, and I entered through the doors with Ezra.

Lit candles covered the floor. Everyone was there. Even my brother kneeled before Her. She sat in Her throne above all with a veil covering Her face, and Her lips widened with a smile at my arrival. She was draped in layers of white tulle, and a flower crown sat atop her head.

The weight of the world fell away as I took a place next to my brother. He sighed when he saw me and gave me a bored welcome nod. Ezra and Sirius walked to stand on either side of Her.

"Our family is finally complete. The Divine favors us."

"The one true path," everyone repeated.

Everyone bowed their heads while Ezra and Sirius kneeled.

Everyone knelt with their heads on the floor. Zach and I shrugged, then did the same.

With my head to the floor, I closed my eyes. When I was a kid, I tried to pray like Mom wanted me to. I'd bow my head and squeeze my eyes shut like her. I'd even lace my fingers together in my lap. Mom believed with her entire heart. So I tried too.

Now I was on my knees again, kneeling to Her. A different god.

Thirty of us didn't fill up the cathedral in the slightest. The usual group of laughing, unruly men were all entranced with stoic reverence.

"Today we come together to anoint one of you. And celebrate the return of our precious Gemini twins." Her voice was unwavering and strong. It was different in a way I couldn't place my finger on. "My agents of chaos. We know the way. The Divine makes the path clear and binds us together. Our unity reshapes the fabric of the world. Nothing can tear us apart."

A hushed rush of prayers filled the room.

"Glory be to Her."

"Show us the way."

"Pick me. Please."

"Glory. Glory. Glory."

"I'm feeling a draw today toward one of you. Soft. Courageous." She stood and let Her draping fall. "One of our newest family members, Connell. Please come sit at my feet."

A hushed gasp echoed, and Connell scurried to the front. He vibrated with excitement and his eyes went wide as She touched his face.

Something in my chest ached. I averted my gaze to the floor again. Was I jealous? Was it because he reminded me of my brothers? My hands tingled like panic was coming for me, but I needed to know what the anointing meant.

"Show me what hurts," She said. Her words were soft, but Her gaze was like a dagger.

"Yes, Beautiful Glorious Honorable One. Thank you. Thank you."

We waited while She searched his mind, and he held out his hands in surrender to Her.

"There. He hurt you, didn't he? Your father was a terrible man. I can take all that pain from you. You'll never have to remember that moment again. Would you like that?"

"Yes, please."

"It's done." She kissed his forehead.

I opened and closed my hands to relieve the tingling, but it wasn't stopping. I didn't want to be there. Everyone fell into Her trance, and all I experienced was panic working its way up my spine and into my extremities. Even my brother was enamored and followed Her every move. There was something wrong. I was wrong. I needed out.

Sirius spoke, "Let's all take a moment to praise Her for performing this miracle for our brotherhood. A win for one is a win for all."

My head hit the floor as we all bowed. I didn't know what I believed or what I felt. That's why they chose me. I was a blank slate for them to mark all over. A place to paint their story. My fingernails dug into my palm.

"Focus, My Love." Her voice was next to me, and soft fingers cupped my cheek.

I was gone. Every sound and feeling fell away with Her touch.

"Focus," She whispered again.

I wanted to please Her. I wanted Her to touch me. For a minute, I let go. The thought of Her took over completely, and peace finally found me. This was my home.

Ascension was coming for me.

I was powerless to fight it.

The prophecy was real.

It would be easier to let go.

That's it, My Love. Her voice was in my head.

Why were we fighting this so hard in the first place? She was a goddess. Real. Vivid. And very much alive. Her blood was in my veins. I was made to worship Her.

"Look at me, and I will bless you."

Before I could think or ponder, She bit into Her wrist and blood flowed in a river of ink.

I had to get out.

After Akira's blood, I felt myself slipping. All that control I'd learned with Kilian became obsolete in the presence of Her blood when I could hear Her pulse racing. I pressed my knees into the floor, willing myself to stay, but my pulse grew louder as She moved closer. All eyes were on Zach and me.

"We are one."

She reached my brother first. The blood on Her fingers resembled ink as She dragged Her fingers over Zach's eyes, forming two lines.

The room was spinning. *You have this. Just get outside.*

She drew a stark black line from his forehead onto his nose.

I turned away. I was sure if I saw the blood touch his mouth, my control would slip. The taste . . .

If I give in, we're all doomed.

I found my footing and resolve, then bolted. When the door shut behind me, I moved to block the entrance with my body and fell to my knees. I couldn't believe I'd made it out.

"Are you okay?" Thane leaned over me.

I shook my head to gain composure, but it was swimming. The blood. It was so close. She was so close. The need gnawed at my insides.

Thane patted my head.

"What are you doing?"

"I'm proud of you. You kept it together. You didn't give in."

"How did you . . . ?"

"I can smell it. I remember how it felt when I had so much. And now I feel empty. I don't know how much blood you've had, but the fact that you were able to walk through that door and shut it is something you should be proud of. I sent Will over there by the garden because he even felt it, and there's a door between us."

His words brought me the relief I needed to not spiral. Even Will felt it, and he'd never drank from Her directly.

"Thanks, Thane."

I hated the circumstances, but it was nice to have him there. Someone who understood the want and need.

"I got you, dude."

I replayed it over again. That look of awe in my brother's eyes. Her attention on him. Her blood on his face. I couldn't cave, or we'd never make it back to our real family.

I shoved the thought down. I was happy to have Thane by my side and thought for a moment on what we'd do when we were out of here. Thane came to sit beside me as I leaned against the door and wrapped my arms around my shoulders.

I'd probably light a fire. I really missed the heat.

Eight

ZACH

The blood wouldn't come off. I scrubbed and scrubbed and still felt it in my pores. That and the touch of Her fingers on my skin. Her eyes bore into mine. This place would ruin me. She would ruin me. As I splashed another bit of water onto my face, I wondered if I wanted Her to.

Fresh steam stretched up into the ceiling lights. The clawfoot tub I bathed in sat in front of a large window that overlooked the maze outside. I could barely make it out between the bits of the stained glass. I ran the hot water when it started to cool. Leaning my head back against the porcelain, I sighed.

She was still everywhere. Her smell lingered like the taste of Her diluted in the water around me. *Darling.*

She *would* ruin me. And maybe I would let Her.

I grabbed the bar of soap and scrubbed my face again.

Nine

LUKE

"Good morning, Luke!" Connell was outside my door.

Zach had left with Sirius, but it was usually Thane waiting for me on the other side.

"Hey, Connell. Where is Thane?"

"Ezra has him and Will doing laundry in the foyer today. I can take you to them if you'd like."

Connell always told the truth.

"I would, but I have to go see the queen first."

"Oh, Ezra told me to tell you not to come today. I'm supposed to try to distract ya."

"Why?"

"He didn't say."

I started down the hallway. Something about it made me uneasy.

"I wouldn't go! Are you sure? He might be angry with you . . . and by that, I mean me."

"I won't let him hurt you, Connell. I promise."

"Aren't you the least bit worried he'll be in a huff?"

"No." It didn't matter because I had to see Her.

As I neared Her door, I realized it had been less than a month and the thought of not seeing Her for a day was sending me into panic. I had to get in there, especially after the prayer night. I needed to be in the same room with Her, just for a minute. And after the prayer not going as planned, I wanted to make sure I hadn't angered Her too much.

"Be careful." Connell frowned as I went to push open the door.

I squeezed his shoulder. "Don't ever worry about me. It's my job to worry about you."

He nodded and bit back a smile.

When I entered, Ezra immediately appeared in front of me, blocking my view.

"I told you to steer clear."

"I know, but I needed to see Her."

"You can't today."

"Move." The word came out harsher than I wanted, but he was blocking my view.

Why was he keeping Her from me? He placed a hand on my shoulder, and I pulled my shoulders back to brace against him.

"Let him stay." Her voice was like rain on a hot summer day.

She lay with heavy eyelids in Her bed, resting Her head on a black satin pillow. I sat next to Her, but Her usual gravity wasn't overwhelming. She felt . . . normal. As She blinked, color returned to Her irises and liquid pools of green appeared.

"What happened to Her?"

"It's the day when Her body is weakest and The Divine draws away from Her."

The girl looking back at me was different. I waited for the gravity of Her to bulldoze me over, but it didn't. It was still there but faint.

"What can I do?"

Ezra interjected. "Nothing can fix it. She needs rest. It is my duty to watch over Her while She does. And I'm the only one who—"

"You can go. Let Luke stay this time." Her eyes were closed, but She reached out for me.

She never called me by my real name.

"My queen. It's too early."

"Please. Luke is safe."

Ezra's shoulders fell like he'd received a blow to the chest. "I . . . yes. Whatever you wish."

I looked to Ezra for permission as I sat at the edge of Her bed. He nodded but didn't meet my eyeline before he left.

"Do you feel okay?"

"Yes, it's only the stars calling me and pulling me to sleep. It's brief. Not painful."

Her skin was blazing hot. To my surprise, there was no pull. Nothing willed me forward to touch or taste Her. I let out a breath at the relief.

"I didn't know."

"Only The Guard are allowed to know. And only Ezra watches over me at my request."

"But you let me?"

"You're safe. You won't hurt me."

"Never."

It occurred that this might be an opportunity for someone. Her gravity was gone. She was weak and nearly sleeping. I should have hated Her so much I might want to hurt Her, but I couldn't. I wouldn't.

"Will you lie with me? I'm so cold."

I moved closer to Her and kicked off my shoes so I could lie next to Her with my head propped on a pillow. There were worse ways to spend my morning.

"Can I tell you a story?" Her voice was different. It was softer, and the faintest remnants of an Irish accent came through.

"Of course."

"I remember layin' in this bed as a young girl. The memory is almost faded. But on days like this, I can feel it on the edge of my tongue. I try to reach for it, but it's so faint. I wish . . . it could always be like this. That I could always be this close to the veil."

"The veil?"

She pulled Herself onto my chest, ignoring my question. "You're so warm, Luke."

"You keep calling me that."

"That's your name."

I moved my hands through the lengths of Her white hair and down Her back. I felt nothing and was thankful for that. For the slightest bit of peace from whatever ran in the queen's blood. That thing that made my blood boil over with need and urgency.

"But you never call me by my name."

When She spoke again, Her voice was soft and far away. "Luke's a good name. It's light. The stars shine brighter when I mention it."

"I like it. My mom named me Luke after my great-grandfather."

My chest ached at the mention of her.

She smiled with Her eyes closed. "Tell me a story."

"What kind?"

"One that you like. One that makes you happy."

I had so many, but I settled on the one that came to mind first.

"Once when I was sick, my mom stayed home with me and let me stay in her bed. We watched movies all day long. She was so busy working and hardly ever took off, but she did it for me. It made me feel special. She let me pick out my own movie."

"That's beautiful. I miss my mother," She whispered. "She smelled of lavender. I want . . . to see her again."

This wasn't my queen. This person I was talking to was different. *Cecily Dooley*. Maybe only The Guard was allowed to know about this because on this day, Cecily was "close to the veil."

This person on my chest, I didn't hate. She didn't kill Sarah. The Thing controlling her did. When she fell asleep clinging to me, I moved to leave but stopped. If it were true, that meant she was trapped there like me. That meant she was scared too. The thought of leaving her to wake up alone made my stomach turn, and I leaned back again and pulled her to me. Her body, usually cool, was like a radiator. I was unsure how to escape and save everyone; I couldn't even save myself.

But I wanted to save her too.

Ten

ZACH

"She was manipulating you."

"No, I'm telling you, She was different. It had to be her. Cecily. And she's trapped here like we are."

Luke and I had been fighting about it all night, and now the morning light came through our bedroom window and we had places to be, but we were *still* fighting.

"Luke, She wants you to let your guard down."

"No, She was burning up. And Her eyes were different."

"Maybe She wore contacts and slept on a heating pad! Are you not getting it? These people will stop at nothing to draw us in. She's a good actor. We know this already."

"But the queen told me these stories. She missed her mom."

"Yeah, like She knows you miss yours. She's fucking with your head."

He sat at the edge of his bed. "No, I think it's real. It makes sense. Maybe the queen is weak on the night of the new moon, and Her human form comes out."

"If that's the case, then all we need to do to get out of here is sneak in Her room and kill Her in Her sleep."

Luke's eyes went wide. "You wouldn't."

"Yes I would! If it would get us out of here faster. Her human side would probably thank me for putting her out of her misery so she wouldn't have to be some Hell Witch anymore."

Luke's wide-eyed horror made the guilt creep in for saying that.

"You wouldn't feel that way if you saw Her like that. She was . . . so weak."

My brother would not make it in a place like this. Everything he said sent my heart into an uneven frenzy. I couldn't sit anymore. He was making me pace the floor, and I *hated* pacing.

"Luke. Please. Consider it for a second that She could have been doing it to gain your sympathy. That's all I'm asking. Don't you think that would work? Pretend to be a sweet, helpless girl who needs you to warm her because she's so cold and vulnerable?"

He stopped paying attention to me and stared at the fireplace while I spoke.

"Don't you think that would be a great plan on making you feel needed and wanted? And don't you think She would pick you specifically for that because She knows it would work on you?"

"I . . . I don't know. Yes. It makes sense. I'm just confused."

I walked over to him and placed a hand on his shoulder. "I just want you to think about it. Because if we start trusting them, we're never getting out of here. Don't you want to get out of here?"

"Yes."

"Good. Because while you were laying in bed with the queen all day yesterday, I think I found a way to get us all out of here. Well, kind of."

I'd wavered for a moment but seeing that look in Luke's eyes gave me the confidence I needed to ensure I'd get him out of this place before She poisoned him.

"Really?" Luke's spark was back.

"No one watches the harbor. There is a ferry that takes people to the island, and they can see some of the property. A few of the members show tourists the far grounds, but other than that, it's always empty. If we can find a way to get Will and Thane on a boat where they wouldn't be missed, it could work."

A loud knock sounded on our door. Probably Sirius. He had an angry knock.

"Talk about this later?"

Luke nodded, and we went for the door. I was right. Sirius, Thane, and William all stood outside our door. Thane looked way too happy to be a prisoner butler, and William was scowling at me. A typical day at the cult castle.

"You're with Her today." Sirius pointed at me.

"What about training?"

"You're doing well. Better. But She specifically requested you today."

"I guess we'll get to test that theory today, then." I turned to Luke. The dark circles under his eyes matched mine. It scared me a little.

"What theory?" Sirius said.

"Nothin'," I said, forcing a bored expression over my face.

"Luke, we'll be with Ezra today. We're meeting clients in Derry."

"I'd rather do that."

Sirius didn't even have to say anything. With the lowering of his brows, I shut up. It wasn't fear but respect. Sirius was clear cut. He loved the queen and was loyal. He didn't hide that he'd throw me into a woodchipper in a heartbeat for this place. I liked the honesty.

"Let me guess, I get to watch over these two as well." I sighed.

"Unless you'd like to lock them up all day. It's your choice."

I cocked my head at Will with a taunting smile, and he flipped me off behind Sirius's back.

"I'm sure I'll figure out something for them to do."

"Are you sure you don't need me? I can ask Her to let me stay with you so you don't have to be alone." Luke rubbed at the skin around his nails.

"I'll be okay. Stop worrying."

Luke knew all my secrets. That's why he was worried. A nasty habit. He was overthinking, wondering if I'd tell him if something went wrong.

"I promise I'll tell you about my shitty feelings if needed. But it will be fine."

He nodded.

Whatever Her plan was, I would not let it get me down. I'd decided to be neutral about it. There was still hope that I would get to hang out with this so-called vulnerable, nice girl Luke mentioned.

I would believe it when I saw it.

I pushed the double doors open.

She had Her hands wrapped around Henderson's arm as She drank from him. Something hot ran through me all at once. I held my breath first, fearing it was Her blood that made me sick to my stomach, but I had a grip. I wasn't losing control.

Was I jealous? *Fuck.*

I couldn't watch, so I looked down at my shoes and thought about how fucking ugly they were. I hated the suits. Day number who knew in hell, and every day, I had to wear an itchy shirt.

When She was done, She smiled at me, wiping the blood from Her lips.

"Ah. I was waiting for you."

Henderson bowed before pulling a hand through the dark curls on top of his head. He flashed those canines at me in a smirk as he walked past me. I clenched my fists. It would be so satisfying to rip his head off and shove it down his throat, and I could do stuff like that. No one would bat an eye.

"You seem tense."

I tried to detect a hint of anything different. Her eyes were the same. No green, but a weird hazy, grayish white that made me feel like I was talking to a corpse. That's all She was. Some holy being that walked around in a girl's dead body.

"You look like hell," I said.

"Didn't your mother teach you how to treat a woman?"

Yep. Same bitch. Different day.

"You're not a woman, so . . . "

"Not a woman? Then this won't bother you."

She pulled down the sleeves of Her white silk gown, and it fell to the floor. Instinctively, I averted my gaze. I guessed I'd have to admire my shoes some more.

"Follow me."

I did. I didn't know why. There was a lot of that. Doing things because I had to. Because there was no other choice or because the demon witch made me feel like I wanted to.

I didn't want to follow Her to Her en suite bathroom, but I did. It had a large pool-like spa with warm moody lighting. The water was already steaming.

"Why am I here for this?" I looked up at the ceiling.

"I like to have company."

"Looked like you had plenty of company before."

"Do I detect jealousy?"

"No."

"Good. Because you don't need to be. We can be as close as you desire."

"Glad you said that. Let's stay at least twenty feet away at any given time." I stepped back a few feet.

"You don't trust me."

"Why the fuck would I trust you?"

I'd been raised never to call women obscenities. Mom hated cussing, but she'd gone ballistic the one and only time I'd called my teacher a cunt during junior year—she had it out for me and deserved it, but the queen was a cunt if I'd ever seen one.

I wasn't buying it. The sweet, innocent act might be working on Luke, but not me.

"Can you pass me a towel?" She said.

I quickly handed it to Her and was ready to bolt. I'd done what She asked. I'd come to visit Her. But something was keeping me here.

Her gravity faltered, but it wasn't the same pull that made me pray to Her in the church. It waned like a flickering light. Her body moved slower, and She struggled for a moment as She went to step out of the tub. Her foot slipped, but She caught Herself on the edge. I would have thought it was another one of Her shows, but I saw a shift in Her eyes. Her jaw hardened, and I reached for Her hand. I kept my attention solely on Her emerald eyes and handed Her a towel.

"Cecily."

Her brow furrowed as I aided her out of the tub. Deep green stained her irises. "I don't know who you're referring to."

"Liar, and a bad one at that."

She scowled, but it was softer. Poutier. She took time to towel dry her hair. Her movements were slow like she lacked strength in her hands and arms.

"Luke was right."

She moved to walk again, but I stepped in front of her. "Oh no. Not so fast. Tell me what you know about me and my brother."

With her head down, she tried to walk past me, but I caught her arm. When our eyes met again, the green was fading.

"What's wrong, princess? You don't want to talk to me?"

Bright emerald seared through. "Queen. I'm a queen."

"Not a good one."

"Why are you being this way?"

"If it keeps your eyes that color, I'll do anything. I've got questions that beg to be answered."

"You're not like your brother."

"No. I'm not. I'm nothing like him. The sooner you realize it, the sooner we can understand each other."

She closed her eyes and rubbed her forehead. "Speak quickly. I can already feel Her near. There are only two days out of the month I am close enough to the veil. And one of them I'm so weak I can hardly stand."

"Good. I won't want to speak to you again."

The green stayed strong in her irises, and her frown deepened.

"How do we get out of here?"

"You don't. You can't. You can't escape The Divine Plan. It is the most likely path, even now. Continuing to fight will only make you and your brother unhappy."

I squeezed her arm. "Don't talk about my brother like you care."

"I wouldn't hurt him."

"You already have. You don't even care about the girl you killed in front of him. You probably don't even know her name."

"Sarah was a threat to The Divine Path, and that is why she was killed. I did not do it. *You* would do well to remember that. If you try to stray from the path, they will punish you. There is no way out of this."

"So we're trapped here—you, me, and my brother—for the rest of eternity?"

She pulled her arm from my grasp and went to her wardrobe. "Unfortunately, yes."

She dropped her towel to the floor and pulled out another silk nightgown.

"Why did She call me here today?"

"To keep you on the path. It's always to keep you on Her path. She likely knew we'd have this very conversation."

Did She know we were going to leave all along? Did She predict that too? Could She see every move? Every possibility and decision we could make. There was something unbelievably hopeless about it and, at the same time, relieving. If She was the mastermind, then we never stood a chance, and that meant it didn't matter what I did. Right?

This was a huge problem. If Luke knew this girl was in the queen's body, he'd never be able to let it go.

"It looks like you and I are going to be stuck together for a long time. Now, understand this, you leave Luke alone. You don't ask for him on the new moons anymore. From now on, you ask for me."

"Are you ordering me?" She'd slipped her dress on and climbed into her bed. The white haze was taking hold in her eyes again.

"Yes, if you really cared about my brother, you'd leave him alone."

He gave himself away too much, and it always left him with nothing, and I wouldn't let him do it anymore. He had nothing left to give.

Cecily stared into my eyes with what was left of her lingering in that body. A better man would have felt sorry for her, but all I felt was rage and hatred that probably had nothing to do with her. I couldn't let her get close to Luke because he would cave. If the queen was going to ruin anyone, it should be me.

I wouldn't tell him about this. I wouldn't tell him anything.

Her eyes turned white again. "I will leave him alone, but it won't work. She'll pursue you both. And She'll win. She always wins."

"What do you know?"

"I can't stay." Her voice was barely a whisper. "She's coming back."

"Tell me, princess."

"I've seen it. You're both standing next to Her, guarding Her. It's written all over the stars. A thousand times over. You look . . . so angry."

Fuck the stars.

Fuck this place.

Fuck Her.

Eleven

ZACH

"I need to talk to you." It took a good hour for me to find Ezra in the vastness of the castle grounds. The obvious solution was a cell phone, which, shocker, still wasn't allowed.

"I'm busy. I've got a lot of things to prepare since the meeting."

My blood was boiling me alive. I hated to beg. I really hated to be asking him at all.

"Would you just help me? You're the only one I can talk to about this. It's important."

Ezra stopped moving to study me. "What's wrong?"

"I was with the queen alone today. I have questions."

"Follow me."

We walked back through the castle. I hadn't been to all the rooms. There were too many to keep track of, and I wasn't exactly trying to hang out with anyone. He led us down a way I hadn't gone before. The floor turned to marble, and the click of his shoes echoed against the arched ceiling.

Finally, we reached a door. Carved on one side was the sun, and on the other, the moon. Inside was an atrium. A dome ceiling made of glass. And through it, you could see the vast night sky and all the stars that filled every bit of darkness. The floor was shiny marble that displayed various arrays of murals in different sections. Lots of winged men and constellations. Under my feet was the phrase "*Sic itur ad astra,*" and next to it was the English translation "*Thus one journeys to the stars.*"

"What did She show you?"

"I know about Cecily. I met her."

Ezra's head shot up. "You spoke with her today?"

"Yeah, we got all acquainted in less than five minutes. Don't think she's going to like me very much."

"I didn't expect her to show herself this early."

"Does Sirius know?"

"Of course. The Guard knows all. He prefers not to spend time with the queen in that state, which is why I am always the one to watch over her. Eros was also very fond of her. Akira didn't mind watching her. But she didn't favor him."

"Yeah, well she favors Luke, and that's my problem. He spent one day with her, and he was giving me that look. Like he's about to do something stupid. So, I went to test his theories today and . . . I'm not going to tell him about Cecily. I told her to leave him alone, and I want you to back me up."

"You want me to lie to your brother?"

"Yes. I want you to lie. That shouldn't be a huge problem for you because you've done it before and probably do it all the time. And I want you to keep him away from her when she's like that."

"What are you most afraid of?"

I swallowed. Not anticipating his question.

"I'm afraid he'll get himself hurt trying to save her. And getting close to Cecily will only make him want the queen more."

His eyes softened. "Zach. It's written. He will be close to the queen, and so will you."

"I know. I just want to help him. I'm afraid for him."

That thing was happening again. Where I spilled all my secrets to Ezra and told him real things about myself, but he already knew how I worried about Luke all the time.

He'd been with me the majority of my life, and there was one thing Ezra understood about me more than anyone else ever had: I needed Luke to be okay. I needed it like I used to need oxygen in the air. And now with the bond we had, it was worse.

I felt my brother's sadness every hour of the day, and since I rarely slept, it was almost constant. Luke's mental health was worse here, but it was more than that.

The bond was getting stronger.

"Is there something you're not telling me?"

I looked down, shielding myself from the stars above. "No."

I didn't want to look at the stars anymore. I was angry at them for staring down at me and telling me what to do. Those little balls of gas were mocking me with their prophecies and shielding the gods and goddesses above.

"I will find out. You'll slip up."

Heat ran through me at his threat. "What's stopping you from shoving your way into my head and taking what you want?"

He sighed as if he could get tired. *Bastard.*

"It's not a threat, Zach. I have no desire to push my way into your head to hurt you."

"There's nothing. I need your help protecting Luke."

Ezra had lied to me so many times. He'd hurt me. He'd manipulated me over and over, but I couldn't help but lean on him in times of need because out of everyone there, he was the only one I knew who would protect Luke like me.

Like he had that day.

"I can't do this." I stood in the emergency room waiting for Luke while he was in surgery from his gunshot wound.

"He'll be all right." Ezra waited with me.

"You don't get it. If something happens to him . . . I can't deal. I won't deal."

"I understand."

"No. You don't. I won't do this anymore. I can't—"

"I understand."

I cried into his shoulder like a little kid, and he told me he wouldn't let anyone take my brother from me.

Ezra didn't try to convince me to be different. He accepted me.

"I'll help. Try to relax. You're on the right path."

I said nothing as I left. Anger was burning me alive. Those gods and goddesses were lucky they weren't down on earth with me. They were lucky I didn't have enough power.

Because I'd take them all down.

Hopefully, the lie wouldn't matter because we'd be out before the next new moon.

Twelve

"You can't keep avoiding this," Ezra said with furrowed brows.

We were in the "green room." The rooms in the castle were flashy and themed with thick rugs and intricate wallpaper. And this one was just green. The couches. The wallpaper. The curtains.

"You picked the wrong person for this."

"How can you be the wrong fit if it's your destiny?"

I wished Zach was here—he was a better arguer, but he was with Sirius, like usual.

"All I'm asking is for you to escort them through town and make sure they don't get into trouble while I meet with a client. It's good practice.

Normally, I do all of it."

"They're not going to listen to me."

"Of course they are."

They weren't. He didn't get it. The men there were many years older than me and hated me. The resentment didn't bother me as much as what I was doing. None of them had a choice. They were my brothers, in a way. Stuck like me, only they were taught to be happy about it. I couldn't save them as much as I couldn't save myself.

"Luke, you're the only one that can lead them."

"Why?" He was doing a pretty good job of it.

"You know why."

"Stop with the prophecy. I don't believe in it."

"Yes you do. You just don't want to admit it to yourself yet."

Is this what it feels like to be "psychoanalyzed," as Presley would say. I understood why it was so aggravating. I missed him.

"You don't know me as well as you think you do," I said.

He didn't understand me and everything he was asking me to give up. This role he wanted me to play was asking too much. I guess I didn't even understand me either. How one part of me could be scared and broken and the other fiercely fighting and excited for the challenge of what came next.

"I'll do it. But Thane comes with me."

Ezra sighed. "Fine. But don't even think you'll be able to sneak him out without me knowing."

He understood me a little more than I thought.

"Got it, captain."

He led me to the yard where a group of fifteen boys dressed in their all-black suits were waiting. A few I knew, like Connell and Henderson, and some looked familiar.

I cleared my throat. "Alright, we're going to town. I've been instructed to make sure no one gets into trouble."

Connell smiled and gave me a thumbs-up while everyone else stared at me with unmoving expressions.

"So, what do you guys do there?"

"We go to the pub sometimes," Henderson said.

The group snickered.

"You go to the pub while Ezra meets clients?"

Connell raised his hand. "No! We're supposed to mingle around town with the shop owners. Collect money, see how they're doing and if they're having any trouble."

"Good. That we can work with. We can split into teams."

"Great idea, sir." Henderson's eyes narrowed as he whispered something to his friend with a sly smirk.

Connell raised his hand again.

"Yes?"

"I can show you the town!"

"That would be great." I tried to hide the smile. It would be nice to have someone who was excited about the prospect of helping me learn the town. None of the others were saying anything, just staring at me with blank expressions. Surely, there had to be things they wanted . . . dreams. A better life. I made myself stop. It wasn't their fault, and I was being a hypocrite. I had none of those things either.

"We move out in ten minutes."

"Sir, yes sir." Henderson winked at me.

"Sorry, I'm late. Got a little caught up." Thane appeared next to me and bowed.

"You're right on time. Let's go, boys."

The town wasn't far. The rolling hills contrasted the gray sky, and the frost lingered on the car windows. We'd taken a few cars into town. They were too flashy, and we all stuck out like black sheep.

"This is Cauldbury. It's one of the oldest towns in all of Ireland." Connell's eyes lit up as he pointed to all the colored buildings that were mostly stone and stumpy. But there was something otherworldly about it. With the cobblestone bridges overlooking a pond, my world didn't seem real. Nothing about it was familiar, and the landscape was covered in a wash of gray, yet it was warm. It was like a dream, and I enjoyed thinking of it like that.

I'd instructed the others to split up and complete their tasks while Connell, Thane, and I patrolled the city.

"This is where I used to live. My house was a ways out, but this is the spot. Ask me anything you want to know." He pointed to a stone fountain in the middle of the town overlooking the pond. "This is a wishing fountain."

A stone cherub tipped a vase into the basin, and the water trickled out of it. At the bottom of its murky depth lay silver chains, jewelry, and a few coins.

"It's bad luck to put anything but silver in, but they say those who sacrifice more to it, get greater rewards."

"Don't people steal from here? That stuff looks expensive."

"Oh, never. It's a bad omen. The deadly kind. They say the gods will strike you down. The last time someone stole from this fountain, he ended up face down in that pond. Freakin' lunatic."

"You ever put anything in there?" Thane asked. Connell was the only one who would talk to Thane and Will.

"Yeah, I threw in some of my mum's old jewelry. There. See it over in the corner."

He pointed to a few silver rings in the corner that were growing moss.

"You must have wanted something pretty big to give up that," I said.

"I did, and I got exactly what I wanted. A real family."

Sadness reverberated in my ribs. All I could think of was Connell's mother. What she'd think of her son turning out this way. Brought into a cult that would only continuously take things from him.

It only made me miss my mother and think of all the things I'd done to make her cry. How she'd never understood. How could she if I could never be honest with her?

Just tell me," my mom said, gripping Zach's arm, tears welling in her eyes.

We'd been beaten to hell and dumped on the footsteps of the hospital after initiation. I always wondered why they'd taken us to Mom's hospital. I remember feeling pain like I'd never known, and I thought it was the worst I'd ever feel. Wishful thinking.

Zach said nothing, turning his head to the side to shield himself from her.

"Baby, you can tell me anything. Tell me who did this. We'll do whatever we need to, we'll move—"

"No." Zach cut her off. *"We're not moving."*

Her red eyes settled on me, and I braced myself for the guilt of making my mom cry, but she didn't know what we knew. We were keeping everyone safe and together.

"Why won't you tell me? You can tell me anything. You know that."

She grabbed onto me, and my resolve slipped.

"I know, Mom. I know. Please don't cry." I let her hug me, and Zach gave me a warning glare.

We say nothing. That had been our rule. He was worried I'd cave. He knew me well.

"I don't understand why you won't tell me. I can help you, baby. Let me help."

I'd buried my head into her shoulder and tried to smother the heat building in my face.

She didn't deserve the stress. All I'd ever wanted to do was to make her life easier. She deserved better sons. Sons who didn't keep secrets and make her cry. I'd only hoped she was happier without me.

"So, are you going to throw something in?" Connell looked at me expectedly. Thane wasn't paying attention to us anymore, and instead, he carefully scanned the area.

I thought for a minute, knowing only one item of silver I possessed. I carried it in my pocket for good luck, and even in the scramble to get to Ireland, I'd held on to it.

"No." *Not today, anyway.*

Connell escorted us through the town, and we greeted the shop owners. Most had lived there for their entire lives. Generations upon generations settled there in the shadow of the castle.

"Anything else you want to know?" Connell practically skipped next me.

"Not really. Unless you know any secret passageways or tunnels."

"Oh, not here. But there are some when you take the ferry over to Ironsburg. The whole town is full of them. They made them during one of the old wars, I think. I don't know as much about the mainland as I do here."

I hid my internal excitement at the news. Our plan was slowly coming together. If we could get Will and Thane out through the harbor, we might be able to hide them in the tunnels and find a way out.

A scuffle down the street caught my attention. Yelling, along with the sound of furniture and glass breaking resonated around us. We followed the sound to a pub, but it didn't look like a bar fight. Henderson was outside with two others, taking a chair to the windows and breaking the glass. Inside, they were beating a man. I smelled the blood.

I was there in an instant, pulling them off him and holding the man up by his shoulders. He couldn't have been younger than late forties.

"He didn't report his earnings for the third week in a row and blatantly shows disrespect."

"Connell, call a doctor for this man."

"Uh, yeah. Sure." Connell disappeared.

"What are you doing?" Henderson said.

"What are *you* doing?" I stood in his face. "I didn't instruct you to take action of any kind."

"You gave shit orders."

"Then let me be clear. Do not touch them. You don't think without my permission. Got it?"

The one next to him spoke, "Respectfully, sir, you don't understand how things work here."

"I do understand. You all listen and do whatever you're instructed to do. This is me instructing you to do exactly as I tell you to. Do you understand me?"

I towered over them, with a familiar fire brewing in my chest. It had been so dim I forgot it existed.

"Yes, sir," they said.

"Good. Now you're going to clean this place up. And I mean every last shard of glass. I want to see you lick the floor to show me it's clean."

A woman tended to the wound on the man's head, and it didn't look deep.

He spoke slowly, "T-thank you."

"I'm sorry about your store. We'll pay to repair your windows. When you're feeling better, we can work out whatever the problem is. I promise."

I wondered if he could even understand me, but he held out a bloody palm for me to shake.

"Good . . . good man."

As we left the pub, Thane whispered, "Can you really do that?"

"I don't know."

But I did. And I intended to keep that promise.

Amid the crowd that had gathered, a crashing of metal trash cans smacked the cobblestone. I easily identified Henderson's voice.

"What does he know? He's wrong for this place. He's going to ruin everything. How could She pick him?"

Another kicking of some trash cans faded behind us.

He was right. I didn't belong here, but I belonged nowhere. Not in Brooklyn or Blackheart. I couldn't stop myself from hoping. From pushing and believing that one day I would belong somewhere, and some day, things wouldn't feel like this.

Thirteen

LUKE

"Luke!" Sarah called.

It startled me. I'd almost forgotten the sound of her voice. Was she here in the room with me?

I was dreaming. I had to be dreaming.

"There you are! The ball's about to drop."

I stared at her for a minute, soaking it in. I missed her so much. The relief washed over me at her proximity. Her smile illuminated life.

It was a dream, but it was more than that—it was a memory.

This particular night was during our sophomore year. Ashley's dad let her throw big New Year's Eve parties, so we always ended up in their

118

basement. It was spacious and bathed in orange and pink lights. Silver balloons lined the ceiling and would shuffle around as people passed.

I couldn't stop looking at her.

She was there. Sarah had a unique smile, pinned dimples, and rosy cheeks that freckled in the sun. My memories of that smile had faded, but my subconscious remembered the best parts.

Her cheeks sparkled with silver glitter and tiny stars. She was obsessed with them.

"Five . . . four!" the crowded room roared.

I'd tried to avoid her that night because I wanted to be elsewhere when she kissed someone else at midnight.

"I know we've already done the first kiss, but I've been saving this for you," she said.

"Three . . . two!"

She leaned in, pressing her lips to mine.

"One! Happy New Year!"

Before she could pull away, I grasped the back of her head and held her to me. In one magic moment, my heart expanded into hers, and we kissed long after the cheers had ended.

She pulled away, dragging her bottom lip between her teeth. "First New Year's kiss."

Her dimpled smile was back.

"I have to tell you something. Come on!"

I let her drag me toward the stairs. We passed Zach with Ashley sitting on his lap. They were celebrating silently, and mouthing words to me I couldn't comprehend. They'd seen it all. When we ascended the stairs, we were instantly in a different place.

It was my old room in Brooklyn. Dark-blue walls. Zach's bed on one side and mine on the other—a different day, a different memory.

"You won't lose me, Luke." She grabbed my hand. *"Even if we try this out and we fight or we split up, you're always going to be one of the most important people in my life."*

"You can't know that." I wasn't worried the slightest in fighting or splitting up.

"I wish you'd tell me the real reason you won't try. Why is this the one secret you won't tell me?"

"Because we promised."

"You and your brother and your promises."

She wasn't upset. She stayed eye level with me, waiting for me to explain, but I didn't know how.

A feeling deep in my gut told me not to. If I bound Sarah to me in any way other than a friend, it would end in disaster. Sarah was my person. I couldn't imagine a day without her. We texted from morning to night. I couldn't risk it.

"You're too important," I said, running my thumb across her knuckles.

"It's okay. Forget I said anything." She smiled, hiding any disappointment beneath her dimples, and moved toward the door.

"Wait." I grabbed her arm. *"I have something I want to say."*

"No, you don't have to. It's okay."

"No, I . . . I love you too."

Her body relaxed as she went to sit by me. "You do?"

"I think I've been hooked since you kissed me on the playground."

"No way you've been holding out on me for that long."

I caressed her cheek. "Because it doesn't change anything."

"I feel like this changes something." She put her hand on my leg, and her breathing slowed to match mine.

I missed that feeling. The feeling of needing breath and the feeling of when it came easily. She was all I wanted. Even then. I never knew what I wanted growing up. It was more of a feeling pulling me from place to place. I wanted my family to be happy. I wanted to be happy. It didn't always matter how or where.

I leaned in to kiss her again. It lasted longer than it had in real life. What had really happened was we both pulled away and laughed, then agreed to stay friends. In this dream, we didn't stop kissing. *My lips stayed on hers, and I lost myself in her completely. Maybe that's how it should have ended.*

Suddenly, it stopped and Sarah spoke again.

"Luke? Why do I feel so cold?" Sarah grabbed at her neck while blood poured from her.

I awoke gasping and checking my hands for evidence of the blood.

It had been so quick.

I hadn't seen the cut on her neck or the look on her face when it happened, but I remembered the warmth. The heat of it on my cold skin would never leave me.

I was confident something in me cracked. It had to be something in my brain or chest. I wasn't sure, but it broke. As soon as the warmth hit, I swear I heard it.

I did the same things I used to—wore the same clothes, had the same routines, but that damned feeling of wetness on my face haunted me. It hit me in the strangest of moments. The breeze on my cheek suddenly felt too hot. I reached up to feel nothing. There was no physical evidence of the break. It was unseen, like broken glass hiding in the sand.

Sarah was gone, and it was all my fault. The dark room was closing in on me, but Zach was asleep after our training, and I didn't want to wake him up. Sleeping after blood loss was a curse I couldn't escape.

I collapsed onto my bed. The feeling of panic surging through every muscle wouldn't stop. I couldn't escape my own body, but I longed to shed my skin and be anywhere else.

I rested my face in my hands and wept.

Sarah, why did this happen? Why did I let this happen to you? What is wrong with me? Why didn't I do more? Why didn't I save you? I can't go back. I can't. My face is hot. I hate it. My hands are tingling. Why is it getting worse? My face is hot. I can't breathe. It won't stop. I need it to stop. My face is so hot.

"Luke?" Zach was next to me in a second.

The dam had broke, and tears streamed down my face. *I didn't used to be like this. Terrified and weak. Broken.*

Zach pulled me into a hug. "It's okay. I'm here."

"It's not. I hate that I'm like this. It's not fair."

"No, it isn't."

I wanted my body to stop betraying me. For my face to stop tingling and the warmth to disappear. I wanted to feel normal again. I wanted it to be a bad dream. I wanted Sarah . . . and she was gone forever.

"Why didn't I save her? Why am I useless?" I barely got the words out.

"Stop." Zach squeezed me harder. "Don't do that."

Now I was hurting my brother with my brokenness; emotionally before, and now with the bond.

"I'm sorry."

"What the hell do you have to be sorry for?" he asked, rubbing my back.

"I'm sorry I'm . . . I'm broken."

Everything would be easier if I wasn't like this. That Luke could have come up with a better plan. He'd have prevented this from ever happening. That Luke wouldn't cry on his bed in the dark. He'd be the hero and bring everyone to safety. He'd get up and give a speech. He'd be braver. I was him once and wanted to be him again, but I didn't know how. That Luke would find a way out of this and get back to his little brothers.

My younger self, full of dreams and optimism, would be so disappointed in me if he knew what I'd become. I imagined it. My younger self sitting in the corner and frowning, then I cried harder.

"Luke." Zach pulled away with urgency, and to my surprise, he had tears too. "You gotta stop. You're safe."

For me? Because of the bond?

"You're not broken. I'd never let that happen. Here." He placed his hand over my heart and mine over his. "Just focus here."

Zach's heartbeat was calm, but it was hard to tune into with a never-ending stream of tears. The pain of the bond fell into me in waves that felt like they'd never quit pulling me under. My hands still felt weird, and my face was still hot. I wanted to peel off my skin.

"Focus," he repeated, squeezing my hand over his heart. "Right here. Nothing else matters."

It had to be a punishment ending up this way.

"Stop thinking and focus on the feeling of vibration. Count it."

I focused harder on the sound of his heartbeat and the rise and fall of our chests. The vibration of his heart in his ribcage was steady and strong.

With my brother, I was in the safest place in the world. Zach didn't need me to be anything. Just alive, and that I could do. Even if it was like this. Painful. Tedious.

Every passing minute grew slower. I didn't focus on my own warmth despite it screaming for my attention. My hand shook, but he squeezed it harder. The pressure helped. I counted the beats in his chest. He was alive. His heart was beating, and it was all I needed at that moment.

As panic let go of me, I let go of him.

"I wouldn't be here without you," I said, sniffling.

"You would."

"No, I wouldn't. You're the only thing I have left. The only thing that matters anymore."

"Luke, don't say shit like that. I hate it when you say things like that."

"Why? It's true."

No one had ever been there for me like my brother. I would have never made it if I'd been alone. My brother would die for me. He'd kill for me and love me no matter what I did. I needed that. Someone who expected nothing from me.

"It's not true. You can live without me."

"I can't. I really can't."

"Well, I couldn't either."

"You could. You just don't want to."

"Exactly. And I don't care how selfish it is either." He wiped his face. "If you go, I go. That's the way it is."

I couldn't and he wouldn't. I chuckled at the obvious dysfunction of it all.

We needed each other in different ways. He needed me to hope, and I needed him to accept me if I failed. I needed him to accept the worst part of me and the worst person I could ever become.

He didn't understand that I was able to hope because he was there to shoulder my failure. With Zach, there was no hiding or bolstering. He accepted me as I was but loved me enough to protect the person I wanted to be. My brother loved me unconditionally, and in my worst moments, that's what I clung to.

Even if I never improved and was stuck this way forever, I'd have my brother, and I was enough for him.

The door opened and we separated. Thane and William quickly made their way into the room. The glow of the fire was our only light.

"What happened?" Thane's eyes softened.

"The usual," I said. It was embarrassing for me to cry in front of people still.

"How the hell are you in here right now?" Zach said.

"You have Thane to thank for that. He's become a little spy." Will nudged Thane.

"I jammed the lock. The person who locks it doesn't check it. It doesn't matter. We've got exciting news."

"It better actually be exciting," Zach grumbled.

"There's talk. Someone is moving and showing their hand. It wasn't super clear, but they know someone is looking for them. We think it's Kilian."

"Who did you hear that from?"

"Sirius." Thane raised an eyebrow. "He was talking with the queen."

"How the hell did you manage something like that?"

"I-I . . ."

"Oh no, tell them how," William said, clenching his jaw.

"I might have snuck into the cathedral during their meeting today." Thane fiddled with things on the fireplace to avoid eye contact with us.

"What the fuck?" Zach said.

"They'll kill you if they find you in there," I said.

"I told him." William folded his arms.

"I know. I wanted to be helpful. And they don't seem that concerned with Will and me. I came up with a theory. I think The Legion is coming. I think they know where we are."

Will tapped his foot on the carpet. "They probably want them to come for us. We think they're using us as bait to draw them out."

"The prophecy did mention enemies."

"You believe the prophecy now, Calem?" Will said.

"No. But they do. They all believe it more than anything. It fulfills itself. They'll make sure they come to ensure the prophecy is complete. And that's great news because we won't be here when they get here. We can help them fight. In the meantime, let's focus on staying alive and finding our opening. Zach thinks the harbor is our best bet for getting everyone out. I've heard there are tunnels in the city. I want to check them out."

"How do we know the opening?" Will said.

"I'll feel it."

Fourteen

ZACH

Nights were hell on earth. One downside of training was the need to sleep to heal.

The nightmares left me feeling like a zombie when I woke up. I never dreamed of Sarah, but that didn't mean she didn't haunt me in the daytime. I couldn't stop remembering those days. A time when I was almost happy. One memory I thought of every morning the moment I opened my eyes was the last time Ashley, Sarah, Luke, and I were ever together at the same time.

"Let's go in there! We should get readings for our first week at college." Ashley pointed to a house across the park. A muted-pink two-story

house with a neon sign in the window that read *Tarot Card Readings.*

Ashley and Sarah were prepped and ready for their time together at the university. They walked arm in arm between Luke and me.

I remember thinking how perfect it was.

"My dad told me to steer clear of that stuff," Sarah muttered.

"It's nothing scary. I do readings all the time." Ash was already steering us toward the building. Once she had her mind set on something, we usually went along with it.

Luke and I weren't religious or spiritual in any sense. Mom tried to get us to go to church with her, but we'd end up in the back playing in the pews.

Luke rubbed Sarah's back. *"We don't have to if you don't want to."*

Ashley shot him a glare. *"It's not dangerous. I wouldn't suggest it if it was."*

"We can try it," Sarah agreed.

We walked up the concrete steps. The door squeaked and a bell rang. An old woman who looked like someone I'd want to party with greeted us. Her arms were covered in tattoos, and she had long catlike nails.

She scanned us over but stopped when she saw Luke and me. Her eyes lingered and shone with some kind of recollection I thought nothing of at the time.

"We want a reading because we're starting classes next week." Ashley squeezed Sarah close to her.

She would always pull Sarah to her like a comfort teddy bear.

"Lovely. Come this way and we'll get started."

She ushered us to a small table covered in green velvet in a room that smelled of old incense. I hated that smell. The walls were full of frilly things like doilies and pink-striped wallpaper.

"You're both . . ." She panned over Luke and me as she took her seat. *"Trouble."*

"That's an understatement." Ashley giggled.

"Geminis. Twins."

"Uh, yeah," Luke coughed out.

"Are you a psychic medium too?" Ashley asked.

"Yes, I have been since I was a young girl. Is it you two girls that want the reading, not the four of you?"

Ashley's eyes lit up as she turned around in her chair, so I said, *"We didn't plan on it. But we can."*

"Please sit. All of you."

"For this reading, you will each get two cards." She pulled out a deck of cards with a deep purple on the backing.

I might as well have been scratching a lottery ticket. It meant nothing to me. Cards were a kid game, but it made Ashley happy, so I didn't complain. She closed her eyes, and a silence settled between us. Luke and I shared a shrug. The girls were pressed together between us. Sarah had her brows scrunched, but Ashley had a calming hand on my knee.

The old woman placed two cards in front of me and flipped the first card. It appeared to be some building being struck by lightning. Ashley squeezed my knee.

"The tower. A great change is coming in your life. I see danger. Sadness. Something shifts, and you will not see it coming."

Typical.

She flipped over the next card, revealing two skeletons embracing.

"The lover. I feel something that you're connected to. Something dark. It calls to you." She looked over at my brother. *"And you."*

She didn't wait this time as she shuffled the deck and drew Luke's cards. His card revealed the same sad little building and dead lovers.

"Interesting. Your fates are set on a similar path. You have a deep connection with each other . . . and another."

I swallowed. No way this lady knew what the hell she was talking about.

We watched as she shuffled her deck and drew for Ashley. Her first card was different— death, but the second was the same. The tower. I sighed. None of this was any fun.

"How often does that happen in readings?" Luke chewed his lip.

"It's rare," the woman said.

She shuffled the deck but stopped before pulling.

"I'm sensing a powerful force here with us."

I had to fight an eyeroll.

"Powerful and malevolent." She squeezed her eyes shut. *"It sees us here. It's watching. Observing. Waiting."*

"We're waiting," I said, and Ashley kicked me under the table.

"Yes, yes," the old woman said quickly. She placed two cards in front of Sarah. A dead man with ten swords piercing his back, and we waited for the flip of the last, and sure enough, the tower stared back at us.

"We all drew the tower card?" Ash's tone had shifted.

"Your fates are all intertwined very closely right now. I'd step lightly in the coming weeks." Her eyes panned over to Sarah, and she rested her hand on the back of the cards. *"Especially you, dear. I don't want to startle you, but I see something life altering happening in your future."*

I scoffed. It was all bullshit.

The woman looked up at me with eyes full of sadness. *"Darkness follows you."*

I wondered if I'd taken it seriously if I could have avoided the future that came after. That was the last time we were all happy together. A week later, Sarah was missing and our worlds crumbled. I'd never be able to forget the hell that followed Sarah's disappearance or Ashley's words to me.

"She could still be out there," I'd said.

I hadn't known what to think about her disappearance at the time. I'd been too focused on keeping Luke's head above water and dealing with the backlash. Like Sarah's father busting into our house and asking Luke and me for answers we didn't have. I was so angry back then. Everyone thought it was us. Sarah's dad even asked the police to investigate us. I'd felt betrayed then, but they were right. It was us the darkness followed.

"You and I both know that's not likely." Ashley didn't waste time on false hope for anything, even her best friend.

I went to comfort her, but she stopped me.

"It doesn't make sense. There is no reason that it was her. She was smart. No one would hurt her. The only thing that connects her to anything bad is . . . you and Luke."

"What? You think I did this?" I remember the stab in my stomach when she'd said it. I didn't understand how she could accuse me.

"On purpose, no. Unintentionally . . . maybe. Tell me what your big secret is. Tell me about this thing you've never been able to say. It used to not matter. I didn't care if you and Luke were doing something you shouldn't be. But now it's the only thing that matters because she's gone. And I think you know who did it."

I was such an idiot back then. Brainwashed child or not, I think it was the last night she ever trusted me. Ashley never started her classes. Not without Sarah. Probably why she wanted to go to San Francisco. To leave the carnage of her planned future behind. And I let her. Looking back, it all made perfect sense. I'd ruined her life. She was lucky to make it out alive after knowing me. Not everyone was so lucky. I would have ruined her, and she knew it, but she didn't leave unscathed. None of us did. Sarah haunted us all, and I hoped she would continue to haunt me for the rest of my days. I owed it to her.

Luke's voice snapped me out of my morning fog. "They hate me."

We were on our way to the training room. Ezra had kept his end of the deal. Luke was spending more time with me than with the queen. He had to see her every morning, but most times, I could come along unless Sirius threw a fit.

It was more of the same mundane stuff. Walking in the cold. The queen put on Her show and tried to charm me and my brother into trusting Her. The scary thing was—it kind of worked. Mornings were quick. Being so close to Her felt like taking a nap. Once we left, I hardly remembered our conversation, but I always remembered how it felt to be close to Her.

"They don't hate you."

"They don't respect me."

"They're delinquents who are brainwashed by a cult. Do you really want them to respect you?"

"Well, they like you."

"Yeah, because I'm an asshole. They respond well to other assholes making them feel like shit."

"You're not an asshole," Luke said matter-of-factly.

"Luke, we've established I am."

"Yeah, but you're more than that. You're a good leader in a different way."

I sighed. "They need someone like you more than they need someone like me."

It was sounding like one of the many talks we kept having over and over.

Luke punched my shoulder. "Shut up."

We walked together where the others were sparring. It was the room Sirius and I used most of the time. You needed little in a room that's sole purpose was to tear people's arms off. Connell was having a hard time with Henderson. They were too unevenly matched, and Henderson had a mean streak, but those were good here. Everyone I'd ever sparred since turning had one. They loved watching others suffer. That's one reason it was so fun for me to make them suffer.

Connell was a weak link, though, and I didn't know where to place him. I didn't like watching the kid get the shit kicked out of him and his limbs almost tore off, but I couldn't help him just because his blond hair was the exact same color as my brothers'. Or the fact that when he laughed it sounded like the laugh I used to make fun of Aaron for.

I couldn't be soft.

"Hey, that's enough." Luke motioned for them to stop.

Luke, on the other hand, couldn't help himself.

"What? We've only started getting warmed up. Connell is my partner."

"Not today. I'm your partner."

Oh shit.

That got everyone in the room stirring and moving in closer. The lower-ranked members had leaders, and Henderson was one of them. Each member of The Guard had their own little squad to look over, but no one was technically under Luke and me yet. We were in a weird in-between stage. Not quite The Guard but not one of them either.

"Luke, can I watch?" Connell was a bloody mess on the floor and could barely move.

"Course you can." Luke beamed.

"You have him calling you by your first name now?" Henderson scoffed.

"There are two Calems here. Can't really identify me that way, can he?" Luke tore a piece of his sleeve from his shirt to help cover the blood gushing from Connell's shoulder.

Pain shot through my chest like someone speared me from behind. It was so sharp that for half a second, it felt as if something had. At first, I thought it was from Luke, but this wasn't the usual dull ache in my chest that could turn from zero to excruciating, depending on the day.

This was all mine.

It was confirmed when Luke shot me a worried glance. He felt it too.

Feelings were more of a suggestion as far as I was concerned. I filed them away in my suggestion box that then got set on fire. Problem solved. I didn't take suggestions. This wasn't that. This wasn't something I could control. I turned away while Luke tended to Connell's shoulder. The sadness crept up my throat, and I beat it down like the vile rabid dog it was. *Nope. Not here.*

"There. You'll be all right," Luke said.

"Come on, sir. We should get this started, don't you think?"

Henderson made it easy to grab on to the only emotion I enjoyed feeling—an unholy amount of anger. He was cocky. From his smirk, I could tell he thought he could beat Luke. They all wanted to beat us because they wanted to *be* us. They thought they'd be next. The missing two from the prophecy. Or maybe they wanted someone else to be chosen.

Luke might lose to me in a fight eight times out of ten, but those times, he showed me he wasn't someone to be messed with. He had something I didn't have. When I was knocked down and couldn't get up, I was fueled by pure spite, but Luke had actual resilience. The kind you couldn't learn and had to be born with.

He tore off his shirt and threw it over the side. With a bite to the wrist, blood ran in a steady stream onto the floor. The drain system in the concrete of the floor was perfect for washing away the buckets full of blood spilled daily.

"Alright. Let's see what you got." Luke was oddly serious, but I knew why. He didn't tolerate bullies.

"May fate guide you, sir." Henderson bowed.

Luke bowed back, though he didn't need to. "May fate guide you."

Sirius taught us that stupid phrase the first time we sparred. More cult bullshit.

Henderson rushed him, and Luke countered easily like I'd shown him. He pushed Henderson to the ground with one hulking arm. Henderson wrapped his arm around Luke's leg and tried to pull him down.

"Amateur," I whispered under my breath.

He may have been older than me and liked to fight, but he had a lot to learn. I guess Sirius and Ezra had other things they deemed more important than training the men like they'd taught me. Luke was a hulking mass, and even if they seemed equal in build, unless Luke was good and drained of blood, knocking him off balance would be nearly impossible.

"See, bad idea. You want to wait to pull me down after more blood is drained." Luke grabbed Henderson from the floor and flung him into the wall with ease. "Okay, try again. This time, keep your chin up. Slow down and watch my movements. Read me first."

Luke rushed him, and Henderson went straight for a cheap shot chokehold and bite at the neck, but Luke flung him over his shoulder into the concrete.

"I said watch!" Luke grabbed him by the collar and pinned him to the ground, holding down his arms and feet.

"What are you playing at?"

"I'm trying to make you a better fighter."

I smiled. He didn't like fighting, but he loved teaching and challenging people to make them better. Luke taught me to be a better fighter. He taught me to be better at everything, and he would teach them too. The medium was right. Darkness had followed us, wrapped us in its arms, and placed us there, and we shouldn't have fit. It shouldn't have worked. If it wasn't true, we wouldn't have.

Something about Henderson softened. He let his shoulders drop and listened to Luke's guidance. Luke's audience of blood thirsty assholes had turned into a more silent group, watching him as he explained things step by step.

I smiled. It was working. He was fitting in. We both were.

Luke and I could be okay if things didn't work out with the escape. I wanted to believe it would stick. That this time would be different, but I didn't know for sure. I had to have a backup plan. I had to be ready for anything.

Fifteen

ZACH

"Follow me to the garden," Ezra said.

I groaned. It was winter. The garden was nothing but old shriveled leaves and gray; there was nothing cool to look at. It was all dead plants. Plus, it was drizzling. It was always drizzling.

He patted me on the shoulder, and I reluctantly followed. I had a few minutes before I had to meet Luke at The Underground, and the sun was setting.

Ezra didn't stop at the gate, and he led me farther into the garden than usual. The whole thing was one giant maze, and that was saying something with the giant hedge maze not too far away from it.

Ezra stopped and turned on his heels. His expression was unreadable.

No visible popping veins. No drooping brows.

"I know."

"Okay, what do you know?"

Ezra stopped me. "I know you have a plan to escape."

"I don't know what you're talking about." This was it. He would force his way into my head, and it would hurt like a bitch.

"You don't understand. I was you. I know exactly what you're going to do before you think it."

"What does that even mean? How are we anything alike?"

"When I turned, I didn't like the things I had to do. I didn't always like the person I had to be. But we don't get to choose our fate."

"This is why I don't talk to you. Fuck all this fate shit. It's bullshit. You could have picked anyone for this. But you've somehow made yourself believe that it has to be us, and you spend all your time trying to brainwash us to believe in some stupid prophecy. And it's all bullshit."

"You really believe that?"

I nod. Rhetorical or not, it was too annoying to answer.

He nodded, running his hand over his face, then speaking with eerie sincerity. "I knew it was you from the moment I met you. It wasn't only a feeling. It was a bond. Something unexplainable. She confirmed it shortly after. It can't just be anyone. Yes, running these businesses and making money, anyone can fill those roles. But protecting Her . . . only a few are ever chosen. Why do you think The Guard is ending?"

I waited.

"I want to hear your answer."

"How the fuck would I know?"

"We were meant to be with Her much longer. The four of us. But when The Legion came and took Eros, the bond became a curse. Without him, our bond suffered. We were missing a vital piece."

"I don't understand. Why? Why does this even matter? Why do we matter?"

"Because these bonds we have are the only thing fate bends its will to. You can't fake bonds. You can't fabricate them with fake memories. And The Divine—a higher power can't create them. It only exists here on earth. That's why they're so important. When Eros died, it was as if something shattered. Imagine it, one of your brothers dying. Would any of you be the same?"

I didn't even need to think about that hypothetically.

"No."

"We were supposed to be together forever, until he was gone. That's when the prophecy came. The Guard is broken, but it will be whole again. And when it's whole . . . when the bonds are iron tight, nothing can penetrate it. Not even if The Legion comes knocking. That is your purpose to serve Her. That's why we're all here."

"That doesn't explain why it has to be me and Luke?"

"You and all your brothers." He corrected. "Your bond together is what will make this Guard the strongest it's been for centuries"

"No, they weren't even part of this until She touched them. It says Gemini twins. That's it. It doesn't say anything about my little brothers."

"So you do believe the prophecy?"

"No. I don't know. But I know they aren't part of this."

"You don't even know your whole part of this yet. You won't just rule for centuries. You will annihilate what's left of The Legion. You will pave the way for greater purpose."

"Why would I do that? Why should I do or believe anything you say?"

"I'll tell you what. You stop fighting me. You and Luke both ascend to The Guard. I can assure your little brothers stay out of this."

"Fuck you."

"I kept my end of the deal, didn't I? Your mother is safe. If you'd left your brothers where I'd intended, they'd be on their way to a quality education right now. They're safe. I didn't have to do all that for you."

"Why did you, then?"

He moved his hands through the gray hairs peppering the side of his head. "I ask myself that all the time. As long as you and Luke ascend to The Guard, I don't care what happens to your brothers. You are the ones The Divine specifically mentioned. I was the only one in The Guard who believed that to be true. And when She touched your brothers, She only said it was possible. But they weren't foretold specifically."

I stared at my shoes, contemplating. "Who would fill The Guard, then?"

"Someone in the lower ranks, I'd imagine. It will show itself in time. Another dark sun is coming, She believes it will be revealed to Her then."

"You can guarantee that?"

"Yes. Stop the planning. Get to Ascension, and your brothers stay out of this."

"Deal. But I'm not planning anything."

Ezra sighed.

"But hypothetically, if I was . . . would you keep your promise? Will you take care of Luke?"

He nodded.

Sixteen

LUKE

"Can I trust you to be good?" Ezra plucked a small hair from my suit and flicked it away.

The air was thick with the stench of salty dead fish. I nodded. It wasn't like William and Thane could come with us to the mainland, but this would give us a great opportunity to explore some of those places Connell mentioned.

"We're always good." Zach threw his arm around me.

Ezra scoffed and stepped back to gawk at us.

"You both look like grown men." The corner of his mouth tugged up. "Now, act like it. Show me I can trust you."

His eyes lingered on my brother.

"Yes, *Boss*," Zach said sarcastically.

I smiled. One of my favorite things about my brother was that he didn't expect me to smile, but he liked it when I did. There was no obligation to be happy. I smiled because it made him happy, and that made me happy too.

Ezra left us at the edge of the harbor, and we got into our town car. It was strange being off the island alone. I'd gone with Sirius and Ezra once, but now we were finally getting some real freedom.

"Hello!" I greeted the driver.

He didn't speak a word and started driving. Zach and I shrugged. He would take us where we needed to go. The cliffs disappeared in the distance, and the rolling hills took their place. I wanted to appreciate the beauty, but I was too busy thinking of a way to get William and Thane in a car like this. To get them off the island and into a car would be challenging, but the hills were bare. Everyone we'd met so far had at least known about The Family. My guess was they'd have this whole place on alert. But if we could get them away from the castle, they could hide out there. Stay away from any small towns. It would be a short window. They had to feed, and that would alert everyone. We'd need to be quick.

My old confidence was coming back. We could do this.

Zach and I endured our car ride in silence, not daring to say anything in front of our driver, which would surely get back to Ezra. After fifteen minutes, rooftops appeared in the distance. The town was bigger than the little town on the island. Much bigger. I finally felt like I was returning to a little of my life. Still real and fighting.

"Meet at Mckinnely's Pub at twelve sharp."

"What's the name?" Zach leaned over the seat.

"They'll find you."

Zach rolled his eyes. "Come on."

I hesitated. "I'm sorry, sir. I don't have any money."

"Already paid, sir."

Zach grabbed me by the collar and pulled me out of the car. His cigarette smoke greeted me first.

"Can I try one?"

That made him smile. "You hate cigarettes."

"In high school. I'm a man now."

"Fine." He pulled one out of his pack and lit it for me.

I inhaled the smoke into my lungs. Ashy. Terrible. I took another puff, trying to hide my dissatisfaction.

"Look at you. Embracing your new persona."

I inhaled again. "That's me."

The ash filled my throat, and I coughed.

We passed various shops. This town was more modern than the town on the island. It was odd seeing chain businesses I'd known from childhood. It felt like a lifetime away. The whole street was bustling and filled to the brim with people. It would be easy to slip into it and disappear. I thought of snatching a cellphone from a bystander's hand, but who would I call? I didn't have anyone's number. No one was coming to save us. If we were going to get out of Ireland, we'd have to do it ourselves.

"Let's go get information on the tunnels."

"You want us to wade around in dirty water for days?"

"Yeah, if it gets us out of here. Think we can stop by one of those fancy historic places before the pub?"

"Fine," Zach said, letting me lead the way through the crowd.

"Don't you want us to get out of here?"

"Fuck yeah. But I'm worried about you."

I stopped to look at him. "Me? Why me specifically?"

"Because you get your hopes up. And I don't want to be picking you up off the floor if this goes poorly."

"It won't." My chest ached.

"Ezra's already on to us."

"He's always on to us. It can work. We can do this. I know we can. You're okay with staying?"

"If it's what needs to be done. If it keeps you from being hurt . . . yeah."

I turned and started walking again. "I don't need you to try to protect me like that."

"A little 'thank you, brother' would suffice. If I don't, no one else will. Someone's gotta protect the one who's protecting everyone else."

"Yeah, but then what about you?"

"Eh, who cares about what happens to me?"

"Don't joke like that. It's not funny," I said.

We reached the historic society. It was a tall two-story building made of red brick. Unsurprisingly, it was not as crowded as the other places in town. It had a large sign with calligraphy lettering.

"Come on, I'm hilarious."

"Not even a little bit." I pushed open the door to a modern lobby that smelled of potpourri.

Our steps echoed in the lobby, so we lowered our voices to a whisper.

"We've got ten minutes," Zach said. "Let's get a pamphlet and call it a day."

I found my pamphlet easily, and happily waved it in Zach's face.

"Wanna memorize the tunnel system with me?"

"No."

"You need to learn too. Just in case the queen gets in my head again."

"Hold up. Again? What do you know?" Zach's tone caught looks from a few tourists.

"Nothing. It's nothing. I let Her see everything with The Legion. She won't if I don't let Her."

Zach furrowed a brow.

"Don't give me that look."

"Well, don't talk about Her like she's a friend. Like you think She's somehow on our side. You can't trust Her. Now I'm worried you're letting your guard down around Her."

"I'm not. My guard is fully up."

"You don't even have a guard to begin with." He sighed. "Show me that pamphlet. It's better if we both know the routes."

We studied the pamphlet of a map that showed a vague route. Under the cobblestone bridge was an opening, and it led under a church on the other side of the city. If we could get out of this city, we might have a chance of getting out of Ireland. The five minutes was enough for me to memorize the routes and the street names. Memorization was my strong suit.

"I've already forgotten everything I just read," Zach said as we stepped back onto the street.

It wasn't his.

We arrived at the pub at exactly twelve o'clock where we met a man who was seemingly unimpressed with our presence. He was easy to charm and made small talk about the city. Something about meeting these clients didn't sit right with me. Everyone seemed to respect Ezra and The Family, and they looked to Zach and me like we needed to earn that same level of trust. My previous thought was that The Family was only a drain on society and its resources, but they were bringing commerce and tourism to the area. The man explained his businesses in great detail and showed us the ones he owned around the harbor. These people relied on them.

Our meeting lasted about an hour, and Zach and I left to explore the rest of the city and get eyes on the entrance to the tunnel under the bridge.

In the middle of town, we stopped at an elegant display. A huge Christmas tree stood in the main walkway. Its green branches supported the weight of shiny bulbs, twinkling lights, and ornaments.

"It's Christmas," I murmured.

Pain sliced through my lungs and traveled up my throat, stinging my eyes. I placed a hand over my chest as if it would help. Unbearable emptiness hit me all at once, and I had to bend over and remind myself it was temporary. It felt like nausea. Like a burning ache that would never stop.

"Ow, fuck." Zach reached to pinch the bridge of his nose. "Jesus, Luke."

It was all of it. Zach's and my normal pain coupled with the new, flaring with the bond at the same time. Zach was subtle with his pain, but it was easy to identify because it was like a hot knife in the chest. It always stung.

"Sorry." I grabbed his shoulder and squeezed despite my own chest aching.

"Don't apologize. Just wasn't expecting it. But let's try to coordinate next time. Only one of us is allowed to feel like shit at a time."

"Yeah, noted." I rubbed my chest.

The blood bond might be the thing to kill us. How had Ezra and Sirius tuned it all out? My own pain was bad enough. It was bearable in

Blackheart, but here, where everything hurt all the time, I couldn't bear it. I had to admit, it was nice to know I wasn't the only one affected by sparkly Christmas ornaments.

"So, you do care?" I hit his shoulder as he straightened his jacket. "I thought you didn't get feelings."

"I don't. Especially not about this. Not because of the stupid smell .. . or the memories."

I didn't need to be reminded. We'd always been together on Christmas. Even if Mom was working, the four of us would be together and cook her dinner and wait for gifts. We did it all. We baked cookies, hid little bottles of liquor in my brother's stockings, and watched holiday movies. Presley loved a good Hallmark movie. He even got us matching pajamas to watch them in.

"I can't be here. It's too much." I looked at my brother, pleading.

"Let's go. Fuck this place and the holidays."

I nodded as he put his arm around me and steered me away from the square.

Christmas was my favorite. Sarah's too.

We left on the last boat out for the day, but when we arrived back on the island, I had my mind set on one place I needed to go.

"I have something I need to do."

Zach followed me along the cobblestones to the old fountain Connell had shown me.

I reached into my pocket and grabbed my silver object. The only object I always kept on me. One of Sarah's silver butterfly necklaces. The one she'd given me before she'd left for college. To remind me "to not forget to keep moving forward." It was her favorite. The one her grandmother had given her. She loaned it to me, claiming I needed its luck more than her. I'd wished that were true.

I never thought I'd part with that necklace, but its luck could be enough to get us out.

"Why do you like butterflies so much?" I'd asked Sarah once in her bedroom. She had stars on her ceilings but paper butterflies that fluttered next to her window.

"They make me happy. Every time I see one in the garden, they make me want to run away with them. They're free to roam wherever they wish. It's full of possibilities."

I rubbed the pendant between my thumb and index finger while Zach waited.

Don't be afraid to dream. Don't be afraid to believe in the best possible outcome. Please. Whoever is listening. Let this work. Let us go home. That's all I want. For us to be together again.

I gave the necklace one final squeeze before chucking it into the murky water and watching it sink.

A singular glint of silver fell to the bottom of the basin.

"You good?" Zach said.

"Yeah, I'm good."

Dear Luke and Zach(Come on. Read the letter, bro),

I keep thinking you're going to walk through the front door. Kinda like you used to do back at Mom's place when you'd surprise us on a random Friday night. You'd bring fancy pizza(anyone else miss stuffed crust?) and we'd play games. Fridays were my favorite after you both moved.

I try to imagine what you might be doing, but I have no clue. Sometimes I imagine you both as secret agents or in some remote jungle on an adventure. Or on a beach somewhere sipping beers. I like to think that you're happy. But I know that's not true.

I'm kinda thankful for Akira's blood. Because without it, I'd have never known you were this miserable all the time. You were both scary good at hiding it. I mean, I knew you struggled, but this feeling is the worst. And it gets worse every single day. Why didn't you say anything? You were great at keeping my secrets. I could have been good at keeping yours. I could have helped you more.

There is this small part of me that wonders if you really wanted to leave. Like you didn't want to be here with us and you'd rather be there. I know you planned to go back because of Kilian, but that wasn't always the case, right? For a minute there, you wanted us all to escape together?

Maybe vampire-cult life is way more interesting than hanging around here with us.

Crazy, I know.

Sorry to be such a sap, but every day here is so gloomy. There's no sun ever.

I know you're sad. If I were with you, I'd tell you a joke.

P.S. Don't worry. I didn't celebrate Christmas without you.

Love you forever,

Presley

Seventeen

The castle was flooding. Little drops of rain fell into the bucket next to me, and thunder shook the painting above the fireplace. It had poured all day and into the night. Will and I sat by the fire in one of the common rooms. The castle was big enough no one would bother us. They were too busy running around patching holes and cleaning up ruined carpet. Ezra said it was the biggest storm Ireland had seen in nearly ten years.

It was hardly the karmic justice they deserved, but it made me laugh a little. Will and I giggled like schoolgirls while watching the others pace the halls in a frantic mess to clean; I hid him so he wouldn't have to help.

The warmth of the fire made me think of Blackheart and my brothers. I wondered what they were doing and if they, too, might be staring into a fire. Presley was probably getting into trouble somehow, and I hoped Aaron was taking good care of Kimberly. He was good at it when he got out of his own way. It was strange. I never imagined my little brother with anyone. All of his high school girlfriends were nothing special, but I knew immediately when I saw that look in my brother's eyes after he met her. It reminded me of when I'd met Ashley.

I wondered how she was. Better off without me, that I was sure of.

I hoped Aaron and Kimberly were happy and together and they'd get to do all that fun couple shit.

"What do you think the love birds are doing right now?" I asked Will to snap him out of dissociation. He was sitting on the floor by the fireplace and staring into it like he might jump in. "I was thinking of them all. Wherever they are."

I wasn't technically breaking my rule because I hadn't said their names.

William grinned and took a swig of his drink. "Probably fuckin' like bunnies, I'd presume. New relationship and all that."

I laughed thinking of that night Aaron came down the stairs to get Kimberly's water. His hair messy and his face glowing with happiness.

"I'm glad someone gets to be happy." I raised my glass, and William clinked his to mine.

The door opened, and Luke and Thane emerged looking more chipper than ever.

"You look happy." I laughed.

"Because I think this is going to work. And because I got this." Luke smiled, pulling a bottle of liquor from his jacket.

"You're drunk." I laughed at first. Then the worry set in. "Wait, why are you drunk?"

Luke almost drank himself to death after Sarah disappeared. Thankfully, he was already a vampire, so he wasn't in any real danger. That didn't stop me from calling Ezra just in case.

"Good news—stop with that look."

"He's okay. Really, I've been with him all day," Thane said.

I grunted an acknowledgment in his general direction and got to my feet to survey my brother.

He smiled from ear to ear. "You worry too much."

"Just about you."

"The guys gave him this bottle and made him take a double shot of it. I think it's pretty much pure alcohol." Thane stumbled. "It's got a kick to it."

"They like me now." Luke smiled radiantly. "That, or they gave it to me to kill me and weed out competition."

I patted him on the shoulder and took the bottle so I could smell it. "Tell me the good news."

"With the flood, they're going to bring in a lot of people for repairs tomorrow. Ezra was really adamant on getting it all done in a day."

"So, that means?"

"It's our opening!" He pushed me playfully, and I had to steady myself.

"You think we'll be able to hide in the chaos," Will said.

"Exactly. Ezra had to stay over on the mainland because of the storm, so he won't be back till after it clears. He wants Zach and I to go meet with a client in the early morning. We can take the main ferry. And you two can sneak in the cargo hold. It can work."

"What about Sirius?" I asked.

"Luke took care of that too. He's going to be with the queen all morning. And then he'll be occupied with all the workers coming in and out of the castle."

"It's going to work! This is it." Luke was too stupidly happy about it.

It's not like I didn't think he was right. It *could* work. Now that we were given more freedom and we only needed a minute or two of really good luck to sneak Thane and Will on the ferry, it was possible. Especially with Will's and Thane's mind capabilities. I wasn't sure I believed, but like every time before this one, he made me want to. It was a shitty curse of believing in unlikely things.

"We could be home in a few days. See everyone, wouldn't that be great?" My brother's eyes sparkled from the light of the fire. *Fuck.*

"Yeah, that would be great." I took a drink from the bottle and recoiled. "Holy fuck. This is battery acid."

"It's good! Come on. Let's celebrate. Let's do something fun." Luke practically vibrated with energy.

I knew that look.

Everyone got to see this tame, fully responsible brother of mine, but the Luke I knew was wild at heart, and though I hadn't seen it a while, that fire burned in his eyes and took over all his other features. His eyebrows were raised, and his smile overflowed with unbridled optimism. *This motherfucker.*

"What type of trouble do you have in mind?" I took another swig of the bottle and handed it to Will. My throat burned down to my stomach.

"You'll see."

The four of us hunkered down in the hall, and a crack of lightning lit up the hardwood floor. We brought the bottle. We really shouldn't have brought the bottle. It occurred to me then, we should have tried to jump in the ocean and escape in the storm or something logical like that. Though I wasn't sure it was logical because we'd probably sink to the bottom.

"Stop pushing me." I elbowed Thane.

"Sorry," he said, then moved to lean into Will.

"Ow, fuck off," William replied.

I elbowed Will. "Be quiet."

"Scoot over.'"

"You're supposed to address me as 'sir' here. Didn't we establish this?"

"You never respected my authority, why would I respect your fake cult Chosen One bullshit?"

Thane fell back onto the hardwood, and Will turned his attention to some plant next to us with long tendrils of leaves touching the ground.

"Oh, god. These people are monsters. Why is this here?" He peeked to check the soil. "Dry as a bone and too little light. I'm taking it."

"Taking it where? Your dark dusty cell?"

"Anywhere is better than this life-sucking hallway with this dated wallpaper."

"Guys. We have a special mission." Luke used the doorframe to keep himself steady.

"Why are we here?" I leaned my face against the cool wood of a door.

"Ezra took my stuff, and I want it back."

"When?"

"When we got on the plane. He took it, and I want it back."

"It better be good, Calem." Will hiccuped, and I had to grab him before he fell into my brother.

"Oh, it's good."

"You're not going to share what it is, are you?"

"Nope. Secret. Come on." Luke grabbed the collar of my shirt, and the world spun.

"Will, get the bottle!" I shouted.

"Got it, your *Most Glorious* Jackass."

I blinked, then we were in another fancy room. They all looked the same, especially when I was drunk, but this one had a similar layout to ours. Bed on the bottom and a loft, but a lot more books and shit all over the ground. Luke hated clutter. He'd never let it fly.

"This isn't Ezra's room," I said.

I knew because I'd been brought to his room many times to be scolded.

"Oh, you're right," Luke said, grabbing our bottle and taking another sip, then I did too.

"You took us to the wrong room?"

"The doors all look the same."

"Wait, whose room is it?"

We all dispersed. I tripped over a stack of records on the floor. Every surface was covered in dust like it had been abandoned. I opened a wardrobe, and the smell of a familiar cologne jogged my memory.

"Akira."

Luke and I shared a look, but there was no pain. The alcohol was doing its job to keep every bad feeling shrouded beneath numbness. I plucked a record from a suitcase record player.

"Akira listened to K-pop?" I snickered. "And Duran Duran?"

"Look at this." Thane pulled a shirt from a drawer. Some boy band.

"I found a diary!" Luke held up a linen-bound notebook.

We scrambled toward the bed where Luke was sitting.

"Get your ass off me, Calem." Will pushed me.

"I don't think I can move." I'd somehow lain across the laps of both Thane and Will in my mad dash to read the diary of some dead guy. "Yeah, I'm toast. Give me a sec."

I lay my head on Luke's arm because the room was spinning. "Tell us what it says."

"It's a lot of poems."

Ashley loved it when I wrote poetry for her. Only, it was a little bit fucked because I was shit with words and didn't actually write them. Luke helped me with all of them. I'd rifle off what I wanted to convey, then he'd take a little blue gel pen and scrawl it out on a piece of notepad paper. She loved it. I was eventually gonna tell her it wasn't me. I wanted it to be me. I knew how I felt but not how to put it into words. It didn't matter anymore.

"What do they say?"

"*She is fortunes high. Marvel at the throne, and behold the coming of the prophecy.*"

He flipped another page. "This one is just the phrase *I adhere to The Divine Path* over and over again."

"Blah. Blah. Blah," I mumbled.

"And he called me an 'altar boy.' I fuckin' hate this place." Will shifted under me. "Move your ass or quit your wigglin'."

Luke flipped another page. "There's a drawing of a . . . I don't know who that is."

I snatched it without looking. "Let me guess, it's the queen."

"Don't you think I'd know it if it was?"

The picture was a detailed sketch of a guy with light skin and dark hair. He had a distinct widow's peak and little facial hair.

"This is that guy Presley liked. Um . . . Harry Styles!"

"No, it's not. Give it here." Luke grabbed it and held it close to his face. "Oh. You're right. This is him. Presley is obsessed with him."

I guess the no-name rule didn't count when we were drunk.

"Apparently, Akira too."

"Wait, there's more. Look."

In the notebook were sketches, shoulder-up portraits of four people easily identifiable when all lined up. The Guard as it had been: Sirius, Akira, and Ezra, and what had to be Eros. He had thick brows and curly hair that curled around his ears and neck, and he was smiling. None of the others were smiling.

"*My guardian. My brother. Wait for me in the stars,*" Luke read the words sketched under the portraits.

"No way." Thane grabbed the notebook. "Can I keep this?"

"If you hide it," Luke said.

"And you say please," I said.

The door opened behind us, and Connell stood in the entryway.

"Oh. I thought I heard a noise. 'Tis forbidden to be in here, sir."

My body moved on its own to grab Connell and push him out the door. His eyes went blank, and his mouth hung open.

"What are we doing in the hallway, sir?"

I looked down at my hand. I must have taken that memory, blocked it or wiped it. Connell might be the only person in the castle I was able to use that power on.

"You were telling me how excited you were to spar earlier today."

He was so shit at fighting it was torture to watch. I tried to straighten my back so he couldn't tell how plastered I was.

"Oh, right! Yes, it was great. And I thought I'd heard . . ."

"Nothing. Only me. Carry on with your duties."

"Will do, sir." Connell's eyes sparkled with determination, and he left as another crack of thunder shook the walls.

I motioned the others out into the hallway when he was far enough away. "I did it. The super mind trick thing."

Sirius was teaching me to use it more, but it was something he assured me I'd get more acquainted with as we got older, and it wasn't that useful in battle when you had an equal opponent. Only something I needed to learn to dodge in someone older and stronger.

"This one is Ezra's room!" Luke plowed through another wooden door, and we followed.

He was correct. The room was more well-kept and had warmer colors. No record player or any band merchandise. Everything was simple and had a place. He didn't look like he collected anything, and I doubted he'd be the type to have a diary.

"We should do something while we're here," I said.

"What are you gonna do? Switch the conditioner with the shampoo?" Will said.

"It would piss him off."

"You're *such* a rebel."

I motioned for Luke. "You look for your thing. I have an idea."

While Luke rummaged through drawers and cabinets, I moved every piece of furniture and tested the weight. With one arm, I lifted the leg of the bed and chipped a piece of wood in the bed frame, that way when he got on it, it would cave, and he'd never know it was me. I moved through various other places in the room, jamming the drawers and removing pieces of the furniture legs. I even pinched the pipe in his bathroom sink.

"I found it!" Luke said.

We gathered around a singular polaroid picture.

"Pres gave me this one. He said it was his favorite."

It was all five of us together sitting by the fire on Kimberly's birthday. Luke had an arm wrapped around me while I held up my drink. Presley was grinning, and his clothes were dirty from where he'd drunkenly fallen earlier in the night. Kimberly wore a tired, content smile next to Aaron, who was looking at her with wide-eyed admiration.

They were out there somewhere. Did they think of us? Were they waiting by the door?

"Totally worth it," I said, and they all nodded in agreement.

Eighteen

LUKE

Will scowled while he moved into his disguise. It was early morning, and the contractors had already come over on the ferry. Thane and Will had them memory wiped and stored in the cargo hold, ready to go back over to the mainland. The outfits helped keep them from sticking out in the stark white they usually wore.

"No one speaks of this," he hissed.

"Where's your little brother with the camera when you need him?" Thane joked while adjusting his collar with a wide smile.

I rubbed my chest, but the dull ache didn't bother me as much because, for the first time in a long time, I hoped this plan could work. I'd gone through all the possibilities. Sirius and Ezra were occupied enough. Zach and I would attend our meeting, and Thane and Will would get to the tunnels. We'd meet up where the tunnels ended across the city. There would be enough distance between us and them. It would work. It had to. We had to try.

"Okay, you have to wait for the window between seven a.m. to eight a.m. Remember?"

"Yes, we fuckin' remember."

"The ferry will dock, and you'll need to get there however you see fit."

"I got it, alright?" William sighed.

I didn't think Will was that hopeful for our plan. That, or he was tired of this place. I was too. Tired of walking with Her in the garden every morning. Tired of training and pretending. I longed to be home with my family more than I'd ever wanted anything.

Thane wrapped an arm around Will. "He means, 'We got it, Boss. Great plan.'"

"This is where we part ways and hope for the best," I said.

Thane smiled. "See you both on the other side?"

Zach shrugged. "I'm not hugging you. But hopefully, this is the end of this nightmare."

"Alright. Enough pleasantries. Don't fuck up the plan," Will said.

Zach and I brought the attention to the front of the ship while Will and Thane came out of the storehouse and jumped on the back. We said little on the way to the mainland. Ezra called me to tell me where we needed to go to meet the client and that he'd meet up after. He'd been happy with me lately. I'd met his clients. I was nervous each time, but it was easy to appease them. And I was good at, molding myself to be whatever they needed me to be.

"We're meeting Aine at some library next to the college."

Aine was lead volunteer coordinator of the blood donor system in Ireland. We hadn't met her yet, but it was "imperative" we get in her good graces, according to Ezra. We were their largest money donor, so they agreed to supply the castle with a small portion of the blood they brought in. It was a new deal now that the castle was occupied.

"Don't talk too much, or we'll be stuck talking to her forever."

"I don't talk too much." A rare smile crept on my face.

Zach lit another cigarette. "I thought Mr. Good Boy didn't like to tell lies."

"Shut up."

Zach joking was a good sign.

Once the boat docked, we passed a few tourists standing in line for the ferry in their rain jackets. It was drizzling, but the worst of the storm had cleared. The city was full of people walking along the sidewalks. The brightly colored buildings stood out against a mostly gray sky, but the clouds dissipated like the sun might make an appearance. I wondered what day it was. How long had it been since we took the ferry for the first time? Was it a weekend or a weekday? I had no way of knowing.

We arrived at an outdoor patio covered by a large awning. I identified Aine right away. She was younger than I'd imagined and couldn't have been older than twenty-five. Her red hair was brighter than Kimberly's. She sat alone with a folder and steaming coffee resting on the table. The cold chill brought red to her pale, freckled cheeks.

"'Bout time you boys showed up."

I would definitely have to take the lead on this one.

"I think we're right on time." Zach checked his invisible watch.

"Two minutes late, actually. Please sit." She motioned to chairs at her table.

"I apologize, Miss. My name is Luke, and this is my brother Zach."

I held out my hand to shake hers. She squinted at my advance but took my hand with a strong handshake.

"Call me Aine." She pushed some hair out of her eyes. "You're taking over for Ezra?"

"Is that surprising?"

I kept smiling. If I'd guessed right, she wanted professionalism but also a friendly face. I could be that for her.

"You both look too young."

"We could say the same about you." Zach clicked his tongue.

"We are." I interrupted. "We've got a lot to learn. But we're willing. Have you worked with Ezra long?"

"Well, I haven't. To give you the short of it, my father has made a deal with your boss that he insists he cannot get out of. Though it breaks the law, in addition to our own moral code. Which tells me you lot aren't my kind of people. The sooner we get this deal sorted, the sooner I never have to see your pretty faces again."

"Sounds good to me," Zach said.

"You're not a criminal—"

"How would you know anything about me?" She had an equal amount of venom in her voice as my brother.

"I'm not either. Sometimes we don't always have a choice in what we're involved in. But my brother and I are doing the best with what we have."

Her scowl softened. "Prior obligations. An unfair consequence of family."

"Family. Exactly."

She reached into her folder, then lay papers in front of us. "I need you to sign and initial all of these. One of you will be a cosigner. All future communication on shipments will be through me."

I flicked through the papers. It would take forever.

"We can't hurry this along?" Zach said.

"Got more important places to be?" She smirked as she leaned back in her seat and took a sip of her coffee. "I can't imagine how anything could be more important than this arrangement. I'm no fool. I think you need us a little more than we need you."

"We have time." I raised a brow at Zach.

We did, but we'd need to hurry. I scanned the documents as quickly as I could without her noticing I wasn't reading them.

"You're a fast reader."

"Have to be. My little brothers loved bedtime stories and had short attention spans."

The sharp pain hit me in the chest, and it almost made me drop my pen as I initialed the final page. I handed it to Zach so he could sign too.

"Little brothers, huh? Where are they?"

"Somewhere that's . . . not here." I smiled, handing her back her papers and pen.

"Hm. I've got a little brother too. He's also anywhere but here. Thank god."

She gathered her things. "Pleasure doing business with ya both."

We shook her hand and said our goodbyes.

"That took too long." Zach groaned.

"I know. We have to hurry."

We needed to deliver word about the meeting to Ezra and make sure we got an eye on his location before disappearing into the crowd. Zach and I had done stuff like this before in Brooklyn and in New York. Pickpocketing was easy as a vampire. I didn't mind it too much because all our targets could afford to lose a little money and not think twice.

After a few minutes, Zach motioned to a girl more worried about her dog than her fluffy keychain hung on her bag. We found our mark. Someone with a phone and a tracker on the keychain.

"There."

I waited to see if she'd unlock her phone. My brother already knew what to do. He bumped into her and distracted her with a cunning smile while I snatched the phone she'd set down and the keychain from her purse. We convened in a small alley between two shops.

"They should be in the tunnels by now," I said as I scrolled through the girl's phone and made sure her keychain tracker worked.

A rumble of thunder echoed in the seaport town, and the drizzle switched from a mist into droplets. I brushed the wetness from my eyes and the phone screen.

"It works."

"Perfect. Let's get the fuck out of here."

We started that way with our heads down. My pulse picked up, but I focused on getting home. A place where I could shed all these clothes and crawl into a warm bed. It felt close. Like if I could keep my head on straight a little longer, it would finally be over.

Ezra was waiting at a pub in town. He ended his phone call as we approached.

"How'd it go?"

"Great. Signed the paperwork. Aine was nice," I said.

"She thought we were pretty." Zach's smile seemed genuine.

"Good. Want to meet me at the ferry in about an hour? I have one more thing I need to do. You can both explore." He handed me a wad of cash. "Buy yourself something. Have fun."

Ezra patted me on the shoulder, and Zach snuck the tracker into his pocket. This was what he wanted. Two obedient pets. He liked this version of me. Agreeable and upbeat.

He didn't like the hopeful version of me. When he realized we were gone, he would be mad. A sinking feeling sloshed in my stomach. Ezra would never stop looking for us. Home might not be a singular place but an infinite number of hotel rooms and hideouts. We may never get to be free from them.

Once we were a safe distance away, I asked, "Did you get it?"

"Yep. So far so good." Zach's hair was soaked.

"Let's meet them at the church."

I remembered the pamphlet well. The bridge tunnel led the way to a church on the other side of the city, and that cathedral was open to the public for viewing during the day. It was a popular tourist attraction. From there, the tunnels led to the next city over.

We worked quicker and darted through the crowd of umbrellas as fast as we could. Their color stood out among the gray and cobblestones. It made it easy to hide. We'd stop between buildings to conceal ourselves if we saw anyone from The Family meandering around.

The cathedral was a warmer stone than the one on the island, and taller. Much taller. As I admired the stained glass on our way in, I thought of Her, and my heart kicked. This feeling of need would never end. I'd always want Her. No matter where I was in the world. As long as we both walked the earth, I'd feel Her waiting for me.

It was too late to worry about it. I wasn't second-guessing, but it was setting in. Running away was running away from Her. It would free me, but I might never fully be free.

Tourists lined the floors of the cathedral. I didn't know exactly where I was going as I darted out of view and went for the halls. I worked solely from the knowledge I had from the pamphlet. A few people tried to stop us but compelling them for a few seconds was all we needed to weasel past them. We walked till we found a door and then another. Until we were face-to-face with a dimly lit set of stairs leading underground.

I checked the phone again. "Ezra's all the way back at McKinnley's."

"Good head start." Zach's eyes were filled with determination.

There was a light at the end of the tunnel. We'd done it. The plan worked. We descended the steps, and Thane and Will were waiting in a narrow concrete tunnel

"Took you both long enough," Will said as he puffed on a cigarette.

"You did it! Did anyone see you?" Thane said.

"No. We don't think so. And we have a tracker on Ezra so we'll be able to see how close he is."

Thane beamed. "Genius."

Zach walked up to Will with his arms crossed. "You smell like dead fish. How'd you like dirtying those pant legs?"

Will flipped him off and offered him a cigarette. All at once, I let in the hope I'd tried so hard to keep in check. We could hide out for as long as it took. Get back to America.

And then . . . we could be together again. Shoveling snow. I'd chop wood for the fireplace. This whole nightmare would be a long-forgotten memory. It wouldn't be perfect, but I could cope. Even if we never got to quit running, I wanted it. I was sure this time.

After our reunion, we moved quickly through the tunnels. It was mostly dry and smelled of moist stones and asphalt. There wasn't much to see other than a few rats.

Then I could see it. A glowing light at the end. I could even hear cars overhead. We made it. The hard part was done. It would be only a few days, then it was over. I imagined it. Embracing my family again and enjoying the shake of their laughter and the warmth of their cheeks on mine. The tightness in my chest would finally loosen.

Someone stepped into the light.

Sirius was waiting.

He stood before us with a look I'd never seen before. There was no smile or scowl. He held my gaze with a bored detachment.

How? The sudden feeling of warmth on my face signaled me to the danger long before my brain comprehended.

"I didn't want to believe it was true. That you boys have traitorous hearts. But time and time again, you show me how wild your spirits are. And wild spirits must be tamed."

How had he known? Even if he'd figured it out, he'd never be able to get on the ferry and get this far in the tunnels. I swallowed. There was no place to escape he wouldn't catch one of us.

"How did you know?" I asked.

"Did you think we didn't keep an eye on them? On you? I know where you are every minute of every day."

"You did it as a test, leaving their door open at night. Giving us freedom."

"Loyalty demands to be tested. Ezra believed you'd stay on The Divine Path, but I knew this rebellious streak would be harder to break. Some lessons must be carved into the brain with a knife, but it eventually gets the picture."

My face felt hot, and my lips tingled. *Luke, focus.*

"Will, take Thane and go."

Thane protested, but Will grabbed him by the shirt and moved toward the back of the tunnel, but that way was blocked too. Ezra stood next to Connell. Both wouldn't make eye contact with me. This was bad. I thought of fighting first. There was no way we could take two members of The Guard.

"Ezra." I moved toward him, but Zach stopped me. He looked at Sirius. It took me a second to realize he was protecting me, but I didn't care about me.

"I guess you boys have to learn the hard way." Sirius darted to Connell's side and took him by the arm. Ezra did the same.

That's when I knew we'd made a grave error. This would be a bloodbath. My body knew already because my whole face was numb.

"Connell, did you or did you not give your superior information on how to escape?"

"I . . . It wasn't my intention, sir."

"Answer my question."

"I told him the history of the city." Connell met my eyeline with soft worry bunching in his brows.

"He's telling the truth. Don't hurt him. Hurt me. I'm the one who decided to escape."

"Oh? Okay, then. You give me your arm."

I moved forward, and Zach grabbed my shoulder. "You're not touching him."

"Punishments must be made. Sometimes, punishment is a gateway to a greater destiny. The faster you comply, the faster we can continue on the path of The Divine."

I blinked, then Sirius was in front of us. There was a blur as we all attempted to flee while simultaneously trying to protect each other, but there was nowhere to run.

Sirius had Will by the throat. There was yelling. My brother said something I couldn't hear over the roar that seemed to fill the tunnel.

"Consequences can be painful. Sacrifices must be made."

My ears were ringing. The lights dimmed. If he'd said anything else, I didn't hear it. I was already gone. Completely detached. I didn't feel myself put my hand over my ears and crouch like a coward. I hated being a coward. Being small when I was supposed to be me. Luke—big, strong, and capable. The hero. I couldn't do it. I couldn't watch someone else I cared about get brutally murdered again. I *had* to close my eyes, or I wouldn't make it.

Will's screams echoed along with Connell's. There was a shuffle going on, but I couldn't move.

"Please stop!" I begged, grabbing at my chest where it burned. Stabbing. Aching.

One brief glance sent a livewire of pain through my entire body. Sirius had bit into Will's neck, and there was blood *everywhere*. A guttural scream came from Will's throat again. Sirius peeled the skin from Will's arm. First with his fingernails, then Ezra handed him a knife.

I couldn't move. I couldn't breathe. I didn't need to, but it didn't matter. My body wanted to breathe again. To fill my lungs, get up, and run far away.

"It's all right. I'm here. I'm here." Zach's arms were around me, holding me to his chest. He pulled me in the other direction, and I rested my head on his shoulder. "I got you."

I was floating. None of it was real.

"I can't do it. I can't."

"It's okay." He put his hands over mine to help me cover my ears from the cries of our friends.

I still heard it. Will, Thane, and Connell all screaming and talking over each other.

"It's my fault. It's my fault it didn't work."

"No. It's not. It's mine. It's almost over. It's okay."

I wasn't used to the sound of fear in my brother's voice, but he hid it well. He was squeezing me so hard.

Like a knife repeatedly being plunged into my chest and back, Will's screaming threw cascading waves of pain through me. All of it was excruciating. I'd felt nothing like it. Nothing worse than what Sirius was doing to him. The guilt was too much. The fear. The hurt.

"It hurts. It hurts. It hurts."

All of it. Everything. I tried to move, but my body was frozen. Shaking. My feet were glued to the floor. I wanted to save them.

"Make it stop, please. You have to make it stop." When would the screaming end? And when it did, would they all be dead?

"Ezra, please," Zach begged.

I wasn't sure of the last time I'd heard him beg. I was happy to hear his voice. It was stronger than mine.

"Sirius. That's enough."

The chaos stopped, and all I heard was my ragged breath and the ringing.

"Are you boys going to behave?" Ezra said.

"Yes," Zach said, more desperately this time.

"Yes, what?" Sirius said.

There was a long pause, and Zach's grip on my shoulders tightened.

"Yes, sir, we'll do whatever you want."

"No more running."

"We won't try to leave again. Just stop." Zach stared at Ezra. I could only look at him. My brother was solid. Safe. All I had and all I needed. I could stand again if he helped me. I could do a lot of things if he helped me.

"We take them to Her."

"You're too soft on them," Sirius said.

"Their bond is stronger than anything we've seen or encountered. It's got to be excruciating for them. Traumatizing them like this isn't going to help them to ascend."

"No, but we kill Legion. We're here to ensure She's safe. There has to be consequences."

"We need them."

"But do we really need both?" Sirius motioned to Thane.

I buried my head into Zach's shoulder. I couldn't look. I couldn't help. I couldn't save anyone. I felt like a child. Small, weak, and useless. Why couldn't I move? Why couldn't I do anything?

Zach was shaking too, but him stroking the back of my head was my only tether.

"We'll be okay. I promise. It's almost over," he repeated to me over and over. *It's almost over. It's almost over.*

"That's for Her to decide," Sirius said.

A foreign feeling fluttered in my chest. Relief. I was going back to Her, but why did that of all things bring me relief?

"So be it."

Nineteen

I was so angry I could've sworn the water was a deep burgundy. I'd held onto Luke while Will and Thane got tied to the guardrail of a small speed boat. William's damage was the worst. He'd forced Thane away from him in enough time to take most of Sirius's wrath. They didn't give him much to cover his bleeding arm, and his blood was all over my shoes. The wetness of it had seeped into my socks. Connell's punishment was the loss of two fingers, but everyone was alive. Bloody and traumatized, but alive.

It's what I'd feared. I hadn't fully believed, unlike my foolish, hopeful brother. He'd let himself believe we could escape, but I always knew we'd end up right back at Her feet.

The queen's eyes softened when She saw my brother, as if She cared about his pain. It had to be a show, but for who?

Luke clung to me, with his eyes fixed on the floor. I think his brain had decided to check out, and it left him vacant and shaking.

"*I don't feel like me. I miss who I used to be,*" he'd whispered on the way over from the mainland while staring at the same spot on the floor for twenty minutes.

I couldn't let them keep doing this to him. Over and over, they played their games with my brother's sanity. Luke's mental health was worse than he ever let on to anyone in our family. Tack it up there with our many secrets. One minute, he'd be smiling with not a care in the world, then night would come and he'd change. It was like a mask he could put on whenever he was with them, but he never put it on with me.

I'd been desperate a few times and tried to get him help. He needed someone to talk to after Sarah disappeared. It got even worse when we found out about her death after getting all those memories back. I'd visited a few clinics in person to try to get them to take Luke. To do something. Anything. He was willing to go, but they never called me back or they'd refuse to take him even if I had cash. Now I was smart enough to see it was always The Family working behind the scenes. One step ahead of me. They wanted Luke to be broken; it was easier for them to control us that way.

The queen's misty eyes bore into mine. "I can help him."

"We don't need your help." I pulled my brother in closer.

"He needs rest. Take him to your room while we handle things," She said.

"N-no," Luke said, "not until we fix this. You can't kill them. We're sorry. It was stupid. I-I was afraid because I didn't trust you not to hurt them. And I wasn't ready for all of this. It's my fault. But I'm ready now. Whatever you want. I'm here with you."

"Luke," I cautioned.

"No. This was a dumb idea. And it was mine. This whole thing was my plan, and it's my fault. Whatever I need to do to show you that it won't happen again, I'll do it." Luke's voice was stronger now.

In the flickering candles of the cathedral, my brother's determination burned steadily in his eyes.

"Can't you see that I don't want to keep punishing you? I didn't want to do those things. All I've ever wanted was for us to be together and for you to take your place on The Divine Path."

"I want that too. I've been afraid of getting too close. But I'm not afraid anymore. I'm ready to do this. I'm willing to commit."

"Give me your hand." Her slender hand extended from Her white floor-length gown.

He pulled from me and kneeled in front of Her with his shoulders straight and tear-stained cheeks. I'd never been so awestruck by my brother, and Luke was nothing but impressive every day of his damn life. He held out his hand, and my shoulders tightened. I was ready to strike at the first sign of pain, but the constant ache that had been in my chest eased.

She smiled and kissed his forehead. "My Love. Thank you."

As soon as She stopped touching him, the pain was back.

When She looked at me, Her eyes hardened. "Now, you. Get on your knees. Let's see if your future favors loyalty."

Luke's gaze bored into me, pleading, so I complied. Mostly for him. I held out my hand for Her to take.

"Kneel. Head to the floor."

I sighed, ignoring the snarling dog of anger that wanted to bite back. It's not like I cared about what anyone in the room thought of me other than my brother.

"Up."

Her hand on my face felt like a kiss. Sickly sweet. Her skin filled the world with Her scent. There was no way to describe it. I had nothing to compare it to. I didn't care where I was, and all my previous worries disappeared. As She searched my future for my betrayal, I stared at Her long, soft lashes and soft pink lips. How many of my futures could She see beside Her? Were there any that didn't end in this place?

Suddenly, I questioned why we wanted to leave. As if there was a place I could exist without Her. Anywhere else would be pure agony compared to the feeling of Her being close. When Her hand left me, I shuddered from the loss.

She stood. "Their loyalty is true."

It answered my question. If She could see them all, She must have seen us choose Her over and over. If it was the most likely one, whose decisions could change our almost certain fate?

"My queen, what shall we do with these two?" Sirius said.

Will and Thane were kneeling on the ground, too weak to bolt. I readied myself for the final decision. Whatever She decided, I'd have to live with and make sure Luke got through it. It's not that I didn't care, but I only had enough feelings for one person, and it was for my brother. Everything else could get buried away in that lovely feeling suggestion box.

"Do we need both of them?" Sirius rolled up his sleeves where the black blood had soaked his cuffs.

"It is more favorable for them to both live for now."

"Don't I get a say in this?" Will lifted his head.

"Not unless you have a death wish," Sirius said.

"What if I do?"

"Will, don't," Thane said.

"I think there's a lot of decisions being made without me gettin' any say. Maybe I'm tired of being here. And I'd rather be anywhere than here with some wicked bitch."

Sirius grabbed Will's head and slammed it into the marble floor. I had my hand on Luke's shoulder in an instant. He pulled us closer to the shuffle, but I planted my feet.

Laughter trickled from Will's lungs, and he groaned as Sirius pressed a boot to the back of his neck. "I come all the way back to Ireland, and this is how I'm greeted? I expected more from all of you. The big bad is surprisingly weak. I can't believe Kilian has been this worried about it. He'll have Her head on a stake in no time."

Sirius kicked Will in the back of the head, and the shock of it rang through my body. I dug my fingers into Luke's shoulders as he pulled us forward.

"Will," I warned.

"It's all right. Let them kill me. I waited my whole life to look your glorious queen in the face and tell Her what a vile cunt She is. My life's goal is complete."

I pulled Luke to look at me before Sirius landed another blow, and Thane yelled in protest.

"Luke. Focus on me. Let Will get himself killed if that's what he wants."

The world spun in the haze of his eyes. He didn't need to say anything. He was torn and panicking. I was too. My hands were shaking. The pain from the tunnel was back and aching in sync with each beat of my heart. Watching Will get killed would hurt like a bitch, but I could handle it. I had to.

"Don't worry, My Love. No one will die. Sirius, hold him up."

She leaned down. "So disrespectful. Let's see where all that hatred comes from."

He convulsed as She dug Her way into his thoughts, forcing Herself into every corner of his mind. Ezra had ahold of Thane while Will writhed on the floor. When She let go of him, he pulled his head into his hands and screamed in stifled sobs.

"Poor little lamb. I think you've taken it a bit personal. Your sister came on her own. It's not my fault she was never meant for divine destiny."

"It's your fault, bitch!" He spit blood in Her face.

Ezra growled, and Sirius was next to Her in a moment, using a handkerchief to wipe Her face delicately.

"Your hatred is admirable. And for that . . . I offer the gift of true hatred back to you. May you be tethered to me and this place forever. My holy offering will become your curse."

She bit into Her wrist, and Luke and I stilled. Blood seeped from Her wrist onto the marble. Luke nearly pulled me to the floor. I only held on for him alone. I should have felt sorry for Will, but all I felt was the thirst consuming me alive. God, I needed Her. All the color had drained from my brother's irises. A fight was futile. She had us exactly where She wanted us. Thirsting for Her.

I took it all in at once. My thirst and my will to keep Luke steady. Thane's wide-eyed horror as Will was forced to drink Her blood. Sirius and Ezra hovering with uneasiness.

He fought it at first, then once the blood was down his throat, he drank like a starved man, and it set my skin ablaze with untamable need. Every second, my resolve slipped away. My blood was alive with a cruel mixture of emotions. Jealousy. Anger. Longing. Sadness. All of it ran through me so fast I couldn't figure out what I felt more.

When She pulled away, Will's eyes were black and his whole demeanor had softened to Her. He licked the blood from his lips.

"There, now you'll truly understand devotion. We'll have plenty of time to have fun together."

The tips of Her fingers grazed Will's face, and he leaned into Her.

"Stay," he whispered.

Ezra tended to Her wrist, and She spoke again.

"Ascension is coming. There's a lot to plan for. Much for us all to do. You'll prep them, Ezra?"

"Yes, of course."

"Sirius, keep an eye on these two. I'd hate to lose them again."

Would it ever stop? This invisible string connecting us all was now pulled taut.

Luke and I sat on the edge of our beds staring at nothing. I was tired. Watching your friends get vigorously tortured was enough to cause the body to feel tired. Psychological wounds needed healing too, I guess. I wasn't sure I'd be able to sleep, though.

"I'm afraid to close my eyes," Luke said.

"What do you think will happen?"

"I'll dream of Her."

"We can do the ole ice trick. I'm sure Connell is dying to do us a favor."

To stay up late when we were kids, we'd dump all the ice trays in a bowl and stick our face in it. I mostly remembered how it would piss Mom off when we'd forget to fill them back up.

He lay back on his bed and sighed.

I did the same. "Fine. If you do, then I'll be here. We'll deal."

"Do you ever dream of Her?"

"Yeah. Every time I fall asleep."

"Mine aren't always bad. Sometimes, I'm so happy with Her that I don't want to wake up. And when I do . . . I feel disappointed."

I remembered the last dream I'd had. It involved sneaking into Her room at night and . . . let's just say it was not an appropriate dream to tell my brother at that moment.

I sat up and moved to his bed to sit beside him.

"We can't go back, Luke. This is who we have to be. This is who we are."

"But . . . I want to go back. I don't want to be here anymore."

"I know."

"I want to help everyone, and I can't. I don't know how. I keep thinking I'm going to be able to, and I can't."

His voice broke, and I broke with it. The weight of his pain was amplified by Her blood and ours mixed together. It was like a siren sounding in my head, screaming for me to help him. As if I needed something to make that need any stronger.

"I know but we can't. We have to stay and try to get to Ascension."

Luke shook his head, and his eyes went red.

"No, no, no, don't fucking do it. Don't cry," I said.

He pressed his palms into his eyes. "I'm sorry. I'm always crying all the time now, and I hate it."

I pulled him into my arms. "That's not what I meant."

He buried his head in my shoulder, almost toppling me over. The fucking brute. His quiet sobs grew louder, and I squeezed him tighter.

"We're never going to see them again, are we?"

I knew it the moment we set foot on the plane, maybe even earlier, but he'd held onto hope this long? Who was I kidding? Of course he did.

"No. I don't think so."

He cried harder, and warmth filled my face.

"I know I'm not funny like Presley or nice like Aaron, but I'll protect you, Luke."

He wiped his eyes. "What if I can't stay away from Her?"

"None of that shit matters. I'll take care of you. No matter what happens, I'll be right here."

"Promise?"

"Fuck yeah, I promise."

I tried not to remember my childhood, but there was one memory I couldn't let go of. I thought of it the most because it brought me comfort like nothing else. When I felt alone, I replayed the memory over and over.

Luke and I were six.

My face was hot where my dad had hit me.

I'd run down to the basement to hide from him. I remembered little about the basement, but I remembered the sting on my face and the headache I got from crying so hard. The light at the top of the stairs turned on, and I cowered in the corner, hoping it wasn't my dad, and Luke emerged. His lip was bloody.

I never understood why Dad liked hurting us. He didn't hit Mom or our little brothers. Just Luke and me. He was good at hiding it. It was rare he'd leave marks and even more rare for them to be on the face.

Mom thought we fought a lot. We lied. Even after Dad left. I think we were afraid he'd come back. He would come and go out of her life, getting her pregnant and disappearing when she needed him the most every time. I never blamed her for it, though. She was lonely. And tired. I understood that type of tired now.

He'd been especially angry that day. I couldn't remember why, only the strong scent of alcohol as he'd yelled in my face.

Luke had smiled when he saw me and sat next to me, then rubbed my back. "We're okay. It's all going to be okay."

I'd been shocked by the way he wiped the blood from his lip and pulled me close to him.

"He won't come down here."

"H-how do you know?" I sniffled, enamored by his unwavering faith.

"I just do." He hugged me tighter. "I'll protect you."

I didn't care who I had to be or what I had to do. I would get us to Ascension, and I would protect him no matter the cost.

TWO MONTHS LATER

Dear Luke (and probably Zach too if he's feeling less broody today),

This isn't fair. That's the only important thing I want to say.

P.S. Do you remember that time I had to get my wisdom teeth out? You both came, and Luke held my hand, and Zach talked to me while they put me under. I used to say it was the worst day of my life because I was one hundred percent convinced they were going to put me under and I wasn't going to wake up again. But I've been thinking of that day over and over. When I woke up from my anesthesia, you were the first faces I saw. If I could time travel, I'd go back to that day. Actually, I'd pick that day in the forest and warn us all so we could avoid this whole situation. That would probably be the smart thing.

But thinking of wisdom teeth day makes my chest stop hurting for a few seconds.

Love you forever,

Presley

Twenty

LUKE

My heart was about to beat out of my chest. *Come on, Luke. You've got this. Don't let this beat you.*

I splashed water on my face to try to stop the wave of adrenaline from taking me under. It shouldn't have been so hard. My reflection stared back at me. I don't know who I expected to find there. Not me. Not Luke.

I rubbed my chest where my ribs hurt. *You're okay. You're safe.*

I'd had a lot of practice with the panic but hoped it would stop showing up. I hoped for a lot of things. None of which seemed to ever turn out.

That didn't mean they wouldn't. Just not yet.

I wiped my face with a napkin and stepped out of the bathroom, and Ezra was waiting.

"You feeling okay?"

"I'm okay. I think . . . I'm going to go see the queen later, though. I want to see Her more often than only in the garden in the morning. I'm ready."

I didn't need to ask permission for anything anymore. For the most part, we were free to roam despite our attempted jail break. I couldn't remember how long ago it had been. It could have been months or weeks. I didn't know. I liked forgetting the days, and not paying attention to how many times the sun came and went was freeing. It was comforting not knowing.

I went to walk back to our table, but Ezra stopped me with a hand to the chest. "You're not drinking Her blood, are you? She's not offering?"

"No, it's not like that." It wasn't. I liked being around Her. The mornings had become my favorite thing. Being around Her was my favorite thing. Not that it made me special. It was everyone's favorite thing, but despite everyone, including my brother, telling me I was being brainwashed, I didn't think it was because of the bond. I grew fond of Her. She was nice to me. Nicer than my new home had ever been. Our garden walks were the only sliver of rest I had.

"Because you've seen what's happened to your friend now, haven't you?"

My chest ached, and he continued with a sigh. "I don't want to see the same happen to you. She's magnificent and calculated, but She can also be self-indulgent. She, too, can get carried away and stray from the path at times."

"I get it."

"No." Ezra grabbed my shoulders. "Listen to me carefully. You've had a lot."

I opened my mouth to tell him he didn't have to lecture me. Again, I wondered if it was how my younger brothers felt. I tried to stop thinking about them completely. That was hard too.

"Just listen, you've had more than most. Not only before when you left with your brother, but after, with Akira. You haven't had any since?"

"No."

"Good. Because She will offer you blood on the day of Ascension, and I want to make sure you're sound."

"I will be."

"You're strong, Luke. But you have to be careful. The amount is different for everyone. At a certain point, your blood can't be cleansed. You go mad and lose yourself, and everything you've cared about becomes obsolete. And I don't want that to happen to you." His eyes softened.

"So we go mad if we don't have blood and mad if we drink Her blood?" I thought of Aaron and the rage in his eyes that day he'd held Presley down by the throat and when he'd been strong enough to take on Akira alone. It's a surprise more people didn't give in to that kind of power, but power didn't matter if you couldn't wield it.

"Too much or too little of something can be a bad thing. The difference is if you don't drink human blood, you turn into a feral animal with no remaining brain cells. But if you indulge too much in Her blood, then you become obsessed with Her."

"I think we're all obsessed."

"No, this is different. It's more than wanting to be near Her. It breaks all ties to your former self, and you don't come back from it. You don't remember?"

"Remember what?"

"What it felt like for you when you gave in the first time?"

I didn't. Not really. All those memories were hazy and hard to access. I remembered drinking Her blood for the first time after changing and fighting with Zach. I remembered feeling lonely. I needed to drink but was scared to, and there She was offering up Her blood instead. It seemed simpler at the time. Everything was hazy after. Until after Ezra and Zach helped "cleanse my blood" of Hers.

The second time . . . I didn't want to think of that time.

"It's hard to remember."

"Well, I remember. You weren't yourself. You wouldn't leave Her side. You were . . . in so much pain."

"Pain?"

"Just promise. Promise me if She offers on any day that isn't Ascension, you'll say no."

"I promise."

"Good." He wiped the sides of my jacket. "Speaking of drinking blood. You look ghastly. You should feed tonight."

I nodded.

"Let's go." I followed Ezra back to a table of men at the pub in town. I'd spend the next hour pretending to like them and feigning my care for their business affairs. All they cared about was my ability to fill their pockets with money. Bending myself into the person they needed was the easy part, and more importantly, the person Ezra needed. He liked the mask. The person I *could* be.

I grabbed my whiskey from the table and took a swig.

There was only one thing I didn't understand. How was it that after all this time all I wanted was to go home?

Twenty-One

"Again," I called to Henderson, and he circled me in the grass inside the front gate of the castle grounds.

The fucker was improving. Because I made him better.

"Can't we stop?" Henderson's chest was covered in blood. All his.

"Don't you want to be better? The best?"

They were an ungrateful lot. I'd even let them have outside fight time on the one day it wasn't raining. I continued to train with Sirius but less. I'd been promoted to teacher, and fuck, was it fun.

He groaned and came at me again. I'd taken the position of his partner since Sirius had taken two of Connell's fingers that day in the tunnels, not that he couldn't fight, but I'd convinced Ezra his talents were better used elsewhere and not as a punching bag.

He was in charge of the tour service that ran to the island. A service that brought in money and more importantly, bodies and blood. The blood from the blood bank mostly went to those of us learning to fight. I trained so much I never needed to drink from humans anymore, but I didn't miss hunting. A quick blood bag every two weeks was way easier.

Everyone there was old enough to wipe memories except Connell, but he loved it from what I could tell. He was personable enough for the job, and it kept him away from Luke, which was a win for me. I'd ordered Connell to stay away from Luke because every time Luke would see him in the hall, he'd spiral.

When Luke spiraled, it put us both on our ass for days. Sometimes, we couldn't leave our room because the pain was so intense. He hurt, so I hurt. Therefore, we both kept hurting and crashing into each other.

Henderson came at me again, and I shoved his face into the dirt. "You have to be faster."

"I can't! I've lost too much blood."

"You think that will stop your enemy? Get up."

I placed a heel on his back, barely weighing him down.

"I-I can't."

"Are you even trying?"

"Yes!"

"I guess that means they win. And do you know what happens when someone else wins?"

"No."

"Do I see tears?"

"No, stop it—"

He tried to get up, but I didn't move my shoe. Someone had to teach him this lesson, and it might as well be me.

"When someone overpowers you, that means they get to do whatever they want with you." With one foot firmly on his back, I moved the tip of my shoe to his face. "Kiss my shoe."

"What?"

"Move me. Or kiss my shoe. Your choice."

"Sir—"

"Kiss. My. Shoe."

He did, and I reveled in the euphoria. I could get used to that, getting stronger every day to where no one could challenge me. A trickling laughter sputtered out as I enjoyed his humiliation . . . until I saw my brother.

Luke stared back at me a few feet away on the lawn, and the sudden ache in my chest jolted me out of my trance. I hated that aspect of it, the pain, but the bond was good in some aspects. Sometimes, it was the only way I could get a read on how he was actually feeling. It made us closer. As if that was possible. Luke's beating heart might as well have been in my chest. I felt every emotion he felt.

"You did good today." I reached down to help Henderson up.

"Uh . . . thanks?"

"Same time tomorrow?"

He groaned, "Yes, sir."

I flung off the dirt and blood clinging to me and skipped out to see my brother. Surrounding us were a few of the other members sparring on the grass.

I called out, "Keep going! Form check in five."

Then I promptly addressed my brother, "Luke, you need some sun or something. Fuck." I grabbed his chin to survey him with Henderson's blood still on my hands.

His dark circles had dark circles, and his golden glow was gone. He reminded me of the time we got the flu. It was this place. It was draining the life out of him.

"I don't think it works like that. Plus, it's never sunny here."

"Still."

"Stop worrying about me."

Luke had stopped smiling. He was struggling. Only, he was having a hard time telling me he was. Another symptom of being here too long. I didn't mind it so much. I got to fight all the time. I'd gotten used to the gray. The monotony.

"You say that like it's not my whole personality. And like we're not bound together by demon witch blood."

He formed a half-smile. "Speaking of, I need to ask you about something. Walk with me?"

I wiped the rest of the blood from my hands and followed him to the covered stone balcony on the second floor. He was right. It was never sunny, and that day was no exception. Dreary clouds hung in the sky like they might pour down any minute.

"I want to see Her more. I think it will help. You don't need to watch over me anymore."

"Luke. That's a shit idea."

"I-I just . . . walking with Her in the morning is when I feel the happiest. Maybe that's what I need. I don't know. But I have to try something else. I don't feel like I've found my place yet."

I'd never told Luke about that night with the queen when I confirmed his theory and Cecily had listened. She'd not asked for Luke during a new moon since that day. Ezra kept his part of the deal too. The first new moon he took Luke over to the mainland for a few days for client work with the blood bank, I'd had to take his place. It wasn't terrible, but since then, I had done nothing but try to distance myself from Her, and it worked. The last new moon, Ezra had to send us away because the pain of the bond got so bad that Luke and I could not stop crying—fucking embarrassing. We spent a full twenty-four hours crying—according to Will who thought the whole thing was ridiculous and a little funny. It was ridiculous but it wasn't funny. No clue what caused it either. I remember feeling so sad I thought it would kill me. Every time we looked at each other, we cried harder, and the usual comfort thing wasn't working. We tried to separate, but that made it worse. Sirius and Ezra had seen nothing like it.

A few nights away in a cabin by the cliffs helped.

"What would She even need you for?" I asked.

"You know . . . making sure She's comfortable."

"She's got Her little servants for that."

They did it all. Combed Her hair. Did Her manicures. Helped Her count Her jewels. I didn't know. I didn't care if I wasn't the one doing it. Everyone fought for their chance to be anointed during our prayer meetings. Sometimes, it was like Connell's with the memory taking, but mostly, it meant getting picked to be Her maid and follow Her around for the week. *Bullshit.*

"I know, but what if She gets lonely? She needs someone to talk to."

"Luke. No. I stand by it being a terrible idea."

"Right." He looked out over the garden and the labyrinth. A few flowers had bloomed.

"You don't need my permission."

"I know that. But I don't like doing anything behind your back."

"You want my blessing."

"Kinda."

I didn't see how it could do anything but spell more trouble for me, but I knew the only time my chest didn't hurt was in the morning during that walk. It could help. Or maybe I was desperate to get Luke relief. I felt guilty for not telling him about Cecily, especially when he was always honest with me, but we'd be worse off than we were now. I wanted him to accept this place because it was killing him not to.

He was right, more time with Her could help him get acclimated.

"Will you promise to tell me if She tries anything weird or offers you Her blood?"

"You don't need to lecture me on that. I already got the full earful from Ezra."

"Good." We didn't need a replay of the last time we drank. That night when we both gave in. Even after we knew what She did to Sarah, we chose Her.

If Luke drank Her blood again, I wasn't sure I'd be able to stay away from Her either.

"I promise. I'll stay away."

"It's not that simple, and you know that. It's not exactly a choosing thing."

There was no way to consent. Not when being near Her made me want Her. To touch Her. Love Her. Worship Her. I knew all of that, but it didn't stop me from feeling guilty for all the times I'd given in. Luke never talked about it, but he knew that exact feeling.

We'd both betrayed Sarah that day.

We'd been in Her room. Donating. We weren't required to do that anymore, but it reminded me of the high I used to chase in high school.

I used to buy Xanax off a friend in class before Luke made me stop. It caused our only physical fight Luke and I had ever had. I'd hit him first for taking the pills from my locker, and he was right to kick my ass for it.

Her blood was a hundred times better.

I tried not to think about it. Her lips on my skin. Being needed by Her, and the feeling of my body growing weaker as She took everything from me. It was so freeing to let go and be Hers. That's why we gave in. I reminded myself like I'd reminded Luke many times. It wasn't fair. There wasn't an even playing field. Luke had grabbed Her first, and I couldn't stop myself from biting Her.

It was the happiest I'd ever felt in my life, but I told no one else that.

"I know, but I'll be careful."

"No blood exchanges?"

"Promise."

"Fine. If it helps." I wrapped an arm over his shoulder. "Come on, let's go walk the pond you like and get a beer at The Underground."

I resolved to abandon my waiting students. My brother needed me more.

Twenty-Two

ZACH

I hated that fucking five-year plan. It made sense for Luke to lecture Presley and Aaron on it constantly when we never had one. Not before we changed and certainly not after. I was staring at my five-year plan, and it looked a lot like bossing around and terrorizing a bunch of grown ass men. So it could have been worse.

I'd turned in for the day. As my bedroom door closed behind me, I spotted Will sitting by our fireplace. Luke must have dropped him off on his way to do something. Ezra and Sirius requested that Thane and Will be locked up more. They couldn't kill them, but they didn't like seeing them around either. For two whole weeks after the escape, they locked them in their room, and in those two weeks, we didn't get to see them.

Thane emerged unscathed and oddly hopeful, but Will . . .

"There you are. Did you see Her today?"

"No, Will."

"I didn't either, but I swear I could feel Her on the other side of the wall. I heard Her heart beatin'. I know that's what it was. She was so close."

Will had gone full off the deep end. He had good days and bad days. It wore off after a while, but he'd disappear and reemerge like this, talking about Her constantly and needing to be close to Her like his life depended on it.

"Have you ever noticed the little lines in Her hands? Last time I saw Her, I couldn't stop starin' at them. I don't remember exactly how long it's been . . ."

"Will."

"They're perfectly symmetrical. Beautiful little lines." He picked at the skin by his fingernails.

"Buddy, I know you can't help it, but I can't listen to another story about the lines on Her hands today or how perfect and glowing Her skin is. Please. Can we try to pivot to something else?"

I think She was torturing him and wiping his memory of it. He could never answer if She was giving him more blood, but it was the only explanation for this. Why She'd take Her time to do that, I didn't know, and I couldn't prove it. I wanted to help, but I could barely keep Luke's head above water, and any complaints to Sirius or Ezra about it would surely result in Will's death. They were neutral to him as long as he wasn't in the way.

Though I think the queen giving Her blood wasn't exactly part of their plan, because I'd heard them bickering about it from time to time. Will having Her blood meant that he was connected to Luke and me. It was faint and not nearly as strong as what I felt with my brother. The only time I noticed was when Will was in a shit mood and his anger crept into mine. Hurting him would hurt us, and the queen and Ezra were adamant not to do anything to agitate the bond further.

It's not like I could help him escape. So it was our only option. Me forcing a drink into his hand and trying to get him to snap out of the delusion every time it came on.

"Right. I'm sorry. I didn't see Her today. I want to, but I feel so . . ."

"Here." I poured us both a glass of whiskey. "Just try to relax."

I'd become mom of the year. If I wasn't helping Luke to not be sad, I was trying to help Will not turn insane. Sometimes, I'd even help Thane with his annoying requests for things like distracting Ezra so he could go into certain parts of the castle. Mostly it was me listening to his theories about what happened to the old Guard. He was obsessed with the idea. I think he thought it would help us somehow, but I could give a shit less about their origin story. I had bigger problems.

Will gripped his pant legs and stared into the fire.

"Few more sips, attaboy." Something about the alcohol seemed to help.

"Ah, fuck off."

"There he is."

He took another long drink and closed his eyes, concentrating I think.

"Come on, think of your sister. And think of how much you hate Her Royal Bitchness. All that hate will come back to you. Think on it."

Another few minutes passed while Will sat quietly.

"What's it like?"

He kept his eyes shut and spoke slowly, "Like a runaway train. Like I'm moving away from myself so fast I can't grab the rail. But suddenly, it slows down, and I finally catch the rail. I'm back on. For now. But I can't stay on. The train moves too fast. I know I'll find myself on my ass again somewhere down the line."

"You poetic piece of shit."

He smiled, opening his eyes. "Bastard."

We let the silence settle, and the fire crackled and popped in front of us.

"I never thought I'd say this, but I kinda miss the college boy problems your brothers used to have. Those fuckin' lunatics were so entertaining."

"Shit. Compared to this place? Anything is better. I'd give anything to listen to Presley tell me an hour-long story about how Jessica from Foreign Studies was totally into him and he got strung along on a double date with her and her friend, only to be told an hour in that he was third-wheeling and her friend was her actual boyfriend."

"That's a real story, isn't it?"

"Yes, and he followed me around for hours to tell me every excruciating detail because Luke was busy and he had no one else to tell. I was so mad at the time, but I'd cut off my own arm to go back and hear that story again."

I hated realizing things about myself, especially feelings, but as I took another drink of whiskey and the burn traveled down my throat, the answer stared me in the face.

I didn't hate college. I wanted to hate it. To be angry and force it away because I knew one day I'd be here. This place was a festering sore. A cancer. Something that demanded my attention. And no matter how many parties I went to or classes I took, I could never escape the truth of knowing my own fate.

"I thought it would hurt less if I cared less. But joke's on me, it hurts either way."

"I hate you," he said.

"Why?"

"Because you're too much like me. It's like looking into a fuckin' mirror."

I scoffed. "I'm way prettier than you."

"You wish."

We were trapped in hell, and I knew right where we'd descended to. Battling each other on the top of the River Styx and doomed to one day fall to the bottom in sullen gloom. I was so angry I didn't recognize what it felt like in my body anymore. It was part of my DNA. Like I'd been born with it, but I knew that wasn't true. Mom said I was a baby who never cried. That I was perfectly content with noise and even the loudest thunderstorm couldn't wake me. She said I was kind and calm, and in daycare, all the sitters loved me because I was an angel to be around.

Dad changed it all. That was before he liked to come around and thought it might be fun to kick around his own kids. He left before Aaron and Presley could even remember what he looked like. I barely remembered until he came back one day when Luke and I were seniors in high school. The bastard showed up unannounced on Father's Day. Like we would roll out the red carpet for him or something. I would have beaten him to a bloody pulp with our baseball bat if Luke hadn't stopped me. It didn't stop me from taking that same bat to our room and destroying our furniture and all my old martial arts trophies.

I thought I wouldn't be able to recognize my father if I saw him again, but that was impossible because he looked like me. Same hair color. Same scowl. Same anger.

"Can you promise me something?"

Will's voice snapped me out of my thoughts.

"Alright."

"Promise me you'll try your best to get Thane out. If I turn into a zombie, I need to know someone is looking after him. Luke, I already know he'll do that. But I need to hear it from you."

I scoffed. Annoyed that he'd even ask. Thane was the least of my worries, and I'd like to keep it that way.

"I know you love to hold a grudge, but Thane is a good guy. He doesn't deserve to be here."

"He's the reason I'm sitting here right now."

"He was manipulated, like you. That's why you hate him so much."

"What's that supposed to mean?"

"I know how much you love blaming yourself for shit that isn't your fault. You can't forgive Thane because that means you'd have to forgive yourself."

"What are you, my therapist?"

"I've lived a lot longer than you. You were both manipulated."

"No. I should have known better. Ezra was a stranger. I should have never trusted him or let it get this far. If I didn't, none of us would be here."

"You were a kid."

"No. I should have—"

"Zach. You. Were. A. Kid."

"Yeah. I guess I was."

I remember the relief I felt when we met Ezra. Like he was going to magically solve our problems, but he caused them. My family would have been better off without him.

"No doubt the most annoying asshole kid in Brooklyn."

"That's what they tell me."

"I still hate you, by the way. If we ever get out of here, you'll never see me again. I'm sailing away to the tropics." Will smiled as he finished the last of his drink.

I did too.

"Will?"

"Yeah?"

"I promise."

Twenty-Three

LUKE

It was early evening when I knocked on the door to Her room. Her scent hit me first. It held a distinctive allure, not like perfume or a flower. I let Her gravity wash over me and cleanse the day. The comfort of it made me whole again. She felt good.

Soft classical music played on a record player across the room.

"My Love." She sat at the foot of the bed while one of the lower members brushed Her hair. "It's late."

"I know. I just wanted to see if you wanted to go for another walk. We could talk."

She held up Her hand for him to stop. "Yes, I'd like that."

"You can leave," I said to the one helping Her. I tried not to learn their names even though I knew I would have to eventually. It was too hard, and getting sad was a bad idea while being so closely bonded to my brother. Everything set me off, and I didn't want to spend any more days so sad I couldn't leave my bed.

"I bought you these today while I was in town." I held up a pair of slippers. "I know you don't mind the cold on your feet, but they looked pretty soft. You don't get to go out and shop or anything, so I thought they might be nice."

She held out Her leg, and the fabric from Her dress fell and exposed Her skin. "You thought of me."

I moved them onto Her feet, which were freshly manicured and free of dirt. The touch of Her skin raised the hairs on my arm.

"I always think of you."

I helped Her into a coat, and we walked toward the garden. It was dreary and cold, but it was always that way. The moonlight blended in with Her Gloriousness. Our full moon complemented Her in a disarray of shadow and light against Her cheeks.

She was at Her strongest tonight and didn't need me to help Her walk, but I gave Her support. I guided Her slowly over each steppingstone. Here, I didn't hurt. It was what I was meant for. To take care of Her. Make Her happy for the rest of eternity. There had to be a reason I was meant to be there and so miserable. I was messing something up or all the puzzle pieces weren't together yet.

"What are you thinking, My Love?"

"I've been unhappy here. But I've been wondering if it's because I'm not using my abilities. Maybe I'm not using my role correctly."

She stopped walking. "Tell me what you mean."

"I want to spend more time with you. I spend a lot of my time thinking about you and how you're doing, and I want to play a bigger role in your day to day. I can do something. I don't know what. But I want to. Please think about it."

Her fingers grazed the stubble on my cheek, and I shivered.

"You don't have to beg for more of my presence. It's a luxury you can have. It's your destiny."

I placed my hand on top of Hers. "I don't know where I factor in."

"You don't need to struggle. Destiny finds you, My Love. It shows up and wraps you in its arms. You will always be with me. I can see your face in so many futures. And you're so happy."

"So, I don't need to do anything?"

"All you need is already yours."

I need you. The words were on the tip of my tongue. If this was my destiny, why did it feel like I didn't belong? Zach had found his groove. Where was my groove? He made it look easy. Every day, he knew what he needed to do and seemed to want to do it. I didn't want to meet clients all day and lie to their faces, and I didn't know how to turn myself into a person who wanted to.

"I know exactly what you want. What you need."

My heart fluttered. "So, tonight I can stay with you? We can keep walking. There are places in the castle I haven't seen yet. I wanna see the places you and your brother used to play."

"I'll show you. Let's walk all night. I'm all yours. I know things are difficult for you now, but after Ascension, things will change for you."

"They will?"

"Yes, it's coming. Sooner than you think. You're almost ready, My Love. The dark sun will be upon us in two weeks, and on that night, we will be bound."

"What's it like?"

I tried not to think of Ascension. There was a lot of talk about it. I guess getting to see Zach and I ascend and usher in a new Guard was exciting business for everyone, but no one ever mentioned what it was or what it would entail. I could imagine nothing more terrible than what I'd already experienced.

"It's peaceful. In many ways, it's like a marriage. You're committing yourself to me and The Divine Path. There is a ceremony and celebrations."

My chest tightened at the thought. It sounded fun, but would I feel that way or ruin it?

"Don't worry. I've seen you very happy there."

"Can you . . . check again? To make sure?"

"You would let me into your head to check your future?" Her eyes sparkled in the moonlight. "Hasn't your brother warned you about letting me in?"

"Yeah. But I've been doing that, and it's not working. I don't want to worry about Ascension. I don't want to wonder if it's something I can mess up."

"Come," She said as She grabbed my wrist and brought me to sit on a stone bench carved with two cherubs on either side.

I held out my hand to Her, and She threaded Her fingers in mine. I was used to crashing into Her like this now. The feeling of Her skin filling me up. It was fleeting, yet every time, I hoped it could last another moment longer. She closed Her eyes, and I waited in silence for Her to search the stars for my future. I hoped She'd see me devoted. Happier. That Luke could do this. He could be whatever She needed. I wasn't him yet, but I could be. I *wanted* to be.

When She opened Her eyes again, a smile curled Her lips.

"You're everything I've waited for, My Love."

I stilled as She leaned in and placed Her lips softly to my cheek.

"You have nothing to worry about. After Ascension, you'll know exactly who you're meant to be."

I didn't think I'd ever be excited to enter The Guard, but it was a comfort to think it would help. We continued our walk in the moonlight, and I felt stronger than I had in months. I could protect Her from the threat of night. I would be the person everyone needed me to be. I'd been praying, and it was finally working.

Something shifted in the night air.

Her scent. Her gravity. It all vanished. The queen blinked and melted into my arms like a ragdoll.

"Are you okay?"

The same feeling washed over as before. I was holding Her, but it was different. It was easier, with no gravity breaking my ribs at Her touch. "Luke," She said, and two pools of emerald stared back at me.

"Yeah, I'm here."

When She heard my voice, tears fell from Her eyes, and I realized I'd never seen Her cry. The woman in front of me was weeping and pulling at my shirt. She pulled away to look at Her hands and shied away from the light as if it were hurting Her eyes.

"I feel strange. This doesn't feel right. This place . . . " She looked around the room. "It can't be real. This is not real."

Her hands shook, and I grabbed them to still Her.

"Everything is okay. You're safe. I won't let anything hurt you."

"I can't stay. I want to stay." She fell into a soft sob.

I wiped the tears from Her cheeks.

This wasn't my queen. She was only a woman with no other powers, and I wanted her to stop crying and to know more than anything she was safe.

"Cecily?" I asked.

I moved the hair from her face, and when she blinked, her eyes were clear with no sign of the gray. It had to be her. The wonderful euphoria of my queen was gone. Everything about her was softer now. Warm and radiant.

"Cecily? Is that you?" I asked again, pulling her chin up.

Tears formed in her eyes, and panic flashed across her face.

"What's happening? I don't understand."

"It's okay. I'm right here."

Her eyes grew wider, and she grabbed my forearm. "Why am I back here? This isn't right. Something is happening. What's happening?"

The tears fell, and I pulled her to my chest on instinct.

"It's okay. You're not alone. You're safe. I won't hurt you."

She was crying so hard her tears seeped through my suit and into my shirt. Her vulnerability startled me. It was strange to feel Her, then to feel Cecily. Two distinctly different sensations. Both of whom I wanted to please in different ways, but I needed Cecily to stop crying like I needed the sunshine on my face, because it hurt to see her so scared when she didn't have to be. I didn't know why.

"Should I go get Ezra?"

"No! Don't leave." She buried her head in my chest. "I need you."

"I'm here."

"I feel so strange . . ."

I stroked the back of her head. "Describe it to me."

"Like I'm floating in the in-between. Not quite whole. I'm splitting apart."

I smiled. "It's okay. I feel like that all the time. It will pass."

She peeked up from my shirt. "The moon is high. I shouldn't be here. I haven't seen a full moon in centuries. It's so . . . beautiful."

When she blinked again, her eyes grew heavier.

"Luke?"

"You keep using my name," I said, stroking the back of her head. Our heartbeats layered in sync. Once both wild and panicked, were falling into a cadence. A waltz.

"Because She knows but never uses it." She sniffled. "Don't tell a soul about this. Tell me you understand. Not even your brother." Remnants of her former accent came through. "Swear to me you will not."

I hesitated. I didn't know this girl, and she was asking a lot, but I trusted her. Or at least trusted that she needed to tell me something and it was imperative that only I knew.

"I swear."

"You cannot trust Her or Ezra. He's not thinking clearly. He wasn't always this way—you are not meant to be here. They are lying to you. And they convinced your brother of their plans. But help is coming."

She brought her forehead to mine to stare into my eyes. "Don't give up, Luke."

The soft caress of her kiss was enough to make my head spin, but not from her touch. The girl in front of me cared about me, and I wanted to be there for her.

I wiped her tears. "It will be okay."

"It will be if they succeed. We'll be free. You and I. It's not safe for you or for me if you tell them about this."

Help is coming. Was this an illusion? Was I imagining the girl? Did I make this up to make myself feel better? Something in me stirred at the mention of help.

But it hurt. Another knifelike pain to the chest. Why was this happening, and why now? What could I do? I could tell Her. This was something they'd want to know, but Cecily looked like she'd been through a lot, and through all of it, she'd only asked that I keep fighting. I wasn't sure if I wanted to, but I promised, and a promise was a promise.

Our faces were so close, and I felt like I was seeing her for the first time. I knew the queen was beautiful, but when I wasn't swarmed with Her gravity, I could see it in her round green eyes and soft plump cheeks.

"You have my word."

It wasn't because she was beautiful. Zach would say it's because she's a vulnerable girl and I can't help but to want to save people, but as I stared into her eyes, I saw myself. Pleading. Hoping. Fighting.

When she blinked again. The color in her eyes was gone. The gravity of Her hit me so hard I nearly fell to my knees in a bow. I let that familiar feeling fall back over me at Her presence. I wasn't as scared of it anymore.

"What did you say, My Love?"

"I said . . . I'm glad I'm where I need to be."

She let me take Her arm, and we continued to walk. My mind reeled with the thoughts of Cecily. Kilian mentioned it was theorized that souls of the girls were trapped in the bodies of the queens. He was right. Cecily was trapped in there, and for some unknown reason, she'd been able to come out. Only, the queen hadn't realized or remembered, and if I was correct—even with looking directly into my future, She hadn't seen it coming.

Twenty-Four

"Zach, I have to talk to you." Thane's voice woke me.

He was standing over me in the dark, and I shielded my eyes as he turned on my bedside lamp.

"This qualifies as annoying me." I sighed.

"I know, but I really need to talk to you."

"How did you even get in here? What time is it?"

"It's almost sunrise. I didn't get locked up because I'm with Luke and he's been with the queen walking around all night. They're still out there."

I groaned and sat up, rubbing my eyes. I'd gone to sleep early so I didn't have to worry about Luke all night. My whole body felt great, there was no pain to speak of, which told me he was happy.

"I have news. There's talk."

"Not this again."

I'd grown tired of Thane's optimism. Unlike the three of us, he'd never given up on the thought of leaving this place. He was convinced The Legion was coming for us. I thought it was bullshit. The Legion didn't care about us. They never had. They certainly didn't care about Thane. I was starting to think Will wasn't any different to them. Kilian was like everyone here. A master manipulator who moved us around like little pawns on a chess board, only he was the worst kind of manipulator. He pretended to care.

"No, seriously, you have to listen to me. Sirius mentioned something a few days ago, and you're going to want to hear. I've been trying to get you alone to tell you."

"Sneaking into the cathedral again?"

"Well, yeah. There's this little spot—"

"Don't tell me. If She starts poking around in my brain, you'll need it as a hiding spot." I sighed as I stood and pulled on my shirt. "Do I need to remind you again if you get caught, you're dead. If you're dead, we're all going to hurt."

Will and Luke would be the most devastated, but I couldn't imagine taking on sadness like that right now. We'd been bedridden from the bond before, and I did not want a replay.

"I know. But this was worth the risk."

"How?"

"Because I know something. Sirius mentioned that he got a phone call from a source. Someone they really want was trying to find our location."

"And you think it's Kilian?"

"Yes! And interestingly enough, they agreed to keep the information away from Ezra. I don't think the queen and Sirius trust him anymore."

"Ezra is Her right hand."

"I know, that's why it's weird."

"What did they say about this 'source'?"

"That he was eager to find them. He wants to find our location, and they're going to give it to him."

"Huh."

"We need to be prepared."

Thane bounced around our room like Kilian might walk in the door any minute. I almost felt sorry for him. At the same time, I was impressed he had this much mental stamina, but I knew better. If it were true and Kilian was coming, what would it change? Could Kilian gather enough people to flood this place and take us down? For all I knew, he might just kill us this time.

"How?"

"We should tell Luke."

"No, do not tell Luke anything." I sighed, pushing my hands through my hair to work it in place.

"Why?"

"Because he's suffering enough as it is. He already hates it here. I don't want to give him false hope. We don't tell him till we know something for certain. I don't know if he can take another disappointment."

"Right. The bond. I get it. I'm . . . sorry about the tunnel."

He'd already apologized about a hundred times since then.

"It's not your fault." It was just us. It was our fate.

"I won't tell Luke. But Will won't help. He's too preoccupied. But you have to know, someone is coming. We have hope. If I hear anything else, I'll let you know."

"Thanks. And Thane . . . be careful."

His beard was getting longer, but he had the same dimpled smile. "Always am."

Gods, it's me again.

I'd lost count of how many mornings I'd spent on my knees in the old church. I was supposed to be praying to Her, and sometimes, I did, but mostly, I stared at the old mural and tried to think of something else. Sirius was watching me, though.

"What do you feel?" he asked.

"Uh. I feel . . . " *Like my knees are wearing a hole into the floor.* "So devoted. And reverential and shit."

"You're still resisting."

The church shit still wasn't my thing. Some days were easier than others. I felt the thing Sirius wanted me to feel at times, but only on certain days, and it wasn't exactly an otherworldly experience. It was lust pooling in my gut for Her.

"A little. My chest hurts."

"I don't want to hear about your brother again."

"I'm saying it's hard to concentrate."

"It's because you haven't given anything. Give me your wrist."

I sighed and held out my arm, and in less than a second, he bit me. It hurt, probably because he wanted it to, and when I went to yank my arm back, he held onto my forearm. It wasn't worth a fight. He was stronger. Something eased in my chest, and I lost the tension in my shoulders. He was taking everything. Emptying me like a well, and I let him.

"There. Feel it. Your loss of control. This is your gift to Her." He handed me a knife. "Give yourself to Her. Ask Her to speak to you."

It's what I imagined people did in the old days when they cut open animals and left sacrifices to their gods. Only, all the power in my body was the sacrifice. Giving my blood was like fasting. From what I'd read in mythology, the gods weren't kind. They played with the souls of mortals. That's what She had to be, because She required so much from me.

It was probably a stupid reason too. Like for Her vanity or Her god-sized ego. I wondered if She was one I'd already heard about disguised as something else, or if she was something else no one had thought to write stories about.

I knew what he wanted from me. With the knife pressed firmly into my palm, I cut until the blood oozed into a pool. I took two fingers and moved the blood down my nose in one stroke, then two more over my eyes.

"Perfect. Now, head to the floor. Feel Her. Give yourself, and see what She gives back to you."

I felt faint when my head hit the wood grain, but I did as instructed. Complying made things go more quickly. I let my mind wander, and it was easier now that I was empty of the blood and pain.

It was only me and Her.

Darling. Come close to me.

The tug in my chest nearly brought me to the floor. I willed myself closer like She'd pop up out of the floorboards. What I really wanted was to be in Her room. On Her bed. Feeling Her breath on my cheek and the coldness of Her skin on my chest.

That's it. Tell me what you want.

I wanted to feel Her in my palms, and Her teeth to embed themselves into my skin. Did I need to be empty to feel the connection? Now that I was empty of my brother's and my blood, I could finally *feel* Her.

It can always feel this way. You know who you are. Give in to your own darkness, Darling. Let it consume you.

When I opened my eyes, I was sitting directly in front of the mural with no recollection of moving.

"There. Your bond to the past is holding you back. You cannot advance while you're holding on to your old bonds."

I fell back, and he pulled me to my feet by the collar of my shirt. I cursed the weakness in my body, but most of all, I cursed the feeling of excitement at seeing Her.

Twenty-Five

ZACH

I said I wouldn't trust Ezra again, but I lied. Well, more like, I didn't have a choice.

The difference between Sirius and Ezra was Ezra was sympathetic. Which was ironic, considering Sirius had an actual blood brother he'd been bonded to. I didn't trust Sirius not to hurt Luke, but Ezra seemed to at least try to help my brother. The only thing I could trust Sirius with was to kick my ass and hang me on a stake and watch me burn if it pleased him or Her.

He'd even asked Ezra to help me get blood to replenish all he'd taken.

Fucker.

"How are you faring?"

Ezra handed me a blood bag while wrapping my wrist. He'd taken me to his room, and I tried to hide my smile at the wardrobe that was mostly intact. It was now sitting on the ground with no legs.

"Been better, I think."

"You let him take your blood? Didn't even throw a punch?" He smirked.

"No. I'm tired of getting my ass kicked. Sometimes, it's easier to let him do his thing. Even if it's . . . weird."

"You were praying in the church?"

"Yeah, and one minute I'm on my knees, then the next I'm right next to that mural and could *feel* it. Like I was in some horror movie."

His voice grew softer. "It scared you."

"Yeah. A little. This felt dark. Uncontrollable. He wants me to take his place and be all Mr. Prayer, and I don't know if that's me. I'm trying. Then when I try and do feel something, it freaks me out."

Ezra was the only one I could talk to about it. The only time Luke had to pray was during our weekly group prayer in the cathedral, and what he described was different. He never talked about Her the way I thought of Her. He was always connected to the soul and The Divine and some shit.

"You're doing well. Luke too. He's safe. You're safe. All is moving along as it should. Sirius would like you to take over his duties, but not all of his roles will fall to you. He wants to teach you because you're the only one he has to teach now. He knows that. You don't need to worry. You can't mess it up, and it won't rush to you before you're ready. Fate comes at the right moment."

I bit into the blood bag as Ezra finished the bandage. I wouldn't need it for long. The blood would heal me quickly.

He continued. "Ascension will change things for you and your brother. The stars are lined in your favor, and it's going to come together in perfect harmony. These things you're worried about won't matter. I promise."

I liked the sound of it even if it was cryptic. Because Luke's feelings were mine now, I'd grown so worried it was eating me alive. No matter which way I turned, I craved something solid to help keep me up. I wanted my hard outer shell back.

"Can I ask you something about Ascension?"

"Anything."

"Is it . . . a sex thing? I want to wrap my head around it so I know what to expect."

Ezra broke into a soft laughter.

"Why are you acting like that's not a valid question when everyone here looks at Her like they're seconds away from humping Her leg?"

"It is. I'm sorry I laughed. It's not a sexual thing. It's the exchange of blood. She'll give you Hers, and you'll give yours. It's very personal but not inherently sexual."

"We've done that before, though."

"The amount and the timing matters. There are certain celestial markers we look for."

"Oh good, then."

"Zach, no one here will make you do things you don't want to if that's what's worrying you. The mortal body has needs, but you don't have to be the one to fulfill them if you don't desire to. All of that isn't the point of The Guard. We serve Her by guarding Her and ensuring the physical body of The Divine is kept safe from harm for eons. So we can continue to live on the earth and bring people into our family."

"No. I only wondered."

"You also don't need to feel ashamed if you do want to fulfill that role for Her—"

"I don't."

"It's nothing to be ashamed of. Shame doesn't exist here in our family. There is only serving Her. And after Ascension, you'll know exactly what that role is. You'll feel it in your being. You'll be joined with Her in pure bliss."

"It will help what's happening with me and Luke, then? The bond is getting worse. It feels like we're the same person. I can't even argue with him anymore without it making me feel like shit. It wasn't like this for you guys?"

"You and your brother were very close before the bond, and now much closer than before."

Being blood bonded to Luke meant I couldn't help but to be a little soft, but being soft here was a death sentence to my sanity.

"What about Sirius? He had a brother."

"Still. They weren't like you and Luke."

Ezra busied himself with the cleanup of our mess by chucking bits of bloodied cotton into the bin.

"You'd think he'd give a little grace."

"He barely remembers his brother's face. Let alone the feeling of being bonded to him. I think he sees his brother in you. It keeps him from seeing you clearly. Eros was very devoted. They prayed in the old church every morning together."

"Well, I wish he'd stop. How did you guys forfeit the bond? Asking for a friend."

"You and Luke are meant to be bonded. Granted, it's quite intense, but it's appropriate for your roles for now. Once Sirius's brother died and our bond was broken, the pain was too much. We couldn't go on. We were in danger of being taken out completely, so with Her help, we severed it."

"By . . . "

"She took specific memories from Sirius and me. No memories. No pain. No memory. No bond."

"But those memories are still there. They're just blocked. You could be bonded."

"Being bonded won't help Her. Sirius and I have accepted the resolve that we must move on and help you both accept your roles."

"And if you were bonded, you'd both be slobbering messes feeling Luke's and my pain. Especially when you end up dead."

He didn't seem scared. Like he'd accepted his ultimate death a long time ago.

"Precisely. Right now, you're both too focused on each other. You need a commonality. You'll acclimate. The bond will soften and snap into place. You'll know when it does."

"It's killing me. I can't have something happen to Luke right now, or I don't think we'll make it. And I mean anything. He stubs a toe, and suddenly, I'm sobbing."

"That's why we're protecting you. Until Ascension, it's imperative you're both kept safe."

I nodded and moved to get up off his bed and continue on with my day. They were likely already waiting on me in the training room.

"Luke told me he was going to spend more time with Her. I'm worried."

"I know. I'll keep an eye out. Make sure She isn't tempting him."

"He should be fine, though, right? Ascension is set in stone."

"There are different fates."

My throat tightened. "Excuse me. Come again."

"The future can change. There's a grand prophecy, but things can shift. Prophecy must be protected. There are bad paths."

"And Luke falling into temptation is a bad path."

"Yes, She's seen it but has no belief it will come true. There are many unfavorable paths, and it's all based on what we choose. Having Her sight only helps us increase our chances of a favored outcome."

"We'll both ensure that doesn't happen, then."

"Agreed." He plopped down next to me.

The wooden bed frame cracked, and the bed came crashing down into a large heap on the floor.

"You wouldn't happen to know why all my furniture keeps breaking, would you?"

I jumped up and headed toward the door.

"Nope. Gotta go."

Twenty-Six

LUKE

"Help me! Please!"

I sped across the lawn to catch a falling crate from Connell. He had a stack of wooden crates fitted with holes. They smelled like a petting zoo, and an echo of squeaking and squawking came from inside.

"Thank you, Luke, The Most Gracious One," Connell said.

Thane appeared beside me and grabbed another of Connell's crates.

"When did you come up with that?" Thane chuckled as he softly placed the crates on the ground.

"I wanted to come up with a name that felt worthy of Luke as a member of The Guard."

"Oh. What is all this?" I asked.

"I'm restocking the pond. I've been put in charge of all of it. Want to help? Sirius said I could name all the animals if I want. I'd love the company."

"What do you think, Thane? Do we have time?"

"I've got all the time in the world."

We made our way to the pond and helped Connell unload his crates. Half were ducks and ducklings, and the others were filled with fish in plastic bags. The overcast of clouds left a chill in the air, and the soft wind from the nearby sea blew the green algae covering our pond.

Our pond. This was my new home. Taking care of the grounds was something I'd need to get used to.

"You see any that are calling to you, sir?" Connell said.

A large white duck sat in a crate surrounded by her ducklings, and I leaned over to see them cuddled together.

"Welcome home."

"What the fuck are you doing?" Zach's shadow blocked the sun.

"Here. Meet Cindy." I plopped the mother duck into his arms. "Isn't she cool? I named her."

"It's a duck," Thane said.

"Yeah, I see that." Zach held out his arms to get her away from him.

"There's one more if you want to name it." Thane kneeled and scooped up a little yellow duck.

"Come on. It won't kill you to name a fluffy animal," I said.

"It might."

I placed Cindy on the shore, and Zach got handed his little duck. Her ducklings pooled around her in an excited flurry.

"Fine. What about Cerberus?"

"That's perfect, sir." Connell put Cerberus next to Cindy, and they waddled toward the water. "Zach, The Just, bestowed you the highest honor, littlest sir."

"What did he call me?" Zach whispered, and I held in my laughter.

The ducks waded into the water. Cindy's white coat stood out in the bluish-green water.

"I had an actual reason for being here. I'm looking for Will. I can't find him anywhere. He was supposed to be waiting for me outside the door when I was with Sirius, and he vanished."

"We'll all help look!" Connell said.

Zach's smile faded. His worry was felt in the pit of my stomach. We all split up. Connell went back into the castle while the rest of us scoured the grounds. The grass was muddy and wet from yesterday's rain, and I spotted a pair of prints leading from the castle and straight through the garden. Whoever it was made a beeline in one direction, walking through the mud and smearing it all over the stones in the garden.

As I followed the steps past the maze, I knew where they were headed. The old church's door was wide open.

"Will?" I called out as I reached the doorframe.

There was a soft stirring, and when I walked inside, he was sitting on his knees in the corner with his forehead pressed firmly against the mural. With no sun, the old church was dim, only illuminated with burning candles.

"I found him!" I called out, and went to Will's side.

His eyes were black, and he mumbled incoherently into the wall.

"Hey, it's okay." I placed a hand on his back.

His fingers grazed the wall. "The Divine. She's so close."

"Will!" Thane gasped as he made his through the door. My brother came shortly after.

It was as we feared. She had to be doing this to him. But why? What purpose did it serve to make him like this? The queen I knew was different. She wouldn't. At least, I didn't want to think She would, but I knew better.

"This shit has got to stop." Zach's stone-cold glare washed through me.

Thane rubbed Will's back and tried to get him to snap out of it, but he didn't respond.

I grabbed Will by the arm and pulled him to his feet. "Come on."

We walked him to the pond that now had a little duck family happily bobbing in and out of the water. Will was dead on his feet. His pupils were blown, and only darkness remained in his immovable gaze.

"Take me to Her. Please."

"Look out at the pond. Smell the air. This is the same air your sister breathed. Remember the rainy winters and think of your house. You told me she got up early and tended to the chickens while you chopped the wood."

Will's stories about his life were brief, but those tiny bits of story made up a much bigger one. A brother who loved his little sister more than anything else, and that love was powerful and couldn't be stopped. In that moment, I had no doubt it was more powerful than the hold She had on him.

He groaned.

"I bet she named them too. Do you remember any of the names? Think really hard. You're standing in the yard with an axe in your hand, and you hear the laughter of your sister as she corrals the chickens close by. You remember. You think you forgot that laugh or her smile, but you won't ever forget because it's so ingrained in you. It's here." I patted his chest. "Remember it. Fight for it."

He closed his eyes and let out a long breath. "I can't. It hurts. I want Her."

I grabbed his hand and squeezed it like my brother had done for me many times. "It doesn't matter. Focus. Remember your sister. The way she used to style her hair and the color of her clothes. The way she sneezed and the things she used to say the most."

A tear rolled down his cheek, and when he opened his eyes again, they were a little lighter. "She had a chicken named Amelia. She loved that name. It was her favorite one. Fluffy and brown with wild feathers. It survived an animal attack, then she started keeping it in her room."

"Sounds like something my brothers would do. They'd probably get along." I smiled.

He finally looked at me, and I wondered if that's how I looked to everyone else. Worn. His dark circles made every feature frail.

"Thanks."

"We should go back to the room," Thane said.

"No, I don't want to go back in there. I'd rather sit here and have someone tell me about why we have ducks in the pond."

"It has to be Her. She's doing this," Zach spat.

"Maybe I should ask Her about it. I could—"

"No. Not you," Zach said.

"Why not? She's the nicest to me."

"Exactly. Let's keep it that way," Zach said while he pushed his shoulders back in solid defiance. "I'll ask Her."

"No. None of you bring it up," Will said.

"Why not?" Thane said.

"Because what purpose would it serve? What could any of you do about it? All it's going to do is give Her reason to fuck with us more. Leave it alone."

Zach rolled his eyes. I could practically see his skin steaming in the cold breeze. Thane seemed to agree, and I did too, for now.

"It doesn't matter. We're going to get out of here soon."

"Thane." Zach's tone startled me.

"What do you mean?" I asked.

"I think The Legion is coming. I heard Sirius mention talking to someone, and it confirms my theory. They're using Will and I as bait." Thane didn't look at me, just my brother.

I thought about my moment with Cecily, where she'd begged me not to tell. She'd mentioned someone was coming and to not give up. This had to be what she was mentioning.

"*They've convinced your brother of their plans,*" She had said.

I turned to Zach. "You knew that was a possibility and didn't tell me?"

"I was protecting you. Waiting till there was more information and keeping your head clean in case She went searching."

I nodded and tried to ignore the heat flaring in my blood. He could feel it. The drop in my stomach.

"Don't be mad. I didn't want you to get your hopes up."

"You just keep secrets from me now? You get to decide things and not tell me?"

"I'm sorry."

"Both of you stop arguing and tell me about these fucking ducks," Will said.

"I named mine Daisy," Thane said.

"Of course you did."

"It's the one with the feather sticking out of its head. The little one behind the mom."

Seeing Zach apologize made my chest ache and all the anger run out of me. I didn't want to be mad at my brother. I understood, but I had to swallow the lump in my throat and ache in my chest to rejoin Will by the water.

I trusted my brother with my life. If he kept secrets from me, it was for good reason. Only, this one confirmed two things I wasn't happy to accept. He didn't believe The Legion coming to save us was a real possibility. And two—the worst one—he didn't think I could handle it.

Twenty-Seven

ZACH

"Just leave it." Sorry, Will, not in my vocabulary.

In fairness, I did the thing Mom always told me to do. Despite being a believer, she told me specifically to let the sun set on my anger. That it was better for *me* to let myself sleep on my anger, or I'd simply go off. She was right. I wanted to hurt the queen less today than the day before.

It wasn't enough to stop me completely. When I opened Her door, She was sitting at Her harp, softly strumming the strings. She didn't even look up as I entered, and I chose not to bow despite the pull to Her.

"Are all of your gowns see-through? Do I need to tell Ezra to buy you some decent clothes?"

She wore a thin satin gown that gathered at Her ankles. If She were a normal girl, I'd say She looked like an angel. There was something angelic about the soft roundness of Her face, and Her fingers were carved like marble.

She ignored me, and I bit my cheek.

"I need to talk to you."

"You can talk when you bow."

"Are you serious?"

Her attention stayed on the delicate strings. My patience was thin and wouldn't allow me the luxury of banter or pride. I did as She instructed and forced my knee to the hard floor.

"My apologies, Your Most High Greatness."

"Stay kneeled."

I sighed but submitted to letting both knees fall to the floor.

"Happy?"

She licked Her lips, then tipped them into a smile.

"I need you to tell me what you're doing to Will."

"Is that why you're really here? For a friend?"

"Yeah, that's what I fucking said."

"See, I think you've been looking for an excuse to come crawling into my room alone."

My heart skipped. How did She know? There was no way She knew about the dreams.

"You're wrong."

"Am I? I can feel you. When you kneel and pray for me to come to you, all I feel is how much you long for me."

I jumped up to my feet. She was trying to piss me off and distract me, and it would not work.

"Stop changing the subject. We're talking about Will."

"I'd rather talk about you."

"No. Because all you're doing is trying to confuse me. You can't feel shit."

She stood and turned from me like I wasn't standing there trying to have a conversation with Her.

"What do you think prayer does? It's for connection. You've had my blood, so when you pray and call me, I hear you. It's the closest most of them will ever get to the connection they desire to have with me. But for you . . . you'll have more. You can have as much as you want."

I followed Her every step as She made Her way over to the bed. She obviously wasn't going to answer my question. I moved to leave but stopped. I wasn't ready.

"You mean after Ascension?"

She nodded, grabbing a bottle of lotion from Her bedside table, then slowly rubbed it over Her legs. What the hell was happening to me? A few minutes in and my resolve was disappearing faster than I could keep up with. I couldn't stop staring at Her legs. The feeling that pulled me to Her wasn't fair. She was a planet with Her own gravity. How could I walk away?

"Yes. After Ascension, you and me. We'll be connected on a whole new level. Wherever you go. You'll have me."

I rolled my eyes.

"As usual. I don't know what that means."

"Darling, would you come over and help me put this on my back?"

Heat rushed through me. A mixture of anger and lust battled it out.

"Uh. Can't you do it yourself? Got enough minions to do that task for you," I said, but I moved toward Her until I was standing over Her. She was so beautiful I couldn't stand it. I tried to refocus.

"Of course. But you're here." She moved the straps of Her gown down to expose Her back.

Oh fuck. I sat down. My eyes darted to the door. I could leave, but I wanted to stay. I grabbed the lotion. My fingers brushed Her shoulder, but I stopped. I couldn't touch Her. Not without giving in completely.

"You like it when women torture you, don't you?" She leaned into me.

"No."

"We both know you're a glutton for punishment. You like being miserable." She moved Her hand to my thigh, and I shivered.

"Do you see now? This is the person you are. This is what you want. You've always known you're different from your brother. But there's nothing wrong with wanting this."

"I hate you."

"You're not looking at me like a man who hates me."

I wanted to shut Her up and stop Her beautiful mouth from talking. There were so many other useful things She could do with that mouth besides threaten me.

"You're the worst thing to happen to me. You're an illusion. You're not real."

"I'm very real. I know you remember. When you asked me to bite you . . . and when I did, you asked me not to stop. Or do you not tell them that part of the story?"

I couldn't grab onto the anger. Before I even thought about it, my body moved to slam my lips to Hers.

It was everything. I didn't care how hard I grabbed Her. Her tongue on mine was the end of all my wandering. I hated Her. I hated that She orchestrated my life, but I couldn't bring myself to stop.

She bit my lip and pulled me into Her. I fell on top of Her and felt every curve. I wanted it all to be mine. My blood filled my mouth, and I licked my bottom lip. I couldn't think.

"Bitch," I said.

Her eyes darkened, and Her presence overtook me. She leaned in closer, and I swallowed. She'd had the upper hand the whole time, and She knew it.

"Say it again."

"What?"

"Don't you remember the last time you called me that?"

"Fuck off."

I needed to devour Her. I took Her bottom lip between my teeth and bit down. The tiniest bit of Her blood sent me into a frenzy. I held Her down and bit into Her neck. My fingers knotted Her hair while fresh blood flowed into me.

"Tell me what you want." Her breath was hot in my ear.

"Bite me."

She pulled away, leaving me without hope of any satisfaction other than Her blood pumping through my veins. My resolve was already gone. It was gone before I even recognized its exit, because I wanted Her. Not in a way that was good or pure in any reality. There was nothing soft or kind about it. It was dark. A deep, deadly need that felt like it might kill me if I didn't have Her.

"Tell me again," She said.

"I hate you." I moved my hands to Her waist, pulling Her on top of me.

"The other thing," She whispered in my ear.

"Bitch."

Then Her lips were on mine, and I was gone. I never wanted to come back to a place of sanity if She was the one touching me. It was greater than anything I'd felt before. I moaned as She grinded into my lap.

The top of Her nightgown was easy to pull back to expose Her chest, and I kissed every glorious inch. Kissing first and then sucking at the skin of Her perfect breasts. The proximity of Her heartbeat only set me on edge with the image of Her blood on my lips. Before I could bite Her, She pushed me into the sheets and peeled off my shirt.

My senses were heightened. There was no inner monologue blocking me from Her. It was only the feeling of Her on top of me.

The things I wanted to do to Her.

Her lips brushed the sensitive skin on my chest.

"Fuck. Don't stop."

She didn't touch me like I ached for Her to. I wanted more. So much more. But Her hands stayed on my chest.

She pulled away, and I reached for Her. "Stay."

"All in good time, Darling. You must be patient. We'll have plenty of time together."

A knock on the door brought me out of my trance. I opened my eyes.

What the fuck was I do doing?

No. No. No.

How could I do this to Luke . . . to Sarah?

The guilt for touching Her slammed into me, and I was right back to where I'd started. In Her room. On Her bed. Looking at Her with the wave of lust pooling in my stomach. I ached for Her.

I left Her on the bed and sprinted out of the room, bumping Ezra on the way out.

"Everything okay?"

Our eyes met, and I felt that familiar pity and sadness in his eyes.

The feeling was so strong it created an avalanche of emotion that nearly knocked me to the ground. I kept walking and pushed out the surfacing memory, but it was right at my heels. I was repeating my past mistakes again. What else was new?

The memory wouldn't stop. It was crashing into me from behind. Biting my legs. I was losing my footing, and the cold was engulfing me.

No. No. No

The feeling of Her hands on my chest. Her teeth in my skin. It wasn't the part of the memory I hated the most. It wasn't the guilt. It was waking up alone. Vulnerable. Shivering. Weak. I'd let Her bite me. I'd wanted it. Begged for it. I'd asked Her to strip me. I wanted Her to do a lot more than She had.

I'd put my clothes back on.

No. Stop. But the memory was there vividly gushing and making me feel.

I'd run out of the Her room with my head down, knowing I had to check on Luke.

But Ezra stopped me.

I could feel his fingers digging into my arm as if it were happening again.

"*What's wrong?*" he had asked.

"*Nothing.*"

I tried to walk again, and he pulled down the neck of my hoodie, revealing the bites all over me.

The look on his face. The horror. My fear.

I felt it all again, and it would consume me this time.

"What's going on?" Will's voice cut through the silence. He'd opened the door to the closet I was hiding in. For a moment, he assessed me and my shaky hands.

With one hand, he grabbed me by the collar to get me off the floor. "Come on."

I let him drag me to my feet, hoping the memory couldn't follow me.

The walk was a blur as other members bowed to me in the hall. My hands were cold and tingling. I didn't know where he was taking me, but I didn't care. We ascended the stairs until we reached the end of the hall on the third floor. He pointed to a ladder, and we climbed. I didn't know there was a ladder to the roof.

We stood on the roof admiring a pitch-black sky. Rain droplets fell onto my face, and I was trapped and achy. I looked over the edge. It could stop this feeling. It would hurt, but I needed pain. I needed the memory to stop making me cold, pulling me under, and suffocating me.

I stared out into the vastness of the dark. Like a magnet, it pulled me to its edge. If I jumped, it wouldn't kill me. That I knew. Not that it mattered anymore, anyway.

I stepped closer to the edge.

"Stop."

"What?"

"Look at the sky," William demanded.

I shook my head, and he stood in front of me and sandwiched my face between his hands and forced me to look up. The sky wasn't pitch black. The moon lingered behind the clouds.

"Feel the rain. Smell it."

He pulled my hands from my sides and set them out, palms up. Tiny droplets pelted my skin and dissolved.

Minutes passed, and I still felt like shit. Like I needed to run.

"Will—"

"Don't talk, just feel."

The time moved like molasses until I finally felt the cold on my skin again. I focused on the sound and the smell, and I let it be my escape.

"Better?"

"Better."

I didn't want to go back in.

"How did you know?" I didn't know why I asked that. I didn't even know if I knew what I meant.

"You have that look. That same look you had at the Halloween party. The look of someone who's about to do something stupid."

He'd found me staring out the window at the end of the hall in OBA with thoughts swirling and pulling me under. It felt like this but with less bite.

"Don't even think about it."

Like he'd read my mind and knew I was about to jump out the window and start running. I wasn't, but I'd thought about it.

I concentrated on him as he stared up into the sky. "I'm always about to do something stupid."

He was calm as he pulled a pack of cigarettes out of his pocket. What kind of world did I live in now that Will was comforting me? It was a symptom of how low we'd descended into this nightmare.

"How the hell did you get those?" I asked.

"Some of them don't hate me so much. They'll at least trade with me."

He handed me one and offered me a light. We stared out into the darkness together, and I let the smoke smother me in the calm numbness.

"So, what happened? What had you shaking?"

"I don't want to talk about it."

"You gonna run off and tell Luke about it, then?"

I hesitated. I didn't want to tell my brother. Not this. This felt like an outright betrayal.

"No, he doesn't need to know."

"Then tell me."

"You'll think I'm an asshole."

"I already think that."

There was silence, then he spoke again.

"You were with Her, weren't ya? *With* Her."

"No. Maybe a little. But not . . . I didn't have sex with Her. I kissed Her, but I didn't mean to."

"You're going to blame yourself for this one, I bet."

"Yeah. Because I know better. I'm betraying my brother, Sarah, myself."

Will took a long drag of his cigarette and blew the smoke in my face. He was smiling.

"This isn't funny."

"It's not. But I find it amusing you're hellbent on always making yourself the bad guy."

"I am."

"No. You're not." He took another long drag. "I want Her too. Me. Someone who's dedicated his life to ensuring She meets a very overdue death. I hate Her with every fiber of my being. She is the reason my sister is dead. And yet, when I'm around Her, I'd do anything for Her to touch me. It's disgusting how much I want Her, and I can't make it stop. There's no consent with this type of obsession. You can't blame yourself. In fact, I'd say She wants you to do that."

"Why do you know everything?" I scoffed.

"Because I've lived for-fucking-ever. One day, you're going to be old too and a fucking know it all. I hope I'm dead by then so I don't have to put up with ya."

The smoke and soft rain accompanied us as seconds turned into minutes.

"Your sister, Eilean. What happened?"

I wasn't one to ask people about their shit, but he would never tell me unless I asked, and we felt close enough. He knew the thing I was most ashamed of. It seemed natural to share our collective pain.

He stayed quiet for a long time but eventually answered.

"My sister is the reason I wanted to join Kilian and The Legion. Back in my day, talk of vampires was common. Now in modern day, it's viewed as a joke. But back then, it was much more serious. People in our village were taken for their blood. The Family had even greater influence back then. There were tales of a great queen hidden somewhere in the lands of the North. She'd performed great miracles for soldiers in war. My sister was obsessed with the idea. She believed in stuff like that. When our mom grew sick, she fled to search for the monastery where the queen was held at the time. She left without telling me because I'd never let her go. She was only fourteen when she ran away. I went to look for her. Only to find it much harder than I thought. It took a year, and when I did, the monastery had been cleared, the queen had fled, and my sister was dead. She'd lived there and grew obsessed. Then became a maiden and was subsequently killed sometime after. I'm not sure how long. That's when I met Kilian."

"Maiden?"

"The queen used to have handmaids. Mostly when She was at the monastery. Only, that jealous bitch often ended up killing them all. My sister included. Kilian thought it had something to do with the queen's past. Her human life was the reason She lures only men."

My mind reeled with the news.

"I'm sorry."

He continued. "I was ready to search for the queen then, but Kilian wouldn't allow it. He made me wait until I was eighteen to change me. Then I could join him. My mom lived, but her body was weak, so she died a few years later when I was nineteen. I decided to finally take Kilian up on that offer."

"Fuck. That's terrible."

"It's not even the worst of my stories."

"Well, then, I don't want to hear the rest. My life is sad enough without hearing your sob stories." I took a long drag of my cigarette and let it out in one long breath.

That made him smile and cough out a bit of smoke.

"You fuckin' asshole."

Twenty-Eight

LUKE

I couldn't find my brother. I'd been lying in bed when the stabbing in my chest brought me to my feet and out of the room. Something was happening, and judging by the throbbing that grew by the second, I knew it was bad. This was the worst part of the bond. The not knowing and the snowball effect that happened after. My heart raced as I searched the halls. All the while, the stinging pain continued to pulse through my veins.

It was kinda like being stuck in an infinite time loop. We were more at ease if we were together. This place wasn't safe, and not seeing him meant he could be anywhere. He could get hurt at a moment's notice, and if I couldn't get to him . . . The thought alone made me sick to my stomach. If he was next to me, we could get the pain to stop and ride it out together. Every second, I felt sicker and dizzier.

"Here." Zach appeared around a corner, and I almost tackled him to the ground. Will was next to him. They reeked of smoke, and Will patted him on the shoulder and gave us some space.

"What happened?"

"What? Oh. Nothing." His tone was oddly nonchalant as he stuffed his hands in his pockets.

"You're really not going to tell me?"

"You don't need to know every little thing happening with me. Blood bond or not."

"Right." There used to be a time when he would tell me. When he didn't think I was so fragile. My chest ached now. The stabbing was there too but faint and concealed.

"Luke." Zach's eyes softened.

Fighting with my brother only ensured we'd both be unbelievably uncomfortable until we made up. It wasn't worth it.

"It's fine, you don't have to tell me. I get it."

"I don't want to add to your plate."

"Okay."

"I don't like this anymore than you do, okay? Being connected to you is the worst thing that's ever happened to either of us."

More pain shot through my chest. At least it felt warm.

"No, no, no. I didn't mean it." He grabbed my shoulders.

My eyes were already burning like he'd hit me. It felt like he had. The bond felt like being cut up. There was no shield anymore.

"I meant . . . " He wiped his hands over his face, and the pain continued. "This isn't sustainable. Being this close to you isn't healthy. It's making us fight."

"I get it."

"Obviously not, because now I feel like an elephant is standing on my chest."

"If you don't want to be around me, then tell me. Don't do it because you feel like you have to or because you think you're going to hurt my feelings."

"What?! Luke, that's not how I feel, and you know that."

I took a deep breath to steady myself and remember the truth.

"I know. I'm sorry. I've been feeling out of place. And I hate the thought that even you don't want me around or that the only reason is because of the bond."

The thought of it brought the sick warmth through my body again.

"Luke, no. It's this place. It's this bond. You're my brother. Bond or no bond. There is no place I'd rather be than enduring this with you. Don't let it mess with your head too much. That's why I think some secrets are healthy for us right now. Everyone tells me this will get better after Ascension, so we just have to make it till then."

I nodded. He was right. The pain eased as quickly as it came. We let out a collective breath.

"This is weird."

"No shit, we have no choice but to bicker like a married couple."

"Why does it feel like it's getting worse?"

"Ezra said it's because we're really close, I guess. We were attached at the hip before, and now, I might as well be living in your skin."

"Gross."

"This is some serious *I'd cut your face off and wear it* type shit."

"Please stop."

He laughed. "Are we good? I was going to turn in for the night. But let's get this ironed out first."

"Yeah, no, we're good."

I put my arm around him, and we walked in stride. I missed the days when my brother didn't look at me like a paper doll on a shelf. More than that, I missed the days when I didn't feel like that fragile doll. Zach was keeping secrets, and I was too. Maybe they were harmless, but secrets had never helped my brother and me before.

Twenty-Nine

ZACH

"Can you give me the day, sir?" Henderson asked me while he rummaged through some papers. He was in charge of facilitating shipping for a client. From what I could tell, his special talent was managing our clients. He was a glorified personal assistant with a knack for dealing with a lot of different types of people. I wondered if that's what The Family saw in him when they recruited him. It explained his ever-changing personality. With his friends and peers, he was an annoying nuisance, but with the higher-ups alone, he was a golden boy, and the longer I spent with him, the more of a kiss-ass he became.

"How the fuck would I know?"

"They still didn't give you a phone, sir?"

"You get a phone and I don't?"

"It's over there. Can you check it?"

We were in one of our many random-colored rooms. This one was themed in purple, and the cushion armchair I was sitting in was lush and, no doubt, expensive. A large window overlooked the back garden and maze. I groaned as I picked up his phone from the table. I was supposed to be helping Henderson. Ezra had given me instructions to get familiar with Henderson and his work, and learn all the clients' names by heart, but upon Ezra's absence, *I* instructed Henderson to do his work without talking while I poured myself a drink. Will would be pissed when I told him I'd spent the day drinking while he and Thane got stuck with window cleaning duty.

When I saw the date, my stomach seized.

"March sixth," I choked out. Presley's birthday.

"Thanks," he mumbled, and left me staring out the window.

I'd never missed a birthday. My heart throbbed in my ears, and I sat down to shake myself of the sudden disappointment. Christmas was one thing, but it was already the beginning of March. We'd been there almost three months. It felt like a lifetime. I didn't feel like the same person. Yet, I was.

I wasn't supposed to care about shit like that. Luke was the real planner and mastermind behind parties. But every year, I would take Presley out just him and me, and we'd do the wildest shit. For his eighteenth, we broke into one of those indoor play areas and stayed the night. Our little secret. The year before that, we'd climbed the water tower and drank till sunrise.

It hurt more than I ever imagined it would.

I composed myself and swallowed the lump in my throat. There was a first for everything. The first year would hurt like a bitch. *Noted.*

I went to find Luke and leave Henderson to his boring job. It didn't take long to find him, because he was already trying to find me. We met in the hallway when he almost barreled into me.

"Are you okay?" Luke said.

He obviously didn't know the day, or I'd have felt his pain on top of my own, and he'd hate to hear how long we'd been in Ireland. I wished I could time travel to a few minutes before I knew.

"Yeah, I'm good."

He wiggled a big bushy brow at me. "You're lying."

"A little, yeah. But don't worry about it. Wanna go beat the shit out of each other for fun?"

"Sure."

I was relieved. The only thing fun to do was fight.

Thirty

LUKE

Zach and I entered the sparring room. Fighting didn't interest me much, but my brother enjoyed it. With the remnants of whatever pain he felt earlier circulating in my body, it only gave me more reason to make him feel better.

We shed our shirts and bit into our wrists. It didn't hurt. My venom control was perfect, and leaving a clean, quick bite was becoming muscle memory.

"May fate guide you," Zach said. His lips twisted into a wicked, sarcastic grin.

Akira's words to me under the bleachers in Blackheart rang in my ears. I pushed out the memory and squared my shoulders.

"May fate guide you," I repeated.

Then he lunged. Zach was great at offense, and though he couldn't immediately knock me to my knees, he was getting better at shifting my balance early in the fight. He wanted to get me on the ground. I dodged him, but he grabbed me from behind and flung me to the ground.

"Ow," we said at the same time.

Our gazes shot to each other in an instant.

"What the fuck was that?"

I popped up to my feet. "Wait. Hit me right here as hard as you can."

When he punched me, we both winced.

"This isn't happening. Are we physically linked now too?"

I punched him in the shoulder, and another wave of pain ran through me. It wasn't exactly like being hit myself, but it was similar and almost as painful. Just slightly less.

"That's—"

"Complete bullshit," he said.

I was confused but not surprised. Anything was possible, but we already shared enough. Physical pain added on top was a nightmare situation.

"Oh good. You're both here. I wanted to get some training time with you both." Sirius came strolling in.

"We can't . . ."

"Why would that be?"

"We think the bond linked us, like physically."

"That's absurd."

"That's what we said, but we came to spar, and when I knocked Luke to the ground, we felt it at the same time."

He looked between us, not saying a word. Then swatted Zach on the back of the head.

"Ow," we said again.

"What's that for?"

"I take it you guys were never linked like this. Not even you and your brother?" I asked.

Sirius wasn't talking, only looking between us with flared nostrils and a hardened jaw.

"Both of you, follow me." We left the sparring room and followed Sirius through the hallway.

"Why are you taking us to the atrium?" Zach asked.

"Privacy."

He led us to an empty entryway with marble floors and stopped right in front of a large wooden door with a sun and the moon carved into it. He turned on his heels to face us. His normally slicked-back hair was falling wildly at the sides of his face.

"Give me your arm." His eyes darkened, and he beckoned for me.

"What the fuck are you doing?" Fear laced my brother's voice.

"Give me your arm," Sirius repeated.

I went to give it, and Zach pulled me away from him.

"No. Not before you tell us what you're going to do."

"What's going on? Why are you afraid of him?"

"Because he knows, unlike Ezra, I might hurt you. And trust me, I intend to."

"We're not doing that," Zach said.

"You say that like you have a choice. *Give me your arm.*"

Sirius's eyes lost all color, then he lunged. There was a scuffle. A push and pull as we all scrambled on the floor, tugging and tearing each other's clothes in an attempt to escape Sirius's advance, but we were already too weak from the blood loss.

Zach yelled for me as Sirius grabbed him by the collar and pulled him through the door.

"No, wait!"

Pure ragged panic took over as I shook the door. "Sirius, no! Don't do this."

I didn't even know what it was until I felt a sharp pain along my forearm. Like someone dragged a knife along my skin, but there was no blood. Frantic breaths sputtered from my chest. The bond pulled me apart from the inside as slices stung my skin, and I heard my brother's screams from inside, but something else was there too—fire. Fire lit up my belly and propelled my feet to the door. Sirius thought he could mess with us and test the bond like weren't real people with real pain.

Not my brother. Not my family.

"Open the door!" I punched the hard wood of the door, growing angrier and angrier.

I didn't know where all the anger was coming from. Was it mine? Was it my brother's? The lines between us blurred, but it didn't matter. I pounded my fists harder into the door, ignoring the pain in my hand and my body while Zach called for me. The bond flared, but somehow, I was numb inside. My only focus was taking out that door that had to be at least five feet thick. The door was coming down one way or another.

Not my brother. No.

Zach's desperate cries on the inside of the atrium echoed, and I hit the door harder.

Connell appeared next to me. "W-what's happening, sir? I heard yelling."

"Go, get Ezra."

"Bu—"

"Go, before I kill Sirius!"

I kicked the door. It was budging. My entire arm was on fire, and my fingernails felt like they were being pried off. The skin on my knuckles peeled and bled, but it only strengthened my resolve. The door was coming down, and I would kill Sirius for doing this to us.

The wood finally cracked and burst open.

Zach was on the ground of the atrium covered in blood, shaking. I didn't understand. Why do this? Why physically torture us to test the bond. My brother knew all along Sirius was capable of this and more.

"There. That's the fight I wanted to see."

I lunged for Sirius, pushing him back a few steps. I didn't care how old he was or how experienced. I'd fight him now. I'd kill him if he thought he could so much as look in my brother's direction.

"This is who you need to be here. Not cowering on the floor. This bond is not your excuse to be weak."

I stepped forward again, but Zach grabbed my leg. "Luke, don't. Please, let it go."

"We're not cowards. This bond doesn't make us weak. It will make us the strongest to ever set foot on The Guard. It makes me strong enough to kill you."

"Want to test the theory, Calem?" Sirius's eyes sparkled with the challenge.

"Yeah, I do." I stared into his eyes, our faces inches apart.

I'd missed the fire in my veins, but it had been there all this time, lying dormant and waiting to strike.

"That's enough," Ezra's voice came from behind and pulled me back.

"No, let's see. Maybe Sirius's time is up."

Sirius didn't shrink away from me, and I waited patiently for his advance.

Ezra grabbed my face in his hands, and his blue eyes steadied me. "Stop. Go comfort your brother."

I turned back to Zach shaking on the floor. His entire arm was covered in blood, with long gashes. A few of his fingernails were cut and pried up.

The emotion of it all hit me like a freight train. I fell on the floor next to him, pulling him into an embrace. Finally, the tears came and we wept. The pain pulsed everywhere. Aching. His wounds were open, barely starting to close, and it hurt. Physically, it hurt, but I couldn't tell if it was worse than the emotional pain as the fear of it left us. This would be a process and another series of days stuck hurting.

"Don't do that again." Zach cried into my shoulder.

"Do what? Save you?"

He said nothing as he buried his head into my shoulder. It felt good to comfort him this time. Holding him was holding me together. It eased all the pain rushing through me. We'd get through this like we always had.

Sirius and Ezra bickered while a few lower members filtered in to watch, including Connell. He, too, appeared to be crying.

"This is over the line."

"The bond needs to be tested. We need them to be prepared."

"They've already been through a lot."

"Haven't we all? They don't get a pass for being damaged. It's up to us to make sure they can face what lies ahead. You of all people know The Divine Path speaks of great enemies coming. What will happen if they catch us here like this?"

Damaged. Squeezing Zach tighter, I understood the fear he held now. Sirius was calloused, and his heart was cold. He called us brothers but treated us like soldiers. Replaceable, beatable, things for him to mold.

"The bond will snap into place when it's ready. It doesn't need molding or testing. You need to apologize," Ezra said.

The hairs raised on the back of my neck at Her presence.

My brother's and my head hit the floor in a bow before we could blink. All of us were on our faces before Her. I didn't need to see Her to feel Her presence, but She rarely left Her room and not without an escort.

I caught sight of the tail end of Her dress as She walked to Sirius, who was kneeling too.

"My queen, I didn't intend to cause harm."

"Do not speak. You carried this mission out on your own volition. For three days, leave my sight. You will not pray. You will not speak to me or anyone. Your punishment is your own loss of connection and a fasting from blood."

There were hushed whispers in the atrium. It was unheard of.

"This is something to be celebrated. The bond has evolved further than we could have ever hoped. Isn't that the true sign of The Divine? That these two will usher in the strongest bond our family has ever seen."

Words of praise filled the room in hushed whispers.

Her attention turned to us, and I wondered if this could be the same person. The one who killed Sarah. Because this felt different. My world was knit together like the stars overhead when She was near. She aligned the cosmos in place and hung the moon in the sky, and more importantly, She came for us when we needed Her.

"Let me see," She muttered, and ran Her fingers through Zach's hair.

I waited for his normal protest, but his tough outer shell had fallen. He let Her take his arm.

"You came."

"You were calling to me. I can help with the pain. Would you like that?"

He looked at me, and I nodded.

She bit into Her wrist and blood flowed from Her porcelain skin like ink. I turned my head, willing myself not to breathe in the scent of Her blood. I had to be strong for my brother. I should have been worried, but She wouldn't hurt him. She wouldn't hurt us. The past was the past. This queen, my queen, was perfect and magnificent. She'd do nothing but care for us.

"Drink a little, Darling."

He didn't hesitate. The euphoria of it hit as if I had tasted Her blood with my own lips. It healed his wounds, and every ounce of pain we'd been plagued with was instantly gone. I marveled in the peace. The sense of safety and love pulled me under with it. She was worthy of all my praise and devotion.

"Ascension is near. On the next new moon, in five days, this pain will be a thing of the past. Until then, you both will not be kept apart. Your wait is almost over. You're both ready."

Dear Luke and Zach,

It's my birthday today, and everyone remembered. I didn't want them to. I've tried really hard to be happy for them. But how am I supposed to do that when you're not here to make my cake or to sing me "Happy Birthday" in that weird chorus you guys do? I've stopped expecting you to come through the door. But today, I kinda hoped for a second or two when I was blowing out the candles.

I'm really sad. My chest hurts and I had the weirdest pain in my hand today. Can you feel it too?

Love you forever,

Presley

Thirty-One

ZACH

I opened and closed my hand. It had been a few days since Sirius took a knife to my fingernails. He'd forced me down with a crazed look in his eye, mumbling about the prophecy and The Divine, when I was too weak to push him off me. I'd since avoided him. Ezra said I should forgive him and that families fight, but I would have never done that to my brothers. At least it was easy to hide the faint scars with my suit coat.

It confirmed what I knew about this place and left a sick feeling in the pit of my stomach. Even if we complied with what they wanted, we'd still get hurt. I was glad it was me and not Luke, or I might have tried to kill Sirius, and that would have ended badly.

I shook off the thought. She was right. Fate was aligning, and Ascension was days away. My brother and I had a set path, and we needed to walk it.

"Sir, are you coming to the bonfire tonight? Everyone would appreciate your presence." Connell was practically jumping up and down at the thought as he scrubbed the deck of the ferry.

I was partially hiding from Sirius and avoiding going to the old church to pray. If Sirius didn't make me go—because he was an ass and got himself in trouble—I would not volunteer.

"I'm so not in the mood for that shit."

After what happened with Sirius, the last thing I wanted to do was mingle with those assholes.

"That's why you should come. We want to spend time with you before you ascend. We're going to make an altar by the cliffside, drink, and tell stories."

More cult shit. Nothing surprised me anymore. I didn't want to burn off the last of my brain cells by participating in some weird ritual.

"Sounds like it could be a good distraction." Luke appeared beside me, oddly chipper for such a gloomy day.

He didn't spend the entirety of the night pacing in the room, thinking of Her. Why did She offer Her blood? It created an itch I couldn't scratch.

I sighed. "What's all the fuss about, anyway? We're ascending. Doesn't mean much for any of you."

"It means everything, sir. The Guard is becoming whole again, and roles will shift. We're coming into a new era of power. Things are aligning in our favor, and The Divine is on our side. Some say She'll do more miracles and we'll find lost brothers from all over who would have never found our family. That your bond will draw us closer together, and we'll be able to serve Her better than ever before. You're both ushering in a new generation. Who knows what we'll be able to accomplish with you both leading us?"

Connell talked so fast his lips could barely keep up.

Luke looked at me with his eyebrows drawn. The last thing I needed was Luke worried or thinking. Thinking too hard about all this was much worse. Sometimes, the answer was to go with the flow.

"Fine. Let's go jump around the fire and sing ancient ritual songs. Sounds like a fucking blast."

Luke's smirk turned into a radiant smile.

"I can't wait to tell them Your Justness is coming! Oh, and Luke The Great, they'll be so pleased."

"Stop calling me that when I'm around," I said.

"But I can when you're not around, sir?"

"Knock yourself out."

"I-I don't think I'm able to, sir."

"I think it's quiet time, Connell."

The night air was bone chilling next to the cliffside, and that was after I asked for another coat. All this shit about not getting cold as a vampire was bullshit. It wouldn't kill me, and I wouldn't shiver, but it didn't *feel* good. Nothing in this place felt good.

I couldn't believe I was sitting next to the fire with brainwashed, unstable scumbags. I guess I was a brainwashed, unstable scumbag too, but at least I knew that's what I was. Most of them had no idea. Luke sat next to me looking way too excited to be a part of whatever the hell the ritual was. No one here had ever heard of a lawn chair. They'd taken their nice dining room chairs and set them up in the grass and dirt. Mom would have had a fit.

Poor Will would probably have to clean them. It wasn't as fun giving him a hard time anymore since the queen was torturing him. He'd had another bad day, and Thane thought it would be better if they got locked in for the night. Doubted rituals would have been his thing anyway.

"Tonight is a very special night." Henderson got up and spoke with a wine bottle in his hand. "Not only do we devote ourselves to our glorious queen as we celebrate the coming of the dark sun—just as it was foretold, but we get to share it with two of The Guard. I can't put into words the honor of being present for your origin story into our family and to see you both grow into your roles. It's a privilege I don't take lightly. You'll usher us into a glorious era."

Luke and I shared the same look of wide-eyed amusement. It was a little funny. We were used to the strangeness by now, and laughing was better than crying. It's possible we were cracking a bit. We should have been asking questions, turning up tables, and causing a scene, probably. Why were Luke and I the chosen ones? What was this "new era" they spoke of? I knew the answers they told me, but was any of it true?

"In two days, our family will be complete. The dark sun will come, and we'll all be one."

"I didn't know he was so poetic." I snickered to Luke.

He gave me the *be nice* look but smiled. Fun, unserious Luke was coming out to play, which meant weird cult ritual or not, it would be a night to remember.

"I'll never forget the night Akira found me standing in a subway in New York. It's a long story I'll have to tell you both sometime but . . . I thought I was alone and my life was over, but he came out of the shadows and showed me a greater life with purpose. This family is all I've ever had, and we're all exceedingly blessed to spend it with both of you. To you."

He held up a wineglass, and they made a toast.

"Here. Take some of the wine. Guests of honor drink from the bottle." Henderson handed the bottle to Luke, and he chugged a good bit of it.

"Well, ya were only supposed to drink a sip," Connell said with a coy smile. "We should have said so."

"Fuck it." I grabbed the bottle and downed the rest.

There were loud cheers mixed with pounding and stomping on the dirt coming from our harmonious brotherhood. I kinda wanted to be like them. Under the spell and immersed into the bond. That could be what Ascension would mean for us.

I may not have gotten straight answers, but there were things I knew for sure. The thought of leaving the queen made my stomach turn, and being bonded to my brother hurt physically and mentally. I couldn't deny those things like I couldn't deny the fact that trying to fight this fate was futile.

Maybe all those guys were right. We were chosen. Somehow blessed with some bond that would make the brotherhood stronger and serve Her better and for longer. That meant the prophecy was real. It meant the entire thing was.

"Please, sir, if you'd both take your shirts off."

"It's cold as fuck."

"Come on. Live a little." Luke shed his shirt and threw it on the ground.

I rolled my eyes and wondered what had gotten into him. The moon bathed us from above, only adding to our temporary madness. I cursed my brother but shed my shirt. The cool air instantly bit into my skin.

"How's it going, boys?" Sirius's voice entered our circle.

I pulled my shoulders down and back and fought the growl in my throat.

Ezra and Sirius invaded our circle, and everyone bowed.

"We were about to start the blessing," Henderson said.

"Don't let us stop you."

"They drank the wine, but it was a lot. Too much probably. I'm a little worried," Connell said.

Sirius and Ezra eyed us with amusement.

"Not surprised. Continue on. We're only observing."

We were the ultimate spectacle. My brother and I watched as the group of men shed their blood into a large silver bowl.

"This is our offering to you. And to Her. May fate guide us all and the dark sun come and bless us abundantly."

Henderson and a few others dipped their fingers into the pool of blood and used it to paint lines on our bodies. I flinched at the sticky wetness that ran from my fingers up my forearm. Three uneven lines. They repeated that pattern on each arm and down our backs and chests.

"What do the lines mean?" Luke asked.

You think we'd have asked when we got the tattoo before we were initiated, shocker—when we unknowingly agreed to join a cult, we didn't care what it meant. We just thought "Hey, we're part of the cool kids now."

And that's exactly how we ended up in the mess we were in.

Connell's hand shot up like a schoolboy.

"Yes, you can say it, Connell."

"The longest line is a symbol of the queen and Her connection to The Divine. The next one symbolizes The Guard and its strength to uphold The Divine's plans and serve Her, and the last line symbolizes the brotherhood."

"Lovely," I said, trying to push out the sarcasm in my voice because no one there ever seemed to pick up on it.

"Let us pray," Henderson said.

Everyone bowed their heads, even Sirius and Ezra.

"We thank Her Glorious Majesty for all She has supplied and endured on this plane for us. May She bless us and bless our new Guard with life and abundance. May the blood overflow and the bonds strengthen. Please Divine, guide us to greater destiny and show this new Guard The Divine Path. May they transform and be molded to Her liking so that they may serve our family with honor and true purpose. Amen."

Hushed amens sounded along with the crackling embers of the fire and the roar of the ocean crashing on the cliffside close by. Their prayers sounded like my mom's. Which meant they'd meant nothing and no one would hear or answer them.

Henderson poured the rest of the blood into the fire, and cheers erupted. Everyone stood, and chaos broke loose with shouts and movement.

"Now the celebration begins. To the maze!"

"To the maze!" the other boys repeated.

Luke handed me my shirt. "See, that wasn't so bad."

"I'm covered in blood, and they prayed about us like we're a sacrificial animal."

The wine hadn't hit me yet, but it had to have hit him because he giggled at my words.

"Come on. Let's do this stupid maze."

I ushered Luke over to where all the boys were standing.

"Ezra says the first one to the end of the maze gets to forfeit all duties for a week. And you get to pick one person to serve you for a month," Henderson said. "No rules. No limits. Get there any way you can, boys."

"So it's going to be a bloodbath, then?"

Nothing these guys ever did was without ruthlessness or blood. I didn't think anyone heard me in the fray.

"Ready. Set. Go!" Those were the last words I remembered as Luke and I moved into the hedges.

My feet left the ground, and my body poised to run and then . . .

I wasn't in the maze.

Sounds of laughter filled the night air, but I was far from it. Alone. Staring at the edge of the cliffside where the sky met the vast darkness of the ocean. The world moved slowly, unlike my heartbeat. I moved my hands over my face, and the world tilted on its axis, almost taking me down with it.

How long have I been out here? Did I miss the maze race?

The water swirled below. I couldn't see far into the blackness, but the entire ocean was blending and moving in a way I could feel on my skin. I moved toward the edge. Why was I out here? And why alone?

You're still holding back.

The queen's voice filled my head, and I fought against the wind. There on the cliff's edge, the soft mist hit my skin.

Prove your loyalty.

My heart kicked my ribs. The dark water churned below and swirled into the black abyss. I stepped closer.

She was right. I was resisting. I let the images flood my mind of what it might be like to give in and let Her consume me. What our future might look like together. I wanted Her to want me like I wanted Her, and I'd do anything to make it so.

Fall.

The word filled my head, and I stood with my toes at the edge of the cliff. I couldn't have Her until I gave in. My skin pulsated, and I swear I felt my blood moving within my body. The water drew me closer. I wanted to jump if it meant She'd be there to catch me and consume all that was left of me. Then I'd finally be free of this place.

The wind picked up, and I lost my footing. I would fall, but I didn't care. If She wanted it, I'd give it. She wanted me to fall. She wanted me to follow Her down to the bottom of hell.

Someone caught me and pulled me to the ground. I held my head, internally reeling at the dizziness.

"What are you doing?" Sirius's voice was next to me, but I couldn't open my eyes to see his face.

"Make it stop."

"Were you going to jump?" He sounded worried.

"She wants me to jump. To show my loyalty. She doesn't want me, but She will." The words were poured out of me before I could even hope to catch them. "She doesn't love me. No one cares. Luke cares. Only Luke."

I felt a hand on my back and then on my head. "It's the wine that makes you feel like that. It's not true. Lay back on the grass for a minute."

I did, and it made the ground shake and melt into me like quicksand. When I opened my eyes, the night sky was a vivid blending of spots and pulsing of lights. I was small and insignificant, like a terrified child.

I covered my eyes with a groan. "Please, make this stop. Do something."

"It will pass soon."

"You don't want to help me. You hate me. You want me to suffer."

"That isn't true."

"It is. I want Her to love me. I just want this to not hurt so much. Why do you hate me?"

"Sit up." He pulled me up by my shirt but held my shoulders to steady me. "Look at me."

"Everything is moving."

"Stop complaining and open your eyes."

Sirius was close to me. "I don't hate you. I can't hate you. It's impossible."

"It's not real," I said. I meant the bond and the blood didn't matter. It was all fake.

"The queen does care about you. I know it feels different than what She has with Luke, but you're special to Her. You test Her. It's different but equally as cared for. If you jumped off the cliff, I'd come after you."

"Because you have to."

"No, because I care about you. You're important to our family."

I was shivering and hadn't noticed. It was the drugs in the wine, but Sirius handed me his jacket and wrapped it over my shoulders.

"I'm sorry about what happened in the atrium. It was over the line. I was shocked to see how far your bond had progressed. It's extraordinary. I just don't want to see you making the same mistakes me and my brother did."

"You never talk about your brother."

"None of us do. None of us fully remember him. We traded our memories of him for peace. Not all of them. Just the good ones, which includes much of my childhood and memories before this place. My brother and I disguised ourselves as crew on a merchant ship in the late 1600s, but we were marauders. She was hidden in the monastery at the time, and we came to 'take from Her extravagant beauty.' Instead, we found Her. You think you and your brother are the only ones who struggled with the bond. But all of us did, aside from Akira. It's different for us all. She told me Akira appeared one day, that he felt he needed to be somewhere, and he found Her on that feeling alone. My brother and I were different. I felt the pull much stronger than he did. We spent too long agonizing and holding onto our own bond that it tore us apart. I fear that's the reason we failed and another pairing for Her was chosen by the stars."

"Because of you and your brother?"

"Yes. Because we could not let go. Once we reached Ascension, we separated. We couldn't care for each other and Her at the same time. And we barely talked after. It was never the same. I think things could have been different if we'd learned how to do both without it killing us. I think you and Luke can do that."

The stars danced in the sky. The light and dark mixed into orbs and shapes that morphed into faces.

"What do the star gods want with me? I don't get it."

Sirius nudged my chest. "The Divine craves connection. It's always looking for the strongest bond . . . *Astra inclinant, sed non obligant.*"

"Are you speaking in tongue now?"

Mom's church used to. It scared me as a kid, and I thought it sounded like gibberish.

"It means the stars incline us, but they don't bind us. The Divine guides us and gives us gifts, but it cannot control the bonds we forge. If the stars gave a gift—a woman that could cure all longing and join the lost, one that heals and gives abundantly more than we could ever hope to have as humans—wouldn't they want us to protect it? That is what this is. A gift and an opportunity, and you are chosen because there is something in you that not everyone has in this world, something that cannot be fabricated even by the stars. Connection."

I nodded, and my eyelids grew heavier. I was busy concentrating on not falling over into grass that seemed to whisper my name, but I felt the comfort of his words. My brother loved me, and I loved him, and for some reason, that made us special.

I moved my fingers to the warmth of my face, and it was wet with tears.

"What's wrong?"

"I . . . miss my brother."

Sirius smiled. "We'll find him. I'll help you to your room."

I was talking about Luke, of course. Even with the world turned upside down, I wanted to see him happy and safe next to me, but I missed all my brothers. I missed Presley being my partner in crime and making me laugh. I even missed Aaron and all his golden boy, goody-two-shoes energy. My happiest moments were of all of us together. It hurt that it couldn't be like that again.

Sirius reached for me.

"I can't walk."

"You're my brother. I'll carry you."

I didn't protest as he flung me over his shoulder, away from the roaring waters and the lingering faces in the stars above.

Thirty-Two

Everything spun around me, and I could feel every particle of dust in my throat and lungs. When I blinked again, I saw Her. Her bloody mural in all its spectacular glory. Nothing in my body hurt. I'd never felt so weightless. It was better than drinking.

Suddenly, I was outside again, no longer moving. I'd been in the maze at some point, then I wasn't. I couldn't find my brother, so I went looking for Her.

Grass, stone, and dirt permeated the air as I tried getting up off my knees. The grass was so soft, sliding between my fingers like velvet. I wanted to rub my face on it forever, but I needed to get up.

Find me, My Love.

She called to me, and oh, how I longed to answer Her. That was the only reason I could get to my feet despite the world spinning. It was worse than any hangover or vertigo I'd ever had. I could barely move, let alone walk, but it didn't matter.

My Love, I need you.

She needed me, and I'd crawl to Her if that's what it took. My fingers sank into the dirt as I pushed myself to my feet, then I stumbled into the castle. No one passed me, but shouts and laughter could be heard in the distance.

I fell into a wall, taking a painting with me.

Closer. Come closer to Me.

Looking down the hall, a flash of white caught my attention. My Love was close. I needed to touch Her like I'd never needed anything else in my life. That yearning pushed me through every dizzying second. I'd find Her.

Closer.

She needed me. I dared to think of that and let the euphoria wash over me until I was picking up my pace. My whole body heated at the thought of Her uttering those words to me. I wanted nothing more than to give Her exactly what She wanted. To fulfill every utterable thought and syllable Her mouth could form, because suddenly, all I felt was my heart in my chest. No pain, no fear, no past. And the only thing left was Her.

I was on my knees, crawling again until the earth stopped shifting beneath me. Just another hallway. Another thing blocking my way to Her.

I need you closer to me, My Love.

This was a sad form of torture. To feel so good yet so empty because

I hadn't found Her yet. She ached for me, and I was failing Her, but the tension in my body shifted as I closed in on Her room. She was close.

She was at Her harp when I entered. Her delicate fingers rested on a string, and Her eyes widened.

"My Love. I wasn't expecting you."

But how? She'd been calling me, and it was so loud. My head spun, and in Her room where the light wasn't as dim, I could see why I'd been so dizzy. Every object was spinning and blooming in its own intricate pattern. I rubbed my eyes, and when I opened them again, She was in front of me.

She radiated light. All Her skin was a sparkling beam so radiant I needed to touch it. My fingers grazed Her arm, and I shivered. She was so cold, but I was warm and could warm Her.

"You're so beautiful. You're all shiney and glittery." The words tumbled out as I ran my finger over Her arm to the top of Her chest along Her bare collarbone.

"Love?" Her fingers lifted my chin for me to stare into Her eyes. Two glowing pools of starlight beckoned to me. "You drank the wine."

She smiled, the worry dissipating from Her features.

"Too much," I said, continuing to move my hand along Her arm.

Closer.

I heard the words, but Her lips didn't move. Now that I was closer to Her, it wasn't enough. All these months, I'd feared this. But why? She felt so good. Nothing could hurt me here.

"Can I touch you?"

Her head tilted to the side as She observed me. I wondered what She was looking for on my face. An answer to a question I didn't know.

"Yes, Love."

Slowly, I pulled at the edge of Her gown, lowering the sleeve so I could kiss Her shoulder and bring Her to me.

There were no words that could describe the feeling that pulsed through my veins when my lips grazed Her skin, but that feeling only left me hungrier and hungrier. I moved up Her neck, over Her chest, and to Her jaw. A soft sigh left Her lips. The room swirled and pulsed in a vivid gush of ecstasy, and every taste of Her was like forbidden fruit that made my stomach sour with need. Vicious, snarling need to take Her and bleed Her dry.

I slid the other sleeve of Her gown down to kiss there too. The night was young. There were so many ways I could make it last and prolong the vibrant euphoria running in my veins.

"Are you trying to undress me?" Her lips held a mischievous smile, and I kissed the corner of Her pale mouth.

"If you'll allow me to."

She invited me with Her lips on mine, and Her nails dug into my scalp as Her tongue entered my mouth. She tasted like ice-cold water on the hottest summer day.

I pulled Her gown to the floor, revealing two sheer pieces of white underwear that left every inch of Her pale skin on display.

With the room tilting, I laid Her over the bed. She watched in silent amusement. Like She was waiting to see how far I'd go and prove how much I wanted Her. Her hands rested above Her, and She let me spread Her legs. I kissed my way up Her thigh to Her throat.

"Do you want me, My Love?"

"You're the only thing I've ever truly wanted." I wasn't surprised by my words. It felt true.

"Show me how much. Show me your devotion."

"Anything for you."

I kissed Her neck and pressed my lower half into Her.

Her absence jolted me as I was pulled backward and off the bed. The movement was so swift I had to cling to whoever was keeping me from falling to the floor. It took me a moment to steady myself while the room spun vigorously.

"He'll be unhappy when it wears off tomorrow. You know that. He'll blame you and he'll blame me. Not to mention his brother will have a lot to say, I'm sure," Ezra said.

"I won't. Please let me stay."

"We can't risk Ascension," he said.

Her starlight irises swirled like a whirlpool, and Her skin glistened like evening stars. What did he mean by that? Why was he doing this to me? Denying me the one thing that made sense.

She watched me like She might protest, with desire burning in those eyes for me.

"Another time, Love." She nodded to Ezra, and he spun me so fast I grabbed on to his coat to keep from falling to the floor.

The world was shaking so much I couldn't think about anything else for a moment.

"Are you angry with me?" Ezra asked as we walked.

He was holding me up much more than I thought I needed. Whatever was in the wine came in waves, because the walls were zigzagging into an infinite pattern that reached to the ceiling, and the floor vibrated my shoes like it had its own heartbeat.

"Yeah, a little."

I thought of Her, the permanent ache of not being there with Her, and how if he hadn't stopped me, I could be there with Her in Her bed.

"Maybe a lot."

He said nothing else as we walked.

"Don't let me drink the wine again."

I was only vaguely aware of not liking the feeling. It was much easier to identify when my thoughts weren't on Her. My stomach churned and things moved too much. I could barely keep my eyes open.

He chuckled. "I'll note it. Don't worry. It will pass."

When we arrived at my room, he helped me to my bed. Zach had a rag over his head but peeked around it to see me. "Luke! I missed you so much."

"I missed you too, dude."

Being in our room was true peace and safety, and I needed more of it. I wanted to wrap the feeling around me, even if it smothered me.

"Take me over there." I pointed to my brother's bed.

Ezra helped me into bed next to Zach. I gripped on the edge of the bedframe to try to stop the spinning.

"I'm so glad you're here," I said, sinking into the blankets.

A sense of calm enveloped me. It was so potent it might have been better than anything I'd felt that night. All the puzzle pieces were together, and I could close my eyes and rest. I needed nothing. I had it all.

"How long was it?" Zach said.

"Too long. Let's never do that again," I said.

"I'm locking you both in here till the morning." Ezra's voice was far away.

"We're getting scolded, I think." Zach chuckled.

"It's okay. They're stuck with us." I smiled at the thought and pulled a pillow under my head.

Thirty-Three

The effects of the wine lasted until morning. I'd shut my eyes and hoped for the best. Lying in the dark was almost like sleep. I'd forgotten about the time and lost myself in the silence.

While bringing the covers over me, I grazed my brother's arm.

"Ah!" We sat up simultaneously.

"Why are you still in my bed?"

"I don't know. I . . . I must have gotten really freaked out last night."

It checked out. Luke and I would take turns sleeping in each other's beds if we were scared, but that was way back when we were children and definitely not anything we did as adults.

"Did something happen? I mean, other than tripping off our asses," I asked.

He paused for so long I nudged him.

"No. No, I was freaked out in general, I think."

"Well, we tell no one. And beg Ezra to keep it quiet."

"Agreed."

I didn't mind it. I was just glad the floor wasn't moving anymore.

"Next time, I pick the nighttime activity, and drug rituals won't be high on the list."

The castle bustled with activity. Whispers of Ascension lingered in the halls, and all regular tasks had been postponed in preparation.

I occupied my time by helping Will and Thane pick up branches in the maze. It surprised no one that the hedges had been demolished in the mad dash to be the winner. I'd heard Henderson won. I didn't know who he chose to torture, but I had a guess.

"Are you still mad at me?" Thane asked while piling branches into a trash bin.

"A little," I said.

"I shouldn't have said anything while Luke was there. I wasn't trying to give him false hope."

"I know. That's why I said a little."

I chucked another huge set of branches in the bin and listened for Will. He was too far into the maze for me to hear.

"Oh good. Because I was trying to cheer Will up, but I'm terrible at it. You guys are better at that kind of thing. You're both so . . . tender."

"Never use that word to describe me again."

"You and Luke are good at navigating these intense moments and saying all the right things. But I don't know how. I've never had a little brother to comfort or family that enjoyed my company. Will is the person I'm closest to in the world, and I clam up when bad things happen. I didn't even know his sister's name until Kimberly asked."

I ignored the ache in my chest at the mention of her. "Why didn't you ask?"

"He seems happier when I don't ask about his past."

"Yeah, most people are."

"I know. I don't want to make any extra trouble for him. I'm a better help in other ways. I want to focus on that."

Thane frowned as he eyed the hedges. He hid his worry for Will well. I'd hardly noticed. But he had hope and people with hope didn't typically bitch and moan about their problems. Instead, they'd run themselves ragged trying to fix them. I wasn't sure who was worse off, me or him.

There was a brief silence as we continued deeper into the maze, picking up branches and empty alcohol bottles.

"Did you find anything in Akira's diary? Anything you're searching for."

"Not much. A lot of it is stories of them together. Like memories Akira wrote of the four of them. There's a lot of lamenting about their loss, but he doesn't mention specifics. I was hoping to get a rundown of the battle or something. I can't believe Kilian never told us."

"I can."

"Akira did mention something kind of interesting. It references Sirius's and Eros's Ascension. The excitement and what he calls 'troubles' and 'growing pains.' There's nothing specific, but it gave me the impression that maybe Eros and Sirius had issues leading up to their Ascension. And he references Eros over and over as The Guardian."

"And knowing this stuff helps how?"

"They're keeping you and Luke in the dark for a reason. It's obvious they're not telling you the whole truth. And knowing why tells us what they're trying to hide. And knowing what they are trying to hide from you gives us a clue in how to defeat them. I know you don't think The Legion cares. But I do think they're coming, and I'll do whatever I can to save you both."

"Why do you even care?" I asked.

"Because I know Kilian ruined any opportunity of you ever trusting the work that The Legion does, but you didn't see the work before Blackheart. All the footwork that Kilian has done for centuries has kept this coven in check. It's one of the reasons it's so small in comparison to some that exist out there. The Family talks a big game, but they've known about us for a long time, and they know Kilian is a threat. He may have been led astray, but . . . aren't we all for the people we love? Is there anything you wouldn't do for your brother?"

I hesitated. He was right. I'd kill for any of my brothers in a heartbeat, even good people. I'd trick, lie, and steal, and if someone killed my brother, I'd never stop searching to hunt them down.

He continued. "I didn't have a loving family growing up. No one really wanted anything to do with me. Will and Sky and Dom were the closest I've ever had to anything. We captured a few members of The Family over the years—these horrible men that didn't pass the trial phase. I had a hard time with it at first. I even thought about leaving, but the hope of seeing people like you be free is worth it. I want to keep real families together and prevent things like this coven from gaining more power."

"How do you prevent things like that?"

"Kilian has a secret. Something they're scared of. Something they'd kill for. That's the only reason we're alive."

"You still believe The Legion is coming for you."

"For all of us. With my whole heart. And if they get here and they don't want anything to do with you guys, I'll change their minds. I'll make sure they listen."

God, he was a hopeful one, sporting that same sunny disposition Aaron had. It was enough to make me smile.

"Well, you're wrong about one thing," I said.

"And that is?"

"I might trust The Legion again if you're in it, as long as you have a say next time."

That made him smile, and we continued our task. I'd listen every once in a while to see if someone was coming. Ezra would be pissed if he knew I was dirtying my suit helping Thane and Will with chores, not to mention Sirius.

"I keep waiting for Sirius to pop up in the hedges and kill me for this."

"Oh, he's busy, I think. She lied, you know? They've definitely been seeing each other in the past couple days, when he was supposed to be banned. I wouldn't be surprised if that's where he is right now."

I raised an eyebrow. "Do you mean what I think you mean?"

"Oh yeah, She keeps Ezra and Sirius plenty of company."

"No. I mean. You're saying She lied?"

"Definitely. I've seen them talking with my own eyes."

Something thick caught in my throat. Anger. She'd put on a show for the others that day in the atrium, but why? They were playing more mind games, only this one I hadn't caught on to. Was this their plan? Getting Luke and me into a vulnerable state to make us think She tried to save us. Was anything Sirius said true? What else were they doing and saying that I wasn't in on?

We continued into the maze until the heavy gray clouds above unleashed rain.

Thirty-Four

LUKE

With the bustle of the castle, I decided it would be safer for Her inside. Ezra let me make decisions like that now. I'd come in the early morning and stayed all afternoon. Her room was quiet and calm compared to outside. Everyone was full of excitement for Ascension, and I wanted to hide. She provided me shelter in that way and didn't mention the night before, for which I was thankful. I remembered it all, even if it was fuzzy.

The smell of parchment was strong, and dust clung to my fingertips as I turned another page of *The Aeneid*. She let me read to Her. I sat with my head resting against the headboard of the bed while She rested Her head on my shoulder.

I wondered if She was listening. Her fingers were wrapped in my other hand, and She traced along my fingers as I read. I had a hunch She knew I needed the distraction, but I hoped we could make a habit of it.

The scent of the fresh flowers on Her nightstand transported me to a memory.

Knocking had sounded at Sarah's door. A bouquet of flowers was in my hand on a hot summer day, back when my world was bathed in sunlight.

"Luke?" Her hair had been pinned up in a white ribbon.

"I thought about what you said . . . about what I wanted. And I was thinking, I think it's about time I took you on that date. Our first."

She smiled. *"I have to tell my dad where I'm going."*

"I told him. He gave me twenty to buy these."

With not even a moment of hesitation, she grabbed her purse from beside the door and followed me to the car. I took her to a drive-in movie. I couldn't forget Sarah or the life she was supposed to have and the life I wanted us to have together. She was made for me. What a lie. Sarah was meant for more, and all I ever did was drag her down with me.

"My Love . . . " She rubbed my chest before I could even feel sad. "Why did you stop?"

"I'm sorry. I remembered something."

"I like your voice. It's calming."

"I'm glad. How are you feeling with the solar eclipse coming?"

"I'm stronger now than I've ever been."

"And you want to sit with me all day?"

"The human isn't the only one who enjoys your company."

"You . . . know?" My heartbeat sped in my chest.

"I do know you met Cecily during the first new moon of your arrival. She's fond of you. It makes me very fond of you as well. Cecily is attracted to kind people."

She still didn't know about that day with Cecily in the garden. Which meant there was still hope of Cecily's words. Someone was coming, but Ascension was close. In less than two days, my brother and I would bond ourselves to Her, and the thought brought me more relief than grief.

I swallowed as a wave of anxiousness fell over me, and I squeezed my eyes shut.

She stroked my cheek. "What's wrong?"

"I think I wanna stay with you. And that scares me."

I couldn't deny that part of myself anymore. That part of me that grew stronger and stronger every day and urged me to give in. To abandon my life and let this place swallow me whole. To let Her take me and hide me in all Her divine power and beauty.

"Why does it scare you?"

"Because I don't think that's what I should want."

"You've always looked after everyone else. Why shouldn't you get something you want?"

"I don't know."

She kissed my cheek, and my unraveling came together again, but as soon as Her lips left me, I was back to the same confusion as before. With nothing but butterflies circling in my chest, I reached for Her, cupping Her cheek and pulling Her lips to mine.

It was gentle and slow. Euphoric. I melted into Her, and She let me slide Her down onto the sheets. It wasn't lust this time but a need of a totally different kind. We were perfect together.

She pulled away first and pushed me off.

"I'm sorry. I should have asked."

"I want you to be settled and levelheaded for Ascension."

"I'm sure," I said, fighting the urge to kiss Her again, "I'm thinking clearly. I know what I want."

"Will you continue to read to me?" Her eyes were softer now, and I wondered how close Cecily was. If she could see or hear me, or if she felt that kiss.

"Of course."

As soon as I left Her room, the weight of my own fate hit me. Her gravity upon me was like a healing salve nothing could permeate, but as soon as it was gone, all of my aches and pains were back. My whole body hurt all the time because of my pain but also some of Zach's and Will's. I couldn't tell what belonged to who anymore. I was starting to think it was only mine.

Thane waited outside the door.

"You need to be alone, huh?"

I said nothing but nodded as he stayed a couple feet behind me. I didn't want to go back to my room where Zach could be waiting, as the sun had gone down for the day. Instead, we walked to the west wing, and I found my favorite room to sit in.

I stopped at the doorframe. "Do you mind?"

"Not at all. You know I'm here if you need," Thane said.

I closed the door behind me. The room was themed in blue and held a fake fireplace and a vaulted ceiling with light-blue walls. When the sun was up, the entire room would be lit up by the turquoise-stained glass on the windows. It was the brightest room in the entire castle.

I collapsed into an armchair and finally let all the emotion fall out of me. Bitter tears welled, and I didn't stop them from falling. I sobbed into my hands. Why was this my fate? And why couldn't I pick something I wanted? The confusion was the worst part. I was tired. So tired. I thought of Sarah. She'd be upset if she knew the things I'd done. The things I wanted to do.

There was a knock but not at the door. Will rapped his knuckles on the edge of the fireplace. He'd made his way into the room, and I hadn't heard him.

"You all right?"

"Oh." I wiped my face. "Definitely."

"You're killing me right now. Feels like someone took a sledgehammer to my chest."

"I know. I'm sorry."

"Don't be sorry." He plopped down in a chair next to me. "You don't want me to get your brother? I'm sure it's only a matter of time till he finds where you're hiding."

"No. I'm fine. I'm good. Happy. Ascension is almost here. It's all good."

He raised a brow, waiting for me to tell him more.

"I was thinking about Sarah and about how disappointing all of this would be to her. How disappointing I'd be." I choked out the last words. "I don't know what I want. I know what everyone wants me to want. But not what I want."

"You know what you want. Do you really think you'd want to stay here if you had any option? No gun to your head or threats to your friends. You want to go home. Don't let them confuse ya."

"You're right. I want to go home. I don't want to go to Ascension. But none of it matters. It never matters."

"I'm going to tell you something, and I'm only telling you because I might be the only one in this world that has any experience in how you feel."

His words caught my attention. He wasn't looking at me but at the painting of Athena that hung over the fireplace. "This is only for you. I haven't told this story to anyone. Not even Thane knows. Kilian is only aware because he was around at the time."

"Okay." I waited patiently for him to speak.

"I was married once or, technically, engaged. Her name was Aurora. She was beautiful. I met her very early on in my life, shortly after I was changed by Kilian and joined The Legion. She was levelheaded. Smart. The better half and all that shit."

A knot gathered in my throat as I listened, understanding this story would not have a happy ending.

"She was fine with what I was, but she wasn't thrilled with the idea of being immortal. She wanted a family, and I couldn't give it to her. Plus, she was close with her sisters. They planned their entire lives together, they even wanted to get pregnant at the same time. She would never leave them. I was surprised when she said yes to my proposal, anyway. She said she'd change, but she needed time, and I couldn't change her myself because my blood is too far removed from the queen, so Kilian offered to change her. But she didn't like the idea. It only made her put it off more." William grit his teeth and looked to the floor. "A few months later . . . I killed her by accident. I waited too long to feed. I lost control. She lost too much blood, then she was gone. Back then, it wasn't as easy to get blood like it is now. I had to tell her sisters. I had to bury her. And when I did, I buried a piece of myself with her, I'll never get it back."

"I'm so sorry."

"I'm not telling you so you'll feel sorry for me. I'm telling ya because I wanted to give up back then. I haven't forgiven myself, and I never will, but I think you could. If anyone can get past this tragedy, it's you."

I remembered Sarah's last words with a twisting in my gut. *"It's okay."*

In the face of terror, she tried to comfort me.

"Me? Why me? Look at me. Seriously, I'm a wreck."

"Come talk to me when you're my age."

I laughed at the absurdness of that comment. We both knew where we'd be for the next two hundred years. Here. Stuck in this place. But his words lit a spark in my chest that warmed me for the first time in weeks. He hoped, therefore, I did too.

"You really think we can leave this place?"

"I think it's possible."

"Do you honestly think The Legion is coming to save us like Thane said?"

"I think . . . if they're coming, you won't be the reason they're here. I don't think saving you and your brother will be their main priority."

"Yeah, I figured."

"Where is that fighting spirit and all those pep talks, Calem?" William smiled. "Tell me, what do you want to do when we leave this place?"

"I don't know."

"You fuckin' know. What obnoxious shit would you and your brothers do?"

I took a deep breath and let in the possibility I hadn't allowed myself to think of. I told myself it was because I didn't want it anymore, but Will was right. It was all I wanted. I wanted it so bad it hurt to think it may never come true.

"I want . . . another Christmas. I don't care where. I want to watch my brothers open gifts, and I want to do all our old traditions. I want to see my mom again and tell her how sorry I am. I just want to be together. Anywhere."

"Well, no doubt, Luke Calem, you'll get there. Maybe sooner than you think."

When did William start to believe in me? When had I stopped?

"You really think so?"

"I do. You may have to go through Ascension, and I don't know what that will mean. But I think you'll navigate it like the golden boy you are. Don't give up just yet."

I think it was a compliment.

"Thanks, Will, this helped."

Thirty-Five

ZACH

No one warned me that Ascension was a rager. I'd prepared for a banquet—a boring one, but every inch of the castle was bathed in red light, disco balls, and melting candle wax.

"What the fuck?" I said as I descended the stairs in the main foyer. The staircase and foyer led to the main hallway that opened to the lawn.

The doors were open, and people—humans—were mingling there dressed up and being served finger sandwiches. I didn't know we had a working kitchen.

"This is for you, sir!" Connell was at my side dressed in some new fancier suit with an ornate flowered shirt beneath it.

"A party?"

"We've been waiting forever to celebrate you. We're so fortunate to see your Ascension. We wanted it to be a surprise."

"Oh, it is."

The entire entryway and the lawn were covered in crimson and people. Men and women of all ages looked at the decor with wide-eyed amazement. No children, though.

"Who are these people?"

"Most are close-client relationships and their families."

"Did you brainwash them all to be here?"

"No. Everyone wants to come celebrate with you. Well, I did bring in some tourists from the mainland. They think this is a super exclusive celebration of this castle's second centennial. A lot of them are history buffs who I found in online forums. Blood for the boys and you, sir."

Connell smiled despite his outright admission he lured humans here to drain them. Little fucker had cards up his sleeve. I bet that's why Ezra recruited him. His good-boy disposition and knowledge of the internet and modern-day technology would do wonders for them . . . for us.

"Don't start talking like that around my brother. He'll bolt in seconds."

Connell's eyes grew wide, and he pulled out a notepad and pen from his pocket.

"Really, sir? He won't like it?"

"No. He won't appreciate you wheeling humans in like cattle to be slaughtered. He prefers to drink from blood bags."

Connell scribbled something down with a bent brow. "What about you, sir? Do you mind?"

"What?"

"Do you care about the humans and the blood?"

I let his words marinate while he looked up from his pen and paper with an unblinking expression. My stomach sank, and heat flushed through my neck and cheeks.

"I—no. I don't care."

"I'll have to make some arrangements." He pulled out his phone and frantically typed something. His shoulders fell from his ears when he was done, then he was back to smiling. "Don't worry. Luke will be joining us shortly after meeting with The Glorious One to ensure the party is kept far away from the church. I was instructed to walk him over myself."

"Well, what am I supposed to do?"

"Have fun, sir!"

"I need to jailbreak Thane and Will."

"Already done. See!" He pointed across the crowd where Will was dressed in a true butler's uniform and holding a platter of deviled eggs.

"Oh no."

Judging from the scowl on Will's face, I could only imagine the seething anger. I think that was the source of heat in my chest that felt a little like heartburn.

"I know. But I did sneak him some cigarettes and got his chores switched to the garden for the next week because I know he likes plants."

"You did that for him?"

"For you, sir. I didn't want you to worry about them. It's your special night, and you should enjoy it to the fullest extent."

"Thanks."

I fought the urge to ruffle his hair like I used to do to Presley when he took a break from being a rambunctious shithead and was actually being nice.

Thane appeared beside me and placed a shot in my hand. His platter was all shot glasses. He winked at me after he bowed.

"I've heard Zach The Just needed a drink."

"The guest of honor always has a drink in his hand." Connell checked his phone. "Oh, I gotta go! I'll be right back."

I downed the shot of whiskey in my hand, then Thane handed me another. *I could get used to this.*

"I've been instructed to keep a drink in your hand all night."

"It's going to be a long night for you, then."

"Mr. Calem." A familiar voice caught my attention. Liam Brennan from the horse track made a beeline for me in the crowd.

He held out his hand, and I made sure to squeeze extra tight.

"Congratulations, sir. This place is magnificent. I'm honored to take part in the celebration."

"I'm sure you are." Me meeting people with alcohol in my system wasn't a great idea.

Liam's smile didn't break. "I'm excited for the future ahead. To you and The Divine Path." He held up his glass, and I held up my shot and downed it a second later.

He retreated into the crowd where a woman was waiting on him. She seemed to be human. These were normal people walking around in the most dangerous place in Ireland. I wondered how many would make it out alive. Another sip and I cared less. Not my problem really.

I'd need to make sure Luke didn't think too hard about it when he arrived.

Just as I thought it, my brother rolled in, mirroring my surprise as he realized what he walked into. He, too, had a drink in his hand in seconds. Those fuckers were thorough.

"From frat parties to . . . whatever this is," Luke said, sipping his beer.

"Cult parties. Much more sophisticated. We've leveled up, for sure. Think there will be an orgy?" I joked.

That made him crack a smile. "Is this all for us?"

"Take a wild guess."

His eyes lit up as he took another sip. Aine from the blood bank was dressed in a cocktail dress with her hair pinned up. She was on the other side of the room with an older man.

"Aine!" He waved her over with a big smile. "Can I get you anything?"

"You're the guest of honor. I think I should be askin' you that."

"Oh, right. It doesn't matter. I'll get you whatever you want."

She rolled her eyes but bit back a smile. Not surprisingly, my brother made her blush. His natural effect on women. Her attention landed back on me, and the smile faded. My natural effect on everyone.

"Pleasure to see you again, Mr. Calem. Congratulations to you both on your promotion."

That's what they were calling it. She scanned the walls and the wrapping staircase while she sipped her martini.

"I'm glad you came," Luke said.

"My father is here. Would you want to meet him?"

"Absolutely."

I let them chat while I greeted a few people. No one else I knew, but they knew me. The alcohol was working faster than it usually did. Damn vampires.

As the day went on, the thumping music grew louder and the lights shifted. Aine and her dad left as the sun disappeared and the crowd got wilder. Luke came back with his face flush and that electric excitement he got in the eyes from meeting new people. It was like hooking him up to a car battery.

"Enjoying your party?" Ezra grabbed my shoulder.

"It's been a while since we've been able to have a party like this." Sirius appeared beside him. "I hope you're both faring well and enjoying your time to relax."

"With someone putting a drink in my hand every five seconds, sure," I said.

I was already feeling the third. Or was I on my fourth? Luke had traded for something stronger and was swaying to the music.

"We want you both to enjoy your night. Worry free. There's nothing for you to look out for. Leave that to us."

"No one will go near the cathedral." Sirius looked directly at my brother. "She's safe."

When they left, Luke beamed.

"Wow, this is so fun. Come on. Let's go dance," he said.

I followed Luke into the middle of the foyer where a horde of people were standing. Everyone was pinned together and swaying to the music coming from the DJ. There was a strange sense of peace as we lingered in the crowd. It went from a party on the lawn to an all-out house party in the foyer with music that deafened me and vibrated me from head to toe. Somewhere in the music, the haze of the lights bathed the room in iridescence.

It could have been the alcohol, but I might have been a little bit happy.

All the faces in the crowd showed me the same expression. Flashes of teeth and chants of praise and encouragement. They wanted me there. It was working. Luke was having a great time too. There was no pain. Not even the slightest hint of ache in my bones.

Why had I fought this so hard? I was meant for this place. It had taken time like Ezra and Sirius said, but I was coming around. This place was perfect.

The bodies pressed against me made me feel warm again. I had new brothers and a new family to keep the cold of winter from ever freezing me again. One that would do anything for me.

That last shot did me in; I was floating in the crowd. Luke and I got lost. There were hands all over me, moving down my back, my chest, and my arms, but I didn't care. It felt good to be wanted. Worshipped. Godlike.

Luke's glow was back as he bounced up and down in the absolute surging wall of bodies. I wasn't worried about him, though. Not there.

Someone grabbed me in the crowd, and I let them take me to the corner of the room.

"This one, sir. Saved for you."

A man lay with his head resting on the back of a red velvet couch. He was smiling and laughing but moving slowly like he couldn't stand. My head was pounding from the alcohol. Somehow, I ended up on the couch.

"Drink, sir," a voice said. I didn't know whose.

I didn't need to drink blood. I'd downed a few blood bags only a few days ago, but I felt empty. Like I needed and wanted to consume. I grabbed the man by the collar and sank my teeth into his neck. It was good. So good. Drinking from a vein was dangerous for him but satisfying for me. There was something else mixed with his blood. The euphoria of it laced itself into my veins, and I drank deeper.

I pulled away with no recollection of how long I'd drank, but it didn't matter. I was full. Full of blood and alcohol and ecstasy. I'd had it wrong. I wasn't in hell. It was heaven. The effect of it was already moving into my body. I was free. I wanted to run anywhere my body would take me, but not to escape. No, I wanted to run in the halls and outside in the rain. I wanted to feel.

I stumbled back into the crowd. This time I felt every brush of skin against mine and the surge of the crowd with the music.

The flicker of a lighter flame caught my attention in my peripheral vision.

Will glared down at me from atop the stairs with a cigarette pressed between his lips.

I pushed my way through the crowd with loud protests and arms begging me to stay, but I had to know why Will was looking at me like that.

"Enjoying yourself?"

"What if I am?"

"I give Luke a pass because he deserves a night off out of hell, but you. Not so easily."

"Little too late to play the holier than thou card, isn't it? Am I not allowed to have fun?"

"You were fuckin' loving it. The attention."

"So what? It's better than what I normally get."

"This is it, then? You ascend and say fuck all to everyone?"

"Please tell me what I'm supposed to do. Luke and I are blood linked, and the only way to fix it is to ascend."

"That's what they want you to think! This. All of this is an illusion. They're manipulating you. They're brainwashing you, and I thought you knew that. But now I think you do know that but ya just don't care about anyone but yourself anymore."

"I'm happy for the first time in months, and I'm not letting Captain Buzzkill ruin it for me. Fuck off." Flipping him off, I hopped on the banister and slid down. I wouldn't let Will ruin my night. Not when it was finally getting good.

"Fuck you too," Will barked in my direction.

I was already tuning him out and blissfully falling back into the rhythm of the music and the sway of the crowd. This place was great. I let my new family take me with their hands in my hair and under my shirt. I'd let this place devour me.

I was finally home. Home sweet home.

Thirty-Six

ZACH

We retreated into our room for the night. The party continued on in the foyer, but Luke was ready to turn in. I collapsed into an armchair by the fireplace and loosened my tie. All the alcohol and whatever was in that guy's blood had worn off, and I felt empty again.

"Will's pissed at me."

"Is he mad because of the party?" Luke's smile vanished.

"Nah, he's not mad at you. Only me. Don't worry."

"He probably thinks we're giving up."

There was a pause as the fire cracked between us.

"Are we giving up?"

"You're Luke Calem, giving up isn't in your vocabulary. No, we're adapting."

"Right. And tomorrow, we'll officially be a part of The Guard. Truth is . . . I'm kind of relieved. It feels right. I've been brought here, and I can do that and be good at it. I'm glad you never let me give up."

"Me too."

I'd fought this place with every fiber of my being, but I couldn't fight fate and what we were destined to be. We'd been blinded by our own family and feelings. This was where we belonged. Will was wrong about me, and he was wrong about this. Luke could be happy here and so could I.

"No, I mean, all the times you didn't let me give up on life. Like when we found out about Sarah."

"Yeah, I remember."

"Do you wanna know why I didn't give up?"

"Because of Presley and Aaron." Saying their names out loud felt odd. I didn't feel connected to them anymore. At one point, they were the most important thing. Soon, their names would disappear like mine and all of our memories with it.

"No. Not them. I knew they'd be well taken care of."

"Oh, so it was pity for me?"

"Not pity. It was because I thought of you and about how I wanted to see how you turned out with my own two eyes. You believed you were good for nothing, and I was excited to see me prove you wrong, then I'd rub it in your face. So every time I considered leaving, I thought, no. Because I hadn't seen you realize it yet."

There was a long silence, and my eyes felt wet.

"You thought of me?"

"Yep." He smiled. "I'm still waiting on it."

He stayed for me. Not our younger brothers or Mom. But for me. Luke—the one person who would never give up on me. I'd have never survived our dad and childhood without him. Because he was the better half of me, and he stayed positive and happy when I gave up.

People in the movies usually resented their brothers who were better than them at everything, but nothing could ever make me hate him. He saved me as a kid, and every day his heart kept beating, he convinced me each day would be better than the last.

Truthfully, I didn't believe in any world where Luke didn't exist beside me. It was a world I didn't care to be in. Because Luke was a part of me that I feared died in childhood, and I was confident it had. And yet, I saw the thing I'd lost in him.

I thought I was doomed. All my brothers got that blond hair, and I got brown like my dad's. There was a phase of my life where I'd had Mom buzz it all off so I didn't have to look at it anymore. When I finally told Luke it bothered me, he spent every day for the next year reminding me of all the great people we knew with brown hair. He'd bring me clippings of magazines and encourage me to grow my hair out. All my life, my brother saw something in me no one else seemed to.

I couldn't live without my brother. I was confident if he went, he'd take all the goodness and light with him, and I couldn't make my own light no matter how hard I tried. No one else in my life could ever bring it back. Not my little brothers. Not my mom. Not even Ashley, who I'd have died for and still would. It was impossible to explain to anyone else. Maybe it was a twin thing.

My brother was my soulmate. We either existed together or not all.

"Fuck. Why would you tell me that now?"

"I don't know. Just felt like I needed to. I don't know what Ascension will bring, but I wanted you to know that I believe in you and that . . . I love you." He smiled with a small shrug.

"Nothing bad is going to happen. It's a blood ritual." I realized the irony.

"I know. But still. I need to know that you know."

"I know that you love me. And you know that I love you. We don't have to keep saying it."

Luke was the only person on the planet I didn't have a hard time saying I love you to, but did we need to keep saying it over and over? It was pretty clear. Someone could turn him into an inanimate object, and I'd drag him around with me, but that was so fucking sappy I would never say that thought aloud.

He laughed. "It doesn't give you that warm fuzzy feeling to hear?"

"I don't need warm fuzzy feelings."

"Sure you don't." His voice oozed sarcasm. "Speaking of, there's one more thing I need to do."

He got up from the chair and went for a dresser, then came back with a notepad and pen.

"Brace yourself, this is going to hurt."

"What are you doing?"

"Writing a letter to Presley and Aaron."

Luke sighed as he put the pen to paper.

"Why?"

"Because I need to say all the things I wished I'd said, and then I can let go. Then I can forget."

I nodded and watched him in the dim light of the fire. He wasn't kidding. That shit did hurt. Every word he added to that page, my stomach dropped. When Luke shed a tear, I closed my eyes and squeezed my nose. Sometimes, inflicting pain helped me stomach it. It wasn't enough. Tears fell from my eyes, and I rushed to catch them.

"Do you want to write one?"

"No." The answer to that question was easy.

I'd said goodbye to my brothers a long time ago and prepared myself silently for the day we'd have to leave. Even after Luke decided that last time we'd try to escape Blackheart, I knew it wouldn't work. It never did. It almost felt like relief to see Ezra come through the trees with my confirmation that all my theories were correct, and it was proved yet again when Ezra and Sirius showed up in the tunnels. This was our destiny, and I'd fought it for him because he deserved better.

But he could make a difference in our new family too. He could bring light to more people who needed him.

"What are you doing?" I asked as he moved toward the fire and held the paper close.

"I don't know. I don't want anyone to find it. Burning it seems right."

And with that, the piece of paper fell into the fireplace along with any lingering hopes of seeing our family again.

Dear Luke,

I'm kinda pissed at you. Why did you leave us here alone? Why didn't you tell me this is how bad you felt? How did you stand it? I don't get it.

You're the one person who was supposed to show up for me. I keep hoping you'll pop up at my window and take me with you. I could have come along. Maybe I could have helped you somehow and you wouldn't be so sad.

I'm angry. I didn't think I could get angry. But that has to be what this feeling is. Aaron is annoying. Kimberly is distracted, and there's nothing to do here other than sit around and be sad all the time.

I'm mad at everyone, but especially you. Because you should have told me. Isn't that what brothers do? Help each other through their pain? You taught me that and still chose to keep these secrets to yourself. I expect that from Zach, but not from you. Did you think I couldn't handle it? Do you think I'm the younger brother who can do nothing right? You're never going to answer me, and you're never going to get this stupid letter.

This pain in my chest keeps getting worse. Who is helping you? Do you have anyone there to make you laugh or distract you from your panic attacks? I would have been good at that I think.

I know you're both not okay. How the hell am I supposed to stay here knowing that?

P.S. Is Zach okay? Tell him I get why he punched walls back at the house now.

Love you forever,

Presley

Thirty-Seven

LUKE

My hair and my face were freshly shaven. I straightened my blazer in the mirror and snagged a piece of lavender from the vase on our table to breathe in its scent and steady myself. *This is right. We're safe here.*

We'd been hiding in our room all day knowing that they'd fetch us when it was time. Hiding in our room wasn't an unusual thing for us in childhood, so it came naturally there too. We talked about nothing important with the dread of the day closing in on us from every angle. I hadn't seen or heard from Will and Thane, and I assumed they would be allowed nowhere near Ascension.

"Ready?" Zach was at the door but stopped to pick up a letter that had been slid under.

"It says. Atrium. Five o' clock. Looks like we're right on time."

"Fate," I said under my breath.

As we made our way into the hall, the air was still and stale. No sounds echoed. The usual voices and movement were absent.

My brother and I kept quiet as we moved toward the atrium. I placed my hand on my chest to feel the uneven, hammering rhythm. I told myself it would be fine and this was what I'd been waiting for my entire life, but a sickness churned in my stomach as we neared the door. The sun and the moon carved into the wood stared back at me,

"Are you good?" Zach was biting his cheek, which meant he was as nervous as me.

I nodded, with my only assurance being that we would do it together. I couldn't do it alone. I'd probably run. But with my brother there, I could do anything.

"I'm ready."

With my hand placed firmly over the sun on the door, I pushed.

Everyone was in there with their knees on the ground and their heads pressed on the floor while the sun shone overhead, bathing the atrium in eerie beams of light. The queen was in the middle of the room, sitting on Her knees with a thick black covering over Her. Everyone surrounded Her, and their nearly silent prayers filled my ears.

Her eyes snapped up to me, and She beckoned us forward, and we sat in front of Her on two flat pillows. Ezra and Sirius were on either side of Her.

"What are we doing?" I asked Ezra next to me.

"We're waiting on the dark sun. Should be coming any minute. Close your eyes and await The Divine's message."

I closed my eyes and tried to focus on something other than my heart racing in my ears. My hands tingled, and I tried to get it to stop by opening and closing them.

I tuned into the whispering around me.

"Please bless us."

"You're worthy of praise."

"Show us the way."

Everything felt too real. Too permanent. Zach grabbed my hand and squeezed. It anchored me to the ground, and I focused on the feeling of his hand. When I peeked up at the skylight, the room was growing dim. The sun disappeared, and the darkness took hold.

She rocked back and forth, holding onto Ezra and Sirius for support. Something was about to happen.

My brother and I held onto each other. The room grew darker and darker, and the light of the candles littering the floor cast everyone in a warm glow.

She gasped. Her eyes opened to a pure white. Her breaths were labored, and She spoke quickly in a language I didn't understand. Latin. Sirius was scribbling it all down in a notebook. His hands moved in a vivid blur as the words poured from Her lips. What was The Divine's message? Would they tell us?

Her cries of anguish snapped my attention to Her. Black blood leaked from Her nose, then Her eyes too. She blinked, and the streams of black fell like tar on Her porcelain skin. Her gravity was waning in and out, and it made me feel sick. Like I was strapped to an amusement park ride rocking me back and forth without mercy.

I squeezed Zach's hand harder. The dark sun was above us. Her body shook, and She repeated the same sounds over and over again until She fell into me. I wiped the tears staining Her face. Her eyes were green, and

She was warm. Cecily was there somewhere. I didn't know how much of her, but I felt it in her rapid heartbeat.

It was dark, but every passing minute, it got lighter and lighter.

Ezra moved to stop me, but Sirius said, "No, let him."

I used the sleeve of my jacket to wipe Her face. She wasn't looking at me, and after every blink, the color left Her eyes. Every second, I was being sucked in. Like the queen was hooking Her very being into my skin. I wanted to kiss Her.

"Shall we move the ceremony to the cathedral?"

"Yes," She finally said. Her voice brimmed with strength, and Her eyes were back to a murky grayish white. "They're ready."

Thirty-Eight

Luke and I entered the cathedral as the last bit of sunlight left the sky and the moon took its place. The whole room was filled from front to back with no overhead light other than from the candles on the windowsills and the thousands of candles covering the floor.

Sirius and Ezra waited next to Her throne while She waited for us.

I wasn't nervous anymore. All of our pain was coming to an end. I stood at the altar ready for whatever was next. Luke was beside me, looking determined as ever. Sirius told me when we finally accepted our roles, we'd know true peace, and I was ready for something other than what we'd been going through.

Luke nodded to me, and we kneeled on the marble floor.

"Sirius, please read The Divine's word."

Sirius stood next to her, paper in hand, and read, "The sun and the moon shall herald in devastation and demise to all save for Thee. Embrace them together, for they were born into ruin and shall sow it upon all who cross their path."

Born into ruin.

Luke was looking at Her with devotion and love in his eyes. This was our path. He'd care for Her in that way he does, and I'd protect us all. I felt it in every fiber of my body. My brother and I were born for this moment. I'd had it all wrong. This place wasn't hell. It was home calling to us before we formed in my mother's womb. We belonged to Her. It finally made sense. All that gibberish Ezra and Sirius spoke over me. There was no way to mess this up, because this is who we were.

In seconds, Her hands pressed firmly to my cheeks. It was impossible to think straight when Her skin was on mine. I clenched my eyes shut, attempting to shield myself from Her, but when Her fingers trailed along my clenched jaw, I knew it was an invitation to let go. To finally give Her every part of me I'd been holding on to. She'd waited patiently for us. She knew us before we were born, and She'd waited for this moment for us to be together.

I opened my eyes. I was ready to stop Her waiting. She was the most enticing thing I'd ever seen in my lifetime. When Her breath hit my face, I didn't pull away.

She bit into Her own wrist and the strangest feeling ached in my chest. Ezra brought over a bowl filled with black liquid. Droplets of Her blood fell into the bowl.

"The blood of our brothers is with you," Ezra said

She moved in closer like She would kiss me, and I'd have let Her. I'd let

Her do whatever She wanted. A second later, Her teeth were in my neck. I didn't fight as She took from me. The world slowed, and Her fingers knotted my hair.

Take it all. Take everything.

The world blurred when She pulled away. I felt slow and human. Empty. Those perfect fingers reached to wipe Her lips, then mingle my blood in the bowl, and She spread the wetness over my wound.

"We're one," She said.

Before I could manage the chaos in my head, She bit Her wrist again to drink and fill Her mouth with blood. My lips parted with Hers, and my blood ran cold as the coolness of Her blood filled my throat. She emptied all that blood into my mouth with a bloody kiss and there were hushed gasps and praise.

Nothing in the world mattered. Not all the assholes watching. Not the future. Not even my brothers. I was gone. Truly gone. Lost in euphoria while Her blood stitched me back together and filled me. So I savored every last drop until I couldn't feel my body anymore. I let go until Zach Calem no longer existed. Just Her. She was pure ecstasy in my veins.

I didn't know what was next, but I was certain I'd never be the same, and as She pulled away to do the same to Luke, I knew something in me had changed because I wanted him to follow me into the same madness. To drink Her blood so we could be lost together. This fucked-up alternate reality was mine, and there was no more holding back.

Thirty-Nine

Who was I? That was my first thought when She pulled away from me. Surely, I had a name, but I couldn't take my eyes off Her as She walked away from me. My heart yearned for Her, but She was only feet away and wasn't looking at me . . .

I'm yours, My Love.

Her voice was in my head.

How could I live like this? If She wasn't touching me or looking at me, how could I function? What was my name again?

"Luke." Ezra grabbed my arm, and the pressure brought enough blood to my brain again where I could focus. His eyes locked with mine,

315

demanding attention.

He was looking for some kind of answer from me, but I looked to Her instead. Catching the tail end of Her dress as it dragged on the floor.

He shook me. "Look at me."

I fought the irritation climbing its way up my throat and the urge to push him off, but he didn't look willing to let me go until I complied.

"Are you okay?"

I steadied myself against him and used his voice to help me fight through the fog.

"Yeah," I spoke in barely a whisper.

Where was She going? She wouldn't—

"Focus on me. Get a hold of yourself." He had my full attention now.

Zach was next to me now, shoulders down and more carefree than normal.

"I've got it." I patted Ezra's hand, and he relaxed. I wasn't sure why he cared or why he'd be worried. There wasn't anything else to worry about. We were home.

Zach didn't skip a beat as he tore me away from Ezra. He laid his hand over my shoulder, and as we descended the stairs, I realized how long I'd been in my dazed state. The room was empty. All other members had funneled out of the cathedral and could be heard celebrating on the lawn outside.

"We're going out to celebrate at the bar in town. Everyone's going," Zach said. My body buzzed from the feeling of Her blood. I looked behind me where Sirius was wrapping Her wrist, suddenly hit with the most powerful fit of worry.

"Sirius will be here with Her. You don't need to worry," Ezra said. He was too good at reading me.

I'll be fine, My Love. Enjoy your time.

She looked over at me with a smile, but Her lips didn't move. She was in my head this time. Loudly and without prayer. I followed Zach into the driveway where two new Scramble Ducati bikes were parked.

"No way," Zach said.

"What is this?"

"A gift." Ezra was smiling too.

"Holy shit," Zach said.

I lifted a leg over to straddle the bike, then ran my fingers along the midnight-black finish.

"You're both free to travel as you please over the island. Figured why not in style?"

"Thank you," I said, running my hand over the handles. I couldn't believe it. Motorcycles were strictly forbidden in the Calem household because Mom was a nurse who had seen way too much, but we weren't human anymore, and now I felt like more than a vampire. We were The Guard.

I turned it on and listened to the roar of the engine. It shook me to my core, only adding to the buzzing jolting my veins from Her blood. I was a god.

Two black sports cars pulled up behind us, and Henderson rolled down the window. "Lead the way, sir!"

"You heard him." Zach gave me a wicked smile and handed me a helmet.

I slammed down my visor and we were off, tearing through the hills. The bikes slid and swerved in the dirt, but we were invincible. Untouchable by anyone or anything. I gripped the handle harder, and my bike jolted forward. We were flying in the infinite darkness.

Zach followed me. When I turned to look, he removed his hands from the handlebars and pounded his chest.

We'd entered a new level. Complete euphoria. And it was better than I'd ever imagined it could be.

We reached the town quickly. I wanted to keep riding all night along the dark hills, but people had to sleep, and the bikes were loud.

"Let's get so drunk we can't see straight," Zach said with a crooked smile.

Plus, Zach had a point. I was ready to celebrate this momentous occasion. It was without a doubt the hardest and biggest goal I'd ever achieved. Who needed to graduate college anyway?

We stepped into the little dive bar. It was packed full of bodies. As we entered, the whole bar seemed to notice. It was likely the only place to go on a night like tonight. Probably a Saturday. The whole thing was filled with the stench of old rotting wood, deep mahogany walls, and booths.

"I second that." I chuckled.

I was positively floating. We headed over to the counter first.

"Two whiskeys, two shots, and two beers," Zach said.

The bartender scoffed at us. "Got a card for that tab?"

Ezra stepped up behind us and pulled up the sleeve of his suit, revealing his tattoo. "It's on the house."

"I'm sorry, sir. My apologies. I'll get that right away."

The crowd surged around us, and the other members funneled in. Everyone one of them bowed their heads in acknowledgment. Connell was the only one brave enough to come and speak with us.

"I'm here for whatever you two need tonight. Or any night. Say my name and I'm there. Ascension was so amazing, wasn't it? Wow, you must feel so good right now."

"Are you a little jealous, Connell?" Zach said.

"Oh, of course, sir. But you were born set apart. I could never compare. It doesn't bother me."

"Go have fun. You don't need to follow us around."

"Why not? Let him serve." Zach grabbed his drink and eyed Connell with a vacant expression.

"No. We're okay." I grabbed my beer and shooed him before my brother could protest. I wondered how long I'd need to stay. I wanted to go home to Her. We'd been separated before, but the wall was gone, and I felt that bond with Her pulling on me. I would go to Her as soon as we were home and wouldn't leave Her side.

Zach scanned the room. No doubt looking for the prettiest girl in the bar. I spied the girl in his line of sight sitting on another man's lap. She was surrounded by a group of men, who didn't look friendly. They all presented scowls in our direction as if they knew exactly who we were.

"Dibs," Zach said, crunching on the ice from his drink.

I chuckled. "That's good with me."

The ice shook in my glass, and I turned to set it on the bar. How he thought about anyone but the queen, I didn't understand.

Until I saw her.

A girl with highlighted warm-brown hair and green eyes. Sarah. She looked like her. Same hair. Same height. Same smile. I forfeited the air in my lungs.

"Don't even think about it," Zach said.

"I don't know what you're talking about."

"Bullshit. Leave her alone. This is supposed to be fun. A new chapter."

"Just . . . how? Look at her."

I'd tried not to imagine what she'd look like now. A little older. Bolder bone structure. I wondered if she would have grown into her feet. She thought they were too big, but she was perfect.

"Doesn't matter. We're letting go, remember? We're supposed to be celebrating."

He was right, but oddly enough, I wanted to keep staring at this girl. I forgot where I was and sipped my drink in silent admiration. She laughed, and my heart pounded harder. It was the way the girl's eyes lit up and her dimpled cheeks flushed. I wanted to talk to her. I'd almost forgotten the sound of Sarah's laugh. It was all coming back. All that I'd once wanted, and all the things about Sarah that made me happy.

A feeling fluttered through my chest like butterflies. It had been so long since I'd felt that feeling, and maybe I needed to trust my gut on this one. The pain in my chest was gone, and I was free to feel. Her cheeks sparkled in the dim lights of the bar, and she caught my eyeline and smiled a toothy grin.

Maybe I needed to follow the butterflies.

Forty

ZACH

The girl was drop-dead gorgeous, with warm-tan skin and long black hair that went to her ass, and I wanted her. No, I *needed* her on my lap, whispering in my ear. I wanted her under me screaming my name, but more than that, I wanted to bite her.

I was full of blood, but a yearning bubbled in my chest since drinking the queen's blood. Then I could go back to the castle and play house, but I wanted warm flowing blood in my throat first.

I'd have gone right over and taken her if Luke wasn't looking at some random girl like that. With the puppy dog eyes and the longing. In his defense, she was the spitting image of Sarah. I didn't believe in doppelgänger shit, but the resemblance was uncanny, and she was surrounded

321

by girls laughing and giggling. Sarah was always surrounded because she was magnetic like that. Not in the way people talk about dead people like they were the fucking second coming of Christ. No. Sarah had that same magic gene Luke had that brought people to her.

I tried to focus on my best memories of Sarah. All those days in homeroom and watching her cheer. Glancing behind me at Luke and her giggling in the back of the classroom. But all that was coming to mind was the image of her sobbing in the basement before she was killed. I chugged my drink at the memory resurfacing. If I drank heavy and long enough, could I permanently erase that memory? Only one way to find out.

It occurred to me suddenly, I should have been on my ass with pain. My own and Luke's from seeing the girl, yet I felt nothing. Comfortably numb. I wasn't even a drink in. The alcohol numbed the pain from the bond, but not that much. She hadn't been lying about everything. Ascension changed something.

We stood there drinking for a few minutes while I soaked in every curve of my girl's body. I was a certified asshole now. If I wanted to eye-fuck a girl in the bar, why shouldn't I?

I didn't like biting women, but I was confident that I wouldn't hurt her, and I might even get her to enjoy it. It was all reckless, but I was riding a high I hoped would never let me come down. Nothing could stop me. Not that guy trying to keep her pinned down in his lap or any of his buddies either.

She'd seen me too, and she wasn't looking away. She wanted me to come over. Not to rescue her. Oh no. She wasn't a damsel. She'd laugh in my face as I got my ass kicked by these guys. But she'd want me to try. At least that's what that hungry look in her eye told me. Her hands moved down the guy's legs and into his lap, and she whispered something in his ear, all while staring at me.

I needed the taste of the queen out of my mouth, then I could think straight. Despite the barrage of drinks, I felt Her, and this girl wasn't drunk. She was a bitch even when sober, and I liked it. I let that word sit in my head a bit. Bitch. I could call girls anything I wanted now. With no mom to lecture me and conscience to speak of, I was turning a corner. A new fuck-boy corner.

I hadn't tried to be intimate with a girl since the Halloween party, and that went to shit.

I was certain if I took this girl to a hotel, I wouldn't have the same problem as I had at the party. Back then, I was like a burning exposed nerve. I felt so far away from that version of myself. Which was the way it should be. One day when my brain had rotted to hell with The Family, I'd forget them completely. I'd forget all about how it felt to be a big brother. I'd forget their names.

Luke and I could talk about it all like a bad memory. *"Remember when we used to be the shittiest big brothers ever and ruined the lives of everyone we came in contact with? Thank god that's over."*

We'd have a few laughs. Shoot the shit at how long it took us to come to the genius conclusion that we didn't belong there. We'd get new names. The name of Zach and Luke Calem would die, and the whole world would be better off for it. It was better this way. Fate was better than anything I'd ever had in Blackheart.

I turned my attention back to the girl. I wanted to feel her blood in my veins so bad I was swaying, and she wanted me to fuck her into the headboard. Seriously, what was stopping me? I caught her eyeline again. Sitting on the guy's lap, she sipped on a martini and popped the olive into her mouth.

Luke would be fine. I wasn't his keeper.

"Don't wait up for me," I called to Luke as I left him at the bar and made my way over to them.

"Can I help ya?" A man with a thick accent stared up at me, pulling her closer to him.

"No. Not really." I reached my hand out to her and leaned next to her ear where he could hear. "But you can. Dance with me."

He tightened his grip on her waist.

"I'd take your arm off her if you want to keep it."

Though he and all his buddies looked like they wanted to try and beat the shit out of me, they didn't. In fact, none of them even mumbled a word of protest. Everyone in this town looked at me like the boogeyman. I could get used to that.

I pulled her closer on the dance floor filled with mostly drunk girls, and wasted no time grabbing her hips and digging my fingers into them. She smelled of expensive perfume. We danced with her ass on my dick, and I moved her hair so I could feel the pulse in her neck.

"You're a good dancer," she said, leaning back into me.

I was not a good dancer, but making a girl want to fuck me was an easy task.

"Is that your boyfriend?"

She wrapped her arms around my neck, and I made sure he got a good view as I grabbed her ass.

"No. Yes. It's complicated."

"I'm good with complicated."

I pressed her back against the pillar, and her eyes widened. With a smile, I went for her neck, nipping her skin and barely holding myself back from biting her in a room full of people. It wouldn't matter if I did. If they all went screaming for the door, someone would stop them. It would be quick for them all. I pulled away, wondering if I'd truly contemplated mass murder to drink one girl.

Give into it, Darling.

My body stilled. I'd heard the queen in my head before, but never like that. Not without praying.

"What's wrong? Do you prefer a girl that likes to hurt you?" she said as she pulled at my hair. Hard. I pushed her into the pillar with my hips.

Drain her. Show everyone who you are.

Fuck. I couldn't wait anymore. As I led her to the hallway, the muffled sound of my boots hitting the hardwood was barely audible with the music. I wasted no time pushing her to the wall and kissing her. She was so hot I couldn't wait.

I traced the pulse on her neck with my tongue, but I hesitated. I didn't want her to panic or scream. I wanted her to feel good. Safe.

Ah fuck.

"I'm going to bite you. But it won't hurt. Does that freak you out?"

"Everyone who lives on this island knows the rumors of this place. Men coming from that castle that need blood. It doesn't scare me."

"You like dangerous guys."

She laughed. "Honey, you aren't dangerous. And I know many. They don't ask before they put marks on me."

I scoffed. "You don't know the type of person I am"

"I know every man in this place turned on a dime as you walked through that door. You're important. What are you? Some prince?"

"I'm not a prince," I growled. Kissing her neck again, I bared my teeth as I went to bite. She gasped in fear.

I froze. "What?"

Her laugh echoed in the empty hall. "I told you."

"You're fucking with me."

"Proving my point."

I pulled at the hair on the back of her neck and brought her neck to my lips. "You shouldn't have done that."

I sank my teeth into the pulse at her neck. The pressure was the most euphoric, but I couldn't drink for long. I savored the taste, hoping to drown in her, but no matter how long I drank, I only tasted my queen.

Drain her, Darling. Then come home to me.

Leave me alone.

I couldn't believe the queen was in my head, and I couldn't believe I was talking to Her. More than that, I couldn't believe I wanted to. I *did* want to go home to Her. The night was young and there was nothing holding me back from having Her anymore.

I pulled away. "Are you too drunk to go to a hotel with me?"

"No. And we can go to my place. I assume yours is off-limits."

"Yeah, something like that."

My queen would not be happy about it. I don't know why I wanted to do it.

As soon as I opened the door to go back into the main part of the bar, Connell appeared beside me.

"Connell, what the fuck are you doing?"

"I've been instructed to follow you."

"Fine, but you have to stay outside."

I passed by Luke who was giving heart eyes to Sarah's doppelgänger. Luke was grown. He didn't need me to tell him what to do. He could sort it out.

We stepped out into the cold and walked toward her car parked in the lot. I couldn't help but overhear a scuffle.

"You hear me, bitch?" American accent. A man towered over a woman with his hand raised to strike. "Answer me."

At the first sound of her cry, I was there. My body moved on its own. I stopped his hand, and pushed him away from her. It took all my restraint not to crush his head in one swipe. No more brothers around to give me the puppy eyes or the "be good" speech. I wasn't good, and he should be scared.

I slammed his teeth into the car door.

"How does that fucking feel?"

That's it. Show them who they should fear.

Connell watched like he was about to jump in front of a bullet for me. Next to him, a girl sobbed into her hands.

I twisted his arm back until I heard a satisfying crack. "That's for making her cry."

My blood pumped in my ears, and every cry and scream that came from him sent me further into a frenzy. He should suffer. He should have cried out and asked for help, because no one would come for him. No one who could stop me.

Another twist at the elbow, and his bones cracked again. "That's for being a fucking asshole. You're lucky I don't kill you right now."

Kill him. Make him suffer.

I grabbed his other arm and placed it in the crack of the door and slammed it shut. His screams carried into the night. He deserved worse.

"Please stop. Please," the man whimpered in a pathetic puddle on the ground.

"Tell her you're sorry."

"I'm sorry. It won't happen again."

"You live with this asshole?" I turned to her.

She nodded.

"If you so much as a mumble in her direction, I will personally come and gouge your fucking eyes out before I have your head. Do you understand?"

"Yes, yes!"

"Good. Because you're moving out. You're giving her the place and all the stuff." I kicked his kneecap, and he collapsed. He wouldn't be walking anytime soon. "Understand?"

"Yes," he moaned.

There was a high to satisfying the need to release the anger boiling in my blood. I'd almost forgotten why I'd ventured outside.

My Darling, you're magnificent.

The queen was tugging on my heartstrings, beckoning me home, but I wasn't done running.

"Connell, make sure this guy is watched."

He nodded with a big smile.

I looked back at the girl from the bar. She was paler than before as she eyed me with her car keys in hand.

"You scared?"

She hesitated longer than I expected her to.

"Get in."

Forty-One

LUKE

I went to the bathroom while the room was spinning. I'd drank too much. Drinking with my brothers was fun, but drinking alone in my current state only made me feel haunted. I adjusted my coat, then I was lost again, thinking of Sarah and of that night. It had to be because of that girl at the bar.

I stared at myself in that mirror, and I was transported back to senior prom.

I could feel Sarah's hands on me and the sweet candy scent of her skin.

"No, Luke, what do you want?"

"I don't know . . ."

"Not what your brothers want or what anyone else wants. What do you

want?"

Her hands were on my coat, pulling me till we were chest to chest. There were a million other places we could have been. Instead, we were alone together in her childhood bedroom. Her dad worked nights. The room was dark, besides the moonlight from the window and the glow from the stars on the ceiling.

What did I want? Did it matter? There was no want. Only what had to be done. What should be done.

"Luke?"

"Sarah. I can't."

"Just answer the question. Don't think about anything else. What do you want?"

Her hair was peppered with glitter and her face painted with glitter stars over her freckles. She was fit to be a queen. I twirled her blue butterfly necklace between my fingers, and our breaths synced. She wore a short iridescent lilac dress, and I tried not to think of her as anything other than a friend. But it was impossible when she looked that beautiful.

"I want . . . "

It never mattered what I wanted. I didn't get to choose things like that.

"It's okay to want something for yourself."

Towering over her, I let my hand fall to her chest where her breath grew deeper. This time I kissed her. Long and slow until her back hit the wall. My hand stopped at the zipper on the back of her dress.

What did I want? I wanted to be normal for a night. I wanted Sarah to be mine.

"I want you," I whispered. *"You're all I've ever wanted."*

In seconds, her dress was on the floor and my suit was crumpled next to it. It was our first time. That night was meant for her, and though it was painful to remember, it was one of my favorite memories.

The only person I ever told was Zach. Had that night never happened, she'd never have been targeted. I should have stuck to my gut. I shouldn't have let things go that far, or she'd be alive. It was my fault.

Stop. Luke. Stop.

Steadying myself on the edge of the bathroom sink, I willed myself into the present with the stench of alcohol in the air and the puke in the next stall. That Luke didn't exist. All the glamour of the night had faded away and all that was left was me. I slammed my fist into the mirror, and it shattered with a satisfying crack.

I forced myself out the door and back into the bar. My brother was gone. He'd let go. It was my turn. I spotted the girl again with her bright smile and her chirpy voice while she laughed with her friends.

"I wouldn't do that." Ezra was next to me again, sipping on his drink.

"I'm only going to talk to her."

"No, you aren't."

"Yes, I am. And why can't I? I didn't see you lecturing my brother."

"You're not Zach. Your path will be different than his."

We shared everything, including the fate of The Guard. Why not this too?

"Who do you think takes my place when I die? That's you."

"And what does this have to do with that? Don't I get a say in what I want to do?"

He sighed. "It's not a good idea."

"Thanks. I'll note it." I walked past him and took my last shot from the bar. A short conversation would hurt nobody. That's all I wanted. I was properly free. Free from any responsibility, and I couldn't remember the last time that had ever happened.

She saw me coming and smiled when I lost my footing and had to steady myself on the wooden pillar.

"Hi. I'm Luke."

Her friend grabbed her arm and whispered in her ear, but she waved them off.

"Hi Luke." She examined me for a moment. "You have kind eyes."

The glitter around her eyes danced in the lights. I was taken back. Her green eyes were soft and full of life.

"You do too." I chuckled.

I didn't have girlfriends, and being with Sarah was easy. I was good at friends, but flirting wasn't my strong suit. Luckily, I didn't need to.

"Do you want to dance?" she asked, and with no drink in her hand, she seemed to be sober.

A dance wouldn't hurt.

"If you'll have me." I held out my hand, and she smiled and curled her hand around mine.

A silver butterfly ring on her finger gleamed in the light. My stomach sank.

"Are you okay?"

I shook off the tightness in my chest and nodded. The time disappeared as I spun her on the dance floor, and she flowed easily with me. She was a natural. I dipped her and we spun in an endless flurry until she needed to catch her breath. That was my que to dip out.

"Where are you going?"

"You should go with your friends," I said.

"Did I do something?"

"No. No. It's me. I'm messed up. You don't want anything to do with me. I promise."

Her eyebrows dipped. "You shouldn't talk about yourself like that."

She grabbed a receipt from the bar and scribbled her number on it. "Call me if you ever need someone to talk to. My sisters say I'm a good listener."

"O-okay."

She kissed me on the cheek before rejoining her friends, and the unfamiliar flutter of happiness warmed my chest. Ordering another drink, I tried to entertain myself. I wanted to talk to Zach, but he'd probably gone home with that girl. The bar patrons had grown sparse, so I tried to spot anyone else I knew. The other members must have started home. I wasn't tired, but something in my stomach made me feel restless. The girl left too, and I gave it only ten more minutes before I decided to go home. My new home where I hoped She'd be happy to see me.

Leaving the bar, the cold wind hit my face. I stood frozen.

Ezra was waiting for me with a knife to the girl's throat. Tears stained her cheeks, and glitter was all over his hands.

"What—"

Before I could finish, the spray of blood from her neck hit my face.

That warm feeling was back, and my ears were ringing again. The night disappeared, and suddenly, I wasn't in my body anymore. I was trembling but didn't feel like myself anymore. I wasn't Luke. This wasn't happening. I couldn't move.

"I'm sorry." Ezra's voice felt far away as I stumbled back into the wall.

My numb hands moved up to wipe the blood from my eyes. I was covered in it. Hot stickiness clung to my skin. His voice was pulling me back to the present, but I didn't want to go. Some of the other members picked up her body, then cleaned up the scene.

The panic spread as my chest tightened. I couldn't even ask for Zach.

I didn't want his help. I didn't want him to see this and try to make me feel better. Ezra inched closer to me, and my body crashed to the ground. Though it didn't feel like my body anymore. I moved away to shield myself from him.

"D-don't hurt me. Please. Please." The voice coming from my lips wasn't mine.

"Oh Luke, I'm not going to hurt you. I promise." Ezra's eyes softened as he took another step toward me. He leaned down till he was eye level, and I tried to squirm away. *I should run*, I thought, but I was frozen.

I hated myself and my weakness at that moment. I should have been able to fight it or stand up for myself, but all I could do was sit on the ground and shake. I was so pathetic.

Ezra's hands were on my face as he used a handkerchief to wipe the blood. "You'll be okay. It's okay. I'm sorry. I tried to warn you. She ordered me to kill anyone you touched tonight. She said you'd be tempted to stray from The Divine Path."

I said nothing. I wanted to push him off me, but his touch was the only thing that didn't hurt. My gaze settled on the red pooling at my shoes, and the sob left my throat. What was my body count up to now? The number of people's lives I'd ruined was in the double digits and climbing. This girl probably had a family and friends who would have to live with the reality that she was gone, killed brutally, and for what? For me?

I continued to cry. Hating myself for every single tear that fell. I didn't deserve to cry for her. It happened because of me, because I was wrong.

"I'm going to help you. You're going to get through this."

I hated him, and I hated what we were. There was no positive in this. For the first time in my life, I couldn't find one or a solution that would make any of it go away.

"I-I didn't . . . I can't." I didn't know what I was saying. It would have been better if he'd left me there to cry in the dirt till sunrise.

"I'm going to help you. I promise. It won't always be like this." Ezra grabbed my head and laid it on his shoulder.

Then I finally came undone. A sob broke through my throat, and I buried my head into his shoulder. I hated us, but he was all I had in that moment, and that gave me the hope that days would get better. I hated The Family, yet loved them all dearly at the same time. I was broken, and he was the only thing keeping me from severing completely. My chest burned, ached, and screamed for my attention.

"Shhh. It's okay. You'll be home soon. You'll be close to Her, and you'll feel good as new."

I relaxed a little at the thought. A confusing mix of emotions made my head spin. I was glad Zach had a different path. I wanted him away from Her, but I wanted him to protect Her. I wanted Ezra to get off me, but his shoulder was warm in the cold night, and I needed *something*. Anything to make the pain in my chest stop.

He caressed my head, the way a dad comforts a child, and I let go. Slowly, I returned to my body. I let him calm me and let the image of going home to Her bring me comfort. I needed no one else but Her. I could get through it if I had Her. It was my fault, and I couldn't remedy it, but I could devote myself entirely to Her. Show Her there was no one else I'd rather be with. Then we could pass into eternity. I'd never be apart from Her, and a tragedy like that would never happen to anyone else ever again.

Forty-Two

I didn't remember the car ride back to the castle. Only the hum of the car engine and the hot air on my face. Ezra's car smelled like leather polish, and that was the only thing keeping me from fully dissociating. Nothing felt real. I was wondering if I had died senior year when I got shot. I hadn't seen it coming. Much like this. That made more sense than everything that followed.

I should be more positive.

My familiar inner voice tried to level with me, but did it matter anymore? What was the point? Zach was fine. Will and Thane were alive. That counted for something.

I blinked, and we were in the castle. Walking like my shoes were filled with lead, I couldn't feel my feet hitting the carpet.

Ezra dragged me beside him, and I tried not to focus on the stickiness of the blood on my shirt or the smell of it.

I knew where he was taking me. I felt Her in my blood as I got closer.

She was in Her room wearing a silk nightgown, and Her hair was braided out of Her face. I'd never seen it braided.

I expected Her to smile at my state or to tell me it was my own doing and I deserved to be hurt, but She didn't. She stroked my cheek with a furrowed brow.

"He'll need a change of clothes. Will you send for them?"

Ezra nodded.

"Would you like to shower?" She said.

I couldn't look at Her. I shook my head. I was already cold.

"I'll leave them by the door." Ezra nodded. The door clicked, but I didn't check to see if he was gone.

She guided me to the bed. Was it possible to lose myself in Her, then She'd save whatever had broken in me? I could be good. I could be the person She wanted. It was my fault, but I could mend it. She'd be merciful. I'd strayed from Her path, but I could do better. I'd do it all. Appease the queen and save everyone else.

The pieces of my former self were scattered so irretrievably I didn't even know how to pick them up again, and for the first time, I didn't want to.

She helped me with my shirt, and a few seconds later, She wiped my face with a cloth. I stopped Her.

"You don't have to do that. You shouldn't."

"Let me take care of you."

A lump gathered in my throat. "No. I don't want you to. I should be taking care of you." As if I could move.

When I looked at Her, I knew I was staring at something otherworldly. Whatever She was, She couldn't love me.

"You don't have to take care of everyone else all the time." She stroked my cheek, and I was crushed under the weight of Her words. "What is it, Love?"

"Don't." I buried my head in Her lap, and sadness swelled like a rushing wave. "Please don't pretend anymore. I can't take it."

Or do. Because it's all I wanted. For Her to care about me and make this pain end. I was crying again and didn't think anyone would ever be able to stop it. No one was coming for me. She was all I had left that made any sense, but She didn't love me. It wasn't real.

She stroked the hair resting on my forehead and pulled my face up to meet Hers. "I'm yours. There's no need to pretend."

I couldn't stop crying. Broken things leaked, and I was open and cracked. Empty and unable to ever be filled again. The pain in my chest was at an all-time high and was killing me.

"Are you upset because you couldn't be with the girl? Because I can give you anything you need . . ."

Her lips caressed my neck, slow and tender.

With two hands on Her shoulders, I pushed Her away. I never wanted Her to stop touching me, but I didn't want Her like that. I did but I didn't. Not when I felt so cold and numb. I knew it would leave me feeling more empty.

"Would you like to see her?"

"Who?

"Cecily. Your friend. She seems to make you happy."

"Y-you could do that?"

She nodded. "The eclipse has made me very strong. She won't be out for another moon cycle. I think she'd enjoy seeing you."

I wiped my face.

"But . . . won't you be angry at me?"

"Why would I, My Love? We are one. You belong to both of us now. I'd like to do whatever will make you happy."

Trust me, My Love.

Her voice sounded in my head, and I pressed Her forehead to mine.

"Okay."

She leaned in to kiss me with Her cold lips. The queen was ice on the heat of my skin, and it burned. When She pulled back, Her irises were flushed with emerald, then her eyes softened.

Cecily immediately pulled me into an embrace. "Luke. I'm so sorry."

"Why is this happening?" I pulled her face into my hands and was comforted by the flush of her skin on mine.

I didn't understand it. I didn't know her. Our time together was built on fleeting minutes and terrible circumstances, but I cared about her. I wanted to save *someone*, even if it couldn't be me. And her touch was soft and sure and comforting.

"I can't help. I'm sorry."

"Tell me what to do. Tell me how to help you. Tell me how to save us, and I'll do it."

"I can't."

"But I can do it. I know I can. Don't you believe me?" Another tear fell.

She kissed me while wrapping her hands in my hair and pulling me into her. It was a hard pull and a different, desperate kind of need. It wasn't Her. It wasn't Her gravity. This was better. This was affection and warmth. It was *real*. She burned hot beneath my fingertips. My tears stopped falling. I focused on the taste of her tongue and the warmth of her breath.

"You can't save me. Stop fighting. Please. It'll hurt less if you stop."

When she pulled away, tears were rolling down her cheeks.

"But you said . . . "

"I know. But I don't want you to keep getting hurt. Please."

"Are you crying for me?"

"Yes. Please. Don't fight. Ask Her to help you, and She will."

I was hurting them. Cecily. My brother. Everyone. Because I refused to let go. Because I was fighting. I was tired of hurting people with my brokenness. My weakness prevented me from saving them. There had to be a different way.

"I don't know how." I kissed her, and I kissed her again. "Tell me how."

"Just let go, Luke. Let go."

Her lips were on mine again. Every press of her lips on my cheek and my neck had me falling. Faster and faster. I pulled at her hair. Her skin. Her face.

Falling. I was falling. And it felt *so good*.

I'd let go with no intention of ever grabbing the ledge again. Falling was peaceful.

I'd finally let go and hardly recognized the feeling of leaving the ledge. As soon as Cecily left, I felt the pull of Her. I kissed Her and fell into Her like it wouldn't kill me.

"Help me." The words were a prayer. "Help me. Please. I'll be good. I'll pray. I'll try anything."

"My Love, I'll take your pain from you, and you'll never have to worry about it again. Would you like that?" She used Her thumb to stroke my cheek.

It would have been easier if She was mean to me. If She was the monster everyone seemed to think. But to me, She wasn't. She was more.

I nodded.

Is this what I'd wanted all along? All those nights spent in pain led me to Her bedroom. It could mean only one thing. She was right all along.

I always wanted my life in ruins. It was my destiny to have Her lips on mine. To be so entangled with Her I'd never get free. That's why it never worked with Sarah. Sarah's death was only a direct consequence of trying to strive for anything other than what was mine. And She was mine. The want that mattered.

She was the gravity and the sun simultaneously pulling me in and dragging me down, but I welcomed the euphoria of falling, even at knowing the ground was coming. She was my queen now and forever.

I was falling. Down. Down.

Forty-Three

The sun was almost up when I snuck into my room. The night, though fun, hadn't made me forget about Her in the slightest. I'd been itching to get home and see Her. Not that I'd ever tell Her that. She probably knew though. She was in my head. I wondered what it meant. Could She hear my thoughts? Was it a one-way street? She seemed able to tell what I was doing, which made it that much more enjoyable to piss Her off.

When I opened my bedroom door, a dark figure was sitting next to the fireplace. Will was alone and waiting.

"Someone let you out of your cage?"

"Where the fuck were you?" He was instantly on his feet.

"Should you really be asking me that? Remember, *I'm* the chosen one."

"Fuck you. Tell me."

"I was fucking a girl. Happy?" *Happy. What a strange word.*

Will covered his face with his hands and sighed. "You weren't with Luke?"

"Uh, fuck no. I wasn't with Luke."

William stared at me with a clenched jaw, like he was trying to gather what to say and simultaneously set me on fire. I wasn't in the mood.

"Will you tell me what you want to tell me so I can get on with my day?"

"You don't feel that?"

"Feel what?"

He grabbed my collar and forced me up against the wall, paintings fell and cracked in their frames.

"Careful," I hissed. I felt hollow and numb. Like if Will pushed me a little too hard, I might tear his head off.

He shook me, and I let him.

"You didn't feel anything? I pulled this out of the laundry."

He revealed a shirt. Luke's shirt from yesterday that was crumpled into a pile. The thick scent of blood coated the entire thing.

"So?"

He slammed me harder into the wall, and I grabbed his collar, snapping the buttons close to his neck. A flash of heat trembled in my fingers. I wanted to gut him for touching me that way, but I let him speak.

"You are going to ruin your life if you don't snap out of it. Listen to me."

"Snap out of what? This is me."

"Do you think you're special? That you're some 'chosen one.' They're brainwashing you to be their perfect little lap dog, and you're letting it happen."

I pushed him and he pushed me.

"Don't grab me again or I'll—"

"Oh, you still feel anger, huh? Well, how about this. You left Luke last night, and he's fucking miserable, and he has no one to help him."

"Luke is an adult. He doesn't need me to help him."

"No. Of course not. Good thing he spent all that time taking care of all of you for you to abandon him in his time of need. I guess that's your destiny. The twin that fucks over his brother when things get a little too hard, is that what you want to be known for?"

"I'm not my brother's keeper."

"That's your life motto, you jackass."

"You don't know me."

"I do! I know you because you're exactly like me. The only difference is that everyone I love is dead. But everyone you care about is still here and you are going to fuck it up if you don't snap out of whatever this is. I felt something last night that was the worst the pain from the bond has ever been, and then when I saw this shirt, I knew Luke was involved."

Will's eyes were riddled with quiet desperation.

I thought back on my night and if I'd felt even the tiniest flicker of pain, but all I remembered was the feeling of the girl beneath me and the obsession of wanting to do whatever I could to taste her.

"What could have happened? He's immortal."

"You and I both know that there are worse things than death. Surely, you can wrap your head around that. Think about your brother. Let it in. Feel what I feel."

"The bond is gone. It doesn't work. I don't feel anything anymore since last night."

"Like hell it doesn't. Focus. Focus on your brother. Not Her."

He pushed his hand into my chest hard, and I let him. There was nothing. No feeling anywhere in my body other than annoyance of Will pestering me.

"This is ridiculous."

"Shut up and focus. Do it for Luke."

I sighed and focused harder as he pressed his palm into my chest till it hurt and I could fight past the numbness. Will's hand was calloused and cold through the linen of my shirt. I thought of my brother. Of where he was. Of how he felt.

The feeling started to come back. That terrible feeling of being bonded. A pain hit me so sharp in the chest I keeled over. I'd felt it before, but it was never that painful. So penetratingly horrible I felt it in the back of my skull. My eyes stung and my stomach turned. I was going to be sick.

"Oh fuck. What is that?"

"That's tame compared to what it was last night. It felt like someone was ripping my heart out of my chest."

Whatever fog I was under before dissipated, and all that was left was my brother's pain. Something had happened while I was gone. Something bad.

"She lied about the bond. The only thing Ascension changed is you got more blood and they got you both exactly where they wanted you."

"Why? I don't get it."

"Use your head, Calem. If She knows all your most possible futures, She knows the people She needs you to be to serve Her. They're going to do anything and say anything to get you on their side."

It was a fact I already knew, but I'd somehow let myself forget.

"The bond is . . ."

"Something She uses to control you. You can't trust anything they've told you about how this stuff works. Always assume it's bullshit."

The nausea grew as the reality set in. Luke needed me, and I'd left him alone at the bar. What was I thinking? The Family knew . . . they knew what I'd do. They used their opportunity to get to my brother.

"It's happening again. I wasn't there to protect him and—"

"Feel sorry for yourself later. You have to go to him. He's with Her."

"Shit!"

I went for the door and ignored everyone on the way to Her chamber. Including Connell who'd been waiting for me outside the door. They made desperate attempts to bow to me. I stopped before opening Her door. What would I find? I hoped I'd at least see my brother fully clothed.

When I pushed open the queen's door, I sighed in relief. Luke was clothed but sleeping seemingly peacefully as She pulled Her hands through his hair. Jealousy hit me first. A blow I wasn't expecting. *Her blood was mixed with mine. It wasn't my reaction. Just the way She wanted me to feel.*

I didn't bow, and barreled toward them until I was standing over them.

"What did you do?"

"It's nice to see you. I knew you'd come looking."

"What did you do to him?" I repeated.

"I didn't do anything. I've helped him sleep. Going out to the bar is tiring business. I'll wake him if you'd like."

"No. Let him sleep."

At least he was getting some peace in his sleep. I wondered if he'd even feel the bond when he woke up or if he'd feel that same numbness I had.

"Do you want to join? You look tired." Her hand grazed the inside of my jacket, and I stumbled toward Her. "Of course, you'll need to shower first. Filthy business you were up to."

I stepped back. "No. I'll wait for him outside."

She wouldn't give me answers, and every minute I was with Her alone, I'd lose my resolve.

Suit yourself.

A smirk danced on Her lips. She wanted a reaction out of me, but I wouldn't give it. Not with my brother so close to Her and Her having all the power.

I let the door shut behind me, leaned against it, then slid to the floor. Pulling a cigarette between my lips and inhaling the smoke was the only relief I had from the tightness in my chest.

I thought the bond was gone, but it was there. Or rather, it was still there for me. What did that mean? I knew one thing. If it wasn't Her that hurt him and Sirius wasn't there, it left one person, and I would find him after my brother woke up. I took a long drag of my cigarette and let the smoke fill the air around me. It would give me time to think and stew on how much I hated myself for letting them hurt my brother again.

I needed to find Will too and apologize for being an asshole. And Thane, where the fuck was Thane? I couldn't move. Not till Luke was up. He'd need someone to be there for him, and I wouldn't let him down again.

I stared at the wallpaper for what could have been days, but I think it was only a few hours. I don't know why I thought hell would be fun. It was wishful thinking that I'd get at least one good night out if it. And it had been. I guess that's the thing about eternal torment, every bit of good is met with twice the bad.

The door opened, and Luke ignored me.

Okay, deserved. He was probably pissed at me for leaving him.

I caught up to him quickly. "Luke, talk to me. What happened at the bar? Are you okay?"

His brows drew together, and his shoulders went rigid. "Nothing happened. I feel fine. Is there something wrong with you?"

"Bullshit. What about the blood all over your shirt?"

"What blood? I don't know what you're talking about."

She wiped his memory of it. I wasn't sure what shocked me more, that or the fact that even when he didn't remember what happened, the pain was still there. All under the surface waiting to be felt and shared.

"When I left early with a girl. What did you do?"

"I went home. That was it."

I stared at him for a moment. It was bad. It was really bad. How much did she take? Why?

"What about the girl? The one who looked like Sarah, what happened there?"

"Who is Sarah?"

My blood ran cold. Of course. Of fucking course. Sarah. She took the memory of Sarah. Something happened to Luke last night, and that something had to be so terrible he'd went to Her for help. My head spun. Why Sarah?

"No one. Sorry. You're feeling okay, though? You're not sad about . . . missing our brothers or anything, right?"

"Why would I be?"

Okay, he remembered them. It was a good sign, but there was something off about his entire demeanor. He was giving me major *fuck off* eyes. If She'd taken the memory of Sarah from his life completely, that meant She took a lot. So much of Luke's childhood was wrapped up in Sarah, and all of the things he enjoyed and wanted to do. If the queen took all of that away, then that meant She took a lot of his pain. The pain of Sarah's death. The thing that pushed us both forward and reminded us of who the queen really was despite the draw of Her blood.

The look he gave the girl at the bar . . .

He'd held on. He probably went up to her and talked with her, danced with her. Luke would never give up Sarah, but She might make him want to. She'd want him to forget. Was this Her plan all along?

"Just curious, because I feel like shit."

"Well, that's on you. I feel great. I really have to go. I've got things to attend to. Now move."

"Gladly."

He turned and left me in the hallway with an aching chest.

We were fucked.

Dear Luke and Zach,

I did a bad thing and you're going to be mad. But I can't take this feeling anymore. I'm sorry I was angry. I get it now. I let you always protect me, and I never helped you. I've been a bad little brother, but you've always been the best big brothers. I promise I'll start pulling my weight. I'm going to help. I'm going to change everything.

Love you forever,

Presley

Forty-Four

I went looking for Will first. That might be a better plan than going straight for Ezra's neck. But he wasn't in my room. He wasn't in the garden, on the grounds, or anywhere in the fucking castle. Instead, I found Connell, or he found me. Connell had been my shadow all night and stayed outside in a separate car while I was with the girl. I suddenly realized that I never got her name.

"Sir, you look well today. I hope I'm not bothering you. I only wanted to see if you needed my help with anything today."

"Have you seen Will or Thane?"

"Oh yes, I passed your friend Thane. He's been assigned outside today, but I didn't see William. I haven't seen him all day. Do you want me to help you find him?"

"First, I have another question. Last night something happened to my brother. And I know you weren't there, but everyone around here talks. Tell me what you know."

"We're not supposed to talk about it. But it's not like I've been sworn or anything. I'd love to be sworn to you or your brother. Not that you would want that. But I'd love to serve you if you thought you needed someone . . ."

Connell kept mumbling to himself, but his words came out too fast for me to catch.

"Back up, what are you talking about?"

"Oh, they haven't told you? Members of The Guard sometimes choose others to be sworn to their service. Like Henderson has been sworn to Sirius for many years now. They say Connery was sworn to Akira. You knew him, right? I assumed you and your brother were sworn to Ezra."

"No." Thank god. Sounds like something I would have happily done at one point. "They don't tell me anything. What does it mean?"

"It's a loyalty vow. They're sworn into that Guard member's care . . . forever."

I bit my thumb till the blood beaded. "Bite your thumb."

Connell did it without even asking me why. I pressed our thumbs together to mingle our blood, and his mouth hung open.

"Swear yourself to me. Swear you'll do whatever I say and I can trust you above all else. You will never lie to me. And you won't keep secrets."

Connell eagerly pressed his thumb into mine. "I swear. I won't let you down."

"Good. Now tell me what you know about last night."

"No one said specifics, but I heard they were needing to dispose of a body. A girl. And that your brother was upset. Inconsolable was the word they used."

They killed her. And I'd bet money I knew why. That glimmer of interest in my brother's eyes came to mind. Luke never left her alone. I should have known. I should have stayed.

"They also said Ezra took him back to the castle in his car."

Ezra. All my problems started and ended with that name. My chest ached for my brother. They'd done this to hurt him. All of that blood on his shirt . . .

They killed her in front of him and made him watch. My eyes stung at the thought. It had to be the bond filling me with all my brother's sadness that he wasn't feeling. Because I should have been vibrating with anger and adrenaline, but I had to fight the lump in my throat. Luke had been all alone. He needed me, and I hadn't been there.

"Connell, I need you to go find my brother and follow him around. Make sure no one hurts him, and if you hear anymore talk, anything that would harm my brother, you need to tell me. But you don't tell anyone about this. Not even Ezra or Sirius. You're sworn to me."

He nodded quickly. "Of course, sir. I'll find him right away."

I sighed when he left. Having Connell be my sworn would help me have eyes on my brother, and I trusted him before he was sworn to me.

Moving to the garden was my top priority. I needed to find Thane and ask about Will. Thane was hiding behind a hedge. I barely caught the curtail of his shirt as he disappeared toward the edge of the garden. He was headed for the cathedral.

"Thane!" I called in a whisper. No one else was around that I could tell, everyone was likely busy making up for all their lost work the day before.

Thane stopped, shifting his feet impatiently. "This is a bad time. Can I talk to you in a second?"

"Have you seen Will?"

"Not since this morning."

"I can't find him anywhere," I said.

"I can help you look in a minute. But I have to go."

"What, why?"

"Someone is coming! I told you it would happen and it's happening. I heard whispers that said in two days' time. I need to go see if I can catch anything else from The Guard and the queen's meeting."

"I'm The Guard, and I haven't heard shit."

"Oh right. Weird. They're still keeping you in the dark?"

I ignored the obvious. "The Legion is coming?"

"Yes! I think so, that's what I'm trying to find out. I'll catch you later. I'll come find you in your room."

"Yeah, see you later."

I didn't know how to take in that new information. I hadn't believed anyone was coming to save us, but if it were true . . .

First, I needed to find Will.

I caught the whiff of his scent in the soft wind, and as I turned the corner of the cobblestone in the garden, I spotted Will and Ezra disappearing into the maze. They were moving fast, because no matter how quickly I followed, I found myself at a dead end. I burst through the thick bushes to where I thought the middle of the maze was. Cussing at the thistles and dead leaves, I broke through the hedges and moved my way toward the center.

Ezra was waiting for me. Only, he was alone with a large marble statue

I'd only been able to see from the top of the castle. It was a statue of a man with wings falling from the sky.

"What the fuck is this?" My mouth was dry despite the wetness of the foggy air.

"Follow me."

Ezra touched the edge of the statue, and there was a soft clicking sound.

A hidden door creaked open, and Ezra disappeared inside. It had once been covered with green vine and thistle. It led down a deep corridor with zero light other than the flicker of a flame and glow at the bottom of the steps. I ran my fingers over the cobblestone and concrete on either side as I descended. Something bad was about to happen. I wanted to run the other way, but Will had to be down there somewhere.

There was a shuffling of feet in the dirt and a shaking of steel.

"Oh god," I choked out.

Will was there, being stored in a steel prison. His eyes widened when he saw me. "Zach, you have to help me. You have to let me out of here. I have to get to Her."

I didn't need Ezra to speak it. I knew. This was the madness he'd warned me of. It was more advanced than I'd ever seen with Luke or Thane. His eyes were pitch black as he reached through the bars toward me. There were scuff marks all over the stone walls and the dirt floor.

"Will . . ."

I wasn't sure he even registered my presence. He knew my name, but there was nothing in his eyes; he wasn't in there.

"Please, help me. Why are you doing this to me? She gives me the world and then takes it away. What have I done? I can be good. I can be whatever She needs me to be. Let me out. I'll be good."

His voice cracked, and something in me did too.

"What happened?" I reached for him, and Ezra stopped me.

Will lunged a half second later. "You fucking promised! Fuck you. You piece of shit."

For the first time, I had nothing to say. Any words of anger I'd felt were suddenly eclipsed by pain. The pain of the bond was still there, only now I was alone to feel it all.

"We can fix this. Like Luke. This is fixable?"

"Take me to Her! Take me!" Will's screaming echoed, making me wince.

"No, it's as I told you. There are some things you can't come back from. He's no longer tethered to you and your brother. It's impossible like this."

Will continued to throw a tantrum and kick and claw at the walls, stopping only to sob.

"I was right. She was doing this to him. Poisoning him with Her blood to punish him."

"Watch it. You're a member of The Guard now. You must filter every word that comes out of your mouth. I know he was your friend—"

"Yeah, he was my friend! Are you really going to try to tell me She did this all for his own good? For mine? And not Her sick twisted games She likes to play."

I'd looked everywhere for him, except Her room. My life was crumbling around me. The ache from the bond flared through my entire body. Will punched the wall repeatedly.

"Will, stop!"

Ezra grabbed me by the shoulders. "Get it all out now. But when you walk out of here, you're not going to speak a word about this."

"Just admit it. Admit that She did this to be malicious. Admit that She did this to hurt me."

"She didn't. She's never done anything to hurt you. Only what was needed for the prophecy."

"Why even keep him alive at this point?"

I didn't want him to die, but he'd have never wanted this. To want Her. It was a mockery to him and the person he was. It was cruel, and She knew that.

"That is for Her to decide."

"Fine. Then tell me, what did you do to my brother?"

I wanted to hear it from his own lips. For him to admit it out loud. Ezra's hardened expression softened for a millisecond. If I hadn't known him and I hadn't been looking for it in his eyes, I'd have never caught it.

"What are you talking about?"

"Stop fucking with me! You know what I'm talking about. Luke was fine when I left. I saw the bloody shirt. You did something to him. I know it was you. You were there watching him. You're always watching him."

"These events are important to The Divine Plan."

"I trusted you to protect him, but you did something even you don't want to admit to yourself. You hurt my brother."

My voice shook with more sadness than anger, though I felt that too. The bond was eating me alive with the pain. It was my fault. I deserved to shoulder it all. Luke had done his shift already.

"No. I'd never hurt him or any member of our family."

"Oh, come off it. Admit it, Ez, this was your destiny. To be an evil bastard. She's orchestrated all of this. It's all your fault."

I can't believe I'd trusted him again. My eyes burned from the betrayal and guilt at my own words, but I had a share of the blame. I'd wanted

Luke to be happy and to have some peace, but I'd led him right into the arms of the people who hurt him the most.

"No."

"You're seriously denying it?"

"You don't know what you're talking about."

"Ha! No, you don't get to be the good guy anymore. Because I see you. You've been parading around playing the part of the morally righteous. But you're the worst one of all of them, and I can't tell if it's because you pretend to care or if you do. Either way, it makes you a manipulative bastard that lured me and my brother here. At least Sirius is honest with who he is. You want to be the good guy, and you want everyone else to believe that you are, but I know the real you. You can't hide from me."

He stepped up to me, squaring his shoulders and shoving me back a step. I shoved him too. I'd finally struck a nerve.

"Come on. You have to start hitting me. You want to, so do it. What's holding you back? That fake moral righteousness? We both know that it's all a lie, so why don't you hit me?"

"Watch what you say to me." He grabbed me by the collar, and I flung him off.

"No. Fuck you. Come on, it will make you feel better for hating me so much. Hit me!"

The pain hit me hard and fast, and I stumbled backward. He hit with the force of a semitruck, and I rubbed my face, reeling through each emotion. First, shock. He actually fucking hit me. Then, pain and the seething anger that bridged on utter hysteria. I couldn't contain the laughter that sputtered out of my lungs.

"See how good it feels when you're not holding back and you're honest about who you are?"

"You don't know everything!" Ezra's calm was finally cracking.

"I would have never been here if it weren't for you. We didn't follow Her. We followed you. We trusted you while you pretended to care. Being a shoulder to lean on so we wouldn't lean on anything else. So when you look at me and my brother and all the pain you caused, I want you to remember you did it. You created this."

"There's your problem. You think you've been the victim, but this is what you wanted. You are the only problem here. Luke is happy. She's happy. We're all happy. And then there's you, going around and blaming others for your own failures. Where were you last night? Maybe if you hadn't run off in your vendetta to hurt the queen, your brother would have never gotten into trouble."

My vision went red, and heat flushed through me so quick it stole the air from my lungs. Bloodlust curdled in my veins, and my shoulders pulled back at his outright admission. I was sure I'd never wanted to kill someone as much as I wanted to kill him then, and I didn't care how long it took or if I had to train morning to night. I would watch the light leave Ezra's eyes someday.

"You'll have to answer for this. I won't let this go. The reason you leave this earth will be by my hand. And you won't see it coming."

Ezra paused as he stared back at me, and his eyes softened. "So be it."

I turned my attention back to Will, but I had to find Thane and warn him. If this was his fate, they'd be out to get Thane too.

"I'll be back, Will."

"Why are you abandoning me? You're supposed to be my friend. Why won't you help me?" Will sobbed again.

"I'll come back to visit you in a little bit. I promise."

"You can't leave me here. I hate you! Fuck you! Fuck you! Fuck—"

Will's words bore into my skull in an echo as the door shut behind me.

Forty-Five

Fuck. Fuck. Fuck. I couldn't find Thane, and he never showed up. I'd waited all night in my room, but my paranoia pushed me back out into the hallway. I hadn't seen my brother or Connell all day, but that was probably because I'd been hiding all day. I couldn't pretend I wasn't. I'd dodged everyone who came looking for me.

I needed to focus on finding Thane and getting more information on The Legion. My new plan was simple. Try to keep Luke safe until The Legion came and hope they didn't kill us in the shuffle. I had to get Luke out though; it wasn't an option not to anymore. Only, I was hoping I'd have *someone* to go over that plan with because the crux of my plan was to ask The Legion nicely not to kill me and my brother.

There was one place I hadn't looked for him, and I was dying to tell the queen what I thought of Her and Her little tirade. I made my way to Her room in the darkness of the castle. At night, the walls glowed with candlelight, and a cool breeze lingered in every hall.

When I opened Her door, She was lying in Her bed with a book in hand.

"Where is he? Where is Thane?" I wasn't in the mood for our usual banter.

"Who is that again?" She blinked, giving me the doe eyes.

I dashed over to Her and grabbed Her by the shoulders. "Stop. Just tell me. Did you hurt him too?"

"I don't know where your friend is. Truly."

"Why did you do that to Will?"

"Will was twisting your mind. He was hurting you. I waited till you Ascended to soften your bond to him. And I didn't kill him. I did you a kindness."

"How?"

"Now you never have to say goodbye. You can go visit whenever you like."

"He isn't a fucking pet. He's a person."

It was so fucked. Thane was likely dead, and Will was gone. And my brother . . .

"Have I made you unhappy?" She stuck out her bottom lip in an innocent pout.

"Don't do that. Don't give me that fake doe-eyed bullshit you give my brother."

"Why not? He seems to enjoy it."

"Yeah, because he wants comfort."

I let go of Her shoulders, but it was too late. I felt the draw of Her gravity holding me to the sheets. Her hair was wet and brushed back from her face in a way that made Her feel bare and open.

"And you don't want comfort? What about in the atrium? You seemed to want me then. I heard you calling for me."

It was so loud.

I'd made a mistake. The anger was running out of me quicker than I could grab hold of it, and Her fingers, light as a feather, brushed my skin.

"You didn't tell me this would happen. That I'd have you nagging me in my head."

She smiled and ran Her tongue over Her teeth. "You'd have put up more of a fight. You'll grow to enjoy this bond. I promise."

She never stopped touching me. Her long nails raked across my chest, and I let Her undo a few buttons. Why had I come in Her room in the first place? I was forgetting and melting into Her as She leaned in closer. I expected Her to hit me. Slap me. Anything that hurt. Instead, She pushed Her hands through my hair. "I'm yours, Darling. Whatever you need."

Darling.

"Where does it hurt?" She moved Her hands under my shirt and over my bare chest.

"Everywhere."

My body felt bruised. I wanted to feel better. Happy. I'd missed that train a long time ago, or I'd never bought the ticket.

"I'll fix it." Her lips grazed my neck, and I groaned.

It was wrong to want. Her lips on my skin. Her hands roaming my chest. She was cold. Every kiss froze me in place, but I couldn't stop. I wanted to bury myself in Her and lose all control. Her lips sucked at the skin on my shoulder, and I undid my belt.

When I opened my eyes, my brother was standing in the doorway.

His eyes were dark as night. Every sense snapped back into my body as Her glamour fell away. I shrugged Her off and went for Luke, who retreated through the door. At the first step of my presence, Luke turned on a dime and slammed me into the wall. Hard. Hard enough to leave an echo trailing through the hallway and make my ribs ache. The lit flames in the hallway flickered.

"What the fuck was that?!"

Luke had never cussed at me before. Ever. Not like that.

"It was nothing."

He slammed me into the wall again, this time busting through the wall. "Don't you ever touch Her."

He flung me, and I hit the wall again.

His absence left me hollow in the silence of the hallway.

She had truly bewitched his mind, and instead of standing up for him or finding a way to help, I'd run to Her. My brother was turning into a monster, and it was my fault. It was all my fault, because I couldn't let him go. He told me it would happen, and I never believed him. The room spun and the realization set in. I was alone.

My composure slipped for a moment. A sob escaped my throat, and I covered my mouth to stop it. The tears forming in the corners of my eyes couldn't be allowed to fall, because I'd never be able to contain them again.

Two members were coming down the hall. I dropped my hands and pulled my shoulders back. Composure returned to me and left me encased in steel. There was peace in perfect composure. They stalked past me, stopping a half a second too slow to bow. I could have let it go and let them pass . . . but why would I?

"Stop," I said.

They did as I said with their eyes averted to the ground. I took a page from Ezra and grabbed one by the collar and kicked the other in the shin.

I couldn't be soft or sad, but I could be a monster for all of eternity. It was better than feeling, and with the ache in my bones from the sheer force of Luke's wrath, I wanted to feel numb again.

"Bow."

They both kneeled but not nearly low enough.

I fisted my hands in their hair and forced their faces onto the ground. "Every time you see me, I want your fucking face on the floor. Do you understand?"

"Yes," they said quickly.

"Yes what?"

"Yes, sir."

Forty-Six

ZACH

It was worse than limbo. Hell dragged me down into its depths, and I shackled myself to the comfort of my bed to stop it from destroying me completely. It was the only thing that was solid. It never moved. Someone came in every day to put on new sheets even if I didn't use them. Connell came in every couple of hours to give me updates, scribble in his notepad, and try to get me up, but he never gave me a good reason to.

I stared up at the stupid skylight in the ceiling and shielded myself with a pillow. *Fuck the stars.*

How much longer could I feel sorry for myself? I had forever, so a pretty long time.

I talked to myself too much, but Luke had barely mumbled a word over the last few days. I could pretend like I didn't care, but who was I kidding? This was my fault. My brother had turned into a lunatic because I didn't try harder to get us out. I didn't want this, though.

I'm such a dumbass. I was the worst kind. The kind who should have known better and instead laid around and let things happen. I'd thought I was fighting, but I hadn't fought hard enough. Luke would have. If our positions were switched, he would have done things differently. He'd have fought.

I wanted to spend every day of my eternity thinking about what a fuck up I was. I'd already spent all night doing that, sitting with Will in his cage while he begged me to let him out and called me every obscenity when I didn't.

I hadn't accepted it yet; all I could do was replay the last thing he'd said to me over and over again.

I should have saved them. If Will were there, he'd have been pissed I didn't keep my promise.

Someone is coming. They're coming.

Was Thane right? Was someone coming to save us from hell?

It was just me and the bond. Party of one. I'd taken death over the pain of the bond any day. Existing hurt because there was no one left to share the pain. There was no point in getting up or trying.

I didn't even notice when the sun came up and went again.

I was supposed to teach in the yard and start my official duties and pick my prized fighters and all that shit, but I didn't go. There was a knock on my door, and I folded my arms over my chest. I wouldn't open the door. I would sulk. The one thing I was good at. Sulking. Killing. Being a shit brother. Ezra never said how I'd spend my time, and I wanted to spend it staring at nothing. Those fucks could make me stay here, but they couldn't make me use my legs to get off the bed. I chuckled at the thought of Ezra trying to drag me, but knowing that bastard, he'd probably try to threaten me with something. Too bad all my nightmares had already come true. Everything bad that could happen, had happened.

There was nothing left even if The Legion came.

Luke appeared, and I braced myself for the pain.

"Come on." He towered over me.

"I don't wanna."

"We need you. Now get up." I let my brother help me up.

"You still mad at me?"

"No." The new Luke wasn't a fun conversator.

He headed for the hallway, and I followed.

"I was gonna ditch today."

That made him pull his shoulder back like he was going to challenge me. "Can't you do something you're told for once?"

"Fine, Mr. Terminator. Who shit in your cereal?"

"It will probably go better if you don't talk."

"Fine by me."

Fuck. The pressure in my chest surged. I'd finally reached the part of hell that hurt, and I couldn't bury it. Thane was right. It was a bad dream, and any minute now, someone would show up on our doorstep. The brigade would come on their white horses to stop this.

I put on a show. All the while, I watched Luke, powering through training. Slinging people like they were ragdolls. Few got hits in, but when they did, I felt the echo of it on my skin. Luke didn't seem to notice when I got hit. Was the bond gone for him?

It worried me, but I paid attention to the sun as it went down over the horizon. Someone would come. Surely.

No one did. The light was almost out of the sky as we packed up and cleaned up the black blood staining the dirt and our clothes. I'd been brought a fresh-pressed suit to change into. They were particular about appearances. I couldn't walk around in just anything. I put it on without fuss. My heart felt bruised, and my body was good and tired from being drained of blood.

If they weren't coming, I had to try something else. I grabbed Luke's shoulder and ushered him away toward the garden. Connell waved, and I shooed him off. If I could get my brother alone, he might snap out of it like Will had done for me.

"What do you want?" His voice was gruff and low.

"I need to show you something."

"Just tell me."

"No. I have to show you."

Luke reluctantly followed me into the maze with his gaze fixed on the ground. The sun was gone, and the moon had risen in the sky like our North Star. I didn't remember the layout of the maze, but the holes I'd made earlier in the week were still there. Luke flinched as I knocked the latch on the statue and the door appeared.

"What is this?"

"You'll see."

The air was stale and musty as we made our way through the corridor. The lit flames flickered at the bottom of the staircase. An almost silent scratching echoed when we reached the bottom. Will scratched words onto the wall. The word "Her" was written over and over.

"Will?" The recollection passed over Luke's face. "What's he doing in there?"

"She did this to him."

"Luke, you're going to help me, right? Please, open the cage. Let me go see Her." Will's eyes were black as he reached for my brother.

Luke's jaw hardened. "He needs to stay here. That's the safest place for him. Away from Her."

"Are you serious?"

"Ah, fuck you both. Some friends you are." Will threw up his hands and went back to scribbling on the wall.

"What is your problem?" Luke spun on me quickly, and we were chest to chest like he would beat my ass.

"Right now, my only problem is you. You have to snap out of whatever this is."

"I don't know what you're talking about."

"I do. She brainwashed you and took your memories, and I need you to come back. I can't do this alone."

"Grow up. She didn't do anything. I asked Her to. I don't want them. Whatever She took, meant nothing."

"That's not true. Sarah meant everything to you."

"Not enough, obviously, because I don't know who you're talking about. Nothing matters except Her, and it should be the same for you."

I scoffed. "You wouldn't feel that way if you remembered the things that bitch did to you."

"Don't talk about Her like that," Luke growled.

"Why shouldn't I? This is Her fault."

He stepped forward to tower over me. "No. You're the problem. You're making this all about you. You wanted me to be here and fit in, and now that I do, you can't let go. This is who we are and who we were always meant to be."

"I never wanted this."

This wasn't right. If it was destiny, why was it pulling us apart?

"You asked me to ascend with you, and I did. I'm finally happy. I have a job that I know I can do. You're a leech. You provide nothing to Her or to me. You don't follow instructions. I don't know why you're here or why She chose you. So be helpful or stay out of my way."

I couldn't fully register the words.

I said nothing.

"She's mine," he hissed. "Call Her a bitch again, and I'll gut you."

He bumped my shoulder on his way out.

My heart cracked.

His absence left me in the cold silence.

My brother was gone. My brother was gone. My brother was gone, and I couldn't get him back. It was all my fault. Everything was my fault. Why was it always my fault? I didn't protect him. I had one job, and I didn't do it. I didn't protect him. I never protected him like he protected me.

I stumbled onto the stairs to hide in the darkness. My legs gave out, and I fell onto dusty steps. Something wet fell from my face. Why was I crying? I hated crying. I hated Her. I hated myself.

It was too much. The weight of it all suddenly tipped, and I wanted to see them. To hug my brothers and go back in time to when I was at least a little happy. Couldn't I go back one more time? I needed to hear one of Presley's stories again. Or to see Aaron smile and do something that made him happy. Anything.

I cried because I missed them. I cried because I hated Her. I cried because I loved Her. I cried because I was so fucking angry. I cried because I wanted to go home.

This wasn't home. It may have been my destiny, but that didn't make it home.

Her voice was in my head again.

You had to keep fighting for control. I've given you so many opportunities to let go.

"Leave me alone," I said.

This is what you wanted, isn't it? Luke will be with you forever.

"No. Not like this."

You said you wanted to keep Luke and your brothers safe. What if this is the only way? The one true path.

"Shut up!" My scream echoed in the empty stairwell, and I made my way back to the maze.

They did this.

They took my brother from me.

And they needed to pay.

My favorite emotion was coming back to me. That's when I knew the queen's blood had affected me. Because all that had been frozen solid burned. No flickering flame, but a sudden inferno. A silent vengeful rage filled my body from head to toe. So quick I had no control. That's who I was. Rage. Destruction. Vengeance.

New plan. I would kill them. Every. Last. Fucking. One. And I didn't care how long it took.

She was a false god, and I would not rest till I tore Her fucking throat out.

Forty-Seven

ZACH

Fuck this place. They wanted to see a lunatic? I'd give them one. They wanted to keep me here? Fine. But I was tired of being a pawn. I was tired of being controlled.

I knew where I was going the moment I got up off the ground. No one feared me. Their mistake. I wasn't surprised. The only people who knew me were already gone. Lost to Her. Well fuck that and fuck Her.

There was a carton of gasoline in the flower garden shed. I had half a mind to set the whole garden on fire and the castle with it, but they'd catch on too quickly for that. I had another place in mind. After snagging a bottle of liquor from The Underground, I made a beeline for the old church.

The grass was wet with dew as I made my way across the field. It left my shoes and pant legs soaked and my feet freezing. The moon mocked me, and I flipped off the stars as I swallowed a mouthful of liquor.

A singular light in the bell tower of the old church shone. That same light that was always on taunted me. The gasoline sloshed next to my side as I picked up my pace. Wind kicked up the salt from the air, and the mist wet my face. At least it wasn't raining yet.

Her voice found its way to me like a siren at sea. ***Why are you so angry? This is all your fault.***

Could She feel the lighter in my pocket? Did She know I was about to let that place burn? I'd need to hurry. I kicked open the door, and it cracked and fell in a flurry of dust on the floor. I thrust off the cap of gasoline and poured it over the floor. The pews. The walls. The stairs. I smiled as I drenched that stupid fucking mural. Her blood melted into a concoction of black and gray paint at my feet.

She called to me again. ***You keep holding on.***

How was this for letting go? This whole building was a lie. I stood at the doorframe. The smell of dry wood soaked with gasoline burned my eyes as I reached into my pocket for my lighter.

You're causing your own problems. Wallowing in your own guilt won't help you. You need to accept this. This is the person you need to be. Let go, Darling. Let the anger take you.

The edges of my lips curled into a smile. *Careful what you wish for.*

I struck the lighter and flicked it a few feet in front of me.

The floor turned into flames, and I stumbled back as the heat flooded my senses. For the first time in months, the warmth carved its way into my body again. The weight brought me to my knees as I stared up at the cracked and burned wood. Flames raged in a cascading inferno that reached up into the night sky.

There would be no saving this place. It would be ash in minutes. I smiled and grabbed the liquor bottle next to me and chugged every last drop. Nothing could touch me.

They'd come soon to stop the fire from spreading. To stop me.

A small chuckle escaped me and kept turning in my stomach until it was a roaring laughter that echoed the sound of the fire. The laughter burned my ribs, but I couldn't stop. The image of Ezra's disappointed face was enough to keep it bubbling up from nothing.

I would make their eternity hell like mine.

The failed prodigal son.

Aren't you proud?

My little pyro heart wasn't done. When everyone was all up in arms about their precious building, the hedges would look so nice burning next to it. I left my empty bottle and took what was left of the gasoline and skipped my way to the entrance of the labyrinth. Taking only a moment to admire the tall hedges that were kept for years, I doused the entrance with gasoline.

Sorry, I guess today isn't your lucky day either. That's when I had the best idea I'd had all day. What if I trapped myself in the middle of the maze? Would their precious fate save me from the growing flames? Would She come running, or would I perish, proving this was one big game? There was only one way to find out.

I grabbed the matches I'd stuffed in one of my shoes and dropped it in the gasoline pail before kicking it under the nearest hedge. A smile crept to my face. I pushed farther into the maze, staggering on my feet. My drunken haze left me giddy as I danced my way through the bushes. The mist was thick, and the night swallowed all the light. Except for that roaring fire that consumed the hedges behind me. Each passing second, the fire bit at the edges of my clothes.

I finally reached the center and fell to my knees at the foot of the statue. I touched one of the marble wings as the flames grew higher around me.

The hysterical laughter came back to me. It was all so fucking funny. They would be so angry.

I don't know how long it took Ezra and Sirius to find me in the maze. I was hot. That I knew.

"What are you doing?!" I swore Ezra had said, but the fire was roaring.

I refused to stand and chose to be dragged. And they did. Grabbing each arm, they dragged me through the mud and ash. I could see nothing. I felt nothing. Not the tug on my arms or the burn in my calves from the grass.

When we were free of the maze, Ezra stood me up. I thought for sure he'd beat me to a bloody pulp, but he grabbed my face in his hands again to stare at me directly. "Are you all right?"

Genuine concern for me as a person? Not likely. He didn't see me that way. I was more like a toy. Didn't he know the favorite toy always gets broken?

Lightning lit up the hills in the distance; the fucking fates couldn't let me have this one thing. Men ran all over the yard in their attempts to extinguish the burning wood of the church. I wiped a few drops of rain that landed on my forehead.

"He needs to go to Her and face punishment." Sirius grabbed me by the collar.

"Give me a minute with him," Ezra said.

"That wasn't Her instruction." Sirius's breath was on my face. "You're lucky She's so fond of you."

"If you want to kill me, Sirius, just do it."

Ezra pulled me out of his reach. "Talk to me. Tell me what's wrong. Is this about Luke?"

He already knew the answer to that question. It was always about Luke. Why was he still trying to make me feel better?

"Get off me." I pushed him, but after training and a bottle of alcohol, I wasn't putting up much of a fight.

"I know it doesn't seem like it now, but things are still adjusting in the bond. He won't be like that forever. The bond is adjusting. It's uneven now but—"

"Times up. She wants to see him."

"Yeah, take me to Her. I want to see Her."

And for the first time, I really did. Because I wasn't done with my rampage. I had one problem, and that was Her. Without Her, none of my other problems existed. The answer was simple. I needed Her gone. I needed Her dead.

"Fine."

Ezra and Sirius escorted me through the halls that were oddly empty. I laughed again, thinking of them all having to clean up my mess outside. Also at the fact that the two sworn guards were taking me straight to the queen that would soon meet Her very timely demise. Did they not expect me to hurt Her? How childish.

Forty-Eight

ZACH

When we reached the cathedral, my ears were ringing. My body buzzed with anticipation of Her. If She wasn't a person, killing Her didn't matter. She wasn't some innocent deer or bunny. She was a predator lying in wait for Her perfect moment to strike. She had no feeling. The only thing She cared about was Her own priorities. I guess I could relate.

"Leave us." She faced away from us with Her hand on the throne.

Their footsteps echoed into the ceiling and the door shut behind me. The only sound was the rain pouring over the roof and hitting the stained-glass windows.

She was beautiful, and She'd be even more beautiful when She was dead.

When She turned, I stopped. Something about taking on the fullness of Her image made me want to bow, but I didn't, and I wouldn't ever again.

She closed the distance between us and placed a hand on my cheek. It was cold on my flustered skin.

"You've come to kill me."

"You had to know this was coming. Can't you see the future?"

"I can. But could you really do it? I thought you wanted to be the good guy." She gazed up at me beneath Her lashes.

"Come on, you can drop the good girl act with me. Whoever you're pretending to be. The sweet blushing girl act doesn't work on me."

Her soft coy smile faded, and another took its place. One sultrier and more sinister.

"Finally," I said.

"I'm not surprised you like me better like this."

"I like you better when you're not pretending to be some poor, weak girl. We both know you're not."

Every minute that passed strengthened my resolve. If She ever was a normal girl, that day was long gone. I was face-to-face with evil. The same evil thing in me was in Her too. And I was ready to snuff it out with my own two hands.

Was I finally going to add murderer to my list?

She licked Her teeth and ran Her black nails over Her palm. "Do you really think you'll be able to kill me? I don't think your brother would approve. Do you?"

"My brother would never hurt you. But I'm not my brother, and you took him from me."

"Did I? I didn't do anything but show him love. It only bothers you because it's stronger than your bond with him. That must be disappointing for you."

Her smile mocked my pain.

"Fuck you."

She stepped forward. "What makes you think I'll go easily?"

Something shifted in the air. My perfect image of Her morphed. The veil was torn, and now I could see Her as She truly was. Shiny, beautiful, evil *nothing*.

"You like me better like this because we're stitched from the same cloth. You don't have to be anything more than what you already are. You're not like your brother. You can't make goodness from nothing."

"I know."

"Did you really think this is where your journey ends? This is only the beginning for us."

"Why me? Why do you need me if you have Luke?"

"Because you were meant for this. For destruction. Carnage and rage. Because you're not weak like your brother. You have real strength."

She placed a hand on my chest, and I pushed Her away.

"Get the fuck off me," I spat. "My brother isn't weak."

"You both have weaknesses. And I've spent time ensuring they're purged. He was afraid of failing all of you, so I made sure he faced that fear head-on. And you . . . afraid of what would happen if you lost your brother. So afraid you couldn't see what was right in front of you. This place was made for you. And that thing you've always wanted is already yours. Luke will be with you forever. Safe and sound with you as his valiant protector."

"That's why you killed that girl. As a test?"

She rolled Her eyes. "You only listen to what you want to hear. The girl was in my way and the perfect opportunity to help him face that fear and squash all that hope lingering inside him. You'll realize some people have so much hope you have to nearly kill them to extinguish it. But not for you. You have no hope left. Only anger."

Her hands made their way to my chest, and I grabbed Her wrists.

"But I thought you came here to kill me? You'll need to be closer." She pressed Her chest up against mine and looked up at me. Taunting. *Fucking beautiful.*

"Don't you wish I'd let you kill me?"

She ran Her fingers up my arm. I said nothing, focusing instead on the rage building in my gut, but it got drowned out by the euphoria of Her touch.

She moved my hand to squeeze Her neck. "Come on. Kill me."

A fluttering pulse thrummed underneath my fingertips. All of Her blood could be mine.

"Did you really think it would be that easy? Darling, you should know better."

That was the last thing She said before I bit into Her neck and I was lost in Her again.

I was at the bottom of hell. The room grew colder. The more I let Her have, the more numb I felt inside. My chest wasn't hurting anymore. I let Her pull me under the frozen lake. The inferno of frost and deception.

She moaned for me. ***Take all you want, Darling.***

I moved Her to the throne and dropped to my knees while loosening my tie. Her foot rested on my shoulder, and She looked down at me with hungry eyes. I was beneath Her. Not even good enough to be trash. Just dust and old rotting bones. And that's exactly where She liked me to be, crawling and groveling for Her.

I didn't care anymore. Let me be nothing. It was all I was good for. All I was destined to be. I brought my lips to Her thigh while Her hands knotted my hair, and She pulled me higher.

Good boy.

I bit Her. The blood trickled down Her inner thigh, and I used my tongue to taste every glorious drop. My whole body buzzed with the feeling of Her in my veins.

I wanted to hide in the shadow of Her darkness.

I was always going to betray my brother. I prayed to Her in silent devotion to let me hide and be nothing in quiet peace. She was my god.

My trance broke when Luke barreled into me and threw me across the altar.

"Don't touch Her," he growled.

There were no traces of my golden brother left in his brown eyes. Something foreign and feral ripped through me. Why did he think he could have Her all to himself? She was as much mine as She was his.

"What are you going to do about it?" The words came out quick and with no thought behind them.

I stepped forward. My body was full again. Full of Her and ready for anything.

"Don't." Ezra stood by the door, letting the moonlight in. The smell of rain wafted in, and the candles in the cathedral flickered.

"No, let them work it out." Sirius smiled, watching me while he tended to the bite mark on Her leg. A mixture of disgust and jealousy twisted in my gut.

Luke pushed me and I pushed back.

My brother was a monster, and I'd let it happen. There were fates worse than death, and Luke knew that. The thing I'd tried to run away from was finally snarling in my face like a rabid three-headed beast about to consume its prey.

No matter what I did, I couldn't save my brother.

Her blood surged in my body and made my vision feel strange and dreamlike. Luke was the last thing standing in my way. The last thing that made me feel anything. I'd dragged my brother to hell with me, and like every time before, I didn't protect him.

That left only one final thing. My brother needed someone to save him, and there was only one way to do that.

He had to die.

That's the brother I needed to be. It's who I was. She'd said so Herself. Carnage was basically my last name. It all made sense.

I, Zach Calem, would kill my brother. That's what I'd be remembered for.

Luke threw me across the room, and the force buckled the marble. The wind blowing through the doors was cold. Sirius closed them and disappeared out of sight.

I could do it. I could make it quick, then he'd be free. My brother was a great fighter, but I was *better*.

I charged him and slid under his legs faster than he could turn. It wasn't a fair fight. He was weak from sparring, and I'd been healed.

That would make it easy for me, then.

Wrapping my arm around his neck, I bit into his throat. I felt the pain too, as the bond flared.

His blood stained my shirt as I spit it on the floor. The last thing I needed was more of Her in my system, muddying my thoughts and confusing me more. He grabbed the edge of my coat and lifted me over his head to toss me to the floor. The marble design cracked all the way to the door.

I twisted him into an arm bar. The imbalance left him on the floor. His blood stuck to my hands and chest and caused my hold to slip. Luke took a chunk out of my arm, and black blood spewed over the floor and into the cracks of the marble.

"Would you like me to stop this?" I barely heard Ezra whisper to Her.

Luke picked me up and slammed me into the marble again.

Focus. I could do it. I could kill Luke. It was saving him. It had to be me. No one else would do it except me. The one who loved him the most in this world.

"Patience," She said.

This time I was faster as I dodged Luke and pinned down his leg. That, or he was getting slower. Weaker. But I could go for days. My heart beat loudly in my ears as I knocked him on his ass again. The pain of it shot through my back.

Luke's movements were sloppy. He wasn't thinking straight. He was thinking of Her.

I would win.

It's better than the alternative, I told myself. Watching Her take advantage of my brother and bind him into servitude.

I put distance between us to wipe my brother's blood off me and make eye contact with Her. "Enjoying the show?"

She smiled. ***You're such a fool.***

Luke charged me again, and I let him take me down and pin me to the marble.

I stayed for you.

Luke's words felt like a scorching hot iron to my chest. I don't know why they popped into my head when they did, but the memory of them burned into the edges of my skull.

I stayed for you.

My brother stayed on this hell of a planet for me.

Despite knowing what awaited us.

Despite the pain of losing Sarah.

Despite knowing he'd never forgive himself.

He did it all for me.

A lump formed in my throat as my brother bit into my neck, and I wrestled away and pinned an arm behind his back, then bit into his shoulder.

The weight of the love I carried for Luke was my undoing. I wasn't nothing. I was a brother. I had a choice, and I couldn't let him corrupt himself. His suffering needed to end, even if it ended me.

I shifted my weight till I was on top of him and pinned his arms at his sides, all while struggling with the wetness of blood coating my fingertips. He wasn't fighting hard enough.

If loving my brother to the extinction of myself was a sin, I'd have done it again and again. This place would continue on without us. They'd find another set of twins to fill that spot. *We weren't so chosen after all.* That's what they'd say, anyway.

We were too broken.

I was unraveling.

It was all meaningless.

All of it was for fucking nothing.

My hands shook around his neck, and fresh tears stung my eyes.

I could do it. I had to.

Memories of my brother flooded me. *My Luke.* Back when we were happy. We were once, and I wanted us to be again.

"Luke, listen to me for a second, please!" I held him down in a flurry of blood spilling over my hands. He tried to lift me up, but he'd lost too much blood. Tears fell from my eyes onto his cheeks. "Please. Come back."

For the first time in my life, I prayed. Not the forced ones I'd do with Mom at dinner or whatever the hell I sat on my knees for and said for the queen. I'd never begged so earnestly in my soul for anything else to whoever was listening. God, gods, the stars. Any or all.

Please, don't make me do this. Anything else. Give me something. Help me.

The door opened, momentarily stopping us both.

I didn't know if it was the wash of cold that fell over us or the sound of a new distinct heartbeat. The only reason I heard it so clearly was because the rain had stopped.

We halted our fighting.

Our savior had arrived. The one person I never thought I'd see.

I let go of my brother. My muscles weren't working. I wasn't sure my heart was beating.

Do you see now, Darling? Sometimes you must let go to see your true potential and the person you're foretold to be. Your family needs you.

"I understand," I said in a whisper.

It had never been clearer.

I had a family to protect, and whoever tried to hurt them would get no mercy.

Forty-Nine

LUKE

Presley emerged.

And everything in me that had separated and deteriorated knit together again. The frayed edges of our bond snapped together like an invisible string tied to my brothers, me, and the queen. It felt tangible.

Our blood bonded us, and I felt the power of it. The thing we'd been missing.

Those pieces of string had been uneven and tattered, but not anymore. When I gazed upon my brother's face, I felt the pull, and any imbalance shifted in our tether.

We were all equal. One heartbeat. Finally whole.

Presley looked different. His blond curls were darker. Dull. And he stood barefoot in a suit. His feet and legs were covered in mud. How had he found us? Why?

"Why is he filthy?" Sirius said to Henderson, who was waiting at the door.

"He took off as soon as the plane landed."

Presley wasn't looking at me or Zach while we sat in a puddle of blood on the floor.

He was looking at Her.

I almost didn't remember our fight, but I remembered trying to struggle against the fog and move toward my brother's voice. He'd felt so far. I reached for him but couldn't quite grab hold of him.

Sirius smiled. "Family reunion."

I should have been angrier, but I couldn't take my eyes off the golden boy in front of me as he walked toward Her. My little brother was here.

"You didn't tell me," Ezra said.

"You didn't need to know. Didn't need the twins mysteriously disappearing again."

"You knew? This whole time you've known he was coming?" Zach said.

They continued to banter back and forth, but I wasn't listening.

I didn't remember who Luke Calem was. I couldn't remember how to be anything that wasn't attached to Her. Like being sedated, I'd been smothered under a cloud, but when I looked at Presley, that cloud dissolved like vinegar in water. Suddenly, I could see him. Like I hadn't been able to see anything for what felt like a long time. The numbness wore off, and I could feel again. Like he fixed something that had been broken.

He closed the gap to Her with graceful ease. His feet sloshed through the black pools of ink on the floor, and he left a trail to Her.

There was barely any light left in his eyes.

She smiled, holding Her arms out to him as if it were a joyful reunion. Her hands grazed his cheek, and a tug of war began in mind.

Get away from Her, some feral part of me screamed, and a growl almost slipped through my teeth, but then I gazed upon my brother's face and his curly hair.

No. Get away from him.

Presley spoke softly, "Hi."

He was completely enamored. Her hands continued to survey him, and he obliged with laughter and snuggled close to Her like a lost puppy. His gaze darkened when he kneeled in front of Her and rested his head on Her thigh.

"You're so beautiful. I knew you would be."

Jealousy burned me from head to toe, but it couldn't stay. It was strong but not stronger than the growing fear bubbling up from my stomach and freezing me in place. I understood the runaway train Will talked about. I reached for the rail using all of what was left of me to hold on. My brother. My sweet, innocent little brother was in danger. I knew it even while being tethered to Her. Even while loving Her with everything that I was.

Presley chuckled and I remembered that little rambunctious kid with his whole life ahead of him. He told me he wanted to be on TV. He wanted to make people laugh, and all I wanted to do with my life was make sure he got to do that.

I missed him. I was sure I missed him.

Get away from my brother.

Her gaze shot through me, and she smiled. She knew. This was all Her plan.

Zach helped me up off the floor. His expression had hardened. He glared at Her through his lashes. All muscle and rage and reverence.

I nodded and he nodded back. No apologies needed. Things were right again.

"Read what The Divine spoke during the dark sun, my dear Sirius," She said.

I could barely hear Sirius utter the words. "Four brothers shall reign and hold the crux of the unbreakable vow."

It's written, My Love.

Of course it was. It could never have been any other way.

"I walked forever to find you." Presley's eyes were wide with amazement. "I could feel you getting closer and closer. I found you. I finally found you."

I knew what I needed to do.

"My queen." I dropped to my knees. "Please, may I ask you a favor?"

She stared at my little brother and ran Her hands through his hair, like he was a shiny new toy. "Of course, My Love."

"Let me be in charge of him. I'll train him. Wherever he is, I must go. I want to swear him to me."

I finally understood the person I was supposed to be. If Presley was there, that meant the prophecy was true and Aaron wouldn't be far behind, and they needed someone to lead them the way Ezra had led me. They'd need me to set them on The Divine Path.

"If that's how you wish to run your Guard, let it be so. You must be so excited. It all is finally coming together."

She spoke to him with a soft smile and kissed his forehead. "I knew you'd find me. It's all as I predicted. Welcome to The Family."

Epilogue

Her

*A*aron Calem.

I'd hardly thought you'd be capable of such destruction. I'd hardly considered you at all. Your entire life you've been only a wimpy, good for nothing, whiny, petulant boy. Not bright. Or brave. Or strong.

Yet I find your face written all over the stars. And they're singing your name in unison. Damn the wretched stars. The stars love a good-boy hero almost as much as they love chaos and death. You've won their favor. But unluckily for you, they speak only to me.

Something great has changed.

The Divine's word revealed your face plastered far and wide over galaxy after galaxy. The future is splitting into thousands because of one boy. Not only for me and my family, but for all the rest of us. If I'd known you'd be this much trouble, I'd have killed you long ago and taken my chances with fate. There were many futures in which your older brothers recovered from the deaths of you and your brother. But none with such great rewards.

But you weren't capable of such things before. You've changed. And the future has changed with it. What have you been up to while you've been away?

We shall see.

There were so many futures in which you were mine, and I can see them in your brothers' eyes. You're coming and I can't wait to take everything from you. I'll enjoy snuffing out that hope with my bare hands.

Cecily

A aron Calem.

    You're in terrible danger. If I was still kind, I'd recommend you run, but I am not kind anymore. I am something else entirely.

I wish I could warn you.

Your brothers need you.

I need you.

You should run.

But don't.

I hope you come. I hope you win.

S.L. Cokeley

Samantha Cokeley was raised in a small town in Oklahoma. Growing up, she always had an active imagination and an interest in crafting stories. She developed a love for writing after college when she discovered anime and fan fiction. If she isn't spending time painting colorful sea creatures or crocheting, you can find her with family, including her pug named Kylo. The This Blood that Binds Us series ends this year. But you can expect many more stories with vampires, heart warming found family, and fluff to come.

Follow Me

Links to my newsletter so you can stay up to date.

Follow me on Amazon so you never miss a release.

Facebook Reader Group

Instagram